ISLANDS OF FORTUNE

Lancarote

By

Ed Kemplar

Acknowledgements

This work wouldn´t have been possible without the support and encouragement of friends and family, who served as sounding boards, test readers and therapists.

Many thanks to Tony, Mike, Dammy, Ann, Debbie, Aileen Sue, Sonja, Kim & Walter who all read some, if not all the story, asking questions and making suggestions. Many asked "what happens next?" which brought a smile to my face to think the story and characters were engaging with their imaginations enough to make them want more.

An enormous thankyou goes to Betty, who had the unfortunate task of reading the early drafts and having her mind truly mushed by my dreadful grammar and disjointed prose. Thanks to her corrections and fearlessness when confronting my sensitive soul, we managed to hammer the original two-hundred thousand words into something which flowed, rather than jerked it´s way to the climax.

The biggest thanks of all are reserved for my lovely Emma. Her unrelenting enthusiasm and occasional foot up the arse ensured I got to the end of the writing process without trashing the whole bloody lot somewhere along the way.

I should spare a mention to all the librarians and archaeologists who not only put up with me interrupting their busy days digging and filing, but who answered my endless questions with patience and good humour.

Most of the historical passages within the book reference the 1872 translation of Le Canarien, written by Pierre Bontier and Jean Le Verrier, translated by Richard Henry Major of the British Museum and Geographical Society. A couple of things Berthin de Berneval was credited with saying, were too good to resist and I blatantly copied the translations from the manuscript. Apart from that, I have to say, I pretty much made everything else up. As is stated on the copyright page, this is not a historical textbook, merely a bit of fiction, based on actual events.   After all, who can really know what the hell went on over six hundred years ago, on a lump of rock in the Atlantic Ocean.

Finally, I would like to thank you the reader.   Without you, there would be no point spending hours, days, weeks, months and years hammering on keyboards.   Hopefully, enough of you buy this and read it to keep the lights on this winter.   Part two can´t be written in the dark.

Thankyou

Ed x

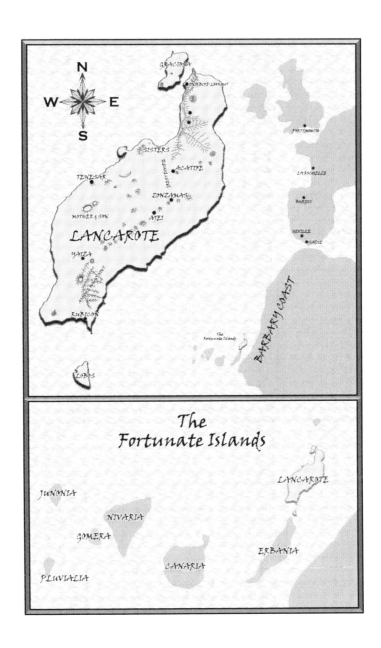

1

Burgos, Kingdom of Castile,

September 1st, 1401

Sir Robert clambered through the tiny opening with as much dignity as he could, forcing his six-foot burly frame through a four-foot skinny doorway. As soon as his feet landed on the floorboards, Ernesto, the King´s steward reached behind him and pulled the door closed. He shot home two bolts and tugged the handle to make sure it was secure before stepping aside to release a hanging tapestry to swing down and conceal the doorway.

"My apologies Señor," Ernesto said, turning and bowing, "but one can never be too careful. Anybody could be creeping around listening in these old passageways."

"It would have to be somebody very small." quipped Sir Robert, brushing dust from his shoulders.

"I don´t think the builders had anybody your size in mind when they built the tunnels señor." Ernesto answered without guile as he led Sir Robert to a highly polished cherry wood table stood on a sumptuous blue Persian carpet in the centre of the room. Sir Robert smiled as his feet sank into the deep pile of the rug. He stretched his toes like a cat inside his boots, imagining what it would feel like to walk upon bare footed.

"Please señor, take a seat. You must be tired after your climb." Ernesto, the King´s Steward proffered one of the chairs arranged around the table.

"Thank you but no." Sir Robert answered, a little perturbed by the Steward´s patronising tone. "I will be fine standing."

"Can I interest you in some wine?" Ernesto asked.

"That, I will accept." Sir Robert brightened as Ernesto bowed and retreated to a small cabinet in the corner of the room where a pitcher and two goblets stood on a silver tray. Sir Robert let his eyes wander around the room. It was a light and airy chamber with lime washed walls and a high, vaulted ceiling. A single door stood in the wall opposite the window and large tapestries hung around the walls.

"Should we be expecting anybody to come tumbling through the walls?" Sir Robert asked, pointing at the tapestries as Ernesto handed him a full goblet.

"What? Ah! No señor. There are no other hidden doors in this room."

Sir Robert raised an eyebrow and smiled at the steward as he took a sip of the wine. It was sweet, a little too sweet for this early in the day.

"I must inform His Grace of your arrival." Ernesto said. "He is most eager to meet with you. Please excuse me."

"Of course." He drank some more as he watched Ernesto walk to the door and leave. He put the goblet down on the table and hurried around the room peeking behind every tapestry. He was pleased to find no other secret doors. He walked back to the table and picked up his wine. He took another sip. His eyes wandered to a stack of velum sheets lying face down across the table. The temptation to reach across and turn one over was great, but he heard footsteps approaching and composed himself, tugging the hem of his tunic down and flicking a speck of dust from his sleeve.

The door flew open. Ernesto stepped inside and bowed deeply as King Enrique breezed past him into the room. He wore a fur-edged, ocean-blue cloak of shimmering satin, so long it swept the floor behind him as he walked. Sir Robert placed his goblet on the table, stood smartly to attention and performed a slow, respectful bow.

"Your Grace." he said.

"Ambassador." the King acknowledged with a bird-like nod of the head. "I trust you are well."

"Yes, thank you Your Grace. I always enjoy my time in this fair city, I find the air most invigorating."

"Indeed. I am inclined to agree. Tell me, how is dear King Charles?"

"When I was last with him, he was in rude health Your Grace." Sir Robert lied smoothly. King Charles was in fact slipping in and out of madness. The last time Sir Robert heard from the French Court, the King was insisting metal rods be sewn into his clothes. He was convinced his body was made of glass and would shatter without them.

"I am glad to hear it." Enrique said. "Please give him our regards when you see him."

"It would be my pleasure Your Grace."

The steward offered a full goblet of wine to the King. "Will there be anything else?" he asked as Enrique took it from him.

"No. That will be all. Leave us. See that we are not disturbed. I will call when we are finished." Enrique waved the steward away. Ernesto backed out of the room, closing the door firmly behind him.

The King walked around the table, sipping at his wine as if it were molten lava. He reached the far side opposite Sir Robert and put the goblet down. Sir Robert was pleased to see Enrique appeared a lot more robust than the last time they had met. His usual pallid complexion sported a couple of rosy cheeks and his hands were steady. He was only two weeks shy of his twenty-second birthday but bore the gaunt appearance of a man twice his age. A fine gold crown teetered atop his head. His prominent brow was the only thing keeping it from slipping over his long face.

"I must apologise for any inconvenience caused by the nature of your arrival señor, but the need for secrecy is paramount."

"I assumed it to be so Your Grace. It has enlivened an otherwise dull Tuesday morning."

"Quite. I will get straight to the point as we have much to discuss." Enrique peeled the top sheet from the pile on the table and held it tightly in his hands. "It has come to our attention that you have been showing a lot of interest in the Canary Islands." He laid down the velum sheet and turned it around for Sir Robert to see. It was a beautifully rendered map depicting the seven Canary Islands, stretching away from the Barbary Coast into the Atlantic Ocean.

"Ah! I see." Sir Robert smiled. "You are correct. I have had cause to research the Islands quite thoroughly in recent weeks." He leaned closer to examine the map. "I wasn´t aware I was being observed."

"I pay my spies well." Enrique commented dryly, "I do believe we have several in common."

"So it would seem." Sir Robert answered, feigning surprise. He knew exactly which of his agents reported to the King. He fed them precisely what he needed King Enrique to know.

"I would like to ask one question, to settle my own curiosity."

"Your Grace?"

"If I may be so bold as to ask, with regard to the Canary Islands, are you acting as the Honoured Ambassador to King Charles of France, or as Special Envoy to His Holiness, Pope Boniface of Rome?"

"You may ask, and I may answer." Sir Robert smiled, tilting his head, looking the King directly in the eye. "I have been commissioned by His Excellency Pope Boniface to survey the Islands. He has a desire to see them civilized and the native Canarians baptized. I am carrying out a logistical study on his behalf."

"Then it would appear we have a common goal. I too would like to see the Canary Islands *civilized*." the King added enthusiastically.

"How fortunate!" Sir Robert smiled and dipped his head briefly. "If *I* may humbly ask Your Grace, what drives Castilian interest in the Islands?"

The King gathered himself a moment before answering. His bearing impressed Sir Robert. Despite his tender years and fragile constitution, he assumed his responsibilities with tireless diligence. Castile was flourishing under his rule. It was rapidly becoming a place where endeavour was rewarded and fortunes made.

"I, or rather we, must resolve a problem we have unwittingly created." Enrique began slowly. "We have been engaging with the pirates along the Mediterranean Barbary Coast for some time now. We attacked their towns and harbours. We made their safe havens unsafe, as you are well aware, having recruited many French nobles to join our cause."

"Indeed your Grace. A most worthy cause."

"Worthy at the time but alas, it would seem that our success at routing these dogs from the Mediterranean has driven them to fresh harbours down the Atlantic coast, here." Enrique ran his finger down the right side of the map. "They swarm into the ocean and attack any ship they can find. The problem is becoming so grave that ship owners are refusing to let their crews sail beyond the Pillars of Hercules into the Atlantic. The Genoese and Venetian fleets hunt the pirates in the Mediterranean but are reluctant, or should I say, unwilling to go further. The Atlantic is turning into a lawless wilderness where good people are afraid to go. I cannot and will not stand by and watch the situation deteriorate further. These brigands must be stopped before they bring an end to all trade in the region.

"To do this, we must garrison troops on the Islands, build fortresses and towns with secure harbours. A strong military presence should drive them further south and away from our shipping lanes creating a safe corridor from the Canaries to Cadiz. To that end it is imperative we secure a solid foothold on these islands as soon as possible."

Enrique moved the map of the Islands to one side and picked up the rest of the sheets in the pile. He laid them out face up, one by one across the surface of the table. Each bore a detailed map of one of the Canary Islands, all rendered in fine detail showing mountain ranges and tiny pictograms of natives and settlements on land, ships and fantastical sea creatures on the Ocean.

"This really is excellent work Your Grace." Sir Robert leaned over the table and examined each of the maps in turn. "If I may?" he asked, pointing to one.

"Of course!"

Sir Robert picked up the velum sheet and held it at arms-length. It felt milky smooth between his fingertips. He squinted to see the minute notations more clearly.

"I appreciate your candour Your Grace," he said. "I will honour you in kind and reply with a truth of my own.

"His Excellency, Pope Boniface has had his eye on the Islands for some time. Until recently, they were merely trading posts, places to acquire high quality tallow and goat hides. They also provided the raw materials to produce dyes and pigments. Indeed, the rich violet and red cloaks worn by Bishops, Cardinals and Kings are coloured using plants and lichens from the Canary Islands. However, Rome´s interest goes way beyond colouring cloth and trade goods.

"His Excellency is engaged in an ideological war of attrition with the Mullahs of Islam who face him across the Mediterranean. He wants a population of Christians on Islam´s western flank. The Canary Islands are perfectly placed to service his needs in this respect. The native population there would become his Catholic army.

"The Church has been probing the Islands for years, sending missionaries to convert the heathens. They all disappeared without trace." Sir Robert paused and looked into Enrique´s eyes. "His Excellency has come to realise that his preachers will not be able to convert the Islands with words alone. He needs martial backing and protection. To those who stand by him, he will grant dominion over the entire archipelago. The first kingdom to establish a Roman Catholic Church on one of the Islands will therefore hold title to all seven islands."

"That should be Castile." The King stated abruptly. "We are the logical choice."

"I agree Your Grace." Sir Robert bowed his head and paused for a moment. "And because I believe wholeheartedly in your claim to the Islands, I am willing to share my personal recommendation for action with you."

"That would indeed be gracious. Your experience and tactical acumen would be most welcome."

Sir Robert lifted the map he held in his fingers and placed it in the centre of the table.

"I believe this island, Lancarote, is the key to unlocking the entire archipelago."

King Enrique looked down at the map, a knowing half smile threatening his lips. "Explain."

"As we speak, King Henry of Portugal is sending warships to the larger islands. He has despatched fleets to Canaria several times but failed to win any substantial victory. He doesn´t possess enough ships to launch a large enough assault to eradicate the island´s defenders in a single blow. The distance between the mainland and the Islands is simply too great to maintain supply lines for a protracted military campaign. Henry´s forces have been driven away time, and time again by the natives. Who, it is said, are ferocious giants, with copper coloured skin and fire in their hair. I have heard it told that the women fight alongside the men, bare-breasted, feral creatures who go into battle with infants on their hips."

"Really?"

"There are many stories your Grace, some wilder than others. The fact remains that King Henry´s efforts have failed, and the islands remain unclaimed.

"Lancarote," Sir Robert continued, his hand pressing on the centre of the map "does not have twenty thousand warriors to repel an invasion force. I believe there are fewer than five hundred natives on the island in total. To claim the Pope´s blessing and dominion over all seven islands, only one island needs to be civilized. Therefore, in my opinion, it makes logical sense to invade at the point of least resistance."

Enrique leaned forward, waving his hand over the other maps on the table. "If one were to invade the eastern isles, wouldn´t the tribes from the west come to their aid?"

"The natives are not a seafaring people. There are no records of them moving between islands, they do not even appear to share a common language. They have no ships and apparently no desire to build any. They are simple creatures who fight with rocks. I estimate that as few as one hundred noble knights could subdue and control the populations of Lancarote and Erbania together." Sir Robert paused and took a sip of his wine. "We have been trading with them for years, they are already half-tamed. If we were to send a small force with a strong, charismatic leader, we would have them eating out of our hands in no time."

King Enrique stood silently, stroking the wispy hairs on his chin. He scanned the maps for a moment then lifted his eyes to regard Sir Robert.

"It could be done." he whispered, clenching his fist.

"Your Grace?"

"I also selected the eastern isles as the primary target for an invasion, although I was thinking of proximity to the pirates on The Barbary Coast." He smiled briefly before continuing. "I must admit, I originally thought you were gathering information on behalf of King

Charles. I was unaware that Rome had such a keen interest in the Islands."

"Not this time Your Grace. King Charles is too consumed by the constant threat of an English invasion to consider sending his armies elsewhere."

"I understand only too well. Enmity with one´s neighbours can be extremely tiresome. We are fortunate to be enjoying a period of peace and prosperity throughout the Peninsula, for the first time in many generations. Skirmishes between Castile and our Portuguese neighbours are finally ending. In the springtime, King Henry and I will meet to sign a treaty of peace between our kingdoms. As I´m sure you will understand, it would not be prudent to commit troops to an enterprise inside disputed territories while brokering this fragile accord between us. Indeed, my council has warned many times against pursuing the Canarian matter until the agreement has been signed. They will not sanction the use of a Castilian army to invade the Islands. However, it is my belief that if we do not act soon, somebody else will, possibly even the Moors. That would make all our lives much more difficult."

"We would all lose." Sir Robert agreed solemnly.

"My thoughts exactly." the King proclaimed. He looked across the table slightly askance at Sir Robert. Sir Robert remained perfectly still under the King´s gaze, not wanting to interrupt his flow. Enrique was moving in all the right directions perfectly well alone.

"Are you still in contact with our old friends?" he asked, sounding slightly breathless after his outburst.

"Constantly." Sir Robert answered confidently.

"I want the Islands, for Castile, and of course for his Holy Father. What would it take for you to arrange it for us, without alerting the Royal Court or offending King Henry?"

Sir Robert struggled to maintain a blank expression. Months of planning and manipulation had led to this moment. He forced calm into his voice. "In theory I could arrange it your Grace, but it would be an expensive undertaking."

"I am in possession of a substantial war chest, to which many interested parties have already contributed. Would that help to persuade you?"

"Oh?" Sir Robert didn´t have to feign surprise this time, he was genuinely stunned. He had no idea the King had already raised a fighting fund.

"We could make twelve thousand pounds of gold and silver available immediately. I also promise to reward a further three thousand to the man who flies Castilian colours from the battlements of the first Castilian fortress built on Canarian soil. Would that be enough incentive for you?"

Robert staggered slightly at the amount the King suggested. By his calculations, it would be possible to subdue Lancarote and Erbania for much less. "It should be enough to get the wheels turning." he answered with a shrug of his shoulders.

"Very well, in that case, release the brakes." Enrique was biting his lips with nervous excitement. "Sir Robert, I am indebted to you." He held his hand out over the table.

"I am your humble servant Your Grace." Sir Robert took the King´s hand and bent to kiss the large signet ring on the middle finger.

"Very well." Enrique drew his hand back and reached for his wine. "Do you have anyone in mind to lead the expedition?" he asked before taking a sip.

"Yes your Grace, I believe I do."

2

Tyterogaka (Lancarote),
September 1st, 1401

The steady north-easterly wind filled the sail of the small boat as it skimmed across the water. The wake it left behind was like a sparkling ribbon of lace in an endless rolling plain of deep blue. The boat ran parallel to the coast, a couple of leagues off the northwest shore. The island rose like a giant sea turtle from the ocean depths, bearing a multitude of volcanic craters like limpets upon it's back. It was possible to see the length of the island, from the Ajache Mountains in the south to the soaring cliffs and Mount Corona to the north. Crowns of brilliant white cloud wrapped around the highest peaks. The island was in its final, parched summer stage before the autumn rains brought new life to the dusty, mustard coloured soil.

The crew inside the boat didn't have time to pay the view any attention. They worked the boat to its limit, squeezing every knot of speed from the wind. The triangular Latina sail swelled with barely a ripple at its edge. The sail hung from a long spar that sat atop a sturdy ten-foot mast. The spar´s leading end was tied to hook in the bow, the rear section rose high into the air behind the mast. The bottom corner of the sail was secured by a pulley at the stern, its tension controlled their speed. In full flight, the small clinker-built boat tore through the water like a monstrous shark fin.

Crouched at the prow, a young girl strung a short bow. She rode the bumps as the boat rode the waves, effortlessly absorbing every rise and fall with her supple legs. Behind her, her stocky younger brother lay back over the side, holding tightly to a rope secured to the top of the mast. His knees flexed as the boat bucked and yawed beneath him, his feet gripped the gunwale as if he were a part of it.

At the stern sat two men side by side on the starboard gunwale. Norstar, the younger of the two held the tiller in one hand, the rope controlling the sail in his other. He pulled the boat closer into the wind over the crest of a shallow wave and then released the pressure slightly as the boat rode down its back into a wide, shallow trough. He tapped the knee of the older man sitting next to him and showed him the course he should follow with his outstretched hand. The old man nodded and slipped underneath the body of Norstar who sprang to his feet and made his way towards the prow, eyes tilted towards the peak of the sail.

He passed by the boy hanging over the side, tapped him on the leg. The boy waved, his face creased into a huge smile. Norstar carried on towards the prow where the girl was tying a length of twine around the shaft of a stone-tipped arrow. He came up behind her and looked past her shoulder. Focussing beyond the sparkles on the water's surface, he caught sight of a brief twinkle of light reflecting off a fish scale.

"They're coming." he said.

Suddenly a twin-winged flying fish leapt out of the water and began to glide a couple of feet above the surface, just off the starboard bow. The girl had it sighted down the length of her arrow in the blink of an eye. She took one shallow breath and released the bowstring. The arrow flew through the air. It's small stone tip punched through the fish's scales and brought it crashing back to the water.

"Ha Hah!" shouted Norstar. He bent quickly to grasp the coil of twine at his feet and yanked the twitching fish into the boat. He turned to where it landed, handing the coil of twine behind him to the girl.

In two steps, he reached the fish, struggling in its final moments, it's mouth opened and closed as it gulped in air. Norstar picked it up with one hand and withdrew the arrow, taking special care not to lose the delicate stone arrowhead inside the fish. He returned to the prow, handing the arrow back to the girl and dropping the fish into a woven grass basket at the foot of the mast.

The water around them erupted as a half dozen fish leapt at the same time. They soared through the air, fins held out like wings at their sides.

"How many do you want?" the girl shouted back down the boat to the old man at the tiller. His face cracked into a huge smile and he waved her away.

"Catch me twelve!" he shouted, cupping his hand around his mouth before roaring with laughter.

"If she gets another one it´ll be a miracle." shouted the boy. "That last one was a lucky shot."

Her bow sprung again, taking a fish through the gill, the arrow burst from its mouth. Norstar yanked the twine, pulling the arrow and the fish back into the boat before it could splash back into the water.

"Lucky shot Eh!" chided the girl looking directly at her brother.

"You are the luckiest person I know" he managed to answer, laughing so hard he nearly slipped from his rope.

The girl looked at him and smiled, picked up the twine once more and re-coiled it carefully. She took the arrow from Norstar and wiped it down with a small square of soft animal skin. She tested the head and tail with gentle probing fingers before pulling the knot of twine tighter around the notch in the shaft. She nocked it carefully and lifted the bow.

"We´re not alone," said Norstar ominously at her shoulder looking into the face of the wave rising at their starboard side. The girl spun to see as one fish ended its flight and plunged back into the water. It re-emerged a heartbeat later, clutched in the beak of a smiling dolphin.

"Don´t shoot the big fish." Norstar said to the girl with a wink.

They sailed with the shoal for a good while, sharing the bounty with the dolphins who danced around the boat, much to the old man´s delight. His laughter rang out from the stern as the girl shot fish after fish and dolphins frolicked in the waves.

Eventually, they veered away and left the frantic pace of the chase behind. The girl unstrung her bow and cleaned her arrow carefully, paying special attention to the flight. She looked up as Norstar bent over her shoulder to study the feathers.

"The new ones are better." he said. "We´ll make more in the winter. You did well today."

"It was a thick shoal." The girl replied, putting the arrow and bow in a soft leather pouch at her feet.

"The season's changing, we'll see much more life passing soon. The birds are already coming south." Norstar paused for a moment, looking across the water to the North. His daughter watched him for a long moment before asking,

"Do you miss it?"

"Miss what?"

"The North, do you miss it? Do you ever feel the desire to go back with the birds after winter?"

"No." He scoffed. "How could I miss something that makes me cold when everything that makes me warm inside is right here." He reached out and pulled her to him. He planted a gentle kiss on her forehead. She held onto him, safe and warm within his strong embrace. "I do admit to wondering about my family from time to time, my Mother and Father, your other grandparents. I wonder how life is treating them." His voice trailed away as he thought for a long second. He pulled away and held his daughter by the shoulders, looked into her eyes and said "Let's go home." She nodded and freed her arms to rub her nose, then turned and busied herself preparing to release the rope securing the huge triangular sail to the bow.

Norstar was already bounding back to the stern. "Ready to come about!" he shouted as he ran. The old man edged himself forward along the rail holding the tiller. Norstar took it from him and spun down into his seat.

"Get ready to switch sides." he told the old man who nodded and crouched down, one hand gripping the side to steady himself. Norstar eased the tiller closer to his body and the boat started a turn to larboard. The boy secured the line he had been riding before leaping over to the opposite side of the boat. He picked up a line connected to the spar that the girl was one knot away from releasing at the bow.

As the boat reached the zenith of its turn, Norstar released pressure on the sail. The girl let the spar loose and the boy heaved it towards him. He caught it in the crook of his arm and bullied it around the pivot point on top of the mast. He walked it back up to the bow where the girl tied it into position.

The old man and Norstar ducked and switched to the larboard rail as the boat approached the end of the turn. Norstar pulled hard on the line to tighten the sail. The boat picked up speed smoothly as it straightened on its new course, heading directly for the sharp spire of White Mountain sticking up from the centre of the island like a pointer to the mid-day sun.

The girl stood and picked her way back to the stern, pausing to lift a line from the water splashing in the bilge. Her brother finished tying off another line and they met behind the mast. The boy grabbed her wrist smiling from ear to ear.

"You´ve been practising." He punched her playfully on the upper arm.

"While you were eating!" she spat back quickly and delivered a barrage of sharp punches into his shoulder. He lifted his free arm to block the blows, laughing to cover up how much the punches hurt. His big sister was stronger than her size would suggest.

"Stop stop stop!" he managed to squeeze out between guffaws. His sister gave him a withering look then feinted with her fist once more, aiming for his face. He instinctively flinched and released her arm. She gave his shoulder a loud slap before turning back to her grandfather. She rolled her eyes and shrugged, tilting her head towards her young brother. The old man laughed again as the girl skipped the short distance to the stern and slid down on to the gunwale beside him.

The boy sloped by, rubbing his bruised shoulder. He took the sail line from Norstar and yanked it tighter, tied it off and perched on the stern rail.

"That was fine shooting my little Fayna." the old man patted the girl´s shoulder. "You must be faster than your father now."

"She´s not there yet, but it won´t be long till she´s beating me with the short bow." said Norstar, feeling prideful of his daughter´s talent with the bow. As with everything she did, she was a quick learner who practised endlessly until she mastered it.

"What were you like with a bow when you were young?" Fayna asked her grandfather.

"What do you mean, *when I was young*? I´m still young now!" he answered in a tone heavy with mock indignation before dipping his head and smiling. "I never held a bow, not many Majos ever did before your father came. The sling has always been my weapon of choice. People used to know my name everywhere, Avago Stone Slinger they used to call me. Did I ever tell you that?" he asked. They all groaned. They'd lost count of the number of times he'd told them that.

"I've been getting good with my sling." chipped in the boy.

"Really?" said Avago, turning to look at him.

"Twelve targets with twelve shots the other day." the boy answered proudly.

"That is impressive. But how many moving targets can you hit?"

"I try, but Ma whacks me for bruising the goats." He looked down forlornly, but soon looked up again grinning as his grandfather laughed.

"I imagine she does beat you boy." He looked into the face of his grandson. "You need to practice shooting leaves in the waves, and then you'll be able to hit the eye of a running lizard from fifty paces."

"Really?"

"A small lizard."

"But what are leaves in the waves?" asked the boy.

"You throw some leaves in the sea and hunt them." Avago answered.

"How do you hunt leaves?"

"The same as you hunt anything. You study how they move. You watch and you learn until you know where they will go next. Then you strike. That is when a toy becomes a weapon, and a boy becomes a hunter. Come and tell me when you hit twelve out of twelve leaves in the waves."

"And then they'll call me Igo Stone Slinger."

"Igo the Arse more like." sniped his sister.

"Fayna the Hairy Witch." Igo snapped back quickly.

"Enough!" Norstar cut them off before they could go any further. If not stopped, the pair could bicker and insult each other all day and he wasn't in the mood to listen. This was going to be the last opportunity to sail before he pulled the boat out of the water and hid it for the winter. These two were not going to spoil his final moments on the sea with their nonsense. Fayna and Igo knew not to test him and sat back to relax into the rhythm of the boat's motion.

A rumble of distant thunder rolled across the sea. Winter was coming early this year, the rains and storms wouldn't take long to arrive and lash the island. Norstar liked to have his family safely inland at their winter home before the autumn storms lifted the waves to pound the shore. Winter also increased the threat of pirates and slavers prowling the seas around the island. The further his family were away from harm the better.

They covered the distance back to shore quickly. The sound of waves crashing against the rocks got steadily louder. Norstar stood and looked to his left where he sighted a large round boulder standing out prominently on the top of a small bluff. Several feet to its left stood a waist high cairn of flat stones. From where he stood, Norstar could sight the stones in relation to a peg on the boat's larboard gunwale. He turned to his right and searched out an identical cairn in line with another peg on the starboard side.

He erected the markers after narrowly avoiding being dashed against the rocks the first time he attempted to sail into the secret harbour. The entrance was almost impossible to spot from the sea. It could only be reached through a break in the sidewall of a small horseshoe-shaped cove. Waves beat the cove mercilessly. They smashed boulders and rocks from the cliff face. It was not only possible to hear them, but to feel them grind against each other when gigantic winter swells moved them around like toys.

Norstar's heart was racing as they approached the cove. The timing had to be perfect, one mistake and they would crash onto the rocks. He released the pressure on the sail to bleed off some speed. He felt the swirling currents beneath the hull with his feet. The sail obeyed his touch, like a team of horses driven by a charioteer.

Igo and Fayna took an oar each and braced themselves at the bow, ready to fend off if they got too close to the walls. A wave lifted them as it undertook the boat, Norstar pulled hard on the line tightening the sail sharply, accelerating to chase the water into the cove before the following wave in the set could catch them.

In the left wall of the cove, the opening revealed itself, a gap twenty feet across between two solid rock pillars. Norstar swung the tiller sharply and steered for the gap. The sail snapped loudly as it filled with air. They lurched forward in a rush of wind and spray with the wave building at their stern ready to break. The boat shot through the gap in the wall and into a channel of relatively calm water.

Avago released his breath in a loud rush. Norstar let the sail go slack, allowing momentum and the wash from the wave that had followed them into the cove to propel them along the channel leading to the secret harbour.

The wall to the right side fell away to reveal a huge bowl-shaped crater, one hundred paces in diameter and fifty feet deep at its centre containing a lagoon of crystal-clear water. The lagoon was sheltered on all sides by the steep crater walls. A beach of coarse black sand ringed the pool like flour pushed from a miller's stone.

The boat glided across the surface of the lagoon. Small fish darted away from its shadow, disappearing into cracks between the smooth boulders cluttering the lagoon's bed. Norstar leapt over to the mast and lowered the spar while Igo and Fayna gathered and tied the sail. The keel nudged ashore. Avago jumped from the bow and landed solidly on the black beach. The others followed when they finished tying the sail and together they dragged the boat up and out of the water.

The beach stretched away from them into a wide low tunnel that burrowed fifty paces underground before reaching a natural rock staircase leading up to the surface through a hole in the roof. Around the opening, hardy succulents grew from cracks in the rock, with gnarled and twisted branches bearing hundreds of bulbous little leaves in thick, juicy bunches. Spike leafed aloe plants grew in a huddled clump at the bottom of the staircase, greedily lapping up the best of the sunlight. The tunnel dived back underground beyond the staircase, stretching underground for another fifty paces before ending at a solid rock wall.

Tiny flecks of shifting dust swirled in the fingers of sunlight reaching through the hole in the tunnel roof. The light flickered when a figure appeared at the opening, followed by another, and another. A loud and deep bark echoed around the walls. Norstar stopped coiling the line in his hands and looked up. The dog barked again, challenging the echoes of its own voice. Norstar whistled through his teeth, two excited yelps answered.

A huge muscular dog dropped through the broken roof and pounded down the staircase followed closely by two young children, who skipped effortlessly down the big stone steps and onto the cave floor. The dog ran over the sand leaving the children far behind as it sprinted to within a couple of feet of Norstar. It leapt to a halt, burying it´s front paws in the sand. It´s rear end stuck up in the air, it´s tail wagged furiously threatening to topple the dog´s back end. It barked playfully with its tongue lolling out from the side of its mouth. It sprang to the side of Norstar who bent and caught it around the middle. He petted it with heavy hands while the dog squirmed and twisted under his touch, folding itself in two as it tried to lift its shovel shaped head to lick Norstar´s face. It rolled onto its back for a second and Norstar gave it a vigorous tummy rub, before it squirmed back onto its feet and bounced off to greet Fayna and Igo with the same enthusiasm.

Norstar looked up and braced himself just in time to catch the two children who ran full pelt into his arms. Norstar scooped them up, one in each arm and planted a kiss on their heads before putting them back down.

They looked like smaller versions of Fayna and Igo. The little boy, Chimboyo, was the elder of the two. He had a mop of curly blond hair which shone like a halo when the sun caught it just right, but he was no angel. His younger sister Nayra was shy and sweet and filled with empathy and wonder. She looked at the world through honey-flecked eyes, peeking out through flower petal lashes.

Avago stepped forward and placed a hand on each of their heads.

"What have you two monsters been doing." he asked, shaking his head from side to side as he studied them both.

Chimboyo answered, squirming under his grandfather´s grip, trying with all his might to pry the old man´s fingers away. "We´ve been up to the mountain caves with everyone." he said through gritted teeth before spinning and dropping to the sand, out of the old man´s reach. He smiled to show a gap where his two front teeth were missing before spinning away through the sand.

"And where is everyone?" asked Avago.

"They´re right behind us." Nayra answered turning to point back into the cave.

Avago let go of Nayra´s head and pinched her gently on the cheek. She smiled up at him bashfully before running off and diving on top of Chimboyo who was rolling in the sand.

"Boyo, Nayra, come here and help." Fayna called out from the side of the boat. They picked themselves up and ran over to her.

"What did you get?" Boyo asked, his eyes wide, looking at the basket at Fayna´s feet.

"A handful of fish and two birds." Fayna replied.

"Can I see!" he asked, bouncing on his heels.

"How did you get birds?" Nayra asked, her eyes flicking to the basket.

"I´ll show you." Igo said shouldering his way past Fayna and reaching for the basket. He lifted the lid, put his hand inside and pulled out the still body of a fat gull. He held the wing between his thumb and forefinger and stretched it out revealing a nasty break in its shoulder. "Two of them, flew straight into the mast at speed and cracked their wings. It´s bad for them but a tasty treat for us."

"It´s so sad. They´re so pretty." Nayra said, looking in genuine pain as she reached out and cautiously touched the break in the gull´s wing.

"You don´t have to eat them." Fayna said, grinning over Igo´s shoulder, making Boyo laugh.

"I won´t!" Nayra replied tetchily.

"Good. More for us." Boyo sniped at his sister who lunged for him. Igo stopped them from coming to blows with a hiss. He turned to look over his shoulder at Fayna, scolding her with his eyes for stirring the little ones up. She pulled a sarcastic face before turning to lift more things from the boat. Igo replaced the gull in the basket and closed the lid.

"You two take these up to the cave out of the sun, quickly before they start to smell". Igo lifted the basket into the little one´s hands. They huffed and puffed and began inching their load up the beach into the cool shade of the cave.

The dog, let out a small gruff and looked up towards the cave. Norstar followed his gaze and saw the sunbeams streaming through the hole in the roof shimmer once more. a whole group of people began descending the stone steps.

Two upright, strong young men led the way, almost identical to look at from this distance. They wore belts of soft animal skin around the waist, with strands of leather hanging from them, reaching down to the middle of their inner thighs to cover their genitals. Each held a binot, a fire-hardened wooden javelin, in their hands, and carried hide bags hung by straps from their square shoulders. They wore necklaces of small white shells and bone fishing hooks that stood out in the gloom of the cave. Anklets and bracelets of the same design shucked gently in rhythm to their steps, taken on feet shod in thick goatskin moccasins.

They were younger, softer versions of Avago. Jonay, the younger of the two wore his sun-bleached hair in a mix of dreadlocks and narrow braids, pulled from his face and tied back with a length of red string. The elder brother Rayco wore his hair loose, the honey-coloured tips brushed his shoulders. Intense hazel eyes stared out from behind the strands of hair hanging across his face.

Following closely behind, or rather tumbling over the rocks like a mini torrent of wild water came four young children. The four-year-old twin boys of Rayco and the four and three-year-old girls of Jonay, all wearing mini versions of what their fathers wore. They bobbled down the stone steps on hand, belly and foot each gripping a stick picked up somewhere along the path.

The children were followed down the staircase by their mothers, Mifaya and Daida. Mifaya, Rayco´s wife and mother of the twin boys offered her hand to assist Daida, Jonay´s wife, who held a sleeping baby girl cradled in one arm. They were dressed in airy linen tabards, tie-dyed with swirls of reds and oranges, clinched at the waist by narrow woven belts. Daida took Mifaya´s hand and the two descended carefully, as there were two babies to convey. Mifaya´s belly was starting to show the new life growing inside her, due to be born in early spring.

Behind them, keeping up a constant level of unrelenting chatter came Iballa, Matriarch of the family, Avago´s wife. A short, elegant woman with a wild head of hair, with wiry, grey strands sticking out at all angles.

At her shoulder, clutching an armful of sticks was her eldest daughter, Gara, Norstar´s wife. She paused at the top of the steps and looked through the gloom of the cave directly at Norstar. He stood squarely on the black beach, his bronzed skin, tight across his lean body. It seemed to shine against the black sand at his feet and the dark rocks at his back. His eyes, his piercing bright blue eyes stared into hers bridging the distance between them, causing her to catch a breath and smile before dipping her head and following her mother down into the cave.

"Yes mother." Gara replied absently to whatever the indomitable Iballa had just said. It didn´t matter, she would always say more. Gara wasn´t really listening, she quivered inside loving the fact that after all their years together, Norstar could still make her bits twirl by simply looking into her eyes.

Fayna plucked her leather bow pouch from the boat and went to stand next to her father. They watched together as Rayco and Jonay stepped from the cave and into the bright sunshine. They paused to remove their moccasins and drop their bags. The pair were almost knocked flying by the irrepressible mass of four small children bursting out of the cave, pushing past them in their race to jump into the water. Avago lifted his arms in the air and made himself as small as possible to avoid getting hit by the tangle of swinging arms and legs as the little ones surged past him and flopped into the pool, smashing the serenity of the lagoon with one huge splash.

The old man started to lower his hands before raising them up quickly to avoid Boyo and Nayra, who followed the lead of the other little ones and flew past Avago. They launched themselves from the edge of the beach, plunging down in the middle of the other children already splashing and screaming in the water. The dog was barking and thumping its front paws down, flinging wet sand in the air as it span and rolled at the water´s edge, eager to join the youngsters at play.

Avago turned back from watching the party in the water to greet his sons with an embrace.

"You survived then?" Jonay quipped as he exchanged a backslapping hug with the old man.

"He did better than you the last time you came with us Uncle," Fayna said smiling.

"Ha! She´s right." laughed Rayco taking a turn hugging his father. "You were green brother."

"And you did much better?" said Jonay, skipping across the sand to slap a hand proffered by Igo, who crouched on the prow of the boat.

"I was a natural." boasted Rayco, moving to grasp arms with Norstar.

"Aye!" Norstar said dryly, "After the first time you threw up you definitely improved your aim." They all laughed, Rayco threw an air punch at Norstar´s midriff before walking away and slapping hands with Fayna and Igo.

Mifaya and Daida stepped from the shadow of the cave and strolled down the beach arm in arm to greet Avago. They reached up to kiss his cheek. He bent and stroked the hair of the baby, sleeping soundly in Daida´s arms and kissed her gently on the forehead. She suckled twice loudly and snuggled back down into oblivion. "She sleeps through everything."

"Just like her father." Rayco quipped, ducking as Jonay flicked a look at him.

"Don´t wake her up!" called Iballa from the mouth of the cave with enough force to wake the dead. "We´ll never stop her screaming."

"Just like her grandmother." Avago mumbled under his breath to Daida, who shared a conspiratorial smile with the old man before turning to greet Norstar.

"What was that?" demanded Iballa, stepping across the sand to face her husband.

"I said, here comes the lovely Iballa! The light of my life." Avago replied, "and look how lovely she looks on this fine day." He wrapped his arms around her, leant in to kiss the cheek she reluctantly proffered before breaking his embrace by flapping her arms.

"Enough of that." She flustered as she stepped away and made a show of straightening her dress. She turned to Norstar, her expression switched from sour to sweet.

"Thank you for not drowning the old goat, he´s still got some uses." She rolled her eyes and offered her cheek for Norstar to kiss.

"He did well today Iballa, I would be honoured to have him in my crew any time." Norstar stated.

"He never says that lightly Mother." Gara said from Avago´s side. "I´d take that as praise indeed."

"Hmmm! And you my deadly hawk." said Iballa quickly to Fayna who stood with her bow pouch held protectively in her arms. "Did you catch us a feast today?"

"Too many fish to count!" Fayna stated proudly.

"And I necked a couple of birds." Igo chipped in.

"Ah well! I suppose that takes a certain amount of skill too my boy." she said, cupping his face before kissing him on the forehead. Little Igo had the heart of a hero. He was determined and driven, perhaps more so because he was smaller than most boys his age. Iballa loved him dearly and always made a big fuss of him. She was tiny herself compared to other Majos, although for what she lacked in size, she more than made up for in volume.

"Well done both of you." Gara said, slipping from her father´s side and moving to stand with Norstar. "And welcome home to you." she said, tilting her head back to look up into his face.

"Good to be home." He bent his head to meet hers and they touched lips briefly. They held each other´s gaze for a second longer before turning their attention to the others.

"We´ve got some work to do." Gara said, her arm still resting round Norstar´s waist. "Fish cleaning and fire building. The sooner we´re finished, the sooner we eat."

******

The sun drifted across the sky, shining down on them as they worked into the afternoon. Norstar, Fayna and Igo set to work breaking down the boat for winter storage. The lines and sail were removed, the mast and oars oiled and placed deep within the cave and covered with rocks to conceal them. They dragged the hull high up the beach, turned it upside down and pushed it into a cleft in the cliff wall. It could still be seen if anybody looked closely from the beach, but it was virtually invisible from the wall looking down into the lagoon.

The rest of the family relaxed around a fire pit in the shade of the cave mouth. The fish cooked on rocks heated around the edge of the fire. The gulls were plucked and stuffed with wild garlic and rosemary and roasted above the hot embers. Jonay twirled the birds lazily as he sat half listening to another of Iballa´s monologues. Igo dropped to the ground beside him, reached out to tear a strip of meat from one of the birds and got a slap on the back of his hand for his trouble. Fayna and Norstar joined the group, Norstar took his place next to Gara and Fayna hunkered down at Avago´s side. Fayna pounced on a pause in Iballa´s story and asked.

"Is it ready to eat yet? I´m so hungry I could eat it all."

"We were waiting for you to join us." Avago replied, beaming down at her.

"Hmmm, I´m here, so let´s eat." Fayna said leaning forward. She tentatively prodded the plump fish roasting on the rock in front of her. She plucked a flake of steaming white flesh with her fingers and threw it in her mouth, blowing and sucking heavily as she flipped it around and around with her tongue in a desperate attempt to cool it down. "Itsch hot!" she tried to say, eventually cooling it enough to chew and swallow. "…and it´s good."

The family let out an exclamation of joy and began to reach out for the fish.

"Slow down everybody." Norstar stopped them. "We have one more provider to thank." He nodded towards his eldest son. "Igo caught the birds, he should take the hunter´s portion." Igo blushed a little and sat a little taller.

Jonay produced a stone bladed knife with a bone handle. He cut a strip from the bird´s breast and gave it to Igo. Everybody looked on as he popped it into his mouth. He took a sharp intake of breath to cool it down and began chewing. The size of his smile told them how good it was. Another exclamation of joy rang out as everybody leaned in to eat.

Norstar pulled out a knife of his own, sliced a leg from one of the birds, blew on it to cool it and turned to the dog. It wagged its tail furiously as it sat on its haunches staring at the meaty morsel as if it would disappear if he let it out of his sight. Norstar clicked his tongue gently and the dog took the meat tenderly in its massive jaws and carried it away a few paces before wolfing it down.

Boyo reached over Fayna´s shoulder and picked gingerly at the fish flesh, trying his best not to wince as it burned his fingers. Nayra sat at her grandmother´s side and listened with genuine interest as Iballa managed to squeeze words out between mouthfuls. Jonay carved strips from the roasted birds and passed them around. They ate slowly, appreciating the food with the time it deserved.

Before long, all that remained of the feast were scraps, which the dog was doing its best to lick off the cooling rocks. The family snoozed, sheltered from the scorching heat of the afternoon sun in the cool cave.

Norstar woke with a start, stirred from his sleep by an almighty explosive snore bursting out of Avago. He sat up quietly and was surprised to feel the hand of Gara brush against his back. He twisted to look down into her smiling face. He gestured with his head towards the lagoon, and she nodded eagerly.

He took her hand and they got silently to their feet. They tiptoed over the sleeping bodies and made their way down to the water's edge. The dog was the only one to notice them go but was more interested in finding another morsel of food to eat than to follow them.

Gara let go of Norstar´s hand and untied the belt at her waist. She let it drop and lifted her dress over her head. Norstar watched as she revealed her skin to the light. She slipped the dress clear of her face and caught Norstar´s eyes roaming over her body.

"Hey!" she called. He looked up into her face.

"You´re beautiful." he whispered. She smiled teasingly as she threw her dress to the sand, kissed Norstar quickly and dived into the pool, breaking the surface with barely a ripple. Norstar was after her in a heartbeat, catching her easily as she swam underwater. They burst through a shoal of tiny silver fish which scattered in all directions, creating a flickering light display as they swirled around the swimmers and reformed as one shimmering shoal behind their feet.

Below them, piles of smooth rocks and boulders littered the bed of the lagoon. Long leaves of vivid green plants reached up through the cracks between them. They swayed in the gentle current like trees in a breeze. A sudden movement caught Norstar´s eye. Between the swaying plants, a small eel wound its way through the rocks. Norstar imagined he was flying over a forest, watching a huge serpent racing through the trees.

They rose to the surface for air in the middle of the lagoon. Norstar swam around in a tight circle to face Gara. She swept the hair away from her face and opened her eyes. Norstar stretched out one hand to brush against her hip as she trod water. His fingers tingled at the feel of her cool skin. He reached around with his other hand to the small of her back and pulled her body close to his. Gara wrapped her arms around his neck and kissed him fully on the lips. They stopped kicking and sank slowly below the surface. Their lips locked together, breathing into each other, slowing down time itself until there was no air left between them and they had to resurface.

They kicked lazily across the pool with Norstar turning frequently to look into his wife´s eyes. Her body had changed as she matured, but that only helped to emphasize her strength and grace more. Her breasts were fuller and hips a little wider but for Norstar, that only meant more of her beautiful soft skin to cherish, and that never ceased to thrill him. The young girl of sixteen he´d first met was still in her eyes, those olive-coloured eyes that had captured him so mercilessly at their first meeting and still held him captive to this day. They lived and grew together. Learned, laughed and loved together. She touched his soul and was a part of him, the best part of him.

He wondered if dreams could still be called dreams when they came true.

He had travelled many oceans to find his wife and his new life. The Fortunate Islands provided well for him, and he missed neither the wealth nor the complications that went with his old life in the North.

He first sailed to the island many years before, from another world where he was known by another name. He came on board the good ship Tilly, captained by his brother Frank. He stayed behind when his brother left, a helpless prisoner of love.

They rolled around each other as they swam together through the lagoon. Their skin was highly charged in the cool water, they delighted in the sensation of touching and being touched. Norstar gently brushed his fingertips across the small of Gara´s back causing her to shudder. She spun round and nuzzled her back into his chest, reaching down she thrilled to feel his desire matched her own. She turned her head and kissed him fully on the mouth. He tightened his grip around her body and they sank under the water once more.

Gara popped back up to the surface first, put her head down and kicked hard across the lagoon. Norstar surfaced a second later and gave chase. He was a strong swimmer but could never catch Gara. She swam with effortless grace, the water flowed across her back as she cut through the pool and along the channel leading out to the open sea. She swam all the way to where the calm water met the waves, a smooth lip of rock just below the surface marked the boundary between wild and tame. She touched the rock and twisted to face Norstar as he caught her. He placed his hands on her hips and pulled her towards him. Their bodies came together. Gara wrapped her arms tightly around his neck and kissed him, her hungry mouth found his equally ravenous.

The kiss closed their senses to anything but each other. Gara pushed her fingers into his long hair and stroked his head. Norstar slid his hands, down over her round, smooth buttocks to the backs of her thighs. He lifted her legs without resistance and pulled her onto him. She let out a gasp of pleasure and threw her head back, wrapped her legs around his back and drew him in deeper and deeper until they were crushed together, locked in the most intimate, passionate embrace. He filled her completely and she enveloped him perfectly. He drew one hand up to the small of her back and held her to him while gripping the rock lip with the other hand to anchor them in place. They moved slowly together, rocked by the waves into a rhythm that suited their unhurried desire, until the desire became too strong to resist and their rhythm became more frantic as they approached their pulsating climax together.

Afterwards, Norstar held Gara crushed against his chest, she held onto him tightly and purred in his ear. They drifted there locked together at the edge of the sea, in love with life and each other.

3

Saint-Martin-le-Gaillard, Normandy, France, September 24th, 1401

It was eleven in the morning and the great and good from miles around were starting to gather at the entrance to the Church of Notre Dame, Saint-Martin-le-Gaillard. Merchants and nobles rubbed shoulders, chatting amiably while waiting for the service to begin in celebration of the Patron´s feast day.

Livestock roamed lazily through the orchards lining the valleys for miles around, gorging on dropped fruit, unaware that they were being encouraged to do so to flavour their meat, a delicacy as desirable as the fine cider the region was famed for.

Sir Robert was looking forward to a pork and cider feast later, but until then he was content to swig the flavours of autumn in the air. He strolled along the lane leading to the church. The earth was dry and cracked underfoot, baked hard by the summer sun. It wouldn´t be long before the rains came and it turned back to a muddy mire, but for now it was pleasant and solid and bore Sir Robert along at a good steady pace.

In his wake followed Piquet, his secretary and constant companion. Piquet carried a sheath of papers under one arm and a leather satchel over his shoulder. He had to skip forward every third step to keep pace with Sir Robert.

They approached the church from the south, partially obscured by the headstones in the small cemetery in front of the limestone church. The sunshine streaming over Sir Robert´s shoulder made the cream coloured, church walls glow. He noticed the congregation were beginning to file inside through the main door on the opposite side of the building.

Perfect! He thought.

He timed his approach to slip through the doors just behind the last people to enter. The interior was bright, light poured into the nave through windows set high in the walls. Dark, low ceilinged, side aisles adjoined the nave behind elegantly carved stone columns. The congregation stood around in small groups, finishing hushed conversations before the service began. Sir Robert cut to his right and stepped between the columns into the shadow of the side aisle. He scanned the congregation and spotted his nephew standing at the centre of a tight knot of people who appeared to hang on his every word.

He looked vibrant and healthy and wore his forty years well with very few lines creasing his boyish features. A mane of rich auburn hair curled out from underneath the brim of a sumptuous blue velvet bonnet. There were a few wisps of grey in his well-trimmed beard but very few other signs of wear and tear to spoil his appearance. As Sir Robert looked, he could see his own sister´s features clearly in Jean´s face. If the son possessed just a fraction of his mother´s character to go with the looks, he would conquer all seven of the Canary Islands without breaking a sweat.

Sir Robert pointed his nephew out to Piquet. The little secretary made his way through the congregation stealthily, slipping between bodies until he was face to face with Jean. Jean recognised Piquet immediately, his eyebrows rose in surprise when he saw him. He excused himself politely and took off after his uncle´s secretary who led the way to the rear of the church.

The main church doors swung shut with a deep thud and a hidden choir began to sing. The congregation hushed and turned to face the altar. A lavishly attired Priest flanked by two clergymen entered the chancel from the vestry on the right side of the building and bowed deeply to the large wooden crucifix hanging above the altar.

Jean hoped he wasn´t noticed leaving as he followed Piquet through a small door in the wall. They passed through a tiny antechamber and slipped out of another door leading outside onto a shaded lawn. Piquet closed the door quietly and pointed to a pathway leading down to the river. Jean hurried across the lawn to the path. The splendid blue cape draped over his right shoulder bounced as he walked while a bejewelled dagger chinked against his hip in time to his steps.

Sir Robert waited in the shade of a huge oak tree, a short distance along the pathway. He turned to appraise his nephew as he came closer.

"Sir Robert!" the young man hailed. "I hope that your sudden appearance brings joyful, rather than woeful tidings."

"Today is a day to rejoice Nephew, not to mourn." Sir Robert replied. "I come to you with a proposal from a mutual friend in the South, one who has served us well in the past."

Jean stopped short. "Not another slaughter in Africa I hope."

Sir Robert shook his head. "Walk with me."

He took Jean´s elbow and led him down the shady path to the river. The gruff squawks of the geese and ducks swimming across the water echoed through the trees lining the banks. The river ran slowly, its deep green water babbled and gurgled against the steppingstones which crossed its span. Sir Robert stopped and looked around, making sure there was no one close enough to hear what he had to say.

"Your letters prompted me to make some enquiries." he began, satisfied they were unobserved. "It appears that the Canary Island problem is causing a great deal of consternation to many."

Jean nodded knowingly. "It has been six months since I took my last delivery from there."

"Quite. You are in good company. There are those who would have me assemble a force to intervene in the crisis. But they do not wish to see a repeat of the slaughter on the Barbary Coast. The parameters of this mission are completely different.

"The savages… the Canarians… are to be welcomed into our fold. They are to be peacefully subdued and converted to the Catholic faith and thenceforth, will enjoy the protection of a powerful kingdom. With a military presence on the Islands, we should deter the pirates and embolden the traders. This would be a long-term solution relying heavily on the cooperation of the indigenous people. The Canarians are a primitive, but noble race. They will make better allies than enemies as we seek to bring order to the region."

Jean nodded quietly, digesting his uncle´s words.

He had written to his uncle decrying the lack of product leaving the Islands. Jean manufactured and supplied the finest coloured cloths to an enviable list of noble clients. His reds and purples supplied royal houses throughout the continent. He had amassed a not-inconsiderable fortune by selling his wares to the Church, a contract arranged by Sir Robert. The best ingredients to produce the colours came from the Canary Islands. Dragon's blood from the dragon plant, and orchil, a lichen which grew in abundance on the archipelago's volcanic rocks.

Pirates had been attacking ships in the area, breaking Jean's supply chain. He had originally written to ask his uncle if there was a way to drive the pirates away. His Uncle was now talking about invading and enforcing nothing less than a theological change on an entire population... Sir Robert didn't disappoint with the scale of his ambition.

"Any who embark on this mission will be rewarded handsomely both financially and in status." Sir Robert continued. Jean's insides jumped at the mention of status. He longed to refute his inferred reputation as a man with little substance who married into all the power he would ever possess. Of course, Sir Robert was aware of this, he continued.

"There are seven inhabited islands in the chain. We shall establish a beachhead on the easternmost of those. Lancarote."

"I know it well. Excellent lichen."

"Initial intelligence suggests that there are fewer than three hundred savages to be found there, men, women and children. They have neither steel nor iron, they are armed with wooden spears and rocks, hardly a worry for a knight in armour. If the need arises the fight could be knocked out of them with a single volley of crossbow bolts, if... and only if, conflict cannot be avoided." Sir Robert paused.

"Am I to understand that by making me privy to this information you wish me to join an expedition to invade the Islands." Jean asked.

"My dear boy... I would like you to lead it."

Jean's eyes flew open in shock. "That is a great honour Sir, and a great responsibility."

"If you don't feel up to the challenge then speak now and I will waste no more of our time discussing the matter." Sir Robert said quickly. "I need not tell you that you are sworn to the strictest secrecy should you choose to decline the offer."

"Of course." Jean replied with a slight nod of the head. "But I think you know I am unlikely to decline. You have never suggested anything without knowing the answer before asking the question Uncle."

"Quite." Sir Robert said with a small smile.

Jean continued. "Would our powerful and dare I say, *wealthy* backers be financing the expedition?"

"Unfortunately, our main backer in the South is unable to be seen to support any acts that could threaten the fragile peace which is being brokered on the peninsula. But you may rely on a considerable war chest being made available in the form of a loan."

"A loan against what exactly?"

"A loan against the successful completion of the crusade, secured by something of great value to offset the loss, should the mission fail in any way. Your estates at Grainville for example could be mortgaged for a sum of, let's say, seven thousand pounds, in silver, which I dare say should be enough to muster enough knights, a ship and crew to get the job done."

"That complicates things somewhat. I would be assuming all the risk."

"…and collecting all the rewards, which I might add are considerable. Have you any idea what the total potential exports are for Lancarote every year?"

Jean shook his head.

"One fully loaded ship every month, fifty barrels of orchil in each. You have what…four barrels a year?" Jean nodded "And they cost a pretty penny I wouldn't wager." Jean nodded again. "The one who controls the market, controls the price, and receives a percentage from every load going through his port. In and out. Hells! You could even mint your own coins. Have you ever imagined your likeness on the money in your purse?"

Jean swallowed even though his mouth was dry.

"The like of what I´m offering to you doesn´t come along in five men´s lifetimes. Your name will be written about and sung by bards throughout the ten kingdoms. That is of course *if* you are indeed my man?"

"You know I´m your man." Jean answered quickly. He bowed deeply, closed his eyes and took the deepest breath he could.

"Good." Sir Robert said simply. "Now get up! Get up." He took Jean´s arm and led him back to the church. He was unwilling to say more, Jean would ask clear, pertinent questions when his mind had calmed enough to think practically. Sir Robert didn´t want to push him too far and make him nervous unnecessarily. Jean was a shrewd man of character, a noble knight and a gambler, but one who knew when to quit and walk away.

They arrived back at the church and stepped into its shadow. Jean finally had his racing mind under enough control to trust his mouth with words.

"How long have I got to assemble my men?" he asked.

"You should be ready to sail in early spring. This venture has to succeed at the first attempt, or all is for nought. I see no need to jeopardise our chances of success by using unnecessary haste."

"Of course not."

"We´ll speak no more about it today. Let us agree to meet two days hence at my house in Tours to begin preparations in earnest. There are many details to discuss."

"I will be there."

"Go back inside now." Sir Robert said, "It wouldn´t do for the Baron to miss the service."

"Of course. Are you coming in?" Jean asked brightly.

"No, I have an important matter to attend to in the city and must leave immediately."

And like that, the meeting was over. They shook hands and kissed. Sir Robert watched as Piquet opened the side door to let Jean back into the church before turning and striding away. Piquet ran to catch him up.

Jean slipped quietly back into the congregation. Nobody questioned the reason for his disappearance. They all stood in silence listening to Father Verrier deliver his sermon. Jean didn´t hear a word, he was occupied compiling lists in his head. He let loose a secret, silent snigger as he imagined his likeness on a coin.

It wasn´t as secret and silent a snigger as he had thought, he could feel eyes burning into the side of his head. He turned to find his wife staring at him from a few feet away.

God it would be good to get away from that sanctimonious sow for a while. he thought. He smiled at her and playfully touched the brim of his cap. She scowled and looked away, searching for some fresh victim to pour scorn upon no doubt.

There wasn´t much love left between them. They had no children, indeed they hadn´t shared a bed for long enough to make one for eight and a half of the nine years spent together. A good lengthy crusade with a risk of violent death was far preferable to languishing here with his wife and having his will to live slowly sucked out of him.

4

Tenesar, Lancarote,
September 24th, 1401

Norstar sliced the excess thread away with a stone blade and held the heavily patched sail at arm's length to examine his handiwork. Satisfied that the new fix would hold, he rolled the sail tightly and slid it into a goatskin sleeve. He placed the long bundle around the foot of the cave wall and thumped it into place.

He packed the needle and thread into a little leather bag and stood to place it in a hole high in the wall before bending again to step through the cave's opening and out into the mottled shade of the yard. The sun's rays hadn't struck the cave mouth yet but they were getting closer, Norstar would have to leave soon to join the rest of his family at Avago and Iballa's home on the southern face of the volcano. It was quiet without the noise of the children playing. Even the dog had left with them this morning, excited by the scent of one of Avago's bitches coming into heat.

Norstar walked out into the yard and stretched his arms high in the air. He'd been at his sewing for a while and needed a good stretch. He grunted noisily as the joints in his shoulders and back popped, the relief was blissful.

Chickens squawked in alarm at the noise. Some ran from the yard through a hole under the gate while others ran to get back in. Norstar laughed for a second before he noticed that the birds were breaking the bottom of the brushwood gate.

Add that to the list of jobs I must finish today. he thought as he rushed over to pull the gate open to stop the mad birds from destroying it completely. They scattered in all directions. He cursed loudly as one scraped his shin with its sharp claws in its rush to escape.

The gate was in the centre of the wall ringing the yard. Norstar crouched down to examine the damage the birds had done to it. It wasn't badly broken this time, but it probably should be replaced with something more substantial if he didn't want to spend year after year fixing it.

The list of minor repair jobs he had to do was becoming so long that he was unsure which to do first. So, he sat down heavily with his back to the wall to think about it for a while.

He looked up at the volcano towering above the family caves to its jagged crown, three hundred feet above. It was an impressive roof to have on one's home. The sight always stunned him. The first rains of the season had washed the dust away, exposing the deep red and black rocks at the heart of the volcano through scars in its sandstone cladding. Wispy clouds skimmed across the cerulean sky, they would get fatter as the day progressed and release more rain to drench the parched land. Norstar endeavoured to catch as much of the rain as possible and store it in underground cisterns to see them through the dry months. He spent a lot of time building small dams all over the mountainside to divert water into the cisterns. It was a constant job to repair and modify them, as it was to service the steep narrow pathways leading to the sleeping chambers higher up the mountain.

Norstar and Gara chose the location of their home together and toiled hard in the early years, shaping the caverns and smoothing the walls with mud and grass. They built stone and timber windbreaks at strategic points to shield them from the worst of the winds, creating a bubble of calm on the western side of the volcano. They could watch the sun dip into the sea every evening from the shelter of their caves, which made the work worthwhile. It required a lot of attention to keep out the weather but Norstar thought it was well worth the extra effort to be able to enjoy some solitude. The rest of the family lived on the southern sheltered side of the mountain. Close enough, but far enough away.

The view to the west was splendid. Looking from the front gate to the left stood the craters of the sacred Mother and Son volcanoes. They lay two leagues to the south and completely dominated the landward horizon. The crater of The Mother was a half league across at its peak and formed an unbroken ring which sat atop a steep slope stretching over a hundred feet down to the sparse farmland fanning out from its base. The Son was an identical crater, but four times as big. It stood protectively over the shoulder of The Mother.

On the plain between Norstar´s cave and the Mother and Son, trees grew in small copses with the huts of Majos clustered around the windswept trunks of the stunted trees. They lived together around springs of fresh water, the only sweet water sources on the island. From his vantage point above the plain, Norstar could see tiny people scattered across the land, driving their goats back home after a long morning at pasture.

Beyond the settlements, Norstar was able to see a full sweep of the ocean, an unbroken line from the north to the southwest. He sometimes caught a glimpse of the snowy peak of the island of Nivaria sixty leagues away across the sea, the holiest and highest mountain in the Canary Islands. It would glisten in the light of the first rays of the sun on clear mornings, some evenings it stood out in dark relief as the sun set behind its peak.

A noise alerted him. He stood and turned to his right to see a small fall of rocks tumbling down the mountainside, followed by his eldest son. Igo hit the goat track at the mountain´s base and started sprinting towards Norstar. Norstar stepped out of the gate and hurried along the track to meet him.

"Pa! Pa!" Igo yelled followed by an incomprehensible torrent of words. Norstar reached for him and gripped him by the shoulders, urging him to slow down and breathe.

"Pa, you´ve got to come. Mifaya and the boys have been taken."

"Taken?"

"Pirates!" yelled Igo, an excess of adrenaline making him jog on the spot. Norstar released him, turned and sprinted back towards the gate, Igo ran at his heels, babbling all the way.

"They went after a couple of goats that ran away. They took the dog with them but one of the pirates shot him. Fayna stayed with him, he´s hurt bad Pa. I came straight back over the tops to get you."

They crashed into the yard. Norstar made for the chicken roost, a squat cave in the corner of the yard.

"Where are they?" he asked as he thrust his arm into the opening causing the birds within to complain loudly, flapping and rolling over each other to get out of the way in a storm of feathers.

"Next to Broken Tooth." Igo answered.

Norstar reached deep into the chicken roost, into a narrow crevice at the rear and put his hand on a tightly wound bundle crammed into the gap. He grabbed it and pulled it out, undoing the ties that held it closed while instructing Igo.

"Go quickly to Avago´s" he said. "Tell whoever you find there to bring weapons." He finished unwrapping the bundle to reveal a weatherworn, yew longbow with a full quiver of iron-tipped arrows. He pulled a coiled-up bowstring from the quiver and made short work of stringing the bow.

"Go quickly!" he urged as he slung the quiver over his shoulder. Igo turned and sprinted through the gate and shot off to the left. Norstar went to the right and sprinted along the track, skipping over rocks and avoiding loose stones. He got to the point where Igo had slid down the slope and began to climb.

He reached the far lip of the crater quickly and looked down upon the land stretching out from the mountain´s base to the sea. He saw the flock of goats grazing in a cleft at the base of the mountain below and to his right. Directly ahead was Broken Tooth about half a league away. It was a small outcrop of rock sticking twenty feet up in the air from the centre of a wide flat field. He could just about make out the stick like figure of Fayna in the shadow of the rock.

He picked out a path down the mountainside and took off towards her as quickly as he could. He was soon at Fayna´s side. She sat cradling the dog´s massive head in her lap, stroking and soothing it with gentle words while tears streamed down her cheeks. She looked up at Norstar pleadingly as he approached. He got to his knees, putting one hand on his daughter´s shoulder before crouching down to lay his other hand gently on the dog´s head. With an almighty effort, it turned to look into Norstar´s eyes and let out a painful whimper before collapsing back onto Fayna´s lap.

"There boy." Norstar cooed, cupping the dog´s muzzle and stroking its cheek with his thumb. There was a short length of black iron protruding from the dog´s chest between its front legs. It was the rear end of a heavy crossbow bolt, and it was ripping the dog´s lungs to shreds with every shallow breath he took.

Norstar threw his head back and cried a silent acid tear, filled with sadness and rage. With an almighty effort, the dog pulled its heavy head round once more and licked the tear from Norstar´s cheek with a hot, dry tongue before falling back, spent. It exhaled one final time, and then, there was silence.

Fayna bent down and sobbed into the dog´s side. Norstar sprang to his feet and rushed to the top of Broken Tooth. Fury drove him. He scanned the ground at the foot of the outcrop, soon spotting traces of a struggle written in the earth.

Footprints were plentiful in the soft dust. There had been four, maybe five men concealed among the rocks, the goats tethered to a bush as bait. The bleating of the foolish animals had drawn Mifaya and her two small boys into the trap. The broken branches of a thorn bush showed where Mifaya had been beaten and restrained. Drops of blood and a long clump of red hair clung to the flattened barbs of the bush.

He saw the tiny footprints of the little ones running away, two men had swooped on the babies and lifted them into the air. The dog´s prints led to a man kneeling in the dirt. There was a splash of blood on the ground where the dart had struck him in the chest, while leaping at the man with the crossbow. A bloody trail led from where it´s heavy body hit the ground to where it dragged itself to die.

There were tracks leading to the North.

"They´ve taken them to the Crabs." he called out to Fayna. "Tell the others when they come." He ran, the arrows bouncing on his back beat out an angry rhythm. He didn´t need the tracks to know where they were. There was only one bay, hidden from view, deep enough to take the draft of a heavy ship at low tide. A small volcano shielded it from view from one side, a steep black cliff towered above it from the other. A narrow crabber´s path led down to the base of the volcano where enormous crabs, scuttled across the rocks at the edge of the sea, daring the waves to knock them off.

Norstar ran until his heart was bursting, his anger gave him speed and the power to feel no pain. He skidded to a halt on the edge of the cliff just as a boat was tying up to the side of a fat double-masted caravel with grimy, grey sails. It was spinning on it´s chain, turning tightly under topsails, manoeuvring to pick up the anchor and leave.

The kicking, tiny bodies of his nephews were manhandled up the side and onto the ship followed by Mifaya, who let out a heart-breaking scream as she was pulled over the gunwale by her hair. Norstar heard the thump as she landed heavily on the hardwood deck. She sat up with her arms crossed protectively around her belly. She called out for her sons and was slapped savagely across the face by a bald sailor with a long red beard who screamed into her face mockingly before striking her again.

Norstar nocked an arrow and sighted down its shaft. A bleating goat was being passed up to the deck from the boat by a cur with a crossbow slung across his back. The dam holding back Norstar´s rage could hold no longer, it burst wide open. He let the arrow fly from his fingertips. It flew straight and true. Those aboard ship heard the arrow zipping through the air. They froze for the long second it took to hit with a dull wet thud. The bowman let out a whimper and collapsed in a lifeless heap in the bilge of the boat. Then the shouting began.

The bald pirate was hoisting a screaming Mifaya by her hair and using her as a shield. Norstar cursed and switched targets, swinging round to the left to find the short, round yet extremely loud Captain who was crouching behind the stern gunwale barking out orders in a high-pitched scream. His head flashed quickly into view over the rail and Norstar released. The captain was fortunate enough to stumble forward, just in time to avoid being shot through the ear. Instead, the arrow cut a deep furrow through the fold of fat at the back of his neck. He began screeching like a pig.

Norstar heard a whistling crossbow bolt pass a few feet over his head. He saw the crossbowman stood on the narrow forecastle of the caravel bending to yank the string back to load another bolt. He never got the chance as Norstar´s next arrow took him in the shoulder, spinning him around and down heavily onto the deck.

"DOG…STOP!" The captain of the ship called out suddenly, using the common tongue. Norstar looked to the stern where he was horrified to see his screaming young nephews held by the ankles, knives pressed to their skinny necks.

Mifaya screamed. The bald man span her around and delivered a jaw breaking punch to the side of her face, knocking her out cold. He carried her limp body to the main mast and secured her to it with a thick rope. Her head flopped as the wind filled the ship's topsails and slowly dragged the caravel out of the bay.

"DOG. NEXT TIME WE TAKE *YOU!*" The captain called. He roared with laughter as they picked up speed and sailed off to the northwest. Norstar was powerless to do anything but watch.

The ship was already a good distance away when he heard approaching feet behind him.

Rayco, Mifaya's husband was screaming her name as he ran to the cliff top. Norstar grabbed him as he ran by to stop him leaping from the cliff. Jonay appeared, dropped his binot on the ground and flung his arms round his elder brother and Norstar, binding to them both and letting out a yell to match his brother's cry. The three of them were joined by Fayna, Igo and Avago along with two other Majos from the neighbouring clan. They all joined together and embraced tightly, screaming into the sky, wailing a heart-breaking song of rage and sorrow.

They screamed until they were breathless.

Their heads dropped. Their tears fell heavily for their wife, sister, daughter, friend and babies, who they would never see again.

5

La Rochelle, France,
December 22nd, 1401

The wind whipped the waves into jagged peaks, fast moving squalls raced them to shore beneath heavy black clouds. A fully loaded ship was tossed from side to side like a toy as it battled to reach shelter within the safe embrace of the harbour walls.

Sir Robert shivered as a peel of rain lashed against the window, glad he´d decided to come by road instead of the sea. He was staying in one of his town houses, a property rented until recently to a young lawyer who was killed under the wheels of a farmer´s cart, after being thrown from his horse. He left neither family nor friends to mourn his passing or to claim any inheritance. Sir Robert was in the process of emptying the house and selling off the young man´s possessions to cover the rent arrears accrued since the young man´s demise. All the furniture and personal items were already gone, all that remained were the desk and chairs in the room he had used as an office on the ground floor of the building.

Piquet had sorted through the books and papers in the desk drawers. Sir Robert kept and copied anything potentially useful, the rest was burned. A dwindling stack of pages stood next to the fireplace. It crackled and spat in the hearth as another almighty gust of wind shot down the chimney. Freezing rain rattled the small leaded windows in their frames. The flame of the candle by which Piquet was writing at the desk flickered in the draft. He couldn´t tell if it was from the wind whistling through the gaps around the windows or the hot air coming from Sir Robert as he dictated his eleventh letter of the day.

"…with that final discrepancy accounted for, I trust we will be able to recommence works before Easter. I await your most gracious instruction eagerly… and you fill in the rest." Sir Robert got to his feet and strolled over to look out of the window. Enough rain was falling now to put out the fires of Hell. Sir Robert cursed, he did not want to be trapped inside this town for Christmas, but if the rains persisted, he would have little choice, the roads would be churned into impassable bogs.

"Your signature Sir." Piquet interrupted his thoughts. Sir Robert snatched the stylus from his secretary and signed his name with a flourish. Piquet laid the paper down on the desk and blotted the page before folding it carefully. He closed it with a considerable dollop of wax and took care to seal it with the appropriate ring mounted crest, one of three he had on a chain around his neck. He placed the letter inside a thick leather satchel at his feet, already packed tightly with outgoing correspondence.

Sir Robert walked back to the window and looked out once more. A hooded figure hurried past on the opposite side of the street, bent into the wind. He held the sides of his hood open while he stopped to look up and squint at the buildings around him. Sir Robert caught a glimpse of his face when it swivelled in his direction; it was his nephew, Jean. He banged on the window to get his attention, nearly putting his hand through the thin glass pane in the process. Jean looked over and waved when he saw Sir Robert beckoning. He hurried across the muddy street and stood at the door of the house.

Piquet flung the door open. Sir Robert stood smiling over his secretary's shoulder.

"Jean my boy. Come in! Come in!" he bellowed, stepping back to allow his nephew to burst through the door and squeeze into the warm dry hallway. Piquet slammed the door against the wind and rain as Jean grasped hands with Sir Robert.

"I was glad to receive your note, I feared you were coming by sea."

"Yes, this ghastly little storm would have made for a dreadful passage. Come in my boy, take off your cloak and come next to the fire to get warm." Jean shrugged his heavy woollen cloak into the arms of Piquet before following Sir Robert into the office and over to the fireplace.

"Tell me, how are plans progressing?" Sir Robert said as he poured two generous measures of deliciously thick brandy from a decanter resting on the mantle. He handed one to Jean who took it gratefully and sipped it. He could feel it slide down his throat all the way to his stomach, warming him from within while the heat from the fire made steam rise from his boots.

"To be completely honest, it hasn´t been as simple as I thought it would be. Almost all those I approached declined without hesitation. There are surprisingly few of my fellow lords and barons who feel confident leaving for a crusade in a faraway land, while under threat of invasion by the English."

"Bother and nonsense." Sir Robert scoffed. "The English are far too busy shagging sheep and drinking ale, they´ll be licking their wounds for years to come after the beating they received last time."

"Still, it is a concern to many to leave their lands unprotected. Also, I´m afraid to say, the lack of treasure on offer is, shall we say, swaying many more against taking up the offer. Few are willing to commit themselves to carry out the work of Christ without the promise of gold and gems."

"Rapine and riches, is that all that interests our noble brethren? Is there any honour left in the world?" exasperated Sir Robert. "Do you have any good news to share?"

"Why of course." Jean answered brightly. "We are not lacking bored knights in this country, especially young ones who are hungry for glory to boost their standing amongst their peers. To date, I have recruited thirty-three who are possessed of the vision, or the hunger, to join our crusade. This evening I have an appointment to meet with a respectable gentleman I am hoping to recruit as my Second, who will in turn I believe, bring with him more knights and possibly even a ship. You may know of him, Gadifer de la Salle?"

"Yes, I believe we are acquainted." replied Sir Robert. He did indeed know Gadifer. In the early days of planning the mission he had briefly considered asking him to lead it. He was a fine knight with a fearsome reputation in his day. However, his sense of honour and duty to the French Throne had weighed heavily against him when it came to choosing someone to lead an expedition on behalf of a foreign king. If Jean showed sufficient strength of character to command him, he couldn´t wish for a better Second. He was a seasoned military campaigner who believed and strictly adhered to the codes and conducts of the chain of command.

"I will have to promise him more than the others to persuade him to join us, there might be a short fall of funds to secure his service. To that end I was wondering about asking him to join us as a stakeholder, put up some of the capital and spread the risk."

"Preposterous!" Spluttered Sir Robert, nearly losing the brandy he had been rolling around his mouth. "This mission is yours, and yours alone to command. That authority must be absolute and without question.

"Your expenses will be returned one hundred-fold, in time, by the King of Castile, His Most Noble Grace, Enrique." This was the first time Sir Robert had mentioned his patron by name Jean noted, a significant leap of faith. "And this crusade has been blessed, lest we forget, by the highest office of the Roman Catholic Church, Pope Boniface has requested that I keep him informed of our progress." They both crossed themselves at the mention of the Church. Sir Robert kissed the ring on his little finger. He lingered there for an instant, looking over his fist to Jean. "Would you really want to share the credit, the honour and the riches, with another?"

"Of course not." Jean answered without hesitation. "But I can see no other way."

"Nonsense! Ultimately, you are wagering your life on this crusade. What is more valuable than your life? Possessions? Promises? Property?"

"I do still have several other assets, not included in the estate I mortgaged."

"Go on."

"But most are tied to my dear wife and can´t be released without her signature."

"So, you will have to talk to her."

"That´s what I´d been hoping to avoid."

"My dear boy, if this isn´t the perfect opportunity to start talking again, I don´t know what is. You are preparing to command a hundred knights on a holy crusade to distant lands, and yet you fear your own wife? Have I overestimated your abilities?"

"She´s fierce and always so damned angry. I´d prefer to cross swords with a thousand Saracens than cross words with her. She hates me with more passion than she has ever loved me with."

"I struggle to see that as a hindrance. Be completely honest with her and explain that you may be killed, in which case she would inherit a stinking fortune to add to her own considerable assets. Or you will succeed and come home richer and more influential than even she can imagine. She will win whether you live or die."

Jean laughed at his uncle´s bluntness and turn of phrase. It was something that few people appreciated, many avoided him because of it, but Jean loved it and had always looked forward to hearing one of his outbursts of *honesty* at family gatherings when he was younger.

"I think she´ll welcome the death option." Jean said smiling. "And what would you like from my properties to add to your collection?"

"I beg your pardon?"

"You know my holdings as well as I do. Which one of them has your eye?"

"I strongly protest at any notion you may have that I am manipulating you for my own gain... But..."

"Paris." Jean interrupted, still smiling. "The Paris house, you never liked that I beat you to that one."

"It does have its charms."

"It´ll cost you a thousand."

"My boy, don´t be ridiculous. You wouldn´t get a thousand if it was in the desirable part of the city, which it most certainly is not. I couldn´t possibly offer more than five hundred."

"You will have to Uncle. If I were to put it on the open market it would sell for at least nine."

"Yes, possibly, but when? The way I see it you need the money now. We could haggle all day, but neither of us has the time to waste. I will give you seven hundred now, which is still more than you stole it for. That is my final offer."

"Once again it would appear that I have little choice but to accept." Jean smiled as he reached out to shake Sir Robert´s hand.

"Very well." Sir Robert said. "Now if you have nothing else to report I have a gift for you." He placed his drink on the mantle and called for Piquet who appeared at the door a moment later. "Give me the letters." Sir Robert demanded.

Piquet hurried over and searched through the satchel containing the correspondence. He pulled out two small rigid leather document tubes. He handed them to Sir Robert who took them without thanks and turned to face Jean.

"The first is a letter from me ordering the release into your custody of two servants to be found at the household of Sir Guy of Bordeaux. They will be accompanying you on your journey. They are natives of the island of Lancarote, spirited away and sold as slaves several years ago. I found them, and at no inconsiderable cost to myself bought their service. I have them safe in Bordeaux. They will be your translators and your guides. They need further religious and cultural education which you should arrange with your priest…"

"Father Verrier." offered Jean.

"Father Verrier…yes… He will be your chronicler no…?"

"Yes, he and a monk from Marnes, Brother Bontier will be keeping a record of our voyage."

"Very well. They need to become acquainted with the Canarians at the earliest opportunity. See to it."

"Of course."

"Do not underestimate the strength of having these two people in your entourage. They are potentially the most important playing pieces in the game. Use them wisely."

Sir Robert handed the two tubes to Jean who shook out the tightly rolled scrolls of velum and opened them out. He had just read the first word on the top sheet before Sir Robert interrupted.

"Read the other one." Jean swapped the sheets bottom to top. "It is a Holy Order from the office of Pope Boniface, bearing his personal seal. It states that you are on a mission from God and are therefore travelling under the protection of the Holy Roman Church. Always keep that on your person. It may save your life."

Sir Robert stopped talking and reached for his drink. He sipped at it slowly, watching Jean's smile grow as he read the words. A touch of immunity would do his nephew the world of good. Sir Robert had discovered from one of his sources that a warrant for Jean´s arrest had been issued in England for various acts of Piracy. He hadn´t asked Jean about the veracity of the accusations, he suspected they were true. There was a touch of recklessness in his nephew which he hoped would be tempered by the rigours of this crusade. If he was successful, Sir Robert planned to approach Enrique´s wife, Queen Catherine of Lancaster and ask her to use her influence in the English court to have the piracy charges against Jean quashed. The promise he had made to his sister to look out for her boy would be broken if he were to have his neck stretched in an English jail. It would be a terrible indictment of his level of care should that be allowed to happen.

"Piquet!" Sir Robert called when Jean had finished reading. Piquet was still standing at his shoulder and coughed politely, causing Sir Robert to jump slightly as he turned and saw him. "Fool!" barked Sir Robert. "Seal the letters for transport now." Piquet bowed to Jean and relieved him of the scrolls. He rolled them tightly and placed them back in their protective tubes. Sir Robert turned back to face his nephew.

"I know I´ve said it before but I will say it again and again. The two Canarians can win this crusade for you without the need for excessive bloodshed. There needs to be an established Catholic presence on the island, a living congregation of converted natives, not a priest overseeing an empty church with a full graveyard outside. Your mission is to convert, not to conquer."

"I understand completely Sir Robert." Jean said earnestly.

"Good. Let that consideration sway you when choosing the final few knights to accompany you. You must not surround yourself with men hungry for blood. Pick artisans and builders rather than blood-thirsty warriors, practical men with experience of life. Yes, a few youngsters are useful should it come to a bloody fight, but don´t put too much faith in them, their inexperience and desire for gold and glory would be your undoing. Remember, build, not destroy. We are there to deliver peace and prosperity, not death and destruction." Sir Robert never stopped pressing the *peaceful occupation* directive to Jean, at least three times in every meeting and writ in every letter he emphasized the same message.

Piquet returned the tubes to Jean, sealed with tight buckled lids. Jean took them and secreted them in a hidden pocket on the inside of his tunic.

"Good. That´s business taken care of, unless there is anything else you need to know?" Sir Robert asked.

"No, I think that is all for now, until I have spoken with Gadifer that is."

"Good!" Sir Robert said, clapping his hands together. "Piquet, hurry along to the kitchen and tell the cook we´re ready to eat now." Piquet bowed quickly and hurried from the room. Sir Robert refilled Jean´s glass. "Tell me now dear boy, everything you know while we eat."

"Everything I know?"

"We will start there and progress to what you don´t know in short order."

****

The rain had eased off slightly by the time Jean made his farewells, a little lightheaded and slightly wobbly on his feet. The evening was threatening to arrive in the middle of the afternoon so thick and dark were the clouds. Jean put his head to the wind and walked briskly down the hill in the direction of the harbour taking care not to step in the river of excrement flowing down the middle of the lane. He could see clusters of masts in the harbour swaying like trees in the forest as the wind continued its assault. Out to sea he could make out a low heavy black cloud heading directly for the town, shedding millions of gallons of water as it came. He quickened his pace, eager not to get another drenching and soon arrived at the tavern where he was due to meet Gadifer.

The steward showed him to a private room where Gadifer already sat waiting. He rose to his feet as Jean entered and snapped the heels of his boots together. He was dressed in sober colours, a dull green woollen tunic without frill or decoration, fastened round his solid waist by a thick brown leather belt. His rugged, sea-burned face was framed by a shock of salt and pepper hair and beard, which were cropped unfashionably short.

"Betancourt! It´s been a long time."

"…and a long way away Monsieur." They had served together in the mercenary force sent by King Enrique to raid the pirate strongholds on the Barbery Coast. They knew of each other but hadn´t had much cause to become further acquainted until now. Gadifer was ten years Jean´s senior but wore his years well, his back was straight and his handshake strong. During the African campaign Gadifer had been Jean´s commanding officer, jean hoped the older man was professional enough to accept a rank reversal. He wasted no time testing his authority, emboldened by the promise of sufficient monies to fund the mission and slightly buoyed up by the brandy already consumed at Sir Robert´s table.

"Please sit Gadifer, and steward, if you would be so kind as to bring wine."

The steward grumbled under his breath as he left the room and closed the door behind him. Gadifer sat back down while Jean took his time removing his cloak. He shook the water from it and hung it on a peg behind the door before turning to face Gadifer. He took the seat opposite Gadifer and leaned across the table. He began to speak quietly, Gadifer leaned across the table to hear him.

"I come to you," Jean began, "with a proposal which could change both of our lives forever."

6

Zonzamas, Lancarote,
December 22nd, 1401

The sun began its final descent to the western horizon, bringing an end to the shortest day of the year. It´s warming light peaked through gaps in the clouds dragging their shadows across the island. The Majo clans gathered around the King´s compound in the centre of the island, to bid farewell to the year just ending and to welcome the new one when the sun rose the following morning.

The event, normally a time for rejoicing, was a somewhat subdued affair compared to previous years. The races and wrestling bouts between the clans, normally an excuse to let off some steam in good-natured competition were fought with a tangible increase in acrimony. There were more cuts and bruises on display around the fires where the people sat and ate and watched the setting sun bring an end to a miserable year.

Norstar and his extended family sat in silence around their fire at the edge of the encampment. Three other families had lost sons and daughters to raiders in the months since Mifaya´s abduction, the latest just two weeks previously. The losses infected the people with a feeling of uncertainty and fear that they were ill equipped to deal with.

Jonay and Daida´s children, normally so adventurous and full of life were huddled close, clutching on to their mother as if they would be stolen away by the wind if they let go. Even Iballa´s constant chatter had ceased, she sat in silence stroking Rayco´s hair. He lay with his head in her lap, staring into the glowing embers of the fire.

Rather than take his mind off his loss, the gathering compounded it. Mifaya had loved the celebrations and would be leaping and laughing with joy, bringing smiles to everyone´s faces with her charm and wit on full display. Overwhelming guilt crushed his heart every time he thought that it were probably better she had died rather than be subjected to the torturous perversions of her captors. A shroud of heavy sadness dampened the anger and rage inside him, he was balanced precariously on the edge of a deep dark pit, only the loving arms of his family kept him from falling in.

Norstar wasn´t able to comfort Rayco with coloured words and platitudes, he had seen the slave markets in Portugal with his own eyes. He remembered with shame the indifference he had felt seeing the strings of slaves shuffling along the street dragging heavy chains on the way to the auction block. He had never looked into their eyes and seen the people inside their broken bodies. Only now did he understand their pain fully and appreciate the fact that the slaves were human, just like him.

He had much to do to atone for his part in the abduction that day, if only he had taken the goats instead of staying at home, things would be different. He remembered the fat man on the ship, cowering behind babies while shouting threats. His face, his fat mocking face was living inside Norstar´s head like an evil genie, the next time they met would be the last time the fat man would draw breath. He hoped dearly to see that dirty, grey sail coming back to the island one day, he would be waiting. He patrolled the coast daily, climbing volcanoes to scan the horizon, clutching his bow and sharpening his knives until they could shave feathers.

He stared across the fire at Rayco curled on the floor with his head resting in Iballa´s lap and felt his ire rising. The Majos were peaceful people living in a society without predation, at peace with themselves and their surroundings. They simply didn´t possess the compulsion to fight. Norstar had lived with them for more than half of his life, lulled by their ways until he too embraced the peaceful, unhurried lifestyle that would see them all wiped out if they didn´t change.

He shared his fears as he lay at night next to Gara. She understood completely, encouraging him to instruct their children how to fight. She herself had learned to draw and fire Norstar´s longbow, no longer hidden in the chicken coop, but carried everywhere he went.

Fayna had helped Norstar to begin construction of two smaller, lighter bows but they took a long time to shape, in the meanwhile, she took the time to instruct Chimboyo and Nayra how to use her own bow.

Igo lost patience with the bow quickly, no matter how hard he tried he couldn´t shoot straight and shattered more arrows against rocks than he shot inside the targets. He had however improved tremendously with the sling. Following his grandfather´s advice he spent many hours chasing leaves in the waves and was getting faster and more accurate every day. He wrestled with Norstar or Jonay and had fashioned a small collection of fire-hardened binots. His adolescence burned away with his puppy fat, he was a lot leaner and stronger than he had been at the end of the summer.

He returned to the fireside now having accepted the challenge to wrestle with a much larger boy from the north. He beat him down easily and with such ferocity that no others dared to challenge him. Instead they mocked him for his blue eyes and *pirate skin*. He sat down heavily next to Fayna who didn´t seem to notice, absorbed as she was napping arrow heads out of the small stones she had collected on the trek to the gathering. Chimboyo sat with her watching closely as she deftly chipped edges and points into the stones. He tried his best to copy her but shattered more stones than he managed to shape. He cursed under his breath every time he failed but words of encouragement from Fayna kept him trying.

Gara kept one eye on Chimboyo and Fayna while showing Nayra how to split gull feathers to make arrow flights. Although little Nayra was reasonably skilled with the bow, she didn´t enjoy it, instead she chose to spend as much time as she could with Iballa and Daida, both skilled healers. She asked about the plants and herbs they used, watched closely how they combined them to make healing drafts and balms. While appearing to be listening to her mother´s instructions she watched Daida closely pulling leaves from her bag to flavour the stew cooking on the fire, her task made more difficult by having to work around the two young ones who clung to her skirt. Jonay was crouched behind them holding his infant daughter outstretched in his arms while she suckled from the teat of the nanny goat they had brought from home. The suckling noises slowed as her tummy filled up with warm sweet milk and she began drifting off to sleep.

In the west, the sun sent its final rays of light up into the sky to flame the underside of the clouds before disappearing out of sight behind the distant mountains. The year's end was usually a wild celebration, with fires burning high throughout the night to ward off evil spirits. There would be dancing and feasting, bonds made between clans, and more than a few sons and daughters conceived. The Majos would watch together in the morning as the sun rose and welcome Magek, the Sun God, born again to give life to another year.

This year the fires burned low.

A few people inexplicably blamed Norstar for leading the raiders to their shores and he saw their scowls from the corner of his eye. He thought himself one of them, he was welcomed as such, but things had changed recently. The Majo's heartache and sorrow searched for something tangible they could hang the blame on for their loved ones' disappearances. He was different, so he became their target. He liked to think he was strong enough to take the unfounded enmity, he knew it would pass eventually, but recently he had noticed his children were being snubbed and that rankled him greatly.

The gloom increased as the daylight fled the encampment. Norstar stood to fetch more wood to stack up the fire when his eye caught the familiar gait of Avago coming down the hill, threading his way around the fire pits. He had spent almost the entire day in conclave with King Guadarfia and the other clan elders. There was much to discuss.

Avago saw Norstar and beckoned him over. Norstar put down the wood he was carrying and went to meet him. Gara watched him leave, put the bag of split gull feathers in Nayra's lap and got to her feet to follow him.

"Come," said Avago to Norstar. "The King wants to speak with you." He turned to Gara. "I think it better if you wait here."

"I don't!" scoffed Gara. "I'm coming with you." Her tone broached no argument, but Avago felt he should try anyway.

"We have to talk carefully in there… and your temper worries me."

"Let it worry others." She walked away, her head held high. Avago looked at Norstar and shrugged before the two of them followed her.

King Guadarfia's compound straddled the crest of the hill looking down upon the Great Divide. It was a sprawling villa by Majo standards, its many rooms built with rocks and boulders scoured from the hilltop. It abutted a huge wind shaped rock at the northwest corner and wrapped around the contours of the hill like a snug fitting cap. The protective outer walls of the compound encircled a sprawling maze of rooms and snugs, connected by passageways linked to an open courtyard at the centre of the structure.

At the eastern end of the courtyard was a squat round hut with a heavy black and white goat hide covering a low doorway. The glow of a fire from within seeped out around the edges as did the sound of raised voices. Avago pushed in front of Gara as they approached the hut and turned to give her a warning look. She returned his look with a fierce one of her own and held out a hand, inviting him to lead the way. He took a deep breath as he turned and grabbed the edge of the hide door covering.

The voices inside ceased as night entered the hut, followed by Avago, Gara and Norstar.

Inside, more than twenty men sat in a wide circle around a small fire that burned brightly in the centre of the floor. Directly opposite the doorway sat the impressive figure of King Guadarfia. He was taller and younger than many of the other men present, and twice as wide at the shoulder. He wore a highly decorated leather mitre on his head, the patterns of highly polished shells it bore reflected the light from the fire and shucked together when he lifted his head to appraise the new arrivals with sharp eyes.

At Guadarfia´s right hand sat Guañameñe Nichel, the King´s chief advisor in all matters spiritual. He had the small eyes and pinched features of a rat, although his nose was decidedly crooked and bent at a peculiar angle. Norstar had never liked Nichel, his feeling of disgust and mistrust rose as he caught the little man´s eyes wandering a little too avariciously over Gara´s body.

"Sit." King Guadarfia said simply, his deep voice filling the hut. Norstar, Avago and Gara sat where they stood, closing the circle of bodies around the fire. The King waited until there was absolute stillness before speaking again.

"There has been much talking here today, too much talking at times." The words caused two men sat at Nichel´s right hand to shift uncomfortably. "Questions have been asked about the lessons you have been teaching your children."

"What?" Gara spat loudly, startling several of the elders in the circle.

"Gara..." urged Avago under his breath.

"Ha! As I told you Mence." Nichel said leaning towards the King. He stared at Gara with a sly expression, a face Norstar desperately wanted to punch. The King took a breath and continued.

"I understand that your family has lost much, we all share your pain. But...there are some, here, concerned that you train your children to fight with strange weapons and will one day choose to settle your disputes with violence." The King tried to cover the distaste he felt for the words he spoke, but it was his duty to speak them.

Every accusation, no matter how implausible was discussed at the gatherings. The clans only came together three times every year and the elders´ resolved to leave bad feelings behind when the clans dispersed at gathering end, snuffing out disputes before they festered in caves. Many of them remembered a time when the island had been divided and fractious, but they had known peace for many years and King Guadarfia took his royal responsibility to maintain that peace very seriously.

Norstar heard the accusation and opened his mouth to answer, but before he could voice his objection, Gara spoke out.

"You are accusing us of making war against our own people. How dare you?" The King´s eyebrows rose in surprise.

"How dare *you* speak to your Mence this way." Nichel said, turning to Guadarfia. "This is exactly how I warned it would be. It cannot be tolerated."

"Why would you doubt our loyalty?" Gara pleaded with the King, deliberately ignoring Nichel. "Why would we wish to harm our own people?"

"You are not all *our people*." Nichel hissed looking directly at Norstar, his black eyes shining with malevolence. "And you." He turned to look at Gara who was struggling to keep what remained of her temper in check. "You have a history of violence against *our people*."

Gara was stunned, her mouth opened. She looked squarely at Nichel and did her best to speak calmly, despite her instincts demanding anything but calm. "I broke your nose when we were young because you demanded an affection I was not willing to give." A small chuckle rippled around the hut. Nichel lifted his hand to cover his nose. "And I would do it again in a heartbeat if you, or anybody else, were to try and harm my family." She shook with rage, Nichel flinched slightly but managed to hold a thin smile on his narrow lips.

"I speak as a proud Majo, a daughter of the volcanoes. I would stand up and fight any of those pig-fuckers from across the sea who would bring harm to any of *our people*, including you Nichel. I teach my children to do the same, to defend *our people*, not fight against them."

"Norstar is my son." Avago broke in. "If you insult him, you insult me and all my family. You insult Majo people everywhere. He has given himself wholly to us and has asked nothing in return. He is the first to offer help when it is needed as many of you sat in this circle can testify to." There was a hum of assent around the ring lifting Norstar's spirits a little, but there were still a couple of openly hostile glares directed at him. One of those came from the man sat at Nichel's right hand, Beselch, the head of the largest clan in the north, who also happened to be the husband of Nichel's sister.

"We know nothing of his origins." Beselch said, his angry mouth growling out the words. "The first years of his life were lived in a different world from ours. How could we be sure that the raiders who have taken our people are not known to him? When he takes his boat out to sea, how can we know he doesn't conspire with them, leading them to us?"

"To what end?" Avago asked incredulously. "Has he caused any harm to come to you or any of your families?" He looked deliberately around the room waiting for an answer, none came. "These unfounded accusations divide us, much more than Norstar ever could. I demand an end to it now before we go too far and cause deeper wounds to open. This is a time we should be working together to fight the threat coming from across the sea, not tearing ourselves apart to reveal a demon who only dwells inside your own imagination." His eyes burned into Beselch and Nichel, challenging them to respond.

"Nothing good has ever come to us from across the sea." Beselch snarled loudly. "We have lost more of our people in recent years than ever before, all since *he* came." He lifted his hand and pointed at Norstar.

"And now." Nichel took over, his voice dripping with contempt. "He teaches his children to kill with weapons no others possess. How can we be secure in our homes knowing he is turning his children into warriors to rise against us one day. I am suspicious of a man who spends more time crafting weapons than caring for his goats."

"Your suspicion is being caused by your own fear and ignorance." Avago snapped angrily. "You have no evidence, no base for your accusations. You share an opinion with others who think like you and dare to call it the *truth*. Norstar came to us and has done nothing to bring harm on any one of us in all the years he has lived with us. He doesn´t covet this knowledge, or pretend to converse with spirits and Gods. He shares *his* knowledge with us freely. He can, and will teach us. We must not close our minds and turn our backs on him. I see you Nichel. It is as clear as the nose on your face why you dislike him." A loud laugh rang out from one of the men in the circle. Nichel stopped it with a murderous glare. He was apoplectic with rage, so angry that words burned in the heat of his throat before they could escape from his mouth.

"The rest of you…" Avago continued, looking around the faces in the circle. "Do the poisonous whisperings of a jealous man infect your ears so completely that all sense of what is right and good is ignored?"

Nichel spluttered, and then was stunned into silenced by the King who raised his enormous hand, obscuring Nichel´s face in its shadow.

"I have heard enough!"

"But Mence…" whined Nichel.

"I said enough." Guadarfia boomed.

Nichel slunk back and peered with undisguised loathing at Norstar, Avago and Gara. The King turned away from him.

"Avago. Wise Avago." Guadarfia began in his deep dark voice. "You are right in what you say. This is not a time for us to seek enemies within our own house." He turned to face Norstar. "You are my brother Norstar, you are one of us." Norstar dipped his head, humbly grateful to receive the King´s endorsement, especially in front of those who would deny him. He lifted his head, the King waited until their eyes met before continuing.

"I believe you would satisfy the suspicions of those within us if you would share your knowledge with us all."

"Mence, it would be a great honour to share what little I know with everybody."

"Do you have your weapon here with you?"

"My bow?"

"Bow…. Yes."

"It is outside."

"I would like to see a demonstration of your… bow." He stood up taking everybody by surprise. "Come." he said, nobody moved. "Now." he urged.

The circle of men all scrambled to their feet. The King strode forward around the fire and took Norstar by the arm. He guided him out through the door with a procession of bemused Majo elders in tow.

They walked down the hill to where Norstar´s family sat silently around the fire. Guadarfia stepped forward and hunched down next to Iballa. She looked up at him, her eyes dark and heavy, filled with sadness. He laid one of his massive hands gently on her shoulder and placed his other over Rayco´s head.

"We all share your pain brother" Rayco raised his hand and grasped Guadarfia´s. "We will wait for you." Guadarfia said.

"We will wait brother." Rayco responded weakly. He squeezed Guadarfia´s hand and then let his own drop back to the dust.

Guadarfia squeezed Iballa´s shoulder and stood.

Norstar stood behind him, holding a long, thin leather sheath.

"This is my bow Mence." Norstar pulled the bow from the sheath and strung it quickly. He plucked the string once and offered the bow to Guadarfia. The King took it and stroked the arc with the tips of his fingers.

"That is beautiful wood." The King said.

"It is a wood of my country, from the yew tree."

"Yew tree." Guadarfia repeated. "We have no… yew trees."

"True, there are none here, but we do have wood which is similar and strong enough to make a smaller, lighter bow. Like the one I made for my daughter." He pointed to Fayna, sat with Chimboyo across the fire pit.

"Show me."

Fayna stood and pulled her bow from its sleeve, it had been lying next to her on the ground. She strung it and held it out to the King. Guadarfia gave Norstar his longbow back and took the smaller one from Fayna. He stroked the wooden arc as he had with the longbow.

"It is similar." It looked like a toy in Guadarfia's hand. "But it doesn't feel the same."

"My bow has aged many years which is why it feels smoother. That one will be the same in a few seasons if it is cared for."

"I want to see what they can do, but not here. Iballa." Iballa lifted her weary face to look up at him. "The care of The Mother to you, proud mother of strong children."

He nodded across the fire to Jonay and Daida, their little girls were stood between them, craning their necks to see all the way up to Guadarfia's face.

"Let us go somewhere else and leave your family in peace."

They found a spot on the far side of the hill away from the fire pits. The entire camp of Majos trailed behind them, enjoying the distraction. A target was found to satisfy Guadarfia, a flat cactus leaf, the size of a man's head which stuck up above a short wall thirty paces from where they stood. Some youngsters rushed away and came back bringing burning branches. They stacked them at the foot of the cactus to illuminate the target.

The King turned and threw his arms out. The crowd hushed.

"Who was the best today with the binot?" He asked, his voice booming over their heads.

"Asche!" several voices called out.

"Asche. Good. Come forward Asche." called the King.

A tall, well-built man with a heavy brow and close-cropped hair picked his way forward through the crowd.

"Of course you won Asche." Guadarfia said, welcoming the man to his side who was one of only a few who stood as tall as the King. "I wished I could have seen you throw. I will now." He pointed to the cactus. "Could you hit that from here?"

"I will try." Asche replied, stroking his chin while he squinted down the range.

Several Majos surged forward, eager to offer their spears to him. He chose two and tested their weight in his hands. He stuck one in the ground and gripped the other over his shoulder. He sighted down the length of the spear and then launched it with an almighty roar. It spiralled in the air as it raced to the target but missed the cactus by a hand's width.

He grunted his disapproval and grabbed the other binot. He snatched his second shot and it collided with the wall, just short of the target. He cursed and demanded another spear while some within the crowd ribbed him mercilessly.

His third throw hit the target. It glanced off the cactus's flat face and landed beyond the wall with a clatter. A thin cheer went up from the crowd mixed with a few cruel laughs.

"And now you." Guadarfia invited Norstar to step forward.

Norstar took a long calming breath and stepped up to the mark. He raised the bow and pulled the string back smoothly. He sighted down the length of the arrow to the cactus head peaking over the wall. An expectant hush spread through the watching Majos. He let the arrow go. It whistled down the range, its iron head pierced the skin of the target with such force it shot clean through and out the other side. A roar went up from the crowd.

"And now yours." Guadarfia invited Fayna to step forward.

She did so confidently and quickly. Her small bow sent her lighter arrow's stone head thudding into the cactus just above the hole Norstar's arrow had punched through the plant. The crowd went even wilder. Young men sprinted forward to retrieve the arrows. A scuffle nearly broke out as they fought over who would be the one to pluck out Fayna's arrow and return it to her.

The King chuckled, a deep comforting happy sound Norstar found to be worryingly infectious. He was overcome with the urge to smile, even though he was determined not to. Guadarfia placed his hands on

Norstar and Fayna´s shoulders and turned them around to face the crowd.

"Our brother Norstar has offered to teach us all to use this…bow. This knowledge will help us to beat those… *pig fuckers*" he dipped to Gara, "…from over the sea and stop our sons and daughters from being taken away."

Another huge cheer went up and Guadarfia joined in, as did the elders, Norstar, Gara, Fayna and Avago, all roaring joyously, defiantly into the night sky.

When the cheering died down, Guadarfia led the elders back to the compound through the crowd. Many hands reached out to touch the bows and arrows held by Fayna and Norstar. They filed back into the hut and retook their seats. The King waited until there was silence before speaking.

"The fighting between us and the accusations will stop here and now." He gave a sideways glance at Nichel and Beselch who sat looking thoroughly miserable at his side. "I want to hear how we will work together to ensure the safety of our children. We need to learn from the past as we walk to the future. I invite you Norstar to share your ideas with us. What would you suggest we do to protect our people?"

"Mence?" Nichel spoke up, unable to keep his bitter tongue still any longer. "Norstar is not an elder, he hasn´t earned the right to speak here."

"I have invited him to speak." Guadarfia answered, "That should be *right* enough."

"But we have traditions, laws which govern us. If we ignore those then we would be disrespecting the memory of our ancestors." Nichel puffed out his narrow chest.

"Would our ancestors approve if he whispered in Avago´s ear and let him speak for him?" Guadarfia asked.

"You are mocking me Mence." Nichel´s face reddened.

"If it pleases the spirits, we will take a vote amongst us to decide whether we let Norstar speak. Will that please our ancestors?" Before waiting for Nichel to answer Guadarfia asked:

"All who would not hear Norstar, raise your hands."

Nichel immediately raised his hand followed by Beselch. They looked disappointed to see no other hands join theirs.

"And all those who would listen." Every other Majo raised their hands.

"Very well, the council has decided." Guadarfia said. "Do you have any other objections?" he asked Nichel.

"I have many Mence, but I will reserve them for another time." Nichel folded his arms and sat back, his face became even more pinched as he sulked in the shadows.

Guadarfia turned to Norstar and invited him to speak with a wave of the hand.

"Thank you Mence." Norstar said humbly. He thought for a moment and then began.

"My sister and her children were taken by slavers who came ashore in a place where they should not have been able to come ashore. We were all looking the other way. They surprised us. They surprised me for which I will bear the shame for the rest of my life." Gara placed her hand on the small of his back, encouraging him to continue before he turned too morose.

"I believe we could remove that element of surprise." he said suddenly. "We need to mount a string of lookouts around the coast who would see the approaching ships, giving us time to gather in numbers and drive them away, or hide in the deepest caves if they are too strong for us to face."

"What you say makes sense." Guadarfia said looking round the bobbing heads in the circle of elders. "But we lack the weapons to fight them with."

"We have weapons aplenty Mence. We have the rocks under our feet and our binots in our hands, we need to use them wisely."

"Explain." Guadarfia demanded.

"I have thought long and hard about this since Mifaya was taken. If we had known the pirates were coming, we could have been there waiting for them on the cliff top. How long would they have lingered if we had thirty, forty or even fifty Majos stood on the cliffs dropping rocks and spears on their heads? We have two archers to still their crossbows, a whole army of slingsmen to launch rocks at them. Pirates and slavers are cowards, they would run away rather than face injury. This is our island, not theirs. They should be wary of us, not us of them."

The men in the hut were nodding vigorously. Guadarfia shared an affirming look with Avago before asking:

"Does anybody else wish to speak?" he asked.

"Mence, if I may." Nichel piped up.

"Of course." Guadarfia answered warily.

"If there are to be men spending days and nights sat on top of the hills looking out to sea, who will be looking after the flocks and the crops? There won´t be any Majos left to protect if we all starve." Beselch voiced his agreement wholeheartedly. The pair of them had the largest bellies in the hut, if not on the whole island, an observation Fayna couldn´t resist whispering under her breath.

"Trust them to be worried about food above all else." Avago heard her and tried to stifle a laugh. He snorted loudly.

"Avago, do you find something amusing?" Nichel spat angrily.

"I do not." Avago choked his mirth. "I had some dust up my nose. I apologise for the interruption, carry on."

"We have more than enough people if we organise well." Gara said quickly before Nichel could speak again. "With just five pairs of eyes we could see any boat approaching from anywhere out to sea."

"I agree." Cheche said, a walnut skinned man from the White Mountain clan who had lost many of his kin to slave traders over the years. His wife had been butchered by a crew of Portuguese pirates ten years previously. They forced him to watch as they raped his youngest daughter in a heart-breaking ordeal that ended with her broken body being tossed into the sea. "I will volunteer to stand watch, and so will my sons, and their sons." he said proudly, with fire dancing in his eyes.

"And I and mine." said another man sitting somewhere to Norstar´s left. They were soon joined by voices coming from all around the circle. Only Nichel and Beselch remained silent.

"Then we are in agreement." said Guadarfia spreading his arms wide. "We will defend our home and our people. We shall lose no more of our children."

"I have something to add." Nichel said quickly before everybody´s enthusiasm found a voice.

"Yes?" Guadarfia said irritably.

"Although I accept your decision to form this *protective ring* around the island, I would have to insist that any fighting force we assemble must be commanded by a full blooded Majo. It would ease the suspicions of those, and there are many, who would feel uncomfortable taking orders from an outsider."

"Pfff!" Fayna couldn´t help herself, she found Nichel´s constant petty objections amusing. She wondered why people still gave him time to speak when everything that came out of his mouth was ridiculous.

"Quiet girl." Avago scolded her under his breath.

"Who would you suggest?" asked Guadarfia.

"I propose Beselch. His loyalty is without question and as head of the Northern tribes already commands a sizeable force of men."

And is completely loyal to you… thought Norstar.

"If there are no objections then we shall agree to your suggestion." The King proclaimed, waiting a moment for anybody to speak. Nobody did. As was often the case, the elders agreed to Nichel´s petty demands to avoid having to listen to his weak, bile-filled arguments any more than necessary.

"Tomorrow we shall speak further." said Guadarfia, eager to draw an end to the meeting and begin the feast. "We will go now to our families and say goodbye to this year, cast our bad memories into the fires and welcome the morning´s new sun with glad hearts. May the strength and love of The Mother, Father and Son watch over us all." he said raising his hands in the air.

"In The Mother´s light we shine." the elders chorused before filing out into the night which was just starting to come alive with the sound of drums and singing.

****

Igo had followed Norstar and Fayna and watched from behind the crowd as they shot their arrows at the target. After the display the crowd dispersed. Igo was approached by a group of boys. They seemed to forget the loathing they had shown towards him previously and asked him a steady stream of questions, many of them about his sister.

He enjoyed the attention at first, but the novelty soon wore off and he found himself wishing it to end. He snuck away as soon as he could without being noticed and made his way over to the spot where Norstar and Fayna had shot their arrows.

There were still some youngsters playing around the target, pretending to fire at the cactus with imaginary bows and arrows. He unwound his sling from around his waist and loaded it with a stone the size of his fist. He swung it in two large lazy circles before whipping it round quickly and hurling the rock. It spun through the air and smashed the cactus head to smithereens. The children watched open-mouthed as the target disappeared in a shower of mulch. One girl started crying and set off running back to her family.

Igo casually wrapped the leather sling back around his waist and sauntered away, whistling quietly to himself.

7

La Rochelle, France,

April 30th, 1402

The Tilly had entered the harbour with the morning tide. She looked tired and worn compared with the magnificent caravel of Gadifer de la Salle, tied astern on the harbour wall. Her forecastle looked down on The Tilly´s poop deck like a vain dragon. It didn´t concern Captain Frank who was immensely proud of The Tilly. Her aged timbers and grubby sails belied her speed. She was one of the fastest tubs on the seven seas and she was due a touch of pampering. She only had to do one final short hop across the Channel before she was hauled out of the water for an invigorating hull scraping. One final dash across the silty sea to Portsmouth and the entire crew would be able to rest. God knows, they deserved it.

Captain Frank tapped her worn rail affectionately before walking down the gangplank and onto dry land. He paid the harbourmaster his due and hurried into town, eager to make one more trade to round off one of his most profitable voyages they´d ever made. Frank had picked up many contracts as they sailed between Mediterranean ports, even carrying passengers from time to time. There were always people willing to pay handsomely for a berth on a fast ship with no questions asked. The strongbox in his cabin contained enough to pay the crew thrice over. The hold was brimming with spices, silks and rare pigments, priceless products in the English markets. He hoped to squeeze a few barrels of fine French wine into his hold at La Rochelle to finish his trading mission with a flourish. There were many customers back home willing to pay well for the finest French wines and cognacs, or at least he hoped there were. After such long trips it wasn´t unusual to return home to find clients dead or missing.

The years had been good to Frank. He not only ran the family business for his aging father but had expanded it successfully too. His father was almost ready to let Frank and his sons take over his empire completely. Frank understood the old man´s resistance to retire. They were cast very much from the same mould and loved the cut and thrust of the trader´s life. Frank had bought two more ships and opened new routes to the North. His eldest son Christopher worked as first mate on one of the new ships and would soon be ready to captain his own vessel. His youngest son, Thomas, a big lad of fifteen, was picking up the ropes from Frank on board The Tilly. His other son Peter ran the operation back in England. He had no taste for the sea, but his mind was sharp as a razor. He kept the books in order, managed the warehouse and ran the dock during Frank´s long absences.

Frank was looking forward to getting back to Portsmouth and hopefully get to see Christopher before he sailed North. It would be wonderful to get the chance to sit down together for a meal as a family, to make up for all the ones he missed. He missed his wife Jane terribly and had not seen his young daughter Elizabeth for over a year, an eternity in baby years, a quick smear to someone of Frank´s age. In the four years since her birth, they had only spent three months living under the same roof. It worried him to think that she might not recognise him.

Memories kept him company during the long nights away. He was always battling voices in his head, telling him he was playing a young man´s game and should give up this life at sea. He was seriously considering hanging up his captain´s hat for good, handing the Tilly over to one of his sons and dropping his anchor for the final time. Able to enjoy the rewards a lifetime of trading had earned him, without being too old to enjoy them.

They had embarked on this latest voyage the previous spring. They called in Lancarote where he spent a few days with his young brother David, dropping off some new oars and pitch for his boat and picking up several hefty bushels of orchil, goat hides and tallow in exchange, the majority of which he successfully traded on in Aragon.

He visited the island every two years. It lifted his spirits to see his savage little brother and his family thriving on the island. He secretly wished David would return home one day and bring his family to meet their parents. They longed to see the man who had left them as a boy.

They questioned Frank endlessly, teasing fresh details with every answer. He would have probably given up sailing many years earlier if not for the desire of his parents to maintain contact with his wayward sibling, although if he was honest, he didn´t want to lose contact with David, he missed him too.

He walked along a narrow backstreet running parallel to the harbour, tucked snugly behind the warehouses on the quayside. He picked his way around the men sat on small stools, their heads bent to the task of making repairs, their hard, scarred fingers deftly working new twine and wire into old nets and lobster pots. Even though they appeared to be completely absorbed in their work, Frank knew that nothing passed them by unnoticed.

Frank ducked through a narrow doorway and along a short dark passage into a small, whitewashed courtyard where a dozen men stood in small groups engaged in quiet but intense negotiation. He scanned the faces in the yard spotting the man he sought quickly. Gabriel was the best procurer in the whole of the country. Partially hidden by the remains of a long dead plant in a clay pot, he leaned casually in the back corner of the yard, his large black hat shielded his eyes and covered a scar running from his forehead to his cheek.

Frank waited patiently while Gabriel finished dealing with a smart young country gent who looked as out of place in this dockside den as a dove sharing a roost with a murder of crows. The pair finished talking and shook hands before the country gent hurried from the yard with his chin tucked firmly into his chest, his eyes locked on the ground at his feet.

Gabriel turned and saw Frank waiting. He smiled and beckoned him over. Frank walked over and they shook hands.

"I have to say I´m pleased to see you´re still alive old friend." said Frank smiling.

"And I you. Not many come back from the Venetians looking so vibrant."

"I am blessed with the luck of the righteous old chap and am eager to share my bounty."

"Selling or buying?"

"A bit of both I hope."

"Good." Double commission was always guaranteed to make Gabriel's day. "If you don't mind." He touched Frank's arm and steered him to the door and back out into the street. "Too many hawkers and thieves in there for my liking today. Let's go discuss business somewhere else, with much better wine and cheese to tempt us with."

"Whatever you suggest old friend. Lead on."

They began walking along narrow streets, bustling with people on every corner. The market traders were doing well, as were the taverns. Even this early in the day people were spilling out of the doors into the narrow streets.

"Is there a celebration I might have accidentally stumbled upon?" Frank smiled to himself at the idea he might have inadvertently arrived at a Saint's day celebration or feast.

"No such luck this time my friend, these will all be gone by tomorrow. I've been filling orders solidly for a month with all they require for their expedition."

"An expedition?" queried Frank.

"A small force of knights and all who follow them."

"Not going to England I hope. I don't want to be fighting my way home."

"Don't worry, you're safe... for now." He turned and delivered a crooked smile. Frank laughed and patted him on the back.

"Here we are." Gabriel said as they arrived at an inn with a boisterous gaggle of men crowded around the entrance. Gabriel pushed his way through the throng at the door and led Frank inside. It smelled of sharp wine and hot bodies, the air cloudy with the breath of a dozen men, drinking and laughing loudly along every passage and in every room. Gabriel led them through a maze of corridors to a relatively quiet lounge at the rear of the building. They found an empty table and sat down. A cheer went up from another room causing an old man sat in an armchair in the corner of the room to chunter loudly.

"Boisterous lot." said Frank, "I imagine there'll be some sore heads when they push off in the morning."

"And they'll leave a sore town behind them. There won't be a whore walking in a straight line for days." said Gabriel. He called a server over and ordered wine and food before turning back to face Frank.

"So! What can I get for you?"

"Wine. The good stuff, not the horse piss you got for me last time."

"Ah yes! An unfortunate vintage as I recall. You have nothing to fear. This year is a year to drink to, not to make war with. The wine is excellent. How much do you want?"

"A dozen to fifteen barrels, depending on the price… and the taste."

"You can try the taste right now." Gabriel said as the server returned with their drinks and placed them on the table. Frank took one of the cups and took a sip. It was divine, the fruity tang brought his salty old tongue to life. He smiled and took a bigger draught.

"If you can guarantee me the same quality as this, I'll probably stretch to eighteen barrels. We don't need to fill up all the water casks this close to home, I can swap some empties for more wine."

"Excellent. I'll see what I can do. And in return you are wishing to trade what?"

"Orchil… if the price is right."

"Wonderful. You have indeed arrived at a fortunate time, for orchil is in great demand. Nobody is selling now, they only want to buy. In a few months' time you may not be so lucky though."

"Why?" Frank asked.

"These bastards making all the noise and filling the town are sailing to a place where its knee deep in the stuff so I'm told. Soon we will have so much on our hands that the price is sure to go down."

"Where exactly are they going?" asked Frank.

"From what I hear, the Canary Islands. Isn't that where you get yours from?"

Frank nodded vacantly, his mind racing.

The server returned and placed some cheese and bread on the table.

"Ah good!" exclaimed Gabriel, "You must try this cheese with the wine. It is unbelievably well matched this year. I can get some for you if you wish." Frank absently picked up a piece of the cheese and asked.

"Do you know which of the Canary Islands these knights are sailing for?"

"I couldn't say with certainty, but I understand they are heading for the Eastern isles."

Gabriel didn't have to say more, Frank knew exactly where they were headed. He took a bite of the cheese and chewed it slowly to fill his mouth while he thought. Gabriel knew everything about everyone who passed through the port. He knew all about David on Lancarote and had brought Frank to this inn for a reason. He had told Frank without telling him, maintaining his bond of confidentiality with his other customers. Frank looked up into Gabriel's eyes, took a sip of wine and nodded his thanks over the rim of the cup.

"I will have our business concluded before the evening tide. I presume you will be leaving at the first opportunity." Gabriel stated matter-of-factly while tearing a crust from the bread on the table.

"Indeed I will… and better just make it the round dozen of wine. I might have need of water after all."

"Of course."

******

The two men pushed their way out of the inn and parted company in the street. Frank hurried back to the harbour and bullied his way up the gangplank on to The Tilly's deck. He found his son Thomas leaning against the starboard gunwale chatting with a couple of boys in a rowboat, trying enthusiastically to sell him a string of herring. Frank grabbed his son's arm and pulled him round to face him.

"Has anyone left the ship?" he asked urgently.

"Only old Hammy."

"Damn. I need you to go find him and bring him back. Before you go, get someone to lift out four sacks of orchil and make space for twelve barrels of wine. Gabriel's men will be here within the hour to make the trade."

"Is something troubling you Father?" asked Thomas.

"Something huge is troubling me." He glanced back to the stern, where the towering forecastle of Gadifer de la Salle's caravel looked down on him. "I´ll tell you when we´re underway. We sail on the evening tide."

"For home?"

"I said I´ll tell you when we´re underway. Now get to your task and be quick about it."

8

La Rochelle, France,
May 1ˢᵗ, 1402

A breeze came from the north and began to carry the mist away, slowly revealing the dock and all who swarmed like busy ants on and around Gadifer's grand caravel. The tide was on the point of turning and if they were going to leave this morning it had to be soon to ride the ebbing current out to sea. Jean stood on the quayside watching, keeping out of the way as the final stores were loaded and lashed down around the ship. He saw a couple of baskets filled with lively chickens being tossed on board squawking loudly in protest. Jean recoiled at the sound and accidentally kicked a dusty sack. Cursing he bent to wipe his boot clean and a passing nanny goat gave him a nudge up the backside nearly knocking him over.

"You!" he roared, then immediately checked himself, "…carry on." he said pleasantly to the sailor leading the animal. They sauntered away, up the gangplank and onto the ship.

The last of the noble knights were also boarding, some of whom looked decidedly un-noble following a heavy few, long days of farewell drinking around the town. Jean heard muffled shouts and a loud thud coming from below decks. Some nobles brought extra squires and household servants not previously on the manifest. They were all down there now, fighting for space, quite literally in some cases. Two hundred and fifty had been planned and provisioned for; knights, tradesmen, servants and crew. Jean suspected that many more than that were already on board and there were still more to arrive.

He was pleased to see one man with a clear head keeping some semblance of order on deck. Berthin de Berneval was an ambitious young man from Caux, Normandy, who had come highly recommended by Gadifer as a possible lieutenant. Jean had been impressed enough at their first meeting to offer the young knight the commission and a generous purse of a hundred francs to secure his service. He was proving his worth now as he steered a swaying pair of monstrous looking knights below decks with a deft display of diplomacy. Jean caught his eye and beckoned him over.

"They were the last of the men monsieur." he said after bullying his way to Jean´s side. "We´re only missing one. The young toff Renaud from Calais got into an argument with the wrong man last night and had his arm broken. He´s laid up in a tavern somewhere nearby. Would you like me to organise a party to go and collect him?"

"Leave the fool where he is, we´re better off without him. We should count our blessings for only losing the one." Jean had feared worse. He had heard the drunken melee spread through the town like a tidal wave the night before as he lay tossing and turning, sleepless in his bed. He had feared they would be leaving behind more young nobles in the port, a common occurrence when wine and men became well acquainted. He remembered a time three years earlier when a handful of drunken knights had brawled with some Dutch fishermen in a brothel. They were found in an alley the next morning with their throats slit.

He heard a loud commotion behind him and turned to see a two-wheeled, covered cart pulled by a monster of a horse, barging its way through the morning traffic crowding the dockside. People were diving for cover as it bounced over the cobbles, slewing from side to side. It came to a stuttering halt a few feet away from where Jean stood. The horse was a big grey with a wide chest and thick legs, more accustomed to the plough than the cart by its girth. It was lathered in sweat and bellowed and snorted angrily. A large friar jumped down from the driving seat and rushed to take hold of the grumpy old nag´s head. He soothed it with soft words and a gentle hand on its neck while it nuzzled him, nudging his arm with its big, solid head. It snorted loudly. The friar calmed it with treats he took from a small sack hanging from his shoulder.

Jean was relieved to see Father Verrier climb down from the back of the cart, apparently unharmed by the wild ride, closely followed by Brother Bontier, who signed himself with a quick cross when his feet hit the ground. A lithe, dusky man in servant garb jumped down behind them. He turned and offered his hand to a young woman who stepped down on to the cobbles to join him. Her legs shook a little as they hit solid ground, but she soon righted herself and shared a quick smile with her companions. Father Verrier said something that Jean couldn´t hear and it made the other three chuckle. It pleased Jean to see a little laughter, there hadn´t been much humour on display during the morning so far.

Brother Bontier started brushing the dust from the back of Father Verrier´s robe while the Canarians turned to gaze up at the ship. Jean watched them looking up to the high tops of the masts where long pennants were starting to unfurl in the rising breeze. He was curious about the Lancarote natives and was eager to learn as much as he could about them and their island before they sailed into Canarian waters. They appeared to have the same tan skin tone as the North Africans of the Barbary Coast, yet had lighter, more piercing eyes, like wolves in cheap clothing. The man had a short-cropped thick thatch of unruly black hair atop his head. Heavy brows and a thick nose dominated his round face, framed by a neatly trimmed, wispy beard. The woman stood demurely in front of him with her hands clasped at her waist. A simple, white wimple covered her head. She peered out of the face hole with large round eyes. Her skin was smooth, youthful, glowing, the colour of golden sand. She was chewing her thick, slightly protruding bottom lip as she looked up, deep in thought. Jean sensed an intelligence and strength behind her eyes which he found to be quite beguiling.

She looked down suddenly, directly at Jean. He quickly averted his gaze, feeling awkward and clumsy for being caught staring. Normally, he would have blustered through such an exchange with a polite bow and a winning smile, but he was unsure how to act in front of the Canarian, unsure even if he had to act differently at all. He couldn´t recall ever having the cause or the desire to know a slave and it shocked him. It had been so easy to dehumanise them in the past, he felt ashamed by the revelation of his own inhumanity. He planned to use the time on the journey south to get to know this *man* and this *woman*. He needed to learn the idiosyncrasies of their people before he had to meet them face to face. He would be standing with eighty bloodthirsty knights at his back, goodness knows how many spears pointing at his chest, and he would have to ask for peace.

He gathered himself and walked over to greet the new arrivals with Berthin by his side.

"Father Verrier, I was beginning to worry." he said loudly, shaking hands with the priest.

"We nearly didn´t arrive at all but for the grace of God." said Father Verrier with a small chuckle. "Our Friar here," he indicated the driver of the cart who was strenuously avoiding looking their way "was fast asleep under the hay. We couldn´t find him. A touch too much holy spirit found its way down his throat last night methinks. He had to whip the horse into a gallop to get us here in time." Jean laughed and turned to Brother Bontier, shaking his hand warmly.

"Good Friar. I trust you have been well cared for."

"Indeed we have monsieur. The brothers and sisters of Saint Bartholomew are very generous hosts. They have been feeding us up with the most delightful food. My stomach needs a rest."

"Have you ever been to sea before Brother?" Jean asked.

"Never closer than a punt on the river." Bontier replied.

"Then let us hope for fair winds and calm seas, you have a lot to hold down."

"Don´t tease the poor lad." Father Verrier said, trying not to laugh.

"And this pair I gather are our translators from Lancarote." Jean asked, smiling.

Brother Bontier made brief introductions.

"My Lord Jean de Bethencourt, may I present to you Alfonso and Isabel of Lancarote, our guides and translators… our friends." Jean watched them bow and curtscy before extending his hand, Alfonso reached out tentatively to acccpt the handshake.

"Alfonso, I am very pleased to meet you." Jean said, "and where I come from, friends shake hands."

"Thank you monsieur." Alfonso replied then quickly withdrew his hand.

"It is my pleasure to welcome you both on our expedition. I expect you are eager to visit the land of your birth once more."

"Indeed we are monsieur." Isabel answered eagerly. "It has been many years since we were…"

"Taken!" Jean finished for her.

"Yes, taken." Isabel said, looking up at Jean shyly.

"Please allow me to introduce you all to Berthin de Berneval." Jean said quickly turning away from Isabel and presenting Berthin who bowed deeply to the new arrivals. "He will see to it that all your needs are cared for as we travel south. Berthin, if you would be so kind as to escort our guests to their berths and arrange someone to deliver their baggage." Berthin nodded.

"Very good." said Jean. "You will all have to excuse me for a moment. I have urgent business to attend to on board. I will leave you in Berthin´s capable hands and see you all shortly."

"Of course, off you go, we´ll be fine." Father Verrier said waving Jean away.

Brother Bontier and Alfonso set to unloading chests from the back of the cart while Jean marched up the ship´s gangplank. He climbed to the quarterdeck and carried on up the steps to the poop deck where Gadifer stood discussing a long list of supplies with his bastard son Hannibal.

"All present and correct below. Father Verrier and his party are the last to arrive." said Jean when Gadifer stopped talking. "We lost one man in the night, fighting in the town and laid low with a broken arm. I told Berthin to leave him where he was."

"We should see about getting the silver back we paid him." Gadifer commented coolly.

"Quite." said Jean raising an eyebrow.

Gadifer strained at the bit like an old warhorse with the smell of battle in his nose. He appeared ten years younger than the man Jean had met in the tavern five months previously. He was fifty-three years old. By all accounts thriving in both business and fortune, but as Jean discovered, his heart lay in the direction of adventure. He lived for the hunt and relished the glory of war.

His son Hannibal was his younger double. He was a hulking thing a couple of inches taller than his father with strong round shoulders and a hero´s jaw to prop up a handsome face with Gadifer´s blue eyes and sharp nose. He would have made a formidable knight but unfortunately had inherited the intelligence of his mother, who, although undeniably beautiful, was as *empty and vacuous as a puff of wind.* Gadifer had commented as much himself one evening when the strength of the wine they were given took them both by surprise. They disclosed many private things to each other that night, much to Jean´s amusement. Gadifer had certainly lived a full life and told some wonderful stories to illustrate it.

"How goes the loading?" asked Jean.

"That should be the last of it now." He pointed to two men squeezing through the low doorway in the forecastle with bulging grain sacks on their shoulders. "I´ll send the men to the boats to tow us off, unless there is anything else we need wait for?"

"Excellent! No no! Whatever we don´t have we don´t need." said Jean, impatient to get underway.

"Monsieur!" Gadifer snapped his heels together and flashed a smart salute catching Jean a little by surprise. This was new. He acknowledged the salute with an amused nod of the head before turning away and walking to the stern gunwale. He put his hands on the smooth wooden rail and took in a huge lungful of air.

There really was nothing else he could do now except be patient. He took a minute to calm his nerves, gripping the rail to stop the shaking in his hands. Until this moment, since the first meeting with Sir Robert, he had been unequivocally occupied hiring, buying and planning. It was only now, with the full complement of people on board, about to embark on a potentially life changing crusade, that he felt the full weight of all the expectations piled upon his shoulders.

He began to offer up a silent prayer to God, but failed. He had no idea what to ask for. He didn´t class himself as a staunch Christian, although he could say all the right things and show respect to the right people. He was a good Catholic, could recite passages from the Bible and quote many verses, but he could never accept accounts of miracles without witnessing them for himself. He didn´t believe in magic and had seen enough debauched behaviour from members of the clergy to doubt that any of them were as pure in their devotions as they claimed to be. He did want to believe that there was a God in heaven and often tried to start a conversation with Him, but after forty years of waiting for Him to answer back, he was beginning to doubt His existence.

Life and death, religion and science, he talked to himself about those things frequently. Most people he had tried to engage in conversation about such weighty subjects were not capable of exploring beyond the accepted schools of thought. It always left Jean feeling more frustrated than satisfied to spend the energy to converse with them. This was why he had taken to talking to himself, sometimes getting into heated arguments as he questioned his own assumptions. He often wondered if he were mad for doing it, but reasoned that talking to himself actually *stopped* him from going mad.

He was too agitated and unable to think clearly so he gave up trying. He let go of the rail and turned around, put his arms behind his back and lifted his chest. Gadifer was shouting down to Robin le Brument, the ship's Master who stood by the tiller on the quarterdeck. Gadifer ordered him to send his men to the boats to tow them away from the dock. Jean was glad to have the old man along. As well as this magnificent ship, he brought more than twenty loyal knights and his bastard son to join the company, experienced fighters and gentlemen all. In his opinion, Gadifer's knights were far superior to the younger mercenary knights he had recruited himself. They were more disciplined and honourable than the youngsters who were hungry solely for riches and glory. He hoped some of the elder knights' humility and grace would spread to all on board during their long voyage south.

Jean felt the movement beneath his feet as the men in the boats heaved on their oars and began tugging at the caravel. They dragged her away from the dock and out into the narrow channel leading to the open sea.

The gunwales on both sides of the main deck filled with people. Jean spotted Father Verrier and Brother Bontier in the throng and called down to them, drawing a withering glance from Master le Brument at the tiller.

The ship had four upper decks. Passengers were discouraged from getting under the feet of the crew, therefore, the raised decks were strictly off-limits during manoeuvres. The tiller was located at the back of the quarterdeck, and it was from there le Brument controlled the ship.

The poop deck was built over the rear half of the quarterdeck giving the master protection from the elements, and crossbow bolts from time to time.

Robin le Brument was already uncomfortable with the size of the load they were carrying. He voiced his objections regularly, only to be told by Gadifer *not to worry*. Gadifer had owned the ship for little over a year. He hired le Brument as Master when he took delivery of her. Gadifer hadn´t sailed in her since that day. Le Brument scowled angrily as he watched the men in holy robes cross *his* deck at someone else´s invitation and climb the steps to the poop deck.

"Come Father, take in the view from up here." Jean called. There was a loud slap on the underside of the boards beneath his feet.

"Is there a problem Monsieur le Brument?" Gadifer called down leaning out over the poop deck rail. Le Brument silently cursed before forcing a smile onto his face and stepping forward to look up at Gadifer.

"No problem monsieur. A fly." he said, holding up his hand briefly. "That is all."

"Good." answered Gadifer, "We can´t be doing with you getting injured before we even leave the port."

Le Brument shook his head and coughed out a small laugh and a wave in response before ducking back out of sight.

"Is everything under control monsieur?" Jean asked Gadifer.

"Yes, nothing to worry about. Excuse me for a moment." He walked to the starboard side and made a show of checking the clearance through the small buoys anchored in the channel.

Jean turned back to Father Verrier.

"How are our guests settling in?" he asked.

"Very well indeed. I believe that seeing the ship for the first time today and realising that they are actually going back home is making them cautiously excited."

"I don´t wonder. I hope to feel the same about this place after a few months away."

"How is the Good Lady Bethencourt fairing?" asked Verrier with the hint of a smile at the corner of his lips.

"She´s the same as she ever will be." Jean sighed. "She gets more agreeable as the distance between us grows. I imagine by the time we reach the Canaries she will be ecstatic."

"You are cruel."

"If honesty is cruelty, then yes, I am." Jean lamented. "She will miss you more than she will miss me. Who will be there to take her endless confessions while you´re administering to your new flock? If we ever come back, she will keep you in the confessional for months without pausing for breath." Father Verrier noticed Brother Bontier stir uncomfortably at the candid way Jean was speaking of his wife. He laid his hand on the young friar´s arm.

"Pay him no mind Brother," he said smiling. "He speaks to get a reaction. I believe the Good Lord sent him to test my faith and my patience." Brother Bontier smiled, his eyes wide as he shook his head a little.

"Yes, pay me no mind." Jean said easily as he placed his hand on Bontier´s other arm and gave him an earnest smile. "The good Father and I have known each other for many years. I imagine our intimacy does sound strange to one not accustomed to it, but I assure you, we would have not remained friends for as long as we have without a great deal of …leeway being allowed between us."

Verrier laughed warmly. "Leeway! Ha! Have you been preparing nautical metaphors in anticipation of our journey?"

"Brace yourself old friend, there will be many… and a drink for every one you spot."

"Including that one?"

"I see it will be hard to slip anything by you Father."

Master le Brument called out loudly from the quarterdeck. The sailors traversing the web of rigging above their heads burst into action. The sails were raised as the ship drifted free of the harbour walls, riding the current of the ebbing tide. All about the ship, sailors were at their tasks, pulling on, coiling up, tossing out ropes. The boats and rowers were hauled back on deck and the mainsail brought around. It snapped loudly as the wind filled it. The ship came to life, with the sails billowed over their heads like the wings of a giant sea bird.

Jean was looking up past the sails to where fat white clouds dotted the clear blue sky, all the way to the distant horizon. Hordes of butterflies whirled around his stomach when he felt the first surge of the ship beneath his feet. As the wooden beams began to creak and the trimmed sails began to hum, a powerful sense of contentment threatened to spill out of every pore of his body.

He chuckled to himself as the bow rode the first small wave and Brother Bontier´s legs wobbled. He and Father Verrier helped the friar over to the side where he gripped the rail tightly. The sound of the keel crashing through the small waves and the wind whistling past their ears quickly overcame all noise coming from the shore.

Jean turned to look astern and bid a silent private farewell to the rolling green hills and forests of home. The joy fled for an instant as he asked himself one final time if he was certain he was doing the right thing.

"Of course you are you fool." he said under his breath.

"What was that?" asked Father Verrier.

"I was saying goodbye to foolish notions." Jean replied turning a placing his hand on Brother Bontier´s back and smiling. Brother Bontier returned the smile with a nervous one of his own and a little *yelp* as another wave passed beneath them. For many on board it would be a long time before their senses, and stomachs would align to the rhythm of the sea.

9

High Bird Lookout, Lancarote,
May 13th, 1402

Tears stung the young Majo´s eyes as he squinted into the chilly morning wind blowing directly into the mouth of the cave, nestling over two thousand feet above the waves in the cliff face at the north-eastern tip of the island. He spotted a speck of white on the horizon in the undefined haze where the sea met the sky. It appeared again, brighter now the sun had crept into the sky and cast it´s light across the tops of the waves.

The lookout reached his arm back and grasped the ankle of his companion sleeping behind him on the cold stone floor, wrapped in a thick woollen cloak. He sat up instantly and wiped the sleep out of his eyes before looking out to sea. They watched together as the sail grew larger and then changed course, bearing off to the left, heading for the western coast of the island.

The lookout scrambled through the narrow opening at the back of the cave and climbed a long twisting tunnel to the top of the cliff. He popped out of a crack in the ground into thick cloud, everything a few paces around his feet was brilliant white. It was wet and damp, the stiff northerly breeze making it feel even colder, but the Majo didn´t feel it. He began running along the edge of the cliff he knew to be there but couldn´t see. He ran flat out for ten minutes, skipping over rocks that appeared out of the mist, he could have done it with his eyes closed he knew the path so well.

In short order the track began to descend to a gap in the cliff face, a break in the towering wall which from a distance looked as if a huge monster had taken a bite from the rock. The clouds thinned as he went lower until all at once they were skimming above his head. A hundred paces ahead he saw a young boy stand and face him from behind a large boulder.

He skidded to a halt in front of the young Majo and pointed to the north. The sails appeared through the haze beyond the farthest islet in the chain of three that stretched into the north from the cliff's base.

The young boy sprang to the edge the cliff where there were several piles of rocks formed in pyramids, fist-sized stones sat atop head sized rocks. He began hurling them over the edge. They tumbled through the air for nearly a thousand feet before smashing with a peel of loud echoing cracks against the cliff's skirts, increasing in volume as the larger stones plunged into the steep curtained valleys, bouncing from one face to another, beating out a tune like a huge stone xylophone.

An unsuspecting pair of gulls soaring close to the cliff face exploded in a puff of feathers as the falling rocks crashed into them. The boy burst out laughing but soon quieted when the older man slapped him on the head and pointed a way down the cliff to the left. The boy looked and saw the flash of a red cloak waving, held by a tiny figure about a league to the west. He quickly took off his own cloak and returned the signal, to let it be known that the stones hadn't fallen by accident.

The signal chain delivered the warning to Norstar's ears in less time than it would take a bird to fly the five leagues to his home. Shrill whistle blasts echoed around the valleys for miles around. Three short blasts meant a ship was sailing along the coast.

"Fayna, Igo!" he called, dropping the three-legged stool he had been repairing on his workbench. He snatched up his bow from next to the gate, put his finger and thumb into his mouth and blew three short loud whistles of his own. Fayna and Igo ran out of the cave, Fayna clutching her bow in one hand and her brimming quiver in the other. Igo paused and stuck his forefingers in his mouth. He tried to whistle but instead expulsed a shower of wind and spit. He puffed twice more but couldn't make a sound. He gave up trying and took off at a sprint to catch Norstar and Fayna who were racing along the path to the top of the mountain.

They soon reached the northern edge of the mountain where it dropped off sharply down to the sea. From there they enjoyed an uninterrupted view across the ocean to the northern cliffs. They stood looking out to sea as still as statues. The wind in their hair was the only movement as they scanned the horizon, soon spotting the ship creeping slowly towards them across the waves.

Rayco, Jonay and Gara arrived, each armed with a brace of sharp binots, with slings tied around their waists and bags of stones hanging from their shoulders. Rayco also carried a well-used tenique, a hefty rock in a leather pouch tied to the end of a three-foot long leather rope. His grief of a few months before had transformed into determination and focus, channelled into the task of helping Norstar create a defensive ring around the southern half of the island below the Great Divide. He practised with his weapons regularly and had all but destroyed the tree stump he used to hone his skill with the tenique. Few would spar with him face to face apart from his young brother Jonay who remained fiercely loyal to him, the bruises upon his body earned in the training ring were testament to that loyalty.

Gara walked to Norstar's side and laid her hand on his arm.

"What is it?" she asked.

"Ship." he answered squinting into the distance. "A big one." There was something familiar about the set of its sails, even from this far away.

The sound of a whistle, almost lost in the wind reached their ears. Four short blasts.

Norstar had witnessed how the natives on one of the other mountainous islands to the west had used whistles to communicate across steep valleys and had suggested the Majos tried the same system to pass messages quickly along the coast. They had taken to it eagerly and even embellished the simple signals Norstar had taught them, building vocabulary with a variety of new whistle patterns that they always delighted in sharing with their neighbours.

Rayco and Jonay whistled together in unison. Four short blasts to call the fighters to the coast and send the old and infirm with the children to the caves.

The whistling was just one innovation Norstar had introduced in the months since the gathering. Even though Beselch was officially in charge of the island's defence, he was fundamentally lazy and rarely wandered west of the Great Divide. Norstar, with Avago and Rayco as willing helpers, had organised the men of the West into a disciplined unit. They regularly drilled together as they patrolled the coast, spending more time practising with their weapons than ever before. They wrestled with wooden knives and took turns to shoot Norstar's bow whenever given the opportunity, impressing Norstar with their natural skill and ability. Norstar redoubled his efforts to make more bows and arrows, but it was a slow process.

The Majos were brave and had shown their mettle in action, turning away a stinking dhow that sailed on a raiding mission from the Barbary Coast. It dropped anchor in a cove near Long Sands close to a small sleepy settlement. A raiding party of dark-skinned Moors, swaddled in grimy cotton pantaloons, with scimitars and knives tucked in sashes around their waists came ashore in a small boat. They were soon leaping back in the boat and rowing for their lives as a torrent of rocks and spears rained down upon their heads. Four of the pirates lay dead on the rocks, their bodies left in the pirate's haste to get away. Every cur who had stepped ashore took an injury back to the dhow with them, they fled south with dozens of Majos lining the shore to chase them away with curses and threats.

Avago arrived to join Norstar with a half dozen men from a neighbouring village, their greetings gruff and perfunctory. They watched together as the ship grew larger; it was sailing unusually close to the land. Passing ships generally gave this coastline a wide berth for fear of striking the reef hidden beneath the heavy swell.

"Frank!" exclaimed Gara smiling.

"Are you sure?" asked Avago.

"I have watched that ship coming many times." Gara replied taking Norstar's hand and looking up at him. Norstar released a breath he hadn't realised he was holding, smiled down at Gara and looked back to the now familiar set of the Tilly, driving a foamy wave before her bow. Norstar was almost disappointed not to have a fight on his hands, even though the joy at seeing The Tilly should have far outweighed that emotion.

"Your brother I think we can call a friend." Avago said, a big beaming smile stretching from ear to ear. "Send out the signals, call the people back to their homes." Norstar nodded absently and returned his gaze to the ship ploughing through the waves, worried that the feelings of peace within him were being overpowered by long-dormant, darker desires.

******

The Tilly´s dinghy skirted a long finger of rock protruding into the sea to create a shallow sheltered bay in its lee. Frank stood in the prow of the boat giving instructions to the four men rowing and the man on the tiller as they navigated the final stretch of calm water to shore. Norstar, Igo and Fayna waded up to their thighs from the pebbled beach and caught the boat before it struck rock. The current was strong and tugged at their feet, but they held fast.

Frank gripped Norstar´s outstretched hand and allowed his younger brother to guide him into the water. He dropped from the side of the boat and landed with a huge splash, laughing heartily.

"Wooah! That´s colder than it should be." he said grinning.

"It's those old bones of yours brother, you should be tucked up under a blanket in front of a roaring fire." Norstar quipped.

"We´ll have less of your cheek whippersnapper. I see more grey colouring your locks than ever before."

"Where´s Thomas?" asked Fayna bluntly.

"My dear girl," Frank laughed, "hello to you too."

"Hello Uncle Frank." said Fayna momentarily chagrined. "Where´s Thomas?" she asked again.

"He´s back on The Tilly. They need all hands to bring her to anchor."

"Could they use two more?" asked Igo eagerly.

"I dare say they could…Igo. My goodness, how you´ve grown. I nearly didn´t recognise you." Frank said. Igo puffed out his chest and stood a little taller. Frank shook his head and addressed the pair of them. "Go on, back in the boat to the ship if you like. Thomas is eager to see you too."

Fayna and Igo yelped with joy, gripped the side of the boat and hauled themselves into it while Norstar and Frank shoved it away from the shore. The men aboard called greetings to the pair while sculling to spin the boat around and point the prow back out to the Tilly.

Frank´s crew had been with him for many years and knew Norstar and his family well, although the children had changed greatly in the year since they had last seen them. Igo was thicker about the chest arms and legs and much more angular. His soft features had hardened into a handsome face, it cracked into a smile as he stepped down the boat and exchanged greetings with the men on board. The sight of Fayna elicited a different response as she followed Igo over the benches. She was turning into a beautiful young woman with her almond eyes and long limbs. Her oval face was framed by her luscious, braided hair which shone in the sunlight. The men at their oars struggled to look into her eyes and not steal glances at her near naked body. She wore just the leather band around her waist as Majo men did, with strands of leather hanging down to the middle of her strong thighs. She was definitely not a little girl anymore. The men pulled on their oars with a rediscovered vigour and wished as one that they were twenty years younger.

Norstar and Frank waded back to shore where Avago and Gara waited on the pebble beach. Gara stepped forward to welcome Frank with her arms open wide.

"Brother." she said wrapping her arms around his neck. "It is good to see you."

"Indeed my dear." said Frank, as usual a little awkward when it came to physical contact, especially with the half-naked wife of his brother. With a sigh he allowed himself to relax a little and gave Gara a quick pat on the back. She laughed and stepped back. Frank stretched his hand out to Avago who took it warmly in both of his and pumped it up and down. Frank was much more comfortable with a rough calloused hand than a soft body in his grasp.

"Frank." Avago said with a huge grin creasing his features. "Welcome."

"Thank you sir." Frank said, genuinely pleased to see the old man, who to his dismay looked a lot younger than he, despite being at least fifteen years his senior.

"Come Frank," Avago said, "Iballa is preparing a feast for you."

"How is your good lady wife, dear Iballa?"

"She will tell you everything."

"I'm sure she will." Frank chanced a sideways look at Avago who raised an eyebrow mischievously.

"She likes you and you are too polite to walk away." the old Majo said with a shrug.

"A curse of my upbringing my dear. Let us go and make haste, before my stomach complains too loudly."

Avago led them off the beach and onto the narrow path that led back to the mountain, so narrow they had to walk in single file. Norstar brought up the rear, sensing that something serious was on Frank's mind behind the small talk he filled the air with. Before long, he slowed his pace, allowing Avago and Gara to walk on ahead.

"What brings you back so soon Brother?" Norstar asked.

"Trouble."

"For who?"

"For you." Frank stopped and turned to face Norstar.

"The French are coming." he said, looking into his little brother's eyes. "A ship full of knights and enough tradesmen to build a small town."

"Coming here for what, goats and fish? Haven't they enough of their own?"

"They're coming for the land. If it wasn't them, it would be others. While you have lived here the world has got considerably smaller little brother. The Portuguese are raiding Canaria and Nivaria, the Azores is within their grasp if not already taken. It is only natural that the other Kingdoms are also looking to expand their territories. This island, indeed this entire archipelago, is the key to controlling new trade routes to the South." said Frank gravely. "We talked about it ourselves when we first sailed here, you must remember."

"Yes, of course. But the French? Are they not still at war with England?"

"There hasn't been any action for some time. The knights seek adventure and plunder wherever they can find it."

"But there is no *plunder* here. No gold, silver, no jewels, other than our food and water, we have nothing of value."

"The land is more valuable than ship loads of treasure. The Italians and the Turks control all the goods coming from the East in the

Mediterranean. The Turks will only deal with the Genoese and the Venetians and once they add their commissions on top of the price there is very little profit left for the rest of us. There has been mounting pressure to find a way to India and China and bypass the Mediterranean completely, but the ships will have to sail south, beyond Africa before they can strike east. These islands are the perfect staging point for that journey, and for that reason alone I am surprised others haven´t tried to invade before now. Your good fortune is running out fast, your sanctuary is about to be invaded... and I measure that in a matter of days rather than years, until the first ship arrives."

"How do you know this?"

"I met them in La Rochelle loading up a large caravel for the journey. We slipped out a few hours before them but according to Gabriel..."

"He´s still alive?" interrupted Norstar.

"And thriving. He sends his regards by the way and hopes to see you soon."

"There´s little chance of that happening unless he´s planning to come here too."

"I very much doubt he´ll be heading this far South. He sits in La Rochelle with his fingers feeling the vibrations from all parts of his web. No, he hopes, as do I, that you will sail back home with me."

"I am home."

"Don´t argue damn semantics with me now you fool. This is much more serious than word play."

"Yes this is very serious brother." Norstar answered, bristling slightly at Frank´s tone. "Who do you suggest I leave behind if I were to come with you. This is my home and everybody on this island is family. Is there enough space on The Tilly to take us all away to safety?"

"Well no, but..."

"Well no but nothing. This is our home, and if need be we´ll fight to protect it. We are not as defenceless as you might imagine, we have had many fights in the year since you were here last, and have tasted bitter loss. Mifaya and her boys were taken."

"Oh my God. I am so sorry." Frank said, genuinely wounded by the revelation. He liked Rayco´s wife. Their marriage had taken place during one of his visits several years earlier. The wedding party had lasted for almost a week and his crew still talked about it, indeed a couple of them still bore the scars they earned in the wrestling rings. "What happened?" he asked, concern creasing his brow.

"Portuguese slavers. A dirty twin-masted ship, with grey sails and a fat pig at the helm. They snuck ashore and took Mifaya and the little ones while they were out with the goats. Since then we´ve organised. We are ready and able to defend ourselves. You were spotted from way out and tracked along the shore."

"Was that what the whistles were for?"

"You heard them?"

"It was hard not to."

"The Majos have had enough of being treated like sheep brother. Our grief has given us the strength to fight back."

"My heart weeps for your loss. I´m impressed by what you have achieved with your *island defenders* but with respect, the knights who follow in my wake are blood thirsty, battle-hardened soldiers in armour, not pirates in pyjamas. Sticks and stones will have little chance against armour and steel."

"We can do it. We must do it." Norstar´s tone was defiant and brooked no argument. He stood tall, his chest thrust forward, he looked every inch like a man of steel wrapped in flesh. However, Frank saw past the façade of bravado and looked into his eyes where a light of uncertainty burned, and as long as that flame smouldered, there was a chance that Frank could talk Norstar around… but not right now, to press him too far would mean pushing him away. Frank decided to withdraw and bide his time.

"We´ll talk more later." he said reaching out to pat Norstar on the shoulder. Norstar nodded, his jaw clenched tightly. The two of them continued to trudge along the path behind Avago and Gara in brooding silence. Frank was determined to find a way to persuade Norstar to leave with him, but finding the words and the correct way to deliver them would take time, and time was a luxury they didn´t have.

He had laid a little trap for the French in Cadiz when the Tilly stopped there briefly, but it wouldn´t delay them for long.

10

Cadiz, Kingdom of Castile,

May 13th, 1402

It had been a difficult and fraught voyage from La Rochelle. Tension between the Normans and Gascons had ignited a feud that had almost led to open conflict on board ship. The wind had deserted them shortly after setting off and while becalmed in the Bay of Biscay, small altercations had escalated into full-blown acrimonious displays of hostility. On one occasion, two crossbow bolts thrown from the rigging narrowly missed Gadifer as he attempted to bring calm to a dispute. Jean had had to plead with both sides to avoid a fully armed conflict.

He had been relieved when they finally approached Cadiz, their last port of call before making the final crossing to Lancarote, only to have that relief turn to dismay as he noticed a company of troops rushing to the quayside to meet the ship.

"Wish me luck Father." he said to Verrier who was stood at the rail next to him.

"How can you be sure that they´re here for you?" asked the Priest.

"Just a feeling." he answered with practised levity. "See if you can administer a touch of the Lord´s love and wisdom to the men while I am away. We are on a mission to bring peace to the heathens, it wouldn´t do for us to arrive there, fighting amongst ourselves."

"I will see what I can do." replied Father Verrier.

The ship nudged gently against the dock and was made fast before the gangplank was lowered. Jean stepped onto the quayside with his head held high. His legs were unaccustomed to the stability of dry land, he felt they might betray him if called upon to move too quickly. He was met on the dock by a platoon of armoured guards and a stern looking officer wearing the red and white diagonal stripes of Castile on his tunic.

"Can I help you gentlemen?" Jean asked.

"We are here seeking Jean de Bethencourt of Normandy and believe him to be aboard this vessel." the officer replied,

"You are addressing him Sir. How may I help you?" Jean asked breezily.

"We have a warrant to detain you. You are to accompany us to the High Court of Seville where His Excellency the Chief Justice has some questions he would like answers to."

"I see." said Jean stroking the hair on his chin and teasing it to a point. "And if I were to refuse your *invitation*?"

"That would not be wise señor." the officer replied lifting his head and flaring his nostrils slightly. The men behind him shuffled, gripping their pikes a little firmer as they glared without humour through the face grills of their helmets. Jean heard a shuffling noise on the ship´s deck behind him and noticed several of the guards shifting their attention from him to the ship at his rear. Jean turned to see the ship´s side crowded with knights, although after a couple of weeks confined in the ship they looked less like knights and more like an army of marauding gladiators spoiling for a fight. Wordless challenges passed between the knights and the immaculately turned-out guards who looked just as eager for an excuse to fight. Jean thought better of provoking the situation into a pissing contest, especially as he stood in the middle of the two sides.

"Very well," he said, turning back to address the officer. "Give me some time to pack some things and we will go and address the issue with His Excellency immediately."

"Of course." answered the officer, his eyes flicking between Jean and a huge unkempt knight stood shaving hairs from the side of his neck with a knife while staring threateningly into the officer´s eyes.

Jean turned away and walked back up the gangplank. The men parted to allow him through and then reformed once he had passed to continue their game with the guards. Jean skipped up the steps to the quarterdeck where Gadifer and Father Verrier stood waiting.

"As I suspected Gentlemen, I have urgent business to attend to in Seville. Father Verrier," he turned to look at the Priest, stood fingering his rosary nervously while maintaining a serene expression on his face.

"If you would be so kind as to ask Brother Bontier to join me. If we are to have an accurate chronicle of our crusade it would be wise for the good Friar to record events in Seville at first hand."

"Certainly, I´ll go below and inform him straight away." replied the Priest. He excused himself and quickly descended the steps to the cabins. Jean watched him go and turned to Gadifer.

"I imagine we´ll be gone for several days. It would be prudent to wheedle out the disruptive elements of the company and bid them farewell here, before we sail any further."

"I thought the same." Gadifer nodded. "Hannibal is in the process of compiling a list of names of the troublesome Gascons in the company, I´ll ask Berthin to do the same with the Normans."

"Good. Get them off the ship and fill up their berths with as many supplies as we can carry. Be careful how much you pay though, this city is a den of thieves."

"Don´t worry Monsieur, I´ve been here many times before. I dare say I still have a few contacts I can count on to supply us at a good price." replied Gadifer with barely restrained humility.

"Of course!" Jean answered with a small smile. "I forget sometimes how long you have been at this business, a few years longer than I, I wouldn´t wonder. It must be your youthful countenance and boundless energy that confuses me so." He clapped Gadifer cordially on the back. Gadifer responded with a short, loud guffaw.

"I may have more years than most in this company, but you can guarantee I´ll still be swinging my sword long after many of these *youngsters* have fallen." he stated with only a slight hint of mirth in his eyes.

"Your longevity proves the truth in your words." Jean replied. "I must take my leave now and be done with this business."

Jean went to his tiny cabin where his valet Philip packed some clothes into a small valise. He took a heavy leather purse from the strongbox under his bunk and strapped it under his tunic along with a small satchel containing the letter bearing the Pope´s seal. He would only use that in an absolute emergency if he had any trouble talking his way out of the charges he was being led away to face. It could be one of several things he was, and wasn´t guilty of at present, and that made him nervous. He tried to mask those nerves as he walked calmly back up on deck.

He met Brother Bontier at the head of the gangplank and together they descended to the dock and the waiting guards. Philip followed behind carrying Jean´s baggage. Most of the knights had given up toying with the guards and had left to freshen up and prepare for a night ashore. There were plans to visit the types of den of iniquity their mothers had warned them never to visit, for many of the stir crazy knights.

"Señor." Jean addressed the officer of the guard. "May I introduce to you Brother Bontier who will be accompanying us to Seville." The officer looked perturbed.

"I was told to bring only you," he said.

"But señor, we are travelling on the Lord´s business. It would not do to leave without at least one of his earthly representatives to accompany us, wouldn´t you think?"

"Erm! Yes of course." replied the officer, finding himself not sharp enough to deny him.

"And Philip of course, my valet." He moved aside to let Philip be seen before carrying on, not allowing the officer time to speak. "I trust you have transport arranged?"

"We have a carriage and horses waiting."

"Very good! Then let us make haste to quench my accusers' thirst for justice. Lead the way sir."

****

From the tip of the ship´s forecastle, Berthin watched Jean being led away. He stood with Gillet de la Bordeniere and Pernet the Blacksmith. Both were younger than he and hoping to make their name and fortune. It was by far the furthest either of them had ever ventured from home before. Gillet had only recently won his spurs in a hard-fought tournament in Paris while Pernet finished his apprenticeship and inherited his first anvil and bellows, but hadn´t yet the funds to build a forge and a house around them.

"Look at the foolish peacock." Berthin said shocking the other two with his outburst. "This venture is doomed to failure if he continues with the pretence that we quest in the name of our Lord."

"I don´t understand Monsieur," said Gillet, "Have you not accepted his coin like the rest of us to follow him on the noble quest to educate the heathen?"

"Pah! A nobler quest would be to capture a few of them for market. They are incapable of higher function and are no better than beasts of the forest. Look." He gestured to the stern gunwale where Isabel and Alfonso were stood together, looking out over the bustling port. "You can dress them in human clothes, but they will always be animals, no better than dancing bears."

"I hear the woman has a rare intelligence." said Gillet.

"And I once heard a man have a conversation with a parrot." answered Berthin glibly. "Look at the man. Have you ever seen anybody look so uncomfortable in their clothes?" Alfonso was leaning over the gunwale, his arm outstretched tempting a gull to hover closer with a small silver fish held in his fingertips. "I hear that they wander around their island naked as the day they were born. It is said that their *King* is only the leader because his cock is the largest on the island." A gull flashed over Alfonso´s shoulder and snatched the fish from his fingers just as the other bird was getting close enough to take it. The usurped gull squawked loudly and peeled off in pursuit while Isabel and Alfonso fell about laughing.

"Animals. But valuable animals. Have you any idea how much they´re worth at market?"

"I confess I don´t." replied Pernet.

"At least a hundred gold crowns a head in Portugal, even more in the Arabian markets." Berthin had no idea whether his statement was true or not. What was important was to appeal to the base desires of the men he spoke to; they would believe what they wanted to hear.

"There is no treasure waiting for us in the Canary Islands. That there is the wealth the islands have to offer." He pointed at Alfonso and Isabel who were trying once more to coax another gull close with a slither of fish. "We could all be wealthy beyond our wildest dreams if we could fill our holds with them and get them to market. Let the Peacock keep the land, I prefer to take the livestock."

"You talk dangerously Berthin." Gillet said, his voice low as he looked around to make sure none were close enough to hear. "What you are suggesting is... is mutiny."

"It can only be mutinous at sea. On land the laws are different, especially as our swords have been bought with coin, not with shells."

"But... our honour!" Gillet blustered.

"To hell with honour. How do you think the Peacock and Gadifer got their wealth and power in the first place?" He looked at the vacant faces of Gillet and Pernet who shook their heads. "Peacock married it and Gadifer's ancestors stole it. Where is the honour in that?

"If an opportunity to make this journey more profitable arises, then I believe it is our right, nay our duty to take it, just as they did when they had youth on their side. They would respect us for it, don't you think?" Pernet flashed him a quick warning look. He turned to see the top of Gadifer's head coming up through the hatch in the centre of the deck.

"Ah! Monsieur Berthin. A moment if you please." Berthin rushed over and lent his arm to Gadifer who climbed out of the hatch, stamped his feet and brushed himself down.

"Gentlemen." he said to Gillet and Pernet, "If you will excuse us."

"Of course monsieur." Gillet said nudging Pernet with his elbow. They walked across the deck to the starboard quarter. Gadifer waited until they were out of earshot before speaking.

"We are to be stranded here a few days more than expected."

"Monsieur?"

"Monsieur de Bethencourt has a pressing legal matter to attend to in Seville and will be away for some time. Therefore, we must make preparations for the final leg of our journey in his absence. I have a very important task for you."

"I am at your service monsieur."

"I want you to make a list of who we can do without. Primarily the troublemakers who have plagued our journey thus far. Bring it to me when you are done. I have business to attend to in the city and will be gone until the evening. We will begin expulsion of undesirables upon my return."

"By your order monsieur."

"Very good." Gadifer returned a salute he wasn't given and made his way down the steps to the main deck.

Berthin watched the old man cross the deck and congratulated himself. Gadifer had just given him carte blanche to rid himself of any knight in the company he found disagreeable. There were many of those. The ones who had ridiculed and dismissed him as inconsequential would be the first to leave, closely followed by the over-entitled titled ones. He wished he could lose the pious troop and the Holy Men they had vowed to protect but there was little chance of that. In an ideal world he would rid himself of Bethencourt too, but he didn't imagine he could get that one past Gadifer.

He hurried aft to his berth to begin preparing his list.

11

Eagle Claw Bay, Lancarote,
May 20ᵗʰ, 1402

Norstar and Frank sat next to each other on the sand looking out to The Tilly. She tugged on her anchor, eager to leave. She lay just outside a horseshoe shaped cove on the southwest coast of the island at the tip of Eagle Claw Bay. Turquoise waters lapped at her hull as she waited for Frank to board and give the order to sail for home. Unfortunately for her and her crew, Frank wasn´t in a hurry to leave. He was savouring moments alone with his brother while Gara, Boyo and Nayra foraged in the rock pools on the exposed reef near the mouth of the cove.

A deep narrow channel entered the bay from the sea, wide enough for a ship´s boat but not for the ship itself. Four leagues to the South the mountains of Erbania were visible through the blue haze under the midday sun. The wind was changing direction, building steadily from the southeast. It was a hot wind and would blow strongly for two, maybe three days. Sand, lifted from the great desert beyond the Barbary Coast would follow later, filling the sky with fine, dry, yellow-ochre choking dust. Frank wanted to use that wind to blow him North, it would shorten his voyage considerably, far quicker than the usual grind of tacking against the trade winds all the way to the Pillars of Hercules. His eagerness to depart was tempered with the knowledge that his little brother was still stubbornly refusing to leave the island.

They relaxed in companionable silence for now, enjoying a rare break in the cloud that had hovered over them since Frank first mentioned the approaching invaders.

A loud scream came from The Tilly and three splashes bloomed at her side. Fayna, Igo and Thomas´s heads popped up, then their arms and legs began thrashing as they raced for the shore.

"I´ll bet you three shells Thomas is first." said Frank who sat with his back against a boulder with his bare feet burrowed into the soft hot sand.

"I´ll bet double that Fayna is on the sand and dry before he even makes it out of the water." said Norstar chuckling.

"You´re probably right. She reminds me a lot of Gara the first time we all met. Remember?"

"Like it was yesterday." said Norstar smiling.

"I wish Mother and Father could meet her… and the rest of your brood of course."

"Don´t start again Frank. We don´t belong in that world."

"Maybe not, but that world is on its way to swallow you up whether you like it or not."

"Frank!" Norstar warned.

"I know I know. I have to try; can you fault me for it?"

"No. I cannot."

Frank looked across at his little brother. It was breaking his heart that he might never see him again. He looked back out to sea before tears came to shame him.

Fayna was leading the boys back to shore as Norstar had predicted. Thomas and Igo swam in her wake side by side, thrashing madly in a vain attempt to catch her, but to no avail, she was on dry sand before they reached water shallow enough to stand in. She tossed her head back and turned around to watch the boys as they raced the last few feet to the beach. They stood up at the same time and began to run through the shallows, kicking the water before them until they hit dry sand. They sprinted, dived and landed together on their bellies at Fayna´s feet.

"It´s the thing between your legs that slows you down boys." she snapped as they rolled over panting. Igo laughed out loud but Thomas suddenly coloured and sat up looking down, horrified that his prick might have slipped from his britches. He was a handsome boy, a little taller and leaner than Igo, the double of Frank when he was the same age. The only nod to his mother´s looks was the mop of white, blond curly hair sat atop his head.

"Could you see it, if it fell out?" Igo asked. Thomas sprang for him and the pair began wrestling in the sand, grunting with effort as they grappled. Fayna stood back looking down on them for a moment before walking away.

"He asked me if he could go with you on the Tilly someday." said Norstar casually nodding towards the boys rolling in the sand.

"What? You jest." replied Frank.

"No, he was being serious, he loves the sea. You should see him handling the boat. He reads the wind and the waves like one of Poseidon´s own."

"What did you say when he asked?"

"I didn´t know what to tell him. Probably if you hadn´t given us the news that the French were on the way I would have been more inclined to let him run with you for a couple of years and see the world... but now we need every man here who can hurl a stone, standing in defence of the island."

"My God man! One boy isn´t going to make a difference. Let me take him, at least keep one of you safe, and introduce him to his Grandparents. Mother would be overjoyed."

"It´s not that easy Brother. Gara wouldn´t let her baby boy go."

"Have you asked her?"

"No, I don´t need to, she thinks the same as I."

"How do you know? If I´ve learned one thing about the women on this island it´s that they don´t appreciate being told how to think by their men."

"It´s not that simple." said Norstar irritably, wishing he´d never brought the subject up.

"What´s difficult about it? The boy wants to travel and see the world. Remember when we started crewing on the Tilly with Father? We were a lot younger than he is now and look... we´re still alive and richer for travelling. What could you possibly object to? Are you afraid I wouldn´t look after him or are you afraid that once he´s had a taste of the world out there he won´t want to come back? I suspect it's you who doesn´t want to let him go and you´re just using Gara as an excuse."

"Let it go Frank. I don´t want to talk about it anymore." snapped Norstar.

"That´s it, isn´t it? It´s you."

"I said I don´t want to talk about it and I mean it!" Norstar turned angrily to face Frank.

"What are you going to do to me, lose your temper and start throwing your weight around?   Listen, you might be the big brave man in front of these people but you`re still my little brother and I could still whip your arse."

"I´d like to see you try." challenged Norstar, starting to rise to his knees.

"Sit down you fool." said Frank with a wave of the hand. "I´m not going to fight you."

Norstar sat back down with a bump, picked a pebble out of the sand and threw it.   He looked at Thomas and Igo rolling in the sand. One then the other gained advantage and then lost it, grunting with effort and laughing in equal measures.

"Listen to me one more time and let this be the end of it." he said quietly so as not to be overheard by Fayna who was standing only a few paces away.   "He is not going with you this time, and yes, it is me who doesn´t want him to go.   It is a sick world out there.   He has no defence against it.   He is not of that world, he doesn´t know how to act, who to trust.   He has no concept of life where the pursuit of coin and glory are the only measure of a man.   Where you can have your throat slit because somebody wants your shoes.   It would chew him up and spit him out and I don´t want my son exposed to that life any more than I would expose myself to it again.   He can´t leave home, we need him here, safe, with us."

"That´s pretty much word for word what Ma and Pa said when you left home.   It took years for Father to give up wanting to bring the Tilly down here and drag you back.   But I fought for you.   I backed your decision to cast your old life aside and start again.   Was I right, or was Father right?   Should I have tied you up in the hold and taken you home against your will because Ma and Pa were worried for your safety?"

Norstar said nothing.   The truth of how much he hurt his parents with his eagerness to leave the safety of their home was only now beginning to register, now that he was facing the prospect of losing one of his children in the same way.

"You know I would look after him as if he were my own, which in a way he is." Frank pressed. "Is that the problem? Is it because I failed to rail you in all those years ago and you jumped ship despite my protestations. Do you fear he will do the same, fall in love with some pretty thing in skirts and dare to make a life for himself?"

Norstar was about to answer when a yell drew his attention down the beach. Igo had pinned Thomas, his nephew´s face was twisted and half buried in the sand.

"I yield!" cried Thomas spitting out sand, "I yield God damn it." Igo laughed as he released the pressure on his cousin´s head, stood and offered his hand to pull him to his feet. Thomas took it and stood. He shook his head and a clump of sand plopped out of his ear and landed at his feet.

"Did that come out of your head?" Igo teased.

"Why you…" Thomas took after Igo who ran away laughing.

"Boys!" tutted Fayna, bored watching them. She walked to the rocks where Gara was making her way back to the beach with little Boyo and Nayra trailing behind, swinging a heavy basket between them.

"You have a beautiful, strong and proud family." said Frank. "I love them as I love you. I wish I could take you all home but have resigned myself to the fact that it will not happen today." Norstar would have rolled his eyes were his brow not too heavy to lift. There was a shout from away to the left where Thomas had dived and knocked Igo´s ankles together, causing him to crash to the sand. They leapt back to their feet and in a moment were grappling again.

"Look at them, there´s nothing to separate them." Frank said. "Young Thomas has been with me for over a year now and no harm has come to him. His eyes have been opened a few times, remember your first time visiting the pleasure houses of Venice?"

"Hmm." mused Norstar, unable to shut out the happy memory despite his mood.

"Igo is a man now. Let him be one." Frank finished allowing the silence to ring loudly around them both as they watched their boys wrestle.

Out on the rocks, Iballa and Avago appeared from beyond the headland. Avago carried a full basket of shellfish collected from pools further along the reef.   Fayna whistled loudly to Igo and Thomas who stopped wrestling and looked over at her. She pointed to Boyo and Nayra struggling over the sharp rocks and shouted for the boys to come help them while she helped her grandparents. Igo and Thomas broke into a run, racing each other across the dry sand. They were neck and neck when they passed Norstar and Frank, their bare feet kicking sand into the air as they ran.

"Fayna´s got the measure of both of them." Frank said with a huge grin on his face as the boys tore past. "I wish my men would jump to my bidding as quickly as they do to hers. You know, she would probably make a good skipper one day." he said casually.

"Don´t you even think…" Norstar looked across and saw the smile on Frank´s face. "If I didn´t know your father I´d call you a bastard." Norstar said scooping up a handful of sand and throwing it at Frank who was roaring with laughter.

Chimboyo and Nayra set their basket down on the rocks when Thomas and Igo arrived. Boyo started to pick creatures out of the basket and named them all for Thomas while Nayra stood back, looking at her cousin through starry eyes. She was besotted.

Gara stepped off the rocks and walked across the sand to Norstar and Frank. Frank, stood as she walked over and remained standing until she had sat down.

"My dear lady, how was the harvest?" he asked.

"Very good. Enough for you and your men to eat well this evening."

"That is very kind of you my dear, but please, don´t leave yourselves short for us." Frank said generously, although in reality, he didn´t relish the idea of boiling shellfish stinking up the ship.

"We will not be short," Gara said, "we have more than enough to go around, we will have one less mouth to feed."

"What! Who?" exclaimed Norstar, his head snapping round to stare at Gara. Gara was looking down casually brushing small stones from the bottom of her feet.

"Our son will be leaving with Frank and Thomas aboard the Tilly." she said calmly.

"What the… How?"

"He talked to me earlier and told me you had forbidden him to leave. At first, I agreed with you and wanted to keep him here. And then I remembered your stories, about the soft wet *grass* and the tall trees that grow so thick the sun cannot reach the ground, the lakes of fresh water and the ice and snow. You told us all about the cities with buildings as big as mountains and the lanes filled with more people than we could ever imagine." She paused and looked Norstar square in his reddening eyes. She reached out to place a hand gently on his thigh before continuing.

"I always cherished the stories you told us. I even hoped one day to see these wonders with my own eyes, to meet your Mother and Father, to sleep where you slept and walk where you walked. To feel snow on my eyelashes and see smoke come out of my mouth on a cold morning. I want to meet Frank´s wife and his children. All of these things that made you are a part of us all." She reached up to Norstar´s face and gently caught a tear on the back of her finger.

"I never knew you felt this way." Norstar said quietly.

"I never told you because you never wanted to go back there. It would have been cruel to ask you to take me somewhere I knew you didn´t want to go. The pictures you painted with your words touched us all, the children more so. Your tales filled their heads with dreams of adventure. They have asked many times, since they were babies, if they could one day see those places with their own eyes. Your son is more like you than you realise and has a desire to travel beyond the horizon. For that reason alone I would let him go and feast his eyes, to learn and to grow in a world bigger than this one."

"But what of the invaders?" Norstar pleaded. "We need him here to fight with us."

"If the men coming here are as blood thirsty and ruthless as you say they are, then we are all in mortal danger. I would meet that danger with peace in my heart knowing that at least one of my children is safe, beyond the reach of those who would carve out his heart. I would send them all away if I could, to avoid ever having to see one of them suffer."

The weight of her words crushed Norstar. He knew Gara spoke the truth. He suddenly hated himself for not paying closer attention to his son, who like Norstar himself had grown in the shadow of an elder sibling and had developed secret ambitions of his own to escape. It was suddenly so clear, how alike he and Igo really were. They were both independent and eager to learn from anybody who would teach them. Igo had spent years wandering the island alone, exploring every hidden valley, cave and mountain until there was nowhere new left to discover.

He stood. "I need to think." he said and walked away. He climbed the path at the back of the beach and disappeared over the crest of the hill. Frank and Gara watched him go. They both knew he needed time and space to think, without the weight of other people´s eyes on him.

"You know I will look after him as if he were my own." said Frank earnestly once Norstar had gone.

"Yes, I know." replied Gara turning to look at him, the warmth in her eyes evaporated in an instant. "And you know that if any harm comes to my son while he is in your care, I will kill you myself."

12

Cadiz, Kingdom of Castile,
May 20th, 1402

Berthin left the ship quietly before Gadifer could set him to work. They had purged the ship of well over a hundred souls: knights, crew and hangers-on in the last few days. Hannibal proved easy to manipulate and agreed to almost every suggestion Berthin made when they discussed their lists of undesirables together. Hannibal and Gadifer, along with a half dozen knights dressed in full battle armour toured the ship ejecting the unwanted men. Those who refused to leave got thrown overboard. With fewer people and less baggage there was more space for provisions. Gadifer set the crew to redistributing the weight of their stores around the decks. It was the kind of work Berthin didn´t care for, so he endeavoured to sneak off the ship to avoid it at every opportunity.

He spent many hours familiarising himself with the port and it´s workings, discretely observing the Harbourmaster and his men as they made their rounds to collect taxes and examine cargo. He learned which warehouses stored which goods and took note of the multitude of strange colourful vessels that travelled through the port. He watched carefully where the different classes of ship dropped anchor or tied up, depending on what they carried.

His curiosity led him to one quay hidden away between the fishing docks and the cattle pens with an unfamiliar aroma, far worse than the smell of rotting fish or livestock slurry. It was the stench of misery. He found four ships tied abreast at the quay sitting in slack water. He could smell stale blood, piss and shit permeating through their stained wooden hulls as he approached. They looked like death, even the catfish swimming through the rest of the harbour avoided them. They were without doubt, slaver vessels. He placed his hand on the rail of the ship nearest the dock and was about to clamber on board to look around when he heard a muffled cry coming from below decks. He almost pissed in his britches and ran away without looking back.

The next morning, he noticed a large double-masted, black-hulled ship sliding into port and making directly for the slaver´s dock. He hurried over and peered out from behind a stack of broken lobster pots as the ship tied up alongside the four wretched hulks already there. The sheen of the brass letters on the nameplate had long since faded, but he could still make out the letters. TAJAMAR.

Berthin watched as a large man emerged from the aft cabin and growled some incomprehensible orders at the sailors on deck before stepping over the side and climbing down into a small dinghy. Two men rowed the little boat across the harbour, the weight of the Master sat on the stern bench almost pushed it below the surface. He was dressed in a long black woollen coat fastened tightly about his monstrous frame. He was like a cold shadow on a hot sunny day, he sucked in heat and snuffed out light. Dank strands of dark greasy hair poked out from beneath a leather tricorn hat pulled down low on his head, shading his eyes from view. The bottom half of his face was obscured by a well brushed and oiled black beard, which was gathered and tied in two thick ponytails under his chin.

Berthin had to sprint around the harbour to keep the dinghy in sight. He saw the Tajamar´s Master climb from the dinghy and onto some iron rungs sticking out of the harbour wall leading directly to the Harbourmaster´s office. He entered the office and came out a few short moments later shaking his head. Rather than return to the dinghy he headed into the city.

Berthin followed at a distance. It wasn´t difficult to keep track of the man in black, people moved out of his way in the crowded narrow streets to avoid him. An aura of malevolence surrounded him, he extinguished any joy that burned too brightly, people were unwilling to brush up against him lest they catch his malaise.

He wandered deep into the claustrophobic streets of the old Arab section and stepped between two buildings to go down a dark alleyway hardly wide enough to contain his bulk. Berthin watched from the corner of the street as the Master ducked inside a small, unmarked door halfway down the alley. Berthin hurried after him and stood next to the door. The smell of sweet liquor and stale fish pumped out into the street along with the unmistakeable hum of hot sweating bodies.

Berthin waited outside for a few moments to make sure his quarry didn´t re-appear, then held his breath and stepped through the doorway. The interior was dark and close. A long corridor led deep inside the building with small rooms on either side. The walls must have been white at one time but were now coloured by soot and dirty handprints. A splatter of what appeared to be fresh blood adorned one wall and Berthin took care not to brush up against it. The corridor ended at a small open courtyard with passages and doorways branching off in all directions. A few small tables were squeezed into the yard, several of which had men sat at them supping and talking quietly.

The ship´s Master sat in a shady corner of the yard, alone at a low wooden table giving his order to a round man who was the same height standing as the man in black was sitting. Berthin crossed the yard and walked confidently up to the table causing the Master to stop, look up and peer at him through bloodshot, chestnut-coloured eyes. His bulbous nose had more pits than a lemon and his beard appeared to begin just below his eyeballs.

"Pardon me for interrupting señor," Berthin leaned over the table and spoke quietly, "I was told I may find you here." The Master stared without blinking, daring Berthin to look away. The young knight held his ground, he was committed, determined to see his plan through. There was no telling how long it might take to find another opportunity if he let this one slip away. Bethencourt could return at any time, they could embark in a matter of hours. It had to be now.

"Allow me to buy you a drink?" he said. The Master nodded once and the small round man went away to fetch wine.

"May I sit?" asked Berthin. The Master gave another single nod of the head. Berthin dragged a stool from the next table and sat down as the round man returned with a heavy clay pot and two cups. He thumped them down and filled the cups before walking away, loud rattling breaths shook his jowls as he squeezed between the tables. Berthin lifted a cup and took a sip. It was foul. It must have already been rancid before it was watered down, it tasted like cold piss. The ship´s Master picked up his own cup and drained it in a single draft. His thick moustache caught as much as his mouth.

"Now fuck off!" he spat and slammed the cup down on the table.

"Señor." Berthin said calmly, reaching for the jug and refilling the Master´s cup. "You haven´t yet heard my proposal."

The Master stood and swept up his cup, downing the contents while staring over Berthin´s head.

"If you´re still here when I finish I may hear what you have to say. Have a full jug waiting." Berthin turned to see a young frail girl standing in one of the doorways in the opposite wall. Dressed in a torn skirt many sizes too big and a tiny white blouse which strained to contain her breasts. She was twirling a greasy strand of hair around her fingers and staring at the Master through dark watery eyes. She looked to Berthin like she needed to take a shit, if she ever ate enough to need one.

The Master pushed past him, snatching the half-empty jug of wine from the table on his way. He followed the girl down a gloomy corridor into the bowels of the building. Berthin turned back to the table and took another sip of the foul wine. He ordered another jug from the round man and settled down to wait.

Berthin smelled the damp sweaty musk of the Master before he saw him returning a few minutes later.

"You´re still here then." He growled as he walked round the table and let his body drop into the seat opposite Berthin. He drained the cup in his hand, banged it back down on the table and refilled it from the new jug.

"Allow me to introduce myself Señor. My name is Berthin de Berneval of Normandy. I am travelling to the new world with my crew…"

"*Your crew?*" asked the Master scornfully.

"Not exactly my crew, but I have men loyal to me amongst their number."

"As I thought." laughed the Master. "How old are you… twenty-one, twenty-two? I have pants older than you."

"I am several years older than Alexander the Great was when he conquered half the known world." The Master smirked as Berthin talked. "And your name is?"

"Unimportant to you."

"Very well señor. This is a large port. I imagine there will be many more master mariners who want to take my gold." Berthin stood and made to leave. The Master grabbed his wrist.

"I like gold. Sit down."

Berthin sat back down and looked the Master directly in the eyes without uttering a sound.

"Very well," said the Master sighing, he took another drink and put the cup down. He leaned over, dropping his voice to a menacing whisper.

"My name is Fernando d´Ordoñez, the Tajamar is my ship."

Berthin smiled in response, leaned forward and in a whisper said "Canary Island savages are considered to be extremely valuable items so I am told."

"And?" Ordoñez said with a raised eyebrow.

"I may be coming into possession of some very soon."

"Then we have business to discuss. Order more wine, I need to piss."

13

Palace of Justice, Seville,
May 20th, 1402

The sound of Jean´s shoes on the wooden floor bounced around the walls and high ceiling of the tiny room. Four steps one way then four steps back. The solitary window was set too high in the wall to see out of. If Jean stood on Brother Bontier´s shoulders, he could possibly see the tops of the trees in the park next to the Palace of Justice, but it wasn´t worth the effort. The shadows had moved from one side of the room to the other during the day, marking the time they had wasted waiting. Jean didn´t like being confined for any reason. Only the absence of straw on the floor and rats in the walls made it feel any different to being locked in a cell, an experience he didn´t want ever to repeat.

Brother Bontier sat with his hands together at his chest on a wooden bench underneath the window, his eyes closed and his lips moving silently, praying they wouldn´t have to wait much longer. He actually found the room rather soothing, with its soft sandstone walls and warm wooden floor, it was far more welcoming than his cell in the Monastery.

Suddenly, the door crashed open and a withered old clerk wearing long black robes walked in. A four-cornered black silk cap sat atop his tiny upside-down pear-shaped head. He had no chin to stretch the skin drooping down at his throat and had just a thin line for a mouth. He looked at a small slip of paper held in his hand, and read Jean´s name in a high, reedy voice.

"Señor de Bethencourt, the Chief Justice is ready to see you now. Follow me please." He turned and scurried off. Jean followed without hesitation. Brother Bontier leapt from the bench to chase them out the door and into the corridor beyond.

The corridor was long with a cold marble floor. Doors lined both walls, each guarded by soldiers wearing red and white tunics under mirror polished breastplates and gladiator helmets. They stood as still as statues as the trio walked past and up to a pair of double doors at the far end. The clerk knocked once and the doors opened by unseen hands. Jean and Bontier followed the clerk into a small, wood-panelled hall.

Opposite the door behind a raised desk sat three Justices having a hushed discussion over a short scroll one of them was holding. They sat beneath a heavy wooden shield bearing the coat of arms of Castile and Leon, the Castle and the Lion. Golden castles on a red background occupied the top left and bottom right quadrants of the shield with red lions rearing on a white background in the other quarters.

Jean and Bontier stood in the centre of the room, waiting for the Justices to finish their discussion. Jean let his eyes wander while he waited. Light flooded through the leaded window in the wall to their right. Opposite the window sat three men on a long wooden bench, *wealthy merchants* Jean guessed by the array of chains around their necks and the richly stoned rings they wore on fat fingers. Looking at them Jean was pleased he had chosen to dress sombrely on this occasion. A silver crucifix on a chain around his neck and his baronial ring were the only adornments he wore with his sombre, green tunic.

The Judges looked up as one, apparently finished with their other business. Jean took a deep breath and lifted his chin as the clerk began to speak.

"I bring before you Señor Jean de Bethencourt, Baron of Saint-Martin-le-Gaillard of Normandy, here to answer charges of piracy, theft and wilful destruction of property." The little clerk finished and scurried forward to take his place at a small desk at the foot of the Judges' platform. He lifted a small quill and charged it with ink, he sat poised to begin writing on a sheaf of blank papers piled in front of him.

"Señor de Bethencourt," said the Chief Justice suddenly, by far the most senior of the three men sat at the desk. He sat between the other two, appearing to be naught but a shrunken head balanced on top of a pile of black silk, with intricate lace cuffs and collars around his scrawny neck and wizened wrists.

"At your service Señor." said Jean bowing his head.

"These are serious charges brought before us. What say you in your defence?"

"Señor," Jean began, raising his hands and shrugging his shoulders. "I regret that I am unable to defend myself as I have no knowledge of the crimes I am accused of committing."

"Then allow us to enlighten you señor. Sir James, if you please." the Judge said barely lifting his right hand and inviting one of the merchants on the bench to speak. The man in the centre of the three stood up and began to unroll a small parchment scroll. He cleared his throat theatrically before starting to read.

"We have been made aware of the actions of the aforementioned gentleman in that he has stolen from, and sunk three ships of English, Genoan and Placentian ownership." He indicated the men sitting to his left and right as he named their cities of origin. "We request of the Court that he should be held to account for his crimes and made to compensate the injured parties for the value of goods he has stolen, for the ships he has destroyed and for the lives he has taken." He finished reading and sat back down on the bench, looking directly at Jean with an ugly smugness as he began to re-roll the scroll in his pudgy hands.

"Is that all there is? This is preposterous, a sham señor!" exclaimed Jean turning to the Judge. "Is there any proof? Are there any eyewitnesses to attest to my guilt? Who has accused me of these crimes? I demand to face him."

"The accuser has withheld his identity for fear of reprisal." Sir James answered from his seat, still rolling the scroll.

Jean turned open-mouthed to face Sir James. He smiled in disbelief and shook his head. "Is that all you have? One anonymous source, who refuses to come forward to accuse me to my face. I cannot believe this is the sole reason I have been dragged all this way to waste all our valuable time." He swept his arm round expansively to include the Judges. "We are here seeking justice for heinous acts in a respected court of law and all you bring to prosecute those crimes, is a sheet of scribbled hearsay from a *secret source*?" Sir James puffed out his cheeks and spluttered at Jean´s unexpected tirade, he hadn´t come here to be humiliated by a pirate. Before he could answer, Jean dismissed him with a wave of the hand and turned to look directly at the Chief Justice.

"Your Honour, I am sure you and your esteemed colleagues have more pressing matters to attend to rather than wasting the court's time with schoolyard accusations."

"These are very serious accusations Señor," the Chief Justice said, "and ones which must be investigated with vigour."

"I agree Your Honour, but I am not hearing anything substantial enough to place the yoke of guilt around my neck. May I ask a question of the gentlemen?" Jean asked.

"Of course."

"Where and when did these acts of *piracy* take place?" Jean asked turning to look at the merchants.

"The ships were all attacked and sunk between April the tenth and April the sixteenth, south of the Balearic Islands." answered the Placentian sitting to Sir James' right, his accent as thick as the oil in his neatly trimmed beard.

"Then pray explain to me how I was able to sink these vessels and be back in La Rochelle by the twentieth of April, a voyage by sea of at least two weeks in fair weather?"

"La Rochelle?" The Judge asked, leaning forward to rest his arms on his desk.

"Allow me to introduce you to Brother Bontier," Jean said inviting the friar to step forward. "He was one of many who attended a feast thrown in our honour by the Bishop of La Rochelle and Saintes on the evening of the twentieth of April." Bontier stepped forward and bowed before the Judges.

"This is absurd." Sir James shouted.

"What is absurd Sir?" Jean turned and asked coolly, "That I have an alibi to refute your ridiculous accusations, or the fact that I am delayed here to answer for crimes I had no possible opportunity of committing, on the word of an *anonymous source?*" Sir James bristled and was about to answer before Jean continued, directing his words towards the Judges.

"If the testimony of Brother Bontier should prove insufficient, I suggest the Court request statements from the Bishop himself, or even the Cardinals who attended the feast in Pope Boniface´s stead. Would the power of their words be sufficient to prove my innocence, or should we ask some of the other thirty or so ordained gentlemen who attended the feast to come and answer these baseless accusations?"

"I don´t believe that that will be necessary señor." the Chief Justice answered sheepishly. Jean held his head high, his face a picture of indignation as the wrinkled old Justice turned to address the three men sat on the bench.

"I was led to believe that you possessed irrefutable evidence of this Gentleman's guilt. Am I to believe that one anonymous note from source unknown is all that you have to present to us?"

"Your Honour. I never actually met him, but he is an honourable gentleman of remarkable standing and... and…" stammered Sir James, his cheeks turning deep purple as the Chief Justice raised his hand to stop him speaking.

"And how would you know of the gentleman´s standing if he is unknown to you?" asked the Judge.

"Signori Giorgio informed me of his credentials." he indicated the Placentian merchant to his right who turned to look at Sir James with his eyes and mouth wide open.

"And how did Signori Giorgio come by this information?" asked the Judge. Signori Giorgio began to lift his arm to point to the Genoese merchant sat at the other side of Sir James.

"Do any of you know the identity of this informant?" the Judge asked, his temper rising as he scanned the faces of the three men who now looked like schoolchildren squirming under his gaze, unable to lift their eyes. The Judge shook his head and sighed.

"Señor." he said turning to Jean, "I humbly beg your forgiveness on behalf of myself and of the Court. You indeed have no charges to answer and are free to leave this place with no stain upon your character and good name."

"But Your Honour!" Signori Giorgio interrupted.

"Signori!" the Judge cut him off, the force of his voice surprising all in the room. "This matter is ended. You can think yourselves lucky that I don´t send you all to the cells for wasting my time." Signori

Giorgio sat back and folded his arms across his chest, his shiny bottom lip protruding between his beard and well-groomed moustache.

"Señor de Bethencourt." the Judge said, turning back to Jean. "You are free to leave at your convenience and accept my personal apology for wasting your time."

"We are humbled by your wisdom and thank you for resolving this unfortunate matter. If you will excuse us, we must make haste back to our company." Jean bowed his head and turned to leave the courtroom. Brother Bontier gave a deep bow to the Judges and took off after Jean who was marching quickly out of the hall.

They left the building by the main entrance and stepped out into the afternoon sunshine. Jean looked up when the sun hit his face and let out a huge sigh of relief.

"A fair outcome monsieur." said Bontier.

"Indeed. It would have been a lot more difficult if they had mentioned another island and a different date." Jean said quietly.

"Monsieur?"

"Perhaps I´ll tell you later good Friar, but for now I am in need of refreshment and something to eat. Shall we go?"

He stepped out into the street narrowly avoiding a speeding carriage. Brother Bontier followed him with questions filling his mind. He hoped Jean lived long enough to answer some of them.

14

Acatife, Lancarote,

July 23rd, 1402

Norstar drew a big breath and squatted down on his haunches, balancing easily on the back of his heals. He looked across the circle of packed earth and eyed his opponent. He was at least ten years his junior, stood a few inches taller and was a good deal broader at the shoulders than Norstar. Belicar was Beselch's eldest son and was his pride and joy. The old man whispered words in his son's ear while grinning across the circle at Norstar. Belicar laughed, the laugh wasn't a pleasant sound and didn't improve Belicar's looks. He had inherited his father's protruding lower jaw and purple lips making him look and sound like a wall-eyed goat in pain whenever he laughed.

He fixed Norstar with a quick furtive look before turning round to the crowd behind him. He raised his arms in the air and got a half-hearted cheer in response. Norstar waited and watched, bouncing gently on his heels, breathing steadily as his opponent preened. Some Majos found Belicar intimidating, but Norstar saw him as a childish bully who only picked fights with those smaller and weaker than himself. That he'd thrown down this challenge to Norstar at all had come as a big surprise. Norstar could only imagine that Belicar had thought him to be old and weak, crippled with grief at the loss of his son. He was sorely mistaken. He cured his sadness with hard work and spent the last two months training with Rayco, Jonay and Fayna. If anything, Norstar felt more strength running through his body than ever before.

Igo's leaving had been hard on them all. For a week following his departure, the atmosphere was strained. Norstar felt a great deal of resentment towards Gara for undermining him as she did, but he eventually came round to understanding that she had been right to let Igo go. He missed his son keenly and was full of regret for not spending more time with him when he was growing up. Time was something he never dreamed they would be short of until they waved their final goodbyes... and then time stopped.

Of all the family, Avago had been the most affected by the departure of his eldest grandson. He built up a wall of silence between himself, Gara and Norstar and spent many hours wandering away from home. He couldn´t escape completely though as one or more of his other grandchildren would invariably follow him and soon have him talking whether he liked to or not. Even now, when all the clans were gathered in Acatife, Avago had volunteered to walk along the cliff tops and take a turn keeping watch on the Northern horizon with Fayna, Chimboyo and Nayra in tow.

The clans met in Acatife, the largest settlement on the island, built on the Eastern side of the Great Divide within sight of the King´s compound at Zonzamas. Acatife was a collection of some thirty round stone huts with cane and mud roofs, radiating out in a circle from the large meeting hall and fresh water well in the centre of the village. The fields surrounding Acatife and Zonzamas were ripe for harvest, with wild wheat growing in abundance on both sides of the Great Divide. In the morning the Majo´s would begin to collect the grain and take the majority of it to the grain store, a stone building on the edge of the volcano overlooking Acatife. Before they worked though, they played.

In front of the meeting hall was an open stretch of ground on which a wrestling circle had been marked out. Men and women crowded in on all sides, eager to see the fight. King Guadarfia stood on one side of the circle next to Nichel, the other Majo´s had roughly divided themselves around the rest of the circle into western and eastern tribes. Already this day they had held the foot race up and down Acatife Mountain. Jonay had almost won, beaten into second place by a youngster from Long Sands. Now, as the afternoon wore on it was time for the wrestling to begin, where anybody was free to offer a challenge to anybody else. An overconfident Belicar had been the first to throw down a challenge to Norstar who had accepted reluctantly. Belicar mistook that reluctance for weakness. He paraded around the ring as if he had already won the bout.

He feinted a lunge towards Norstar, hoping and failing miserably to illicit a reaction. Norstar didn´t even blink, he just continued bouncing gently up and down. A flicker of doubt crossed Belicar´s face as people laughed at him.

"C´mon you little shit!" jeered Rayco from the group of Majos behind Norstar "This is an arena for men, not boys. Get on with it or get out of the circle."

The words stung Belicar. "I´ll beat this old man and you will be next." he snarled.

"Anytime boy." replied Rayco. Belicar snarled and spat on the ground before taking his place opposite Norstar in the ring.

He leaned forward slightly and rested one hand heavily on the ground in front of him. Norstar leant forward slowly and deliberately, maintaining eye contact with the youngster. His left hand reached down, fingertips barely brushing the dirt. His legs held his weight easily, ready to explode into action.

Suddenly Belicar burst forward with a huge roar, his long muscular arms outstretched, his face distorted into an ugly snarl. In three steps he crossed the ring and lunged at Norstar who ducked under his flailing arms and hit him hard just below the ribs with his shoulder. He heard the crunch as one of Belicar´s ribs cracked. Norstar wrapped his arms around his opponent´s chest and drove up with his legs, using Belicar´s momentum to propel him high into the air. With a twist at the waist, Norstar steered him around and down. They crashed into the ground, Norstar´s full weight drove into Belicar´s chest as they struck the earth. Belicar opened his mouth to scream but couldn´t. There was no air left in his lungs to make a sound. He gasped like a drowning fish as Norstar peeled himself away and got to his feet, casually brushing dirt from his arms and legs.

The people cheered. Norstar reached down and offered his hand to Belicar who was trying unsuccessfully to sit up. The young man batted away the hand and fell back on the ground clutching his side. Norstar shrugged his shoulders and stepped over Belicar´s writhing form and into the waiting arms of Rayco and Jonay who were laughing and cheering wildly.

Rayco looked down at Belicar and shouted "It must be my turn now boy. I´ll give you time to catch your breath." Laughter erupted around the ring. Belicar looked about to speak but thought better of it. He got painfully to his feet and limped back across the circle to his father.

"Enough!" bellowed Nichel. His face was burning red as he shouted once more for quiet. The sound trickled to a stop around Norstar. All the gathered Majos turned to face Nichel and Guadarfia.

"Well done Norstar," Guadarfia said, his arms crossed across his massive chest, "You will have to teach me more of your fighting tricks."

"It will be my honour Mence." replied Norstar with a dip of the head.

"Tricks." said Nichel suddenly. "We wrestle to test strength and courage, not to test trickery."

Norstar took a long breath before replying.

"I wrestle to win, training for the day when I am called upon to defend my family. I have no time to play games when life and death are in question."

"Maybe you should have *trained* a little harder," Nichel purred, "you appear to have lost some members of your family."

Rayco roared and launched forward but was caught and checked by Norstar and Jonay who held onto him tightly.

"Stop Brother." whispered Norstar in his ear. "It is what he wants... Wait and see where he is leading us. Leaves in the water brother, leaves in the water." Rayco relaxed a little and Norstar released him, turning back to face Nichel.

"Your aggression spreads Norstar." Nichel hissed. "I worry it will infect us all before long."

"We must prepare to defend ourselves from the people coming from the North. A bit of aggression will be a good thing." Norstar said, trying to keep the anger from his voice.

"When are they coming, these people from the North? It has been more than two moons since you told us they would be here *tomorrow*." said Nichel gaining a murmur of approval from several Majos on Beselch´s side of the ring. "I am beginning to wonder if *you* are the northern enemy that we should be afraid of."

This brought angry responses from around the ring. Norstar hung his head and closed his eyes. Nichel´s barbed comments were beginning to grind him down. Norstar always felt the need to act differently to everybody else because he was different. To those who thought as Nichel did, he would never be good enough because he hadn´t been born on their island. If he reacted violently, he would be reinforcing Nichel´s arguments. He had to be patient and tolerant, even though he was fighting deep-rooted intolerance.

He forced himself to bite his tongue and closed his mind to the baying voices lashing back and forth across the ring. He searched for peace within his own mind, wondering not for the first time if life really would have been better for them all if they had simply sailed away with Frank and Igo and left this place behind. He no longer felt welcome here.

He heard something cutting through the noise of the crowd which brought him back to reality.

He opened his eyes and stood up straight, craning to see over bobbing heads to where the trail leading up to the cliff top entered the village. Fayna came running into view with Avago, Chimboyo and Nayra close on her heals, moving as fast as they dared down the loose path, calling out and whistling.

The Majos quietened and turned to see. Norstar broke through the ring and ran to meet his children. Fayna flew into his arms while Boyo and Nayra grabbed for his legs and hugged them fiercely. He was shocked to feel Fayna´s tears on his chest.

"What is it my girl?" he asked gently.

"They are here!"

15

Lancarote,

July 23rd, 1402

Jean´s excitement grew as the ship neared the island. The cliffs on the northeast coast reached high into the air like an impenetrable shield wall. A ring of dark volcanic peaks stood like sentinels around the scorched earth beyond the cliffs to the west. Jean had never seen a more desolate yet vibrant sight, the reds and browns of the land stood out in stark contrast to the cerulean hues of the sky and the sea. It was a meeting point of the elements, earth, air, fire and water. He wished he could bottle the colours and use them to dye satin and silk.

The caravel dropped its anchor into the shallow waters of a sandy bay on the southern coast of the tiny island of Graciosa. The mainland lay half a league across a stretch of water through which a ferocious tidal current flowed like a raging river. Jean stood on the poop deck as the stern swung round to face the magnificent view of the cliffs soaring high into the sky, where small white clouds kissed the jagged tips of the summit as they raced by.

Jean´s heart was racing and his head spun as he contemplated the enormity of the task ahead. The natives could simply avoid him and his men for years if they so desired, turning his crusade into an elaborate game of hide and seek. Every tool, weapon and person he had available to subdue the island was with him on the ship. Standing here in the shadow of the cliffs, with the size of his objective literally blocking out the sun, the ship and its contents felt far too small and ridiculously inadequate for the task.

Gadifer joined Jean at the gunwale.

"It is much larger than it looked on the charts." said Gadifer. "We should have brought more men."

"Don´t be deceived by the size Monsieur. There are only three hundred at most living there. Men, women, old and young. I doubt they have enough bodies to put together an army." Jean tried to sound more confident than he was.

"Didn´t you tell me the women fought alongside the men?"

"Yes, I did. But having spent the last few weeks in the company of the lady Isabel, I find it hard to believe that anybody with a similar countenance as her could turn into a violent, crazed, warrior woman."

"You haven´t met many women then." Gadifer said raising his eyebrows.

"Probably not." Jean said with a chuckle. "You are correct of course. If it comes to it, we will have to fight men and women. Let us hope it doesn´t come to it."

"If this were my home, I would fight to defend it." said Gadifer staring up at the huge cliff wall, buttressed by towering pillars of black basalt, thrusting out of the deep blue sea.

"We can only pray that there are no men of your mettle living here." The smile disappeared from Jean´s face. He really did hope there were no warriors with Gadifer´s fortitude waiting for them. It would mean a long and bloody campaign, with more dead than alive by the end of it.

"Do you think they are watching?" asked Gadifer.

"Undoubtedly."

"How do you suggest we proceed?"

"Carefully."

****

The ship stood out like a big brown bug squatting in the turquoise bay below. Majos peered from vantage points all along the cliff top, hardly daring to breathe.

"How many people will be inside?" asked Guadarfia, standing with Norstar, Beselch and Nichel behind a tall cairn of flat rocks.

"There could be up to four hundred. One hundred or more of those will be fighting men. It´s difficult to say from here." answered Norstar.

The King´s face betrayed no emotion while Beselch and Nichel fidgeted nervously.

"Are they the ones your brother warned us about?" asked Beselch.

"I believe so. See the pennants flying from the highest points?" Beselch nodded. "They are the colours of Normandy and Gascony, with others from the Kingdoms of France and Castile if I am not mistaken."

"There are two Kings with them?" asked Nichel.

"The Kings own many ships and command many thousands of men. I would be surprised if they had ever seen this ship with their own eyes. They wield power and influence from afar, ordering men to kill and die in their stead." Nichel blanched. The silence stretched for a long time before Guadarfia broke it.

"What do you suggest we do Beselch?" he asked.

"We watch and wait. Stock the caves and prepare for a long time below ground."

"And you Nichel?"

"The same. I urge caution until I have had time to consult with the spirits."

"What would you suggest Norstar?"

"We kill them as they land and don´t let any get away. If we allow them to land unopposed, more ships and men will come until no corner of the island is left for us to hide in. They come to take the land from us. Whether we live or die is of no consequence to them."

"How can you know this?" asked Nichel scornfully "They could be here simply to trade as others do."

"As you never cease to remind me, I come from the same world as they." He pointed at the ship, "I know what drives them."

"Look!" Beselch called. Two boats were lowered into the water and people swarmed over the side of the ship to board them.

"They cannot all come at once." began Norstar. "They´ll land in small numbers and then form up into a fighting unit. Men like these favour grand battles over small skirmishes. If we lay traps and ambush them as they land, we can avoid meeting them on an open field. We must show no mercy and strike fear into their hearts from the outset if we hope to prevail."

"And how many people do we lose?" asked Beselch "No no no. We must hide and wait underground until they tire of searching for us. If they leave empty handed, there will be no reason for them to return."

"They won´t leave and they won´t tire. They are here to stay. If we don´t stop them now, we are lost. They will keep coming until we are dead in our caves."

"Not all of us are as comfortable with death as you." cut in Nichel "We shouldn´t put any of our people in harm's way unnecessarily."

"If we don´t stop them now, they will kill us all eventually."

"Enough." said Guadarfia. "Send the children and the old ones to the caves. We will watch them from the high ground."

"But Mence…" pleaded Norstar.

"I have made my decision." Guadarfia turned back to look across the water at the ship. Norstar´s head dropped. He knew to argue further would be pointless so excused himself and left. He picked his way along the cliff to where Rayco, Fayna and Jonay waited.

"What did he say?" asked Rayco stood upright, gripping his tenique in both hands.

"We must do nothing but watch." Norstar spat. "The children and the old ones are to go to the caves and hide."

"And what shall we do?" asked Fayna.

"We shall do nothing until ordered differently by Guadarfia. I want you to go with Avago back home, help your mother and Iballa to prepare the deep caves for a long stay."

"But I want to stay with you and fight."

"There´ll be no fighting if Guadarfia gets his way. He ordered us to wait and see what happens next. He has already decided to concede our advantage. The man´s a fool if he believes doing nothing is the way to get something done."

"What are you going to do?" Fayna asked forlornly.

"For now, I must follow Guadarfia´s orders." He turned to Rayco and Jonay. "You two need to spread the word and get the people underground."

"I´ll help." Fayna said eagerly.

"You'll help by telling the people you meet on the path home. Go, please. Help your mother and Avago with the little ones. They need your bow there."

Fayna gave Norstar a dark look and turned away. She bounded off along the cliff top path.

"Stay below the edge!" Norstar shouted after her.

"Spread the word." Norstar said again to Rayco and Jonay. "Bring as many of our men as you find back here, we may have to fight despite what the Mence says."

The brothers sprinted away leaving Norstar alone. He looked down at the ship sitting in the bay. The boats were disgorging their loads of tiny black figures onto the clean white sand of the island opposite. They had only been here a short time and already their stain was spreading.

16

Graciosa, Lancarote,

July 24th, 1402

Jean was awake before the sun had risen. He lay still under his sodden blanket, dripping wet from the night's dew fall. He Looked up and watched the clouds tearing across the sky getting brighter in the pre-dawn light. The air was refreshing without the taint of shit, piss and sweat so prevalent onboard ship. Almost all the company had jumped at the chance to spend a night in the open air. Only Gadifer and his bastard son Hannibal elected to stay on board with a handful of knights and the ship's crew.

Jean heard coughing and muffled voices coming from somewhere amongst the dunes. He sat up and threw his blanket back, sending a shower of water across the sleeping form of Philip. The little man jumped to his feet, rudely woken from the grip of a vivid dream. His eyes flew open but didn't see. He pulled a knife from the sheath in the small of his back and turned around and around in the sand. He was as nervous as a box of chickens in a doghouse. Jean determined to find a worthwhile task to keep his mind occupied before he accidentally stuck his knife in someone.

"Relax Philip, we're not under attack yet." he said standing and stamping his feet to shake the sand from his britches. Philip sheathed his knife and hurried over to brush the sand from his back.

Jean lifted his head to the mainland while Philip rubbed him down vigorously. The cloud was low and hid the tops of the cliffs. The black rock wall hung down below the cloud base like an impenetrable curtain. The sea was slate grey and choppy. The wind whipped the tips of the waves into leaping white horses, charging through the narrows between the islands.

Shouted orders and the sound of a ringing bell drifted in the wind. The men on board ship were moving.

"Thank you Philip, that's enough for now." Jean said moving out of range of his valet's enthusiastic hands. "Clear the camp and find some breakfast. We have a busy day ahead of us."

Jean set off at a brisk walk in the direction of the ringing bell. At the water's edge, he looked out at the ship drifting on its anchor in the bay. The unmistakeable form of Gadifer was prowling around barking orders. Three men dropped from the deck into a boat tied at the foot of the ladder and took up their oars followed by Gadifer who climbed down and stepped over them to get to the bow. They were soon darting across the water. The old man stood with one leg up on the bow rail, looking every inch the conquering hero with the wind blowing through his white hair and whiskers. Jean rolled his eyes and walked over to meet him. The boat skidded up the shallow beach and Gadifer leapt out.

"Good morning monsieur." hailed Jean.

"Monsieur," replied Gadifer, "I trust you slept well."

"Very well indeed." Jean lied smoothly. "The island is devoid of life save the odd lizard. It is unfortunately also without fresh water so we'll need to conserve our supply for the time being until we find a source."

"I saw evidence of a spring high in the cliffs late in the evening when the sun cut across its face. There is a patch of greenery with a path leading up to it. I was about to send Hannibal across to investigate."

"Belay that order for now. I don't want to linger here any longer than is necessary. We need to find some of the natives we came here to civilize."

"Monsieur," Gadifer acquiesced with a tiny bow.

"The cloud will have forced them lower. Our chances of running into them are therefore greatly increased. We need to move on, we've wasted enough time. As soon as the men are ready, we march."

"In which direction?"

"I intend to lead an exploratory force along the Southeast coast. The translator, Alfonso is from that region and claims to know the terrain well. I would like to put his knowledge to the test. I'll take half the men and one of the boats."

"Why not take the rest of us and the ship?" queried Gadifer.

"No. I want you to take the ship around the northern coast and land in the South. Secure the anchorage and establish a beachhead there. We will walk to you, it can´t be more than ten leagues. If we are not with you by midday tomorrow, then sail back up the coast to find us."

"Are you sure that splitting our forces would be wise?"

"Splitting doubles the chance of making contact. We need them to come to us or we´ll never find them. In smaller groups we are much less threatening."

"…and easier to attack." added Gadifer.

"My heart refuses to believe these people have the wherewithal to fight us. They are as timid as rabbits. We need to approach gently lest they take flight and disappear down their holes. We need to coax them out into the open, not scare them deeper underground."

"But these rabbits are armed with spears."

"True, but only wooden spears. I do not imagine them foolhardy enough to attack us. Courage, and God´s will, will see us prevail."

"With God´s will Monsieur."

"Which famous General once said "It takes more courage to act peacefully in a hostile environment, than it does to start a war."?"

"That was Julius Caesar Monsieur."

"Are you sure? I always thought it was Alexander."

******

Berthin sat on a little wooden stool stretching his feet to a small fire. He tore a piece from a tough flat loaf and passed it on. There were eight other knights, all loyal to him, huddled in a small circle sharing a breakfast of bread, cheese and watered wine.

"When do you think we will find the savages?" asked Gillet tearing a chunk from the bread and passing it on to Pernet the Blacksmith.

"They saw you coming and shat themselves!" roared Big Perrin, a red-faced bald knight sitting across the circle. Even though the air was chilly, sweat oozed from the scarred folds of flesh wrapped around his head, "We´ll spend weeks digging them out."

"You swing your shovel and I'll swing my sword Monsieur."

"You have a quick tongue little one. Maybe we should see if you have an arm to match." Big Perrin took a bite from a wedge of cheese stuck on the end of his knife, eyeing Gillet.

"Calm down Big Man." said William Blessi sat at Perrin's side, eating quietly with his head down. "It's too early for that."

Big Perrin stuffed a chunk of bread into his mouth, his lips making wet smacking sounds as he chewed, all the while staring at Gillet over his red veined nose.

"I meant no disrespect Monsieur." Gillet conceded "I am merely eager to see some action after being cooped up on board that ship for the last three months."

"As are we all." said William, "I do not imagine Monsieur le Bethencourt will have us lazing here for long, it costs him too much. As for the savages, you'll meet them soon enough."

"He tells the truth." said Pernet the Blacksmith. "They are up there watching us. I counted at least thirty of them and saw a dozen fires in the night."

"How could you see all that from way down here?" scoffed Big Perrin.

"My eyes, Monsieur, like my arms, are young and strong." He stared defiantly across at Big Perrin.

"Ha Ha Ha! I like this one." Perrin barked, his face twisted in an ugly snarl. "Maybe I'll have him after I finish my breakfast. What say you Blessi, would you like to share him?"

Berthin shut them up with a sharp click of the tongue as he spotted Gadifer step out from behind a low sand dune and walk towards them.

"Gentlemen!" the old man called. "Don't get up." Nobody did. "Berthin, if I may have a private word with you?"

"Of course monsieur!" Berthin followed Gadifer out of earshot of the others.

"I trust the men's spirits are high." said Gadifer. "It is good to see everybody mixing together without trying to tear each other apart."

"Oh yes Monsieur, peace has been restored."

"Good, good. Monsieur de Bethencourt has a mind to march down the coast in search of the natives while I take the remainder of the men and the ship to the South. I want you to break camp and divide the men. I know they will all be straining at the bit and itching for a fight, but you are only to take the ones who are capable of a long march with Monsieur Bethencourt, the others are to come with me."

"Yes monsieur, I will see to it right away."

"Very good. I will leave it in your capable hands. I want to be off this island within the hour. Carry on."

Berthin watched him leave before returning to his seat. He bent down, picked up his cup and drank slowly while all the men watched on in silence.

"Well?" asked young Gillet. "Are we going?"

Berthin finished his drink and lowered his cup. He looked around the circle at the eager faces staring back at him.

"Get your things together." he smiled. "We are going on a savage hunt."

****

Norstar watched with Rayco and Jonay from a sheltered hollow in the cliff wall as the ship edged out of the anchorage. It swung to the right and began ploughing eastwards across the current.

The three of them raced back to the misty tops of the cliffs and ran blindly along the path to the East. Within no time, they found Guadarfia standing with fifty other men on a high ledge peering down through the thinning clouds. The ship hove into view, clearing the sharp finger of land reaching out into the sea to mark the island´s northernmost point. It turned to starboard and sailed into the bay below them.

"They are coming." Norstar said.

"We have seen." Nichel answered.

"Have you given my idea more thought Mency?" Norstar asked hopefully. "Now would be the time to end them." Nichel tutted and opened his mouth to say something

"Nothing has changed." Guadarfia´s deep, commanding voice cut Nichel off. "We will keep to the high ground."

Norstar hoped Guadarfia knew what he was doing. If his gamble went sour, Norstar resolved to get his own boat ready and take his family away to safety, to hell with the rest of them.

"They are stopping." Rayco called out.

The ship turned into the wind and dropped anchor. Two heavily laden boats rowed from the ship and shot through a narrow gap in the reef. They rode on the small swell to a sheltered beach tucked under the cliff, directly below the Majos. The ship swung on its anchor beyond the sharp black reef. Norstar could see the deck crowded with people watching as the boats dropped men onto the sand before returning to the ship.

The ship upped anchor and left. She steered west and rode the current back between the islands, soon disappearing around the headland. One of the boats had been left behind. The men on board hoisted a small sail and sailed beyond the outer reef, keeping pace with the knights onshore walking along the coastal path.

"What are they doing?" Guadarfia asked.

"They have split their forces to divide us, possibly to attack us from two sides at the same time." Norstar answered. "The small boat is carrying four men, extra provisions, possibly bowmen hidden in the prow. I imagine the big ship is heading west to let more men ashore further along the coast. Acatife, Ajei, even Zonzamas are all within striking distance of the Divide."

Guadarfia pondered for a long second before turning to face Norstar. "Take your men and follow the ship. Stay out of sight. Do not fight them." Norstar affirmed with a single nod of the head.

Guadarfia turned to Beselch. "You follow the others from the hills."

"As you say Mence." answered Beselch. "My men will not be seen."

"I will return to Acatife and from there go on to Zonzamas. Send messengers to me there."

Norstar turned to walk away.

"Norstar!" called Nichel. Norstar half looked back over his shoulder. "Do not fight with these men. Do you understand?"

Norstar didn´t answer, he began running up the hill. Jonay and Rayco fell in with him. All three soon disappeared in the clouds.

"I´m not sure I trust him." said Nichel.

Guadarfia closed his eyes and took a deep breath.

17

Lancarote,

July 24th, 1402

They had been hiking for a couple of hours. It was impossible to see too far ahead as the path twisted and turned around rocky outcrops. It dipped and climbed through dry gullies where long sharp spines on old, twisted cacti stopped them from straying too far from the path. The experienced fighters amongst them were nervous; they took quick furtive glances to the left and the right between every step. It made for painfully slow progress.

Jean followed Alfonso at the head of the column. The young man bounced along the path while Jean trudged, his head bent to watch where he put his feet.

"Come, come, hurry Monsieur." Alfonso urged as they rounded a huge boulder heavy with dusty yellow lichen. "We are nearly there."

"Slow down man." called Jean through his teeth. His legs were tiring and he was struggling over the rough terrain in the heat. His mail shirt got heavier with every step.

"Over the next rise." encouraged Alfonso without looking back.

"Wait!" Jean called out too late. The wiry Canarian slipped through a gap between two tall rocks and disappeared. "Curse you, you little shit." muttered Jean putting on a burst of speed to catch up.

He stepped through the gap between the rocks and looked down into a rough bowl-shaped clearing where six small stone huts with domed roofs stood around an open yard of flattened earth. If Alfonso hadn´t led the way, Jean had no doubt that they would have walked by without seeing it.

One by one, the men in the column caught Jean and pushed through the gap behind him. They spread across the hillside and looking down into the tiny hamlet as Alfonso ran from hut to hut calling out words in his own tongue. Nobody answered. The place was deserted. Jean was amazed how loud silence could be as he walked slowly down the hill and out of the wind for the first time since they had landed.

The men followed him and started poking through the huts. They were identical, thick-walled one-room structures with domed roofs, built in a ring with low doorways opening out onto the central yard. The interiors were bare. Whoever lived here had left in a hurry and left nothing but ashes and bones. A large old tree offered shelter, it´s tortured branches swept to the South and refused to grow above the lip of the hollow. The thick leaves sprouting from its branches offered the first patch of shade Jean had seen since landing on the island.

He ordered the men to rest and went to find Alfonso. He found him in one of the huts, sat cross-legged in the centre of the packed earth floor, looking bedraggled and forlorn.

"Was this your home?" Jean asked.

Alfonso answered with a shallow nod. His shoulders drooped further.

"Where do you imagine the people have gone?" asked Jean.

"The caves."

"How unfortunate." Jean lamented. Alfonso sat staring at a point on the floor, his face slack and vacant. "I will give you five minutes to yourself and then we really must press on." Alfonso nodded and Jean ducked out of the hut. He ambled slowly over to join the men resting in the shade.

They had found a small stone trough, filled with cold spring water near to the tree trunk. Jean splashed water on his head and across the back of his neck and stood up, letting drips of water run under his collar and down his back. He shivered with delight as the cold water dribbled between his shoulder blades.

******

"If I may Monsieur." Berthin approached Jean as he was smoothing water from his beard.

"What is it?"

"A couple of the men are keen to hunt. They asked if you would allow them to track the savages to their hiding place."

"We haven't got time for that now. I want to get back to the coast before the boatmen think us lost and sail away."

"It wouldn't take long. A couple of the men reckon they could track them easily. Why wait?"

"We are not hunting them Berthin. They will come to us."

"Whatever you say Monsieur," Berthin shrugged.

"Good. We should move on. Rouse the men. Stay at the rear and make sure we don't lose anybody."

"Monsieur." replied Berthin with a tiny flick of the head.

Jean stalked off to collect Alfonso. Berthin turned round and kicked out at a pair of feet.

"Oy!" The knight pulled his feet away.

"Come on you lazy dogs." Berthin said, looking around at the men clinging to the shade as if it were a life raft. "The sooner we get moving, the sooner we get there."

"Get where?"

"To wherever our Lord and Master is leading us." answered Berthin. "Come on, get up and get moving before we lose him." Berthin could see Jean was already following Alfonso out of the hamlet by a path leading to the south.

"I miss my horse." Big Perrin whined.

"Don't worry," answered Pernet the Blacksmith "we'll find a goat for you to fuck before long."

"Didn't I say I liked this boy." Big Perrin laughed, clapping his hand on the grinning blacksmith's shoulder as he passed him. "Maybe I'll wait until we're back in France before I open him up… in front of his mother."

Berthin hung back and watched them all follow Jean and Alfonso out of the hamlet. Gillet was the last to leave and Berthin fell in with him. He noticed the young knight teasing the string of his bow with his fingers and reaching down to touch the arrows hanging in the pouch at his right hip. Berthin laid his hand on the youngster's shoulder.

"You seem tense." he said. "Do you think we have reason to be worried?"

"They've been following us since we landed. I've seen them up in the hills. Don't look!" he said as Berthin began to turn his head. "They think they move without being seen. It's best we keep it that way or they may get a little more cautious and disappear."

"How many?" asked Berthin, suddenly a little more attentive.

"It's difficult to say, I've seen a few on the hill tops, but I fear there could be more. There could be an army of them a dozen paces away behind the rocks and we wouldn't see them."

Berthin stopped. He checked his sword was free in its scabbard and followed Gillet. Suddenly, everything was beginning to feel real, no longer the ghost of a plan somewhere in his mind.

****

Norstar reached the Three Sisters Mountains with well over forty Majos in his company. They crouched amongst the red rocks of the tallest peak watching as the blooming sails of the caravel bobbed in the swell half a league from the shore to the north. Norstar estimated she was travelling at a little under ten knots. He looked along the coast to the West. The waves pounding the shore were growing in size and frequency as the day wore on. An endless parade rolled in to dash against the rocks sending brilliant white plumes of water high into the air with every strike. It was too wild to put a boat ashore. Norstar guessed they would head directly for the shelter of Eagle Claw Bay.

He sent a messenger to Guadarfia before leading the men down the western slope of the Three Sisters and onto the sun burnt sandy earth beyond the mountains' skirts.

They struck out due west on a direct course to Tenesar, two leagues across the plain. They ran together like a pack of wolves, stalking the ship that prowled menacingly offshore. Norstar loped along in the centre of the pack with his bow hanging in his left hand. He looked around with pride at the men surrounding him. They were fit and strong. The muscles in their legs coiled and stretched easily as they flew across the uneven ground, leaping over rocks and hopping across the deep, dusty scars in the land criss-crossing their path. Onwards they ran in silence, occasionally looking out to sea to make sure they were keeping pace with the ship.

Norstar allowed his mind to wander while they ran. He refused to accept defeat even though the best time to strike the invaders had already passed. If it came to an open battle, there was no doubt in his mind that the French would run amok and slaughter or capture all the Majos. He had to make sure they avoided that scenario at all costs. The men´s confidence was riding high following their easy victory over the pirate raiders, but the French soldiers were not the same type of animal. They were organised and experienced. The only way the Majos could beat them would be by controlling as many elements as possible, using their strengths and exploiting the enemy´s weaknesses. It would be a long bitter campaign if it came to it.

The men surrounding him were strong and fast, in any other setting they would probably be fearsome warriors or hunters. But here they had grown on an island without predation and natural enemies, in a society of sharing rather than taking, they were like an army of swallows facing an army of hawks.

Norstar had no authority to lead them. They followed him because they trusted him. He had never fought in a war, he wasn´t a soldier, in the world of conflict they were all innocent.

He begun to see the wisdom of Guadarfia´s decision not to fight. Yes, they could have won a small victory on the beach but at what cost? If what Frank had told him were true, then these were only the first of a huge wave of Northerners coming to lay claim to the island. The Majos couldn´t fight forever, they simply didn´t have the numbers to absorb any losses.

He looked ahead to Jonay leading the pack across the dry land. He was honourable and brave, but no amount of noble attributes would prevent a crossbow bolt from piercing his golden skin and ending his beautiful life. The modern world had no respect for beauty and honour, it was rapacious and all consuming. It rewarded avarice and violence… and now it was here and the brave Majos were running to meet it.

Norstar suddenly felt like running the other way.

******

"I can smell them. I can smell their sweat and their fear. I can even smell their savage little cunnies!" snarled Big Perrin, his head glowing an angry shade of red under the burning sun. "Why don´t we go and get some and make the journey through this hell hole worthwhile."

"You´re welcome to try," said William at his side. "But you won´t see anything down there without a torch."

"I don´t need a torch. I can smell the fuckers!"

The men stood around the jagged edge of a hole in the ground thirty paces across and a hundred long. It sank another forty feet below their feet and had two narrow caves at either end leading further underground.

"What say you Berthin?" asked Perrin. "I reckon we could go in there and find us a nice little prize waiting."

"Like an axe in the head." said William.

"Listen to your friend." said Berthin. "The savage with the Peacock reckons those caves are like a huge maze. You´d be wandering around until you starved."

"Fucking rabbits!" snorted Perrin.

"Quite!" said Berthin.

"They´d smell you coming before you got anywhere near them." said William. He tugged at the leather collar of his jerkin willing some cold air inside to cool his skin. It was getting hotter. The metal helmets some of them wore were too hot to touch.

"Move out!" called out Jean from the other side of the hole.

"I´m getting mightily fed up with this." grumbled Big Perrin. "If I´d known it was this difficult to walk on this shit I would´ve stayed on the ship." He kicked at some loose rocks, sending them showering over the edge.

Berthin left them and hurried to catch up to Bethencourt. It served his purpose for the men to be disgruntled with Gadifer and Bethencourt, but he didn´t want them turning on him too.

"Monsieur!" he called out as he came within a few paces of Jean.

"What is it?" he asked peering out from beneath the rim of his floppy cap. *Bloody typical*, thought Berthin, *the bastard's even brought a fancy sunhat. He's got no plan, but he has a fucking hat.*

"The men are burning up and in dire need of rest Monsieur. We will have to stop soon." He spoke loud enough for as many men to hear as possible. It was important for them to think he had their best interests at heart.

"I couldn't agree more." said Bethencourt. "A little further and there is a bay where Alfonso tells me there is shade, water and a place to bring the boat in. We will rest there until the midday heat passes."

"Very well Monsieur. I will inform the men."

"Good man." Bethencourt said as he turned and hurried along the path to catch Alfonso.

The land was getting less hostile the further they marched. Larger clearings were appearing between the rocks, some of which had clumps of a wild cereal growing in them. The path passed more huts and small settlements, all deserted. The silence was eerie. The only sounds were the buzzing of insects and the scrape of lizards scurrying across the rocks to hide. Tiny birds flew by at breakneck speeds, whirling like leaves in an autumn storm. Shrill cries pierced the air from time to time as hawks circled high above them.

They passed an orchard of stunted fig trees hunkering down in hollows in the ground sheltered from the wind. Only the shape of their leaves resembled the tall fig trees they knew back home in France. Flat leaved cactus plants grew in clumps between the rocks. Some knights risked the sharp spines to pick the fruit that grew along the edge of the leaves like red pimples. They peeled back the prickly skin and sucked at the flesh inside declaring them to be delicious.

Berthin found no satisfaction in discovering new types of fruit, the flesh he craved was warmer and much more valuable. He had spotted some savages high in the hills an hour earlier. Their silhouettes stood out clearly against the bright sky as they leapt across a wide ravine. He was expecting a horde of them to be lying in wait around every corner, or to creep up on them from behind.

He worked his way forward deftly through the column and established a new position in the middle of the line. His life was worth more than the others´. He wasn´t about to waste it stopping a spear meant for somebody else´s back. He felt a little more secure with knights in front and behind.

The sun was directly overhead when they stopped in a hamlet by the sea to rest. Berthin could have happily gone to sleep there and not moved another step, but Bethencourt had them up and moving again as soon as the sun had passed its peak.

It was mid-afternoon before Berthin realised they would not be able to make the whole journey to the meet up with Gadifer in one day. They rounded a bend in the path and saw their goal. The Ajache Mountains stuck up like a row of broken teeth, a long, long way to the south.

The Peacock pointed excitedly beyond the mountains even further south to where the peaks of the island of Erbania could just be seen through the haze. His enthusiasm for adventure seemed to energise him and he drove the men even harder along the rocky pathways. Berthin´s anger drove his feet forward. He would have dearly liked to place one of those feet up Bethencourt´s arse.

******

Norstar stood with Gara, Fayna and Avago on the high peak of the Tenesar volcano watching the caravel slip out of sight to the southwest. The rest of his men had carried on shadowing the ship along the coast, but Norstar decided to wait for the messenger returning with word from Guadarfia.

Fayna was the first to spot the young Majo approaching from the East. They went down to meet him and offered him a full skin of water. He took it gratefully and drank deeply. He spluttered a little when he pulled it from his lips and wiped the sweat from his eyes.

"Mence Guadarfia is in Zonzamas. Beselch has sent word that the others will get no further than the Big Reef before nightfall. They are slow." The messenger sucked in a big breath of air and took another swig from the water skin. "Beselch also believes that they are being guided by a Majo."

"One of us?" asked Avago, his eyebrows raised in surprise.

"He leads them along paths unknown to outsiders."

"This is a good sign." said Avago.

"Armies in strange lands often take local guides with them, it doesn't mean they travel without the intention to kill." added Norstar.

"Is there anything else?" Avago asked the messenger, hearing but not answering Norstar.

"Only that Nichel requests that you, Avago, travel with Norstar and his men in case the intruders attempt to make contact with us." The messenger paused before continuing, looking uneasily between Norstar and Avago. "His words were: *Only a true Majo should speak for us. Norstar will remain silent and use his ears to hear for us.* That is all."

"Thank you." Avago said, "Rest a while, we will leave for the South soon."

The messenger nodded and wandered away to sit on a rock in the shade. Norstar shook his head.

"*Only a true Majo.* He never misses an opportunity to remind us of what I am not." he said, his tone tinged with bitterness.

"Don't let Nichel's words upset you." Avago said. Gara walked over and placed her hand gently on his arm.

"They don't upset me, that would be admitting the old fool riles me," he said forcing a grin. "He never stops trying though, trying to make me feel less because I don't have Majo blood running through my veins. I am forever being pushed to the outside."

Gara spoke calmly. "You will always be one of us. Nichel can be a fool sometimes…"

"Only sometimes?"

"Very well, a lot of the time, but he has wise moments too. His words are clumsy, but his intention is sound. He has asked Father to speak and you to listen. Judge their words, listen to them speak without letting them know you understand."

Norstar looked at Gara. She always spoke the sense to cut through the noise created by his emotions.

"I am sorry," he said bowing his head, "I misunderstood. My mind is full and my hearing bad."

"Our lives may depend upon your hearing." Gara said, cupping Norstar's face in her hands.

"Enough." Avago said turning to leave. "I have to gather my things, we need to leave."

"I need to collect my cloak too." chipped in Fayna.

"No you do not." said Norstar.

"Oh yes she does." said Gara. "And I need mine too. We are coming with you."

"And the little ones, who will keep them safe?" asked Norstar.

"They will be safe with Iballa and Daida. I would not rest not knowing what was happening on the other side of the island. You need us to watch your back. Fayna is the only one who can shoot as well as you."

She turned and led Fayna and Avago away. Norstar shook his head as he watched them go, his mouth open, full of words he wouldn't get to say.

****

Jean finally called a halt with less than an hour of daylight remaining. He waved the longboat ashore while the men set about collecting scrub and driftwood to build a fire. Within a short time, those lucky enough not to be taking their turn on watch were sprawled on the ground around a raging fire while the boatmen descaled and gutted a long line of fish.

Jean removed his boots carefully and set to popping a half dozen blisters on his feet. He hobbled down to the water's edge and waded in up to his knees. The cool water washed over his sours and took the fire out of his tight calf muscles. He closed his eyes and breathed deeply as the salt water penetrated the flaps of skin on his heels and toes. He was so completely emerged in the sensation he didn't notice Alfonso wade out next to him.

"Monsieur?" Alfonso said gently, making Jean jump.

"Alfonso!" he said as he righted himself. "What can I do for you?"

"Take this," Alfonso proffered a foot long flat green leaf with small sharp spines along its edges. Jean recognised it as a leaf from the aloe plant, several thousands of which they had passed during the day. "The plant has soothing properties if you rub it on the parts that ail you."

Jean took the leaf which was rubbery to the touch and edged with short, sharp spines. He turned it over in his hands, unable to see how such a hostile looking plant could ease his pain.

"Thank you, but how?" Alfonso tutted and took the leaf back. He bit the bottom corner of one of the long edges and pulled at it with his teeth. Once it started to tear, he gripped the leaf in both hands and stripped the edge all the way to the tip. He then inserted his thumbs into the gooey green sap between the faces of the leaf and opened it along its length to reveal a viscous slime within. He handed it back to Jean who tentatively touched the slime with the tip of his finger and lifted it to his nose. It smelled funky, almost meatily green.

"You rub it into your skin." Alfonso explained while making a rubbing motion with his hands. "There on your face where the sun has burned you, and on your feet."

Jean scooped out some of the goo with his fingers and dabbed his red nose with it. The burning sensation fled and the dry skin on his nose softened perceptively. Jean scooped out a larger dollop of the plant slime and started rubbing it into his cheeks and across the back of his neck. The plant soothed and cooled his angry sun burned skin almost immediately and Jean couldn't help but moan with pleasure. He began to rub the leaf all over his head.

"My God! This is marvellous." he said to Alfonso who smiled for the first time in many hours as he watched Jean pull the plant from his face leaving big blobs of green sap stuck in his beard and hair.

"Berthin!" Jean turned back to face the beach and called out. "Berthin, come here!" A few seconds later Berthin splashed to Jean's side.

"What is it monsieur?" he asked with slightly more irritation in his voice than Jean would have liked to hear.

"Try this." Jean thrust the aloe leaf at him. "Rub it in to your skin where the sun has burned you."

"Monsieur?"

156

"Do it man!" Berthin began to rub the leaf along his red forearms. The relief hit him like a wave. He found despite his anger he couldn´t help but smile.

"It´s soothing, no?" asked Jean.

"Extremely so." purred Berthin as he began to rub the open leaf on the back of his neck.

******

Alfonso crept away. He walked stealthily around the periphery of the camp and found a secluded spot behind a large stand of rock a hundred paces from the fire. As the last rays of sunlight fled the land, he fixed his gaze on the tall mountain peak less than two leagues away to the north behind which he knew the palace of Zonzamas lie. He remembered the stories his father used to tell him when they attended the gatherings there, the games they played and the singing and dancing. He knew the current King would be up there now, whoever it was, looking down at these invaders polluting their land. Alfonso wished he were up there with his people.

He had considered, albeit very briefly, leading Jean and his men directly to the King´s palace, but had decided against it. Although their leader Jean seemed respectful and trustworthy, many of the armour-clad idiots under his command were not worth pissing on if they caught fire.

For years, he had feared that he would never set foot on this land again and now here he was. His people were tantalisingly close. He had wept when entering the village of his family earlier and discovered them gone. He thought for maybe the fiftieth time that day about slipping away into the mountains and leaving the French behind, but his worry for Isabel kept him tied to his Gallic masters… for now. He resigned himself to wait, but, if an opportunity arose to escape with Isabel and re-join his people, rediscover his Majo name and his Majo tongue, he would take it.

The long shadows squeezed the final colour from the day as the sun dipped out of sight behind the Ajache Mountains in the West. Alfonso stood and walked slowly back to the camp and found himself a spot near the fire. He watched the flames dance, illuminating the weary faces of the men. Burns and sores were being eased by aloe leaves which Jean and Berthin had shown them all how to use. An occasional moan of satisfaction escaped into the night sky as the plants went to work.

Alfonso began to relax as the sound of lapping water and crackling fire filled his ears. The boatmen had dragged glowing embers from the fire and were laying cleaned and gutted fish directly upon them to cook. The aroma of the roasting fish filled the air and for a moment the foul smell of sore feet and sweating bodies disappeared. Alfonso lay back and looked up at the familiar stars in the sky. Without too much effort he was able to block out the presence of the strangers surrounding him and fooled himself into thinking he was alone, and he was finally home.

****

Majos crouched in little groups looking down on the camp the invaders had set up in the middle of Eagle Claw Bay. The sun had set long ago and only the faintest line of red light still bled over the western horizon.

The bay was shaped like a huge talon two leagues from point to point and gave shelter from the strong sea currents that flowed constantly from the North. Across the sea lay the island of Erbania, the peaks of its volcanoes betrayed not the slightest hint of life upon them. The small island of Lobos stood out clearly half a league from Erbania´s northern shore and although appearing barren and desolate from this distance, Norstar knew it was teeming with life. He and Frank had hunted sea wolves there, although it had felt less than a hunt and more like a slaughter as the big lumbering seals hadn´t thought to flee from the men with their spears.

His thoughts switched to Frank and Igo. He hoped they were safely back in Portsmouth by now. They would be eating one of his mother´s pies and supping on farmer´s ale, sat around the big table in the cosy kitchen with candles spitting on the mantelpiece. He wondered what Igo made of the horses in the paddock and would have dearly loved to watch him take his first walk through the woods behind his parent´s house, to see the look on his face as he heard the first cuckoo´s call or the tapping of a woodpecker´s beak.

He was surprised how much his son being there made him miss things he hadn´t thought about for years. Since Frank had left with Igo he had begun to understand the sacrifices his parents had made and the love they gave to him when he was young which he hadn´t appreciated at the time. He found himself missing them terribly.

He remembered many things he would like to see again and show to his young family. He would love to hear a babbling brook, swim in a lake of fresh water and wander for miles across springy moorland. He could imagine the look of ecstasy on Gara´s face lying down on a bed of perfumed flowers in a summer meadow.

The sound of feet crunching along a stony path brought him crashing back to reality. He stood and turned to see one of Beselch´s men approaching. He ran right up to them and stopped, bent over gripping his side as he struggled to get his breath back. A circle of curious Majos gathered around him.

"The others…" he began breathlessly. "The others…" he started again.

"Slow down." said Rayco, offering him the skin of water from around his neck "Drink, then talk." The young man accepted the water gratefully and took a couple of gulps before starting again.

"The others have stopped for the night close to Big Reef. Beselch says to wait here. He will join you tomorrow."

"Is that all?" asked Norstar.

"That is all. I am to wait here with you." said the young man, still breathing heavily.

"Very well," said Norstar, "pick a spot and get some rest."

A handful of Majos led the young man away, eager to question him further.

"We may as well get settled in for the night." said Norstar. "I doubt they´ll be going anywhere in the dark."

He looked down at the ship resting at anchor in the bay below. Torches and lanterns were being lit around the deck and up in the masts. Onshore adjacent to the ship, a few tall tents had been erected around a large fire. They could just pick out the tiny forms of people moving around but not straying too far from the flames.

159

18

Lancarote,

July 25th, 1402

Jean woke when the sun climbed over the horizon and shone it´s light directly into his face. He squinted against the bright light for a moment before trying to move. His body did not respond as he would have liked. It ached and creaked and resisted when he told it to sit up. His legs were painfully stiff and his whole torso complained. His mail shirt felt as heavy as an anvil on his chest. He had to roll onto his stomach and peel his body off the ground slowly. He finally got to his feet and tried stamping out some of the stiffness.

He looked to his right in the direction they would soon be travelling. The Ajache Mountains were still a fair way off and they had to cross them to get to Gadifer and the ship. He debated whether he should get the men up and walking or wait for Gadifer to sail back up the coast and pick them up later in the day. He quickly rejected that idea. There was the possibility that Gadifer had run into trouble of his own and wouldn´t be able to come looking for them. He began to doubt the wisdom of splitting their forces.

He turned to look over the bodies huddled around the cold embers of the fire. Some men were already awake and were talking quietly to each other, others lay as still as corpses cocooned in their blankets. He looked up at the hill overlooking their camp and was relieved to see two sentries stood upright and alert.

Although everybody was bone tired and sore from the previous day´s hike, they broke camp quickly and were eager to get under way. All except for Big Perrin, who insisted he couldn´t walk because his feet were *broken*. Jean lacked the patience to listen to the man´s griping so sent him off in the boat. Everybody´s mood improved perceptively as the boat shoved off taking Big Perrin away. Jean almost felt sorry for the men in the boat, he saw their expressions of misery as they rowed away.

Jean was weary. His bones, muscles, even his skin ached. His mail shirt was ridiculously heavy, it had been a long time since he had worn it for such a long period and he wasn´t getting any younger. He cursed himself for not wearing it during the voyage on the ship and getting used to the weight. He felt his blisters re-engaging with the leather of his rigid boots. It took all his concentration to block out the pain. His interest in plants and wildlife waned since the day before and he asked very few questions of the native guide. He just concentrated on putting one foot in front of the other. Sharp stones and large rocks littered the path. The column of knights walked with their heads down taking care not to slip and turn an ankle. The land was getting drier the farther they walked, with very little life breaking through the dusty earth. The wind was lighter and warmer. The sun beat down mercilessly from a clear blue sky, getting hotter the further South they marched.

****

They passed by several deserted hamlets, one of which still had fish drying on lines between the huts. Bethencourt stopped the knights from helping themselves. Signs of life were few, but there were absolutely no signs of wealth. Many of the younger mercenary knights were getting more disheartened with every step. Berthin was working on their disillusionment carefully. He noted which of them balked at the idea of capturing slaves for profit and avoided them. He held a walking court with those who were bending to his will, always careful to speak out of earshot of Bethencourt. He was walking near the back of the column with Gillet, Pernet the Blacksmith and William Blessi when Pernet stopped and pointed offshore.

"It looks like the big man has had enough rest." The boat was making directly towards them with Big Perrin waving frantically from the prow.

The knights grouped together on a small bluff overlooking a sheltered bay to watch the boat get in close enough for Perrin to leap ashore. He mistimed his jump and flapped his arms furiously to stop himself from falling backwards into the water. The sailors were already rowing away with all their might, glad to have the big oaf off their hands. Perrin eventually got his bulk under control and began climbing. He puffed, panted and swore his way up the rocks to reach the other knights.

"Fuck this place." he gasped as he took his final few steps up the bluff.

"What's the problem?" asked Berthin as Perrin paused to take a breath.

"I've seen the fuckers!" he grinned. "There's a whole army of them just beyond the hill over there." He pointed to a steep rise a hundred paces inland.

"You saw an army?" Bethencourt asked excitedly, pushing through the crowd.

"I saw the dust kicked up by their feet. I swear I can smell their filth on the wind now I'm here." Perrin replied, sniffing the air like a hound.

"Then we should go take a look." Bethencourt said, his face breaking out into a huge grin. The men busied themselves loosening swords in their scabbards and checking the strings of their bows. Alfonso started running up the hill.

"Hold fast boy." Berthin called. "We don't want you warning them off now do we." The guide stopped and looked to Bethencourt. Bethencourt was suddenly busy looking elsewhere. Alfonso shrugged and sat down on a rock.

"Gillet, if you please." Berthin directed the young knight who already had an arrow nocked in his bow string. "Lead the way. The rest of you spread out in a line and follow, but do not get ahead of him."

Bethencourt nodded. "Very good Berthin! Carry on."

Berthin raised his head and caught a faint whiff of musk riding on the breeze. He drew his sword and followed Gillet up the hill.

****

Alfonso waited until the line of men passed him by. He sprang to his feet and scurried off to the side, well beyond their left flank, and began climbing again. He scanned the ground as he went, pausing briefly to pick up two palm-sized rocks. He moved silently, which couldn´t be said for the body of French knights to his right. Their boots skidded and kicked, dislodging rocks that were send clattering back down the hill. Scabbards struck rocks and the plated tunics some of them wore clanged like dull bells as they climbed. They made enough noise to warn people living on another island they were coming.

A few feet from the top of the hill, Gillet stopped and raised his hand. The knights following came to a loud grinding halt. They waited as Gillet crept up the final few feet to the crest of the hill. He paused behind a boulder and slowly leaned out to see what waited for them. After what seemed like an age, he finally waived his arm and set the men in motion again.

Alfonso was a hundred paces away. He flattened himself against a tall stand of rocks on the hillcrest and slowly crept forward. His heart was pounding in his chest. He couldn´t believe the sound of it wasn´t giving him away as he looked with one eye, and then the other to see the Majo army.

At first, he was dismayed, and then laughed with relief. The large flat plain at the top of the hill was alive with an immense flock of multi-coloured goats. It stretched to the base of the Ajache Mountains half a league to the west. The goats were grazing on the sparse scrubland, oblivious to the army stalking them. He looked carefully above the heads of the animals to try and spot any herders but saw none.

He heard a roar of laughter away to his right and looked across to see the knights stood on top of the hill, pushing their swords back into their scabbards. The goats nearest the French began bleating. The call spread slowly across the plain, it soon sounded like the entire herd was laughing at the feckless warriors. With no small satisfaction, Alfonso watched as Big Perrin was mocked mercilessly by the other knights. The big fool snatched a bow from one of the men and loosed an arrow into the herd. It struck with a heart-wrenching thud. Goats scattered in all directions leaving one of their number lying on its side, an arrow sticking out of its heaving ribcage. The animal struggled to take its final, shuddering breaths.

Alfonso was pleased to see Jean snatch the bow from Perrin´s hand and shout up into the big man´s face. For a moment it looked like the Big Man would pound Jean into the ground, but he soon backed off and hung his head while Jean turned away in disgust.

He heard a scrape of stone on his left and turned, expecting to see a goat searching for a tasty root. There was nothing there. He checked to his right to make sure none of the French were looking his way before carefully creeping back around the rock. He spied a dark hole on the far side where the rock met the earth. He heard the stone scrape again and saw a little puff of dust against the dark shadow of the hole. He leaned out as far as he could to look down into the black opening and saw a small foot wearing a well-worn moccasin.

He stopped breathing, took another quick look to make sure none of the French were looking his way, then crept around and crouched down to look inside the hole.

Two sets of frightened eyes stared back at him from the darkness. Two young boys, skinny with matted hair and dusty skin pushed themselves as far back into the hole as they could, their hands clamped firmly over their mouths. They were trembling with fear. Alfonso smelled the sharp tang as one of them pissed down his leg. Alfonso nearly cried. He held his hands out and spoke quietly, the boys´ eyes flew wide when they realised he spoke their language. Alfonso told them to stay quiet and still. They pressed their hands even tighter across their mouths.

"What have you found there?" Alfonso looked up and was horrified to see a French knight walking towards him.

He stood up quickly and shouted "It´s nothing… I thought it was another goat, but it was a fat lizard."

"Are you sure?" the knight replied, moving closer.

"Yes, just a big fat lizard on a rock!" The knight was still coming. Alfonso jumped out and trotted a couple of paces towards him. "Help me catch it and I´ll share it with you. Tastes good."

That was enough to stop the knight in his tracks.

"Not this time my friend, maybe the next one." He laughed and began to turn away. "Come and help carry this goat." He walked away, shaking his head as he went.

Alfonso went back to the rock and stuck his head into the hole. He warned the boys to stay where they were before following the knight to the dead goat. He didn´t look back at the rock. He dare not. He fizzed with joy as he caught up to the knight and tried his best to mask it.

"Did you catch it?" the knight asked, bending over to pick up the goat´s front legs, Alfonso grabbed the rear.

"No. It got away."

****

At midday the ship left the shelter of the bay. The wind blew strongly from the northeast, the ship began sailing away to the southeast. It made slow progress tacking against the wind, Norstar and his men kept pace with it easily. They walked around the southern peaks of the Ajache Mountains, arriving at the eastern end of the range long before the ship began its final tack to shore.

Rayco called their attention to a little boat with a tiny white sail bobbing in the waves a few hundred paces along the coast to their left. Soon the eagle-eyed Majos spotted the column of knights marching along the rocky path adjacent to the boat. They must have seen the ship out to sea and began waving and cheering frantically. The wind carried their voices to the Majos in the hills who settled down to watch the ship sail past them and swoop in to pick up the knights. When they were all on board, the ship turned back to the south and left.

Rayco pointed back to the place on shore where the knights had been. Beselch and his men materialised from the rocks above and scrambled around searching for anything left behind by the French. Norstar let out a piercing whistle. Beselch´s men looked up and started running towards them, bounding along the skinny mountainside tracks.

The first arrived quickly and exchanged greetings. They were drinking and talking with Norstar´s men when Beselch arrived, bringing up the rear. He was breathing heavily as he took the final few steps up the path, pushing down on his knee to mount the final steps. Norstar met him and took him to one side.

"Any trouble?" he asked.

"None. These Northerners are slow." Beselch answered gulping in air. "And you?" he wheezed.

"No trouble. The others made camp in Eagle Claw Bay and are building walls. They seem peaceful enough, but I still have an uneasy feeling about them."

"Would your uneasy feeling be lessened any if you were to learn they travel with Majos?"

"It is true then?"

"We saw one of them yesterday and suspected but didn´t know until we found two boys who said a Majo had talked with them earlier."

"If he didn´t give them away to the men he travels with? It suggests to me he doesn´t entirely trust them."

"That puzzles me also." Beselch nodded.

"Have you sent word to Guadarfia?" Norstar asked

"Yes. I sent a runner."

"Then there is little else we can do but wait and watch some more." Beselch nodded. "Come with us, we have made camp at the top of the valley."

"Lead the way." Beselch said taking a huge breath.

Norstar turned and whistled. His men turned as one to look at him. He flicked his head in the direction of the summit. They set out at a quick trot.

"After you." said Norstar.

"No. I will slow you down." Beselch replied, looking greyer than Norstar had ever seen him as he stared up at the steep twisting path to the summit.

"We will go together." Norstar replied smiling.

****

Jean stood with Gadifer, Father Verrier and Brother Bontier inside an airy tent pitched on the rocky prominence overlooking the ship at anchor in the bay. They hunched around a table on which was spread a large map of the island. Brother Bontier was carefully adding settlements and other features onto the map as Jean described them to him. Bontier finished another section and stood back to check his work. The others crowded round to see.

"Fine penmanship Brother." said Jean putting his arm around the friar's shoulder. Bontier had rendered mountain ranges, volcanoes, villages and springs in exquisite detail.

"Is there anything else of note you remember?" asked Father Verrier.

"Not that springs to mind right now…" at that moment Berthin entered the tent leading several other knights. "…unless you remember anything of note Berthin?" asked Jean.

"Erm, no, nothing. Pardon?"

"Anything of note from our little walking expedition?"

"Oh that," Berthin said, more than one snort sounded from the men behind him. "I am sure that everything that needs to be told has been said by you Monsieur."

"Quite." said Jean with a clap of the hands. "Now gentlemen, if you please, spread out, find some space. The men fanned out around the walls of the tent while Jean walked behind the table. He looked down at the map and waited for silence before lifting his head and addressing the gathered nobles, comprised of the most senior in the company in rank and age.

"Gentlemen." he began. "I believe we can declare the first stage of our campaign to have yielded promising results. We have made solid progress charting the coastline, as you will see from this excellent piece of work by Brother Bontier here." He spread his hands over the map. "As you are all aware," he continued, "we have thus far failed to make contact with any of the natives. We have come here to introduce the heathen horde to the Holy Word, a task made so much more difficult by not finding any members of that heathen horde." He smiled warmly as a couple of knights responded to his mirth. "I am open to your suggestions gentlemen. How would you suggest we proceed?"

Gadifer was quick to speak. "I believe it would be prudent to use every hand we have to finish the defences here Monsieur, before we strike out for the interior and go on the offense."

"I disagree," Father Verrier said, "I feel the defences you are constructing here are already stating an offensive intent to the natives. I was led to believe that we were here to convert these people, not conquer them. Building high walls, on their land, without their permission is an act of wanton aggression."

"Let us see if you still feel the same when one of them creeps into your tent and slits your throat in the middle of the night." Gadifer replied, drawing several grunts of approval from around the table.

"How would you feel monsieur, if a caravan of squatters appeared on your lands near the river Sevre and started building walls and houses?" Verrier asked haughtily.

"That is hardly the same Father." Gadifer answered.

"No? And why not?"

"Because…"

"Yes?"

"Because it is not. This is ridiculous." Gadifer complained.

"Surely, if we were going to encounter any hostility it would have come yesterday when our forces were divided?" continued Father Verrier.

"They could be waiting and gathering numbers for an attack." Gadifer replied. "We know nothing about them."

"And they equally know nothing about us." Father Verrier snapped back. "Look, I do not question your military expertise, nor your ability to plan for battle, but it is not a battle we are planning for. I have spent many days conversing with our native guides and from what I understand, the people here are as ignorant of warfare as I am. They welcome many visitors to the island with whom they trade freely. They live a peaceful existence and are probably up there now scared out of their wits, watching us sharpen our blades and build walls on their land. We need to adopt a less threatening stance if we are to persuade them to come to us."

"With all due respect Father, I have seen Saracens plead piety and speak of peace before stabbing a soldier in the back. We cannot ever totally trust an opponent, or it will be the last thing we ever do." Gadifer´s words drew a chorus of *Ayes* from the other nobles, even Jean quietly nodded in agreement. He had seen his fair share of men killed by *innocents*.

"If they haven´t come to us yet they are not coming." added Remonnet de Leneden, an old confederate of Gadifer. "We could take a small group of men into the caves where we know they hide and drag them out."

"You would only find women, children and the elderly underground." Jean added.

"What if we made a push with all our men to the large settlement here." Gadifer suggested, stepping forward and placing a finger on the blank interior of the map approximately where Acatife was. "Did you not say to me yesterday Father that the woman mentioned a sizeable town in the interior where the island´s King had a palace?"

"The Lady Isabel did make mention of such a settlement, as did Alfonso, although his recollection was that the King´s palace was a little further away from the town." answered Father Verrier.

"If there´s a King there´s an army." spoke one voice from the back.

"Oh, there´s an army. Big Perrin found it for us earlier." Jean quipped to a murmur of amusement. "But, joking aside. We know there are armed men prowling the interior of the island." His hand drew circles above the blank space on the map. "How organised they are, is impossible to say."

"If it were an experienced *army*, they would have attacked when we were at our weakest yesterday." Gadifer offered, "They know the land, they control the high ground. If I were to defend this place I would have hit hard yesterday while you walked along a blind pathway, and then come south and slaughtered everyone in this camp while we slept." Jean nodded thoughtfully, stroking the hairs on his beard. "But they did nothing except watch us from a distance."

"You are correct." Jean said.

"Correct monsieur?"

"You are perfectly correct in assuming that if they wanted us dead then we would be. We are whole, which suggests to me that the natives want to talk to us as much as we want to talk to them."

"I have a suggestion if I may." Father Verrier volunteered.

"Of course!" replied Jean, "Speak freely Father."

"The key to breaking the impasse is to offer the hand of friendship."

"Go on…" Jean encouraged.

"Isabel and Alfonso are Canarians. They are from here, yet they dress like us. We need them to be seen wearing native garb. We could use them as bait, a lure to entice the natives down from the hills."

"That could work." Jean remarked turning to Gadifer who nodded in approval. "Then this is what we will do. We leave with two companies. I will take the Lady Isabel with me. Alfonso will go with you Gadifer. You and your men walk back along the western coast here." He traced a line with his finger on the map. Gadifer affirmed with a crisp nod of the head. "I will lead a second patrol into the mountains here, next to the camp."

"I would like Brother Bontier and myself to accompany these patrols." Father Verrier volunteered.

"Are you sure Father?" Jean asked, "It will be a hard, rocky path to walk."

"My Boy I have been walking the path of Christ for many years now. I cannot imagine this trail being harder or rockier than that one has been."

"Very well." Jean laughed. "You shall come with me, Brother Bontier will accompany Gadifer and Alfonso." He looked to Gadifer who again nodded approval.

"And so gentlemen, unless there are any questions…" Jean scanned the faces in the tent, "No? Good! We will adjourn for now and make provisions for the morning, we leave at dawn."

The knights filed from the tent. The tantalising aroma of a hearty meal being prepared in the kitchen block wafted into the tent as the knights left.

"That smells delicious." Jean beamed. His hunger demanded some attention. "Do you have any idea what we´re having for supper this evening?"

"Goat stew I believe." answered Gadifer.

19

Las Ajaches, Lancarote,

July 26th, 1402

Rayco jumped back from the edge and pushed Jonay in the chest.

"I tell you, it´s her." he shouted in a whisper.

"Calm down brother." pleaded Jonay, grabbing his brother by the arm.

"What´s happening?" asked Norstar jumping down into the lookout nest to join them.

"It´s her, I know it is." Rayco replied, breaking free from Jonay´s grip. "It´s Mifaya. She has come back home."

"Are you sure it´s her?" asked Norstar.

"Look! Look!" Rayco said pulling Norstar to the edge. Norstar lay out flat and peeked over the lip of the nest. He saw a long line of soldiers picking their way along a narrow track some way below them. They were led by a woman in a short dress.

"I don´t know brother." began Norstar "She is about the same size and shape as Mifaya, but she doesn´t move the same. I don´t think it´s her." Norstar pushed back from the edge and turned around, but Rayco was no longer there. "Where´s he gone?" he asked. Jonay spun around.

"He´s jumped." Jonay said rushing to the side of the nest.

"Shit!" spat Norstar springing to his feet and pushing past Jonay to see Rayco bounding down the steep slope. Norstar leapt out after him with Jonay in pursuit, mouthing curses at his brother´s back as they descended, leaping from boulder to boulder at breakneck speed.

Rayco made no sound as he made his way down the mountainside. He finally stopped on a ledge twenty feet above the track. The sound of the knights´ boots crunching on the stone path halted as Norstar and Jonay landed on the rock behind Rayco. The pair of them grabbed his arms and pulled him back from the edge. Jonay tripped him and he crashed to the ground, Norstar climbed on his chest and clamped his hand over his mouth.

"Hello?" A small voice rose to them from the pathway below. The three of them froze.

"Is there anybody there?" A gust of wind carried the voice away, but not before Norstar and the others heard the Majo words.

"Please show yourselves to me."

"That´s not her!" said Norstar letting his hand slip away from Rayco´s mouth.

"I can hear you. I beg you to let me see your faces."

"Mifaya!" shouted Rayco desperately. Norstar clamped his hand back over his brother´s mouth and looked at him with undisguised fury. Rayco looked defiantly back into Norstar´s eyes. He was tense and shaking wildly, a dam of emotion ready to burst.

"I once knew a girl with that name, she was kind to me, Mifaya, but I am not her."

Norstar fumed, threatening Rayco with a glare before taking his hand away from his mouth once more and releasing him. Rayco nodded weakly and sat up, the tension left his body.

"Who is your tribe?" shouted Jonay. Norstar spun round and looked at Jonay, apoplectic with silent rage. Jonay looked back at him and shrugged. "I think I know her." he said quietly and smiled.

"My mother was Rama. We were taken when I was young, too young to remember much. We were separated many years ago and I never saw her again, but now I have been brought back home. Please show yourself, so that I might once more see my people."

"Wait!" urged Norstar. "We can´t go stumbling into this like half brained goats." He gripped Rayco by the shoulders. "Are you back with us yet?" he asked, Rayco nodded feebly, "Can I rely on you to do something without losing your mind again?"

"Yes." whispered Rayco. "Yes!" he said more forcibly as Norstar punched his shoulder.

"Then get your arse back up the mountain and tell Avago to come. He is the only one permitted by Guadarfia to talk to these people." He fixed Jonay with a withering gaze. "We must let Avago do all the talking. Understand?"

Jonay looked away, his face colouring deep red. Rayco got out from under Norstar and took off back up the steep slope.

"*Are you still there?*"

"Tell her to wait." Norstar hissed.

"Wait. One comes to talk with you." Jonay called out.

"You stay here and wait for Avago. Do not speak to her again." Norstar told him sternly and waited for him to nod agreement before leaving him alone on the ledge and climbing back up the mountainside. He climbed upwards for a few feet above where Jonay waited. He cut to the right and crawled along a narrow ledge until it dropped into long thin gulley. He followed it down to where an enormous boulder jutted out from the loose scree of the mountainside.

Norstar crouched down behind the boulder and raised his head slowly. He could clearly see Jonay on the ledge fifty feet away and slightly below him. Norstar stretched up a little higher and saw below Jonay's perch to where the French knights stood waiting on the path. Several of them had arrows nocked and were scouring the mountainside for targets. Norstar was amused to see a colourfully dressed man wandering between the knights, physically dragging the bows down and reprimanding the archers. That several of the larger knights hadn´t swatted him away like a fly told Norstar he was their leader. Several words reached his ears in the wind, the distinct sounds of French vowels, a sound he hadn´t heard in a long time.

"*Hello?*"

Norstar's eyes flew to the Majo woman who spoke again. He was pleased Jonay resisted the urge to reply this time. She stood near the head of the column, looking so tiny amongst the heavy metal of the knights pressed in around her. An old priest in simple robes with sandals on his feet was asking something of her. Norstar watched and noted that the young woman did not appear to be suffering any discomfort, indeed all the men appeared to treat her with deference.

His attention switched to the steel tipped arrows and spears tickling the air. He counted the crossbows and paid special attention to the high-quality mail and armoured tunics the knights wore, looking for any gaps he could hit with an arrow. He wished he had more bows to give to his men. With twelve good bows shooting steel tipped arrows, they

173

could kill all the knights with two swift volleys. He calculated their chances without the bows; Rocks would bounce off the armour, obsidian knives would crumble in the mail and binots would be chopped to kindling by the knights´ swords.

The Majo woman laughed at something the foppy general said to her. The laugh tinkled like the peel of a glass bell, it sounded fragile and delicate. Norstar realised that he did remember the girl, or at least had known her Mother, Rama, many years ago. She had left two husbands and a healthy farmstead behind when the slavers took her and her daughter, eleven, maybe twelve years earlier. A few short days later, the husbands were both found dead on the rocks in a cove near to Norstar´s secret harbour. Some said they threw themselves from the cliffs, overcome with grief for their lost wife. Others were more inclined to believe that the two of them had stumbled while fighting to determine which had the bigger claim on her land and possessions. Either way, the poor girl would not be enjoying a family reunion.

She was maybe five years older than Fayna but looked a lot older. Her hair was smooth, tamed by fine combs and fresh water. Her skin was white from her neck to her feet, she hadn´t lived outdoors for a long time. She wore a Majo style dress, but it felt wrong somehow, almost too rigid. It hung stiffly from her shoulders where it should have flowed like a second skin.

Norstar heard a small *click* away to his right and looked to see Avago staring back at him. Norstar nodded and made to rise. Avago held out his open hands, signalling Norstar to stay put. Fayna ducked under Avago´s outstretched arms and crossed the mountain to join Norstar, closely followed by Gara. Fayna carried her own short bow with Norstar´s in her other hand. He took it gratefully. She pulled three full quivers of arrows from her back and laid them on the ground. Gara carried a small sack of rocks over her shoulder, a sling hung from her fingers, already loaded.

Norstar eyes wandered up the mountainside and saw Majos hiding behind boulders and squeezing into cracks and folds. Norstar stole another look back down at the French knights below and was relieved to see that they appeared to be completely oblivious to all the action going on above their heads.

Avago reached the ledge where Jonay crouched and shared a few silent words with him. Beselch followed Avago. He skidded down the final three feet sending small stones skittering down the mountainside. Avago caught him and stopped him from sailing over the edge. The noise alerted the French below and all chatter between them stopped. The tension in the air thickened, even the wind held its breath, not daring to break the peace with an ill-timed gust.

****** *

It took a large force of will for Jean not to reach for his sword when he heard falling stones. He looked around, noticing for the first time just how vulnerable their position was, perched on a narrow path with loose rocks underfoot, a steep drop-off to one side and a near vertical hillside on the other. The heights above them were full of massive boulders and deep shadows. There could be a whole host of natives up there, ready to crush Jean and his men beneath a murderous rock fall.

He fidgeted nervously. Sweat poured down his face, his heart beat so hard he felt it would burst from his chest. He jumped out of his skin when Isabel called out in her strange tongue.

He took a breath and then froze as a deep voice answered her from somewhere up above. He released the air in his lungs, relieved it was only words falling on his ears and not rocks. He edged closer to Isabel.

"What did he say?" he asked, scanning the mountainside above.

"He calls me by my old name. He knows my family!"

"Well that's good... That's Good!" Jean stood up straight smiling from ear to ear.

"Ask him if they still live." She did. When the reply came, Jean could tell by her reaction the news was not good. He allowed her a moment before pressing her to ask the man his name.

"Avago."

Avago asked a question. Jean listened carefully, trying to pick words from the stream of strange syllables flowing through the air. He turned to look at Isabel.

"He asks who you are and wants to know if I am your slave."

"Can you translate as I speak?" Jean asked. Isabel nodded.

"Monsieur Avago… Please allow me to introduce myself. I am Jean de Bethencourt, Baron of Saint-Martin-le-Gaillard, loyal servant of King Charles of France and agent of King Enrique of Castile. I come with the offer of friendship from my royal patrons, who offer their protection, with the blessing of the Holy Church of Rome.

"We travel with your people as companions, not as slaves. We freed them and brought them back home to you. They will help us talk to each other."

There was a long pause. Jean waited, scanning the mountainside for movement. At last Avago replied.

"He will send word to the King that you wish to speak with him." Isabel translated, "It will take time. Return to camp and he will deliver a message to you there."

"I would gladly await your King's answer in my camp but request one thing." Jean said, sweeping round, his palms held up to his shoulders. "I would like to look into your eyes. Show yourself to me so we can make acquaintance."

There was another long pause. Jean had to tell more than a couple of knights to put down their bows as the silence stretched on. Suddenly a trio of Majos appeared, stepping to the edge of the ledge only twenty feet above his head.

One stood in the middle of the trio. Jean guessed he was Avago. He stared deeply, unwaveringly at Jean through piercing, olive-coloured eyes. He was a little older than Jean but was fit and lean with broad shoulders and a straight back. A shorter man stood at his left shoulder, his face half hidden by a thick greying beard and carried a small paunch. The third man was a younger fitter version of Avago. A study in strength and poise. The tight muscles across his burnt-butter stomach and square chest looked solid yet fragile at the same time.

All three stood almost naked save for a belt with weighted leather straps hanging down to the middle of their muscular thighs. Each held a wooden spear, planted in the ground at their feet. The sight stirred a strange emotion within Jean. They were living bronze statues, as striking as Greek Gods.

Avago and Jean exchanged silent, respectful nods before the three natives stepped back and disappeared again.

Jean breathed a huge sigh of relief and turned to clasp Isabel´s hands.

"We owe you an enormous debt of gratitude for what you have done here today. I know it is small compensation for the news you have had to hear from our friend Avago up there, but imagine, soon you will be able to speak with many people who knew your mother." Isabel looked up and nodded.

Jean was genuinely sincere in his concern for Isabel. She was probably *the* most valuable asset he had at his disposal. She was the bridge between him and the Majo people. He found her much more personable than the dour Alfonso. This girl was perfectly charming. Although shackled by her lowly status, she was surprisingly well educated and spoken.

"My Dear, that was simply marvellous." Father Verrier bustled along the path and congratulated Isabel enthusiastically. He turned to Jean and spoke

"I won´t lie to you My Boy, I nearly shat my pants there."

******

Norstar watched as the last of the knights disappeared down the hill. He had seen and heard everything clearly during the exchange, it made him slightly uncomfortable. There was something in the word "*protection*" that didn´t sit easily with him. Protection was a word used by bullyboys and toughs, the ones who roamed the docks and the streets surrounding them. They extorted money and ruled the sewers they inhabited with fear and violence. Would the Frenchman act the same way? Was this Bethencourt just another thug, dressed as a toff? Or was he a true gentleman of honour and substance, one who could be trusted?

Gara put her arm around Norstar´s waist.

"I knew Rama." she said, "She wasn´t much older than Mifaya when she and the girl were taken. It was a sad time."

"I don´t want to lose you two." said Fayna turning to hug them both.

"Don´t worry little chicken, we´re not going anywhere without you." Norstar said gently, kissing the side of her head. "And if anyone were stupid enough to drag you off to be their slave, I would follow them to the ends of the world and rescue them from you." He laughed as Fayna punched him in the stomach.

"You are a bad man." Gara snorted and punched him in the arm.

"I yield." he said wrapping his strong arms around the pair of them and hugging them tightly to him. "If anyone were to take any of you away, I would sail across every sea to find you and bring you back home. That I promise with every beat of my heart."

****

A messenger returned long before nightfall. King Guadarfia was on his way and would meet with the French the following day. Avago decided to take Norstar and Beselch´s son Belicar with him to deliver the message.

Norstar was surprised that they got within a hundred paces of the tall tents and the low walls surrounding the French camp before any alarm was raised. A cacophony of clanking metal and shouted orders broke the tranquil evening air.

Knights came rushing out to the jagged boundary wall, bristling with menace, regarding the tribesmen walking majestically towards them with hostile eyes. There was a commotion from the back of the crowd. The leader Bethencourt appeared, trying to push the people aside, accompanied by the girl Isabel and a large white-haired man wearing a full suit of armour. The knights blocking their path soon jumped out of the way when the white-haired old man barked at them.

Avago slowed and halted twenty paces from the wall. He planted his binot in the ground with his left hand, the sign of peace. Norstar and Belicar did the same. They watched impassively as Bethencourt walked stiffly out to meet them, flanked by the shiny big man and Isabel.

The groups came together. Avago and Jean met in the middle with Norstar facing Isabel on one side and Gadifer eye to eye with Belicar on the other.

Jean surprised them all by extending a greeting in Majo. Avago nodded his approval and returned the greeting. With Isabel translating, Avago delivered the message from Guadarfia and arranged to accompany Bethencourt and no more than twenty of his knights to meet with him the following day.

Jean agreed effusively before holding out his hand to the left. "Monsieur Avago, where are my manners. Allow me to introduce you to Monsieur Gadifer de la Salle, my second in command, and warrior of high esteem." Norstar saw Gadifer flinch slightly when called Jean's second in command but he recovered quickly and nodded respectfully, if not a little stiffly towards Avago. An uncomfortable silence ensued while Jean waited for Avago to introduce his companions. He made no effort to do so.

"I don't believe it!" Belicar bellowed suddenly. "Is that really you back there with the short legs and the skinny arms?" He looked over the shoulder of Gadifer. Everyone turned to see who he was shouting at. Alfonso stood leaning against the wall, grinning from ear to ear.

"I may be skinny, but you're getting uglier every year. You lost another fight with a goat?" he called out. Belicar laughed wildly, the strange braying sound coming from his mouth captivated Gadifer. The old man stared at Belicar's mouth in wonder as it contorted.

"Ah! Alfonso, join us." Jean shouted redundantly as Alfonso was already running to embrace Belicar.

"I never thought I'd see your face again brother." Belicar gushed slapping Alfonso's back.

"I thought the same. It's good to feel the earth and the sun kiss my skin again. It has been many cold years since I have felt warmth beneath my feet."

"Alfonso," Jean said, the grinning guide turned to face him. "If Monsieur Avago has no objections, I would like to suggest that you return to your people this evening and spend the night becoming reacquainted with them. However, I would like you there when we meet with the King tomorrow."

"Yes, Yes, Yes monsieur. Thankyou!" Alfonso beamed his happiest smile showing all his uneven teeth. He bowed deeply before scuttling away back to the tents.

"Well, we've made one man extremely happy tonight." Jean laughed and clapped his hands together.

"It is a good thing you have done." said Avago through Isabel. "We will come in the morning at first light to accompany you to meet with King Guadarfia."

"I shall look forward to seeing you then." replied Jean.

Alfonso came sprinting back carrying a leather satchel. He skidded to a halt at Belicar's side bouncing on his feet like a puppy.

Avago took Isabel's hand and spoke softly to her. "And you my noble lady, I know many people will want to meet you. It gladdens my heart to see you back home and looking so very well."

"Thank you, Avago. I think I remember you." Isabel said, lifting her eyes to meet his.

He smiled for an instant. "You are most welcome home." he said, then stood tall.

He nodded to Jean and Gadifer, hoisted his spear and turned, touched Norstar's arm and broke into a steady trot, leading the way back towards the mountains. Norstar fell in behind him, Belicar and Alfonso brought up the rear. Alfonso jumped around Belicar excitedly, asking many questions without waiting for answers.

****

Jean, Gadifer and Isabel watched Avago lead his men away. Father Verrier came out from behind the wall to join them.

"My dear." he said to Isabel. "If you could give us a minute?"

"Of course." she said and walked back to the camp.

"I must congratulate you Jean. I am truly impressed that you have led us this far without the need to spill any blood."

"Long may it continue Father." replied Jean.

"We must prepare for our meeting with the King tomorrow. I'm worried that you might let Isabel slip away from us too. Are you sure it was a good idea to let Alfonso leave tonight?" asked Verrier.

"I have to agree." Gadifer said. "I question the wisdom of allowing one who could provide vital information to the enemy to simply go with them."

"What could he tell them that they haven't already seen with their own eyes? They have been watching us since we arrived. Besides, I want Alfonso to talk." Gadifer looked at Jean like he was mad. "I want him to tell tales of enormous cities, the wealth of Kings and Queens and the ferocity of their armies. I want them to know from where we came, to know it would be pointless to fight us." He clapped Gadifer on the shoulder and looked into his eyes. "I would like to dazzle them with the shine of our armour tomorrow." Gadifer nodded enthusiastically. He would have his knights polishing their armour and weapons all night long.

"*An enemy who is defeated before he reaches the battlefield is an enemy no longer, he is your servant.*" Which famous general said those words monsieur?"

"Alexander the Great." Gadifer replied without hesitation.

"Was it?" asked Jean. "I thought it was Julius Caesar." Jean had no idea if it were a real quote or not. The words just fell from his mouth, but Gadifer had seemed so confident with his response that Jean decided to play with him again. The game amused him.

"Now you mention it, it could very well have been Caesar." said Gadifer stroking his whiskers thoughtfully. Jean smiled.

"And Father," Jean turned to Father Verrier. "Isabel will not be leaving us, but we must protect her. It would be a good idea to assign a guard to watch over her tonight."

******

Berthin saw Jean, Gadifer and Father Verrier walk back to the tents. He stood just outside the wall with Gillet, William and Big Perrin.

"What did I tell you." he said when they had gone.

"Did you see the size of those fuckers?" said Big Perrin "There's a whole lot of gold in that skin."

"Our *friend* Alfonso is the runt of the tribe I reckon." William added.

"It certainly is good merchandise." replied Berthin, struggling to hide a smile.

"But how do you plan on getting a shipload of them out from under the noses of Gadifer and Bethencourt?" asked Gillet, twirling his bowstring.

"The plan is already in motion." Berthin said quietly. "I´ll let you know when it´s time for you to know the how and the when. Until then, we need at least a dozen more men."

"We´ll get you the men." Big Perrin sneered. "But we need to agree a better share of the profits."

"You´ll get what you deserve." said Berthin and walked away.

****

"It was as big as this mountain and had tall walls as thick as three men laid end to end." Alfonso stood next to the fire surrounded by a huge ring of Majo´s, sat hanging on his every word. His arms whirled wildly as he recounted the wonders *and horrors,* he´d seen in the North. Beselch and Belicar sat at his feet captivated by everything he said.

Norstar and his family sat on the opposite side of the fire. Norstar looked at Fayna who was listening intently as Alfonso was trying to describe a cathedral. Fayna was totally immersed. He worried that she might choose to go North alone without his protection. If more ships came, the passage would be easier. She would soon discover however, that women in the civilized world did not enjoy the same freedom they enjoyed in Majo society.

He had seen several maidens scuttling around the French camp earlier with their hair covered and long skirts brushing the floor. He couldn´t imagine Fayna or any other Majo woman dressing that way, waddling around at the beck and call of their men folk. There were far fewer women than there were men on the island. Many women had two or even three husbands who would dote on them until it was their turn to share the marital bed. They weren´t forced to hide beneath long skirts and blouses to cover their *shame*, a shame given to them by men to hide *their* desires and weaknesses. Majo women chose their husbands and decided how long to keep them. They walked around dressed in as much or as little as they liked every day.

Fayna and Gara both turned to him suddenly. He was surprised to notice everybody else around the fire had turned to look at him too. He had been so far away with his own thoughts that he hadn't heard Beselch ask him a question.

"Are you there?" asked Beselch with an easy smile upon his face, something Norstar couldn't ever remember pointing in his direction. "I asked what your God name was before you came to us."

"My *God name* was David." Norstar answered, surprised how alien the name sounded to him now. A few Majos in the circle tried with varying success to say it out loud. It made Norstar smile to hear Gara saying it, just like the first time they met. *"Daybee."* He looked across at her and she smiled briefly before turning away coyly. "I expect you will all have to change your names soon if you welcome the Christian God to the island." he said swinging back to face Beselch.

"Did you not worship the same God?" asked Beselch.

"I choose my God by what he allows people to do in His name. The last time I saw the cross of Christ it was painted on the shield of a noble knight, much like the ones who camp down in the bay. He chopped the hand off a young boy for taking a loaf of bread, in the name of God."

"But our Lord Jesus is kind and just," spluttered Alfonso, "he died for our sins."

"Upon a cross, like the one you wear around your neck." Norstar answered quickly, Alfonso's hand flew up to grip the small wooden cross hanging from a frayed string, his eyes narrowed as he looked at Norstar.

Norstar felt himself being drawn into an argument he didn't want to have. He stood up. "I am neither a preacher nor a believer. Who you choose to follow is your own business. My mind is clouded with other thoughts this evening. Please, Alfonso, this is your night. I will not spoil your homecoming with my foul mood. Continue with your tales and excuse me, I will go and take my turn on watch."

Norstar bent to retrieve his bow and cloak and lurched off into the darkness. Alfonso turned to look at Beselch with his hands held out.

Beselch scratched his head, "Pay him no mind. Continue with your story."

Gara got to her feet and hurried after Norstar. He heard her approach and turned to meet her.

"What troubles you?" she asked, searching his face with her eyes.

"The man's words stir disturbing memories within me, but they are not your concern." he put his hand behind her neck and drew her into a brief embrace. He kissed the top of her head and took a step back. "Thoughts are flooding my mind and I need to get them under control. Go back to the fire my love and listen to his tales. He does tell them well."

"Are you sure?" asked Gara.

"I need some space to think, and you need to listen to stories of gods and monsters...Go!"

Gara gave him a quick kiss on the cheek and turned to saunter back to the fire. Norstar carried on to the lookout nest and relieved the two young men sat there.

He settled down close to the edge and watched the fires of the camp burning far below. Tiny figures worked by torchlight to shift large rocks into the defensive wall. It certainly appeared as if they intended staying for a long time judging by the amount of work they were putting into their construction.

Frank had been right to be concerned. This wasn't just a casual raiding party, these people were well prepared with wealthy sponsors. The time to chase away them away had passed and Norstar wondered if he could ever be happy sharing his island with them.

There was one advantage in having a garrison of knights on the island. Their presence would deter the pirates and slavers, of that there was no doubt... But would the Majos simply become slaves on their own island under French control? They were inviting a bear to scare off a dog. When the dog had been chased away, they would still be left with a hungry bear.

Once more Norstar found himself wishing he had buried the knights under an avalanche of rocks.

His thoughts were interrupted by the sound of approaching feet. He looked up to see Rayco climbing down into the nest to join him.

"Brother." Rayco said quietly as he leaned out to look down at the camp below. "Any change?"

"No, they're still building.   Has he finished?"

"No!   He is making animal sounds now."   Rayco breathed out as he thumped down on to his backside and crossed his legs, "It will be a long night."

Norstar knew his brother hadn't wandered over by chance, something was on his mind.   He waited in silence until Rayco was ready to speak.

"I have been thinking." Rayco said, after a short while.

"About what?"

"The two of them, Alfonso and the woman…"

"Isabel."

"Isabel, yes, Isabel.   Is there a chance that my Mifaya could still be alive somewhere and seeing the same things Alfonso describes?   That one day she will be brought back home as they have?"   His eyes held back tears, a sight Norstar had become familiar with.   For the first time in over a year however, there was a hint of optimism with the tears.

"We must always have hope brother," Norstar said softly.   "Even when it feels like the Gods have deserted us."

20

Ajache Mountains, Lancarote,
July 27th, 1402

Jean had to shake Philip awake. The valet was exhausted, having spent the previous night sewing the Majo dress for Isabel, working from the vague descriptions she had given him. He mumbled to himself in the candlelight as he adjusted the bright red and blue tunic around the shining coat of armour plate Jean had chosen to wear.

Jean was fizzing with impatience. Philip worked as quickly as he could to get rid of him. He shooed him out of the tent as soon as he snipped the final thread.

Jean did a quick circuit of the camp. It was beginning to come alive as the sky lightened in the East. The fires were hot in the kitchen block and the cooks were already hard at work. The baker had built a rudimentary oven and was making his first batch of bread. The warm, comforting aroma drifted between the tents. It soothed Jean to smell something so familiar in this strange place. He made his way to the bluff overlooking the bay.

He stopped at the edge and looked out over the masts of the ship and past the hazy silhouettes of the islands of Erbania and Lobos. He searched for the horizon, where the sea met the sky but was unable to see it, a huge cloud bank linked the two seamlessly. He closed his eyes for a moment and took a lungful of cool, damp air, chasing stillness. It wouldn't come. He opened his eyes again and looked out at the misty slopes of Erbania. He would have been there already if not for the delays in Cadiz. His strongbox had lost a lot of weight while tied up in port. He needed success quickly to replenish it.

A noise down to his left caught his attention. He looked down into the small bay and saw Father Verrier and Brother Bontier down by the water's edge, taking communion. Jean bowed his head and offered a silent prayer of his own. He asked God to watch over him this day, give him strength and wisdom. He couldn´t ask for more, he was too full of energy to linger. He crossed himself quickly and hurried over to the latrine, hoping his head would clear when his bowels emptied.

The first rays of the sun were streaking through the camp when a warning shout rang out from the wall. The camp erupted into life, knights raced between the tents, armour plate clanging and feet pounding as they pushed past servants who were struggling to get out of the way.

Jean marched through the melee as calmly as he could, arriving at the outer wall relatively unflustered, on the surface. Gadifer was already there, stood in his full suit of armour with a hand on the hilt of his sword. The metal encasing his body was so highly polished it seemed to radiate with a heavenly glow. He made an imposing spectacle, even the whiskers poking out between the cheek guards of his onion-shaped helmet looked vibrant. Jean for once felt decidedly underdressed as he went to stand by his side.

"Here they come." Gadifer said without turning to look at Jean. He kept his eyes fixed on a group of Majos walking over the crest of a low hill, four hundred paces away.

"Let us give them a warm welcome, line your men up." Jean said to Gadifer who launched into action, barking out orders and harrying his knights to form up into a long line with their backs to the wall. Jean was impressed with their turnout. Their armour was resplendent in the early morning sunshine, tunics sponged and brushed. He walked along the line inspecting them, nodding with approval when he got to the end of the line.

"Monsieur Martin!" he called out. A knight stepped forward from the line and lifted a small trumpet to his lips. "Carry on." said Jean.

Martin blew a breathy revelry that rolled across the landscape to meet the Majos. Jean was amused to see the natives' steps falter briefly as the sound wave struck them. A few knights laughed until Gadifer silenced them with a harsh glare.

"You underestimate your foe at your own peril. You are knights of the King, not children. Act that way." he said loudly.

Father Verrier and Brother Bontier rolled out of the camp with Isabel sandwiched between them. They pushed their way through the throng of spectators gathered around the wall. Jean waved them forward and they hurried over to stand by his side.

The Majos halted twenty paces away. They carried out their own inspection of the troops from there. Their eyes roved over the metal clad knights. If they were impressed or intimidated, they didn't show it. They seemed to be much more intrigued by Martin's instrument and gazed at it glinting in the sunshine.

The final notes of the trumpet revelry floated away in the breeze and Jean stepped forward followed by Isabel and Father Verrier. Avago stepped forward from the Majo side to meet them in the middle. He smiled and spoke directly to Isabel much to Jean's annoyance. He turned quickly to see Isabel smile before replying. Avago spoke once more, Isabel answered again and then turned finally to Jean.

"Avago would like to know if you and your men are ready to travel?" she asked.

"Inform Monsieur Avago that indeed we are ready. We are eager to meet with King Guadarfia and see more of his beautiful island." Isabel translated as he spoke. Avago watched Jean closely, waiting until he finished before turning back to his men and holding three fingers in the air. Three Majos broke away from the group and began trotting back the way they had come. Avago turned back to Jean and said through Isabel:

"Come, my men will lead the way."

He invited Jean to walk beside him with Isabel in the middle. Father Verrier and Brother Bontier followed with a couple of natives close behind them.

Half the Majos had left and were blazing the trail in a long line before Gadifer had formed his knights up into a satisfactory double file and got them marching. The remaining Majos fell in behind the knights.

******

They had been walking steadily, but achingly slowly for almost three hours before they called a halt for a rest. They had come north, sticking to a gently undulating pathway that traversed a long plain of rocky, windswept scrubland. The march stopped at a small hamlet of six huts overlooking a sheltered inlet of calm water. Tiny coracles sat on a shale beach below the huts, but there were no other signs of life. The clanking of armour plates on rock as the knights sat down was the only sound carried away in the wind. The island was silent.

Norstar had walked alongside the knights during the march, straining to pick up snippets of conversation. The dozen at the front of the column, marching behind the big old shiny knight Gadifer were highly polished Gascons. They complained and worried the least. Their well-maintained armour had the patina of use.   A pair of pious knights followed the Gascons wearing armour and swords inlaid with crosses and Latin text. They always stood close to the Priests whenever the march halted for whatever reason. They said very little, but what little they said usually had a *Praise Him* somewhere. Norstar amused himself for a few minutes by counting each *Praise Him* they said during one exchange. He counted eight.

There was a small gap between the pious knights and the half dozen Normans who brought up the rear of the column. They were the most vociferous of all the knights and kept up a steady stream of banter. One bear of a man with a scarred pink head under his grubby helmet seemed to think everyone wanted to know what he would like to do to *"these bare breasted savages and their whores"*. At one point, he turned to speak to Norstar who was walking close by. He asked him if he had a beauty hidden amongst the rocks who would *"appreciate a proper cock"*.

Norstar had smiled dumbly at the man while imagining Gara punching an obsidian knife through his ear.

The knights crowded under the trees surrounding the hamlet. Many took off their helmets, following Gadifer´s lead. He lifted his helmet away with a huge sigh of relief. The hood beneath was drenched. He ripped that off and shook his head like a dog, spraying sweat into the air. The old man impressed Norstar, the heat had been rising in waves from his shiny armour during the walk and he was in obvious discomfort, but he hadn´t complained once.

Gadifer settled with a small group of mature Gascons and remained on his feet, alert, taking fleeting glances at the horizon all the time. Norstar saw the Normans crowd under the trees as far away as they could get from Gadifer. He ambled over, as close to them as he dared and sat on a small rock. He reached into his pouch and pulled out a small cake of toasted corn flour and pig fat wrapped in green leaves. He bit off a chunk and let it melt slowly, working the pasty substance with his tongue into the roof of his mouth. He wrapped the remains of the cake and put it back into his pouch.

"Oy savage!" Norstar swung round and looked into the eyes of the pink bald man. He looked like an angry pig without his grubby helmet on. Short stubby strands of white hair clung to his scalp enhancing his porcine appearance.

"You don´t understand a fucking word I´m saying do you?" the knight tried to smile innocently, but his face couldn´t do innocent and delivered a constipated grimace instead.

Norstar reached into his pouch and pulled out his food. He peeled back the leaves and held out the cake to the knight. He mimed taking a chunk and putting it in his mouth.

"You´re a fucking monkey." said the pink knight with a dismissive wave of arm. He twisted away.

Norstar rewrapped the cake and got up to leave. He needed some time away from this savage before he was forced to do something he would regret.

****

"Fucking savage." scoffed the Big Perrin as he put a strip of dried beef in his mouth and chewed it loudly.

"Be careful who you curse Perrin." said Berthin moving to sit next to the big man.

"Pah!" scoffed Perrin, spraying flecks of meat and saliva. "He doesn´t understand a word I´m saying."

"I wouldn´t be too sure about that one. I´ve been watching him. He looks at us differently than the others. There´s an understanding in his eyes when we speak."

"You give him too much credit. He´s as dumb as a sausage on a plate of turds."

"Just be careful what you say around any of them. They've been trading with the outside world for years, some must understand what we're saying."

"You worry too much."

"I worry just the right amount. Remember, we're getting paid for flesh and blood, we'll get nothing for a hold full of corpses. Try to remember that when you're looking for a fight. Every one of them you kill is two hundred francs less, and it will all come off your share." Perrin grunted an unintelligible response and threw another meat strip in his mouth.

Berthin was getting more concerned about Perrin. He was a mad dog on a frayed leash. It would make more sense to lose him than a valuable savage, but Berthin was stuck with him. He prayed that the big fool would control his fundamental impulse to be an arse, but he knew he prayed in vain.

******

Avago was waving for Norstar to join him from the edge of the hamlet. He sat with Isabel and the two holy men. Norstar walked over to them, observed from the shadows by the two pious knights who stood at a discreet distance watching.

"Norstar, come sit with us a moment." Avago said. The others shuffled round to make room.

"This is Norstar, the husband of my daughter," Avago placed his strong hand on Norstar's shoulder as he sat down. "This is Isabel, Father Verrier and Brother Bontier." Norstar grunted at each of them in turn.

"The holy men here want to introduce us all to their God. What say you my boy?"

"I ask what their God can do for us that our Gods cannot." he replied looking from one to the other of the priests. Isabel translated smoothly. The old Priest's face creased into a smile.

"I have heard that question many times before, and not so eloquently put." he dipped his head toward Norstar before continuing.

"I do not know what your God *does* for you, I can only explain what my God does for me.

"There are some who believe that all the Gods; yours, mine, the eastern and the northern deities are one in the same. One God, one Creator, one shepherd guiding his flock. He uses different names and faces depending on where He speaks. I confess, I have never seen His face, but I have read his words and they touch me deeply."

Norstar listened carefully to the way Isabel translated. He was impressed. She was honest in her interpretation of the priest's words. She was clear and precise.

"I have been to many holy sites where I have seen artefacts touched by Him. I have read words written by the hands that had held His hand." He spread his arms wide. "God has guided me here, to this beautiful Eden, to share His word, as taught by his Son, The Lord Jesus Christ who sacrificed his own life to show us the true path to Paradise. Where the strong protect the weak and the quietest voice is heard." He finished and sat back while Isabel finished translating.

Norstar was surprised by how much the man's voice made him feel homesick. The words didn't mean anything to him, they flew over his head, pure God twaddle just the same as every other holy man. But the sound the words made, and the rhythmic way they fell softly from the Priest's mouth reminded him so much of his mother. He thought back to dark nights when his father was away for months on end, when his mother would sing as she walked around the house, telling him and Frank stories and playing games by candlelight. His heart felt a sudden pang to see her again and listen to her sweet voice.

He looked up at Father Verrier who was smiling serenely back at him. Norstar turned to Avago.

"What do you think?" he asked.

"I think Nichel might have his hands full with this one."

"I think you're right." said Norstar before standing and looking down at the holy men.

"It was good to meet you." Isabel translated his words.

"And a pleasure to meet you my boy, I hope we will have further opportunities to talk." Father Verrier said standing to shake Norstar's hand. Norstar was surprised to feel the Priest's soft and warm palm.

He couldn´t remember the last time he had touched a hand so smooth and unblemished by hard work.

He walked away and made his way down to the water´s edge. He craved a moment of solitude. He knelt on the little sharp rocks, splashed water on his face and looked up at the sun.

"Do you have a plan for us all Oh Majek the Magnificent?" he asked and then dipped his head and closed his eyes. "And you God of the Cross. Which of us have you chosen to be a saviour to?" He waited for whatever came. No voice answered, no lightning bolt struck. He wondered for a moment if he should ask the God of the Moors but couldn´t remember ever hearing his name. He chuckled to himself and sat down on a rock, took off his shoes and shook the pebbles out.

The knights were not long resting. Norstar heard a jangling of clanging metal as they got back to their feet. He ambled back to the hamlet and took his place alongside the column as it began to slog inland. Norstar looked up into the mountains from time to time and saw movement. He hoped Gara and Fayna had listened to his advice and returned home, but doubted they had. He wanted them safely away from the knights he was hearing bragging, swearing and spitting their way across *his* land.

He wished there were some way to wipe the stain of these people away. He imagined going along the line and slitting their throats one by one. He got close enough to hear one of them comparing Avago to a shabby old donkey´s arse and pictured himself smashing the knight´s face to a pulp with a rock.

****

A little before midday their destination came into view. Jean had been expecting something a little grander than the village peeking out from a nook in the base of the mountains. It was a little larger than the other settlements Jean had seen thus far but it was built in exactly the same way, a ring of domed huts radiated from a central plaza and a larger meeting hut in the centre.

They walked past a large coral and a row of stone pig pens on the leeward side of the village. The sweet aroma of dung and hay hung in the air. For a brief moment, Jean was transported back to his own farm the familiar smells of livestock and feed were the same everywhere in the world. He also detected a faint rotten tang of stale blood. Jean spotted tanning racks dotting the land behind the corral. Swarms of flies buzzed around the half-scraped hides stretched out upon two of them. Whoever lived here had left in a hurry.

They walked to the centre of the village to a circle of hard packed earth in front of a much larger hut than the others. The knights stopped, shifting uncomfortably as the Majos spread out around the plaza.

Gadifer sidled up to Jean who was having the tanning process explained to him by Avago. The sun bounced from Gadifer's armour into Jean's eyes and he had to squint through its sheen to see the old man's face.

"The place appears to be deserted monsieur." Gadifer said, looking from side to side.

"Yes indeed…" began Jean before the clear note of a horn cut through the air. Gadifer and Jean looked up and saw a solitary Majo stood holding a conch shell to his lips on a ridge high above them. He took a big breath and blew again. The mournful note was joined by another from further away. Jean searched the hills but couldn't see where that one came from.

The knights stood in the square started to fidget. A few hands flew to grip their swords as the natives surrounding them began making whooping noises and stamping their feet.

"King Guadarfia comes." Avago said. "We will go to meet him."

"Certainly. Just one second." Jean turned quickly to Gadifer. "Form the men up and tell young Martin to come to me." Gadifer hurried away to hustle the knights into order. He arranged them in two ranks and walked along the front line. He stopped a couple of times to rearrange a folded cloak or bent collar before taking his place in front of them.

Martin trotted over to Jean.

"You asked for me Monsieur?" he asked.

"Yes. Let me hear something regal from your horn young man. A tune fit for a King."

Martin nodded nervously then slowly lifted the trumpet up to his mouth. He licked his dry lips and tested the keys. He thought for a moment, took a deep breath and blew a quiet long thin note, harmonising with the conch shells in the hills. The Majos around the village stopped whooping when Martin raised the note´s volume in a smooth crescendo. He used the sound of the conch shells as a drone and played a stately march. It was a tune Jean recognised immediately, the Battle Cry of the Crusaders, normally sung in cider houses in Normandy where cups would be thrust in the air as they got to the chorus. Jean began singing the words under his breath and turned to look at Gadifer and the pristine knights arrayed behind him. They thrust their chests forward, some were mouthing the words. Sweet notes echoed back from the steep walls of the mountains. It sounded like a chorus of trumpets playing in a round. The swooping scales dipped and soared into the air and soon the conch blowers blew to Martin´s rhythm with added gusto.

Jean smiled as he caught sight of Avago looking at Martin with his mouth open. The sweet music hypnotised the old man. The spell broke when a great shout went up from the other side of the village announcing the arrival of the King.

Avago snapped back to attention and hustled Jean and Isabel to the foot of a path snaking down from the heights. Jean looked up and saw Guadarfia for the first time walking slowly down the pathway towards them.

The King looked magnificent. He towered over his small entourage, the decorated leather mitre atop his head made him seem even taller. A heavy, black, brown and white goat hide cloak hung from his broad shoulders, his chest bare beneath the flaps of the cloak led down to a narrow waist, over stomach muscles, straining through his skin. About his waist he wore a loincloth, similar to the other Majos, barely concealing his more than adequate manhood. He walked tall and erect on strong legs, his steps measured and sure. On his feet he wore goatskin moccasins, above those he wore anklets of small, polished shells which shucked together with every deliberate step he took.

To his left walked the old man with the potbelly Jean remembered from the day before. On the King's right walked a smaller man with pinched features, swathed in a cloak more colourful and intricate than the King's, with tufts of feather and fur around it's edges. On his head he wore a hood of small fur pelts sewn around a decorated goat skull. Unlike the other men who carried long binots in their left hands, he wielded a short stabbing spear with a soft leather handle.

Jean recognised Alfonso walking with the men behind the King. His smile was as broad as his face was wide. Jean felt a surprising jolt of joy to see him.

Avago stepped forward a pace and greeted Guadarfia with a shallow bow. The King looked down at Jean. It was a long way down. Jean tipped his head quite a way back to return the stare.

The pot-bellied man stepped forward and gestured with a sweep of his arm. His voice was much deeper than Jean had expected.

"The Mencey of Tyterogaka, King Guadarfia, son of Guanarame and Ico, welcomes all who come in peace to his Kingdom. By his side stands our Spirit Guide Nichel, the voice of our ancestors and keeper of laws." The men stood like exotic birds of prey, with their capes folded over their shoulders like wings. There was a moment of silence. Beselch stepped back to his place at Guadarfia's shoulder.

Jean stood to his full height and began.

"Your Grace. Allow me to introduce myself. I am Jean de Bethencourt, Baron of Saint-Martin-le-Gaillard, loyal servant of King Charles of France and agent of King Enrique of Castile. Here with the Blessing of His Holy Father Pope Boniface of Rome."

Jean waited for Isabel to finish before going on. He didn't get the chance to say more as Guadarfia strode forward and placed his heavy hand on Isabel's shoulder. He looked down and spoke some words gently to her. Jean was shocked not by the depth of his voice, but by the tenderness he was able to convey with it. Isabel blushed when he finished. She stood up tall, a bright smile lighting up her whole face. The men behind the King grunted with appreciation and Alfonso stepped forward and hugged Isabel before turning to Jean.

"King Guadarfia has welcomed Isabel back to her home and wishes to show his thanks." he said while another man stepped forward leading three snow-white goats on a leather leash. The goats complained loudly as they were dragged forward, the leash holding them was thrust unceremoniously in front of Jean´s face.

"Oh! Well... Thank you." he said having no choice but to take it. "Very... very fine animals." he said, bending to study the beasts. He looked up at Guadarfia. "Thank You Your Grace."

"From his own flock monsieur, the best on the island." Alfonso said patting the rump of one animal, straining against the leash. "Allow me monsieur." Alfonso took the goats from Jean and pulled them away to the side. Jean glad to be free of the animals rubbed his hands together and invited Guadarfia to step forward with a wide sweep of his arm.

"Please!"

They walked the short distance to where Gadifer stood proudly at the head of the knights neatly lined up in two shining rows behind him.

"Allow me to introduce to you Gadifer de la Salle." Jean said, "trusted leader of men and veteran of a hundred battles." Gadifer was nearly as tall as Guadarfia. He puffed his chest out and lifted his head before giving the shallowest of bows. Guadarfia studied the metal breast plate. He muttered a few words.

"The king asks if he may touch your metal skin." Isabel translated.

"Well of course monsieur, of course you may." he smiled as Guadarfia reached out and ran his fingers slowly across his mirror-polished chest plate. Much to Gadifer´s surprise the King rapped his knuckles against it and uttered some words.

"It would make a good drum." Isabel said. Gadifer looked slightly affronted, but Jean laughed and stepped forward to steer the King towards Father Verrier who stood fizzing with energy a few paces beyond the knights with Brother Bontier at his side.

Jean introduced them to the King. The King enquired why servants of a powerful god dressed so modestly. Nichel sneered behind the King´s back as his eyes dropped to see the Priests´ simple sandals on their dusty feet.

Jean watched the holy man closely. Winning him over could mean the difference between success and failure. The King didn´t introduce him to Father Verrier. Jean detected the slight, he saw it delivered and felt. If there were a rift between the two most important men on the island, it would make his task so much easier.

****

Berthin was counting shekels in his head. The big savage would be worth a fortune in the Arab fighting pits. He was working out exactly how much when Gadifer marched over. Berthin stepped forward to meet him. The old man got as close to Berthin as his armour plate would allow and spoke quietly.

"We are going inside to discuss terms. Stay out here with the men and keep them under control. I want no fighting while we talk peace, understand?"

"Understood monsieur." replied Berthin sharply. Gadifer flicked his eyes over the knights and noticed Big Perrin leering and snarling at a young Majo stood a few paces away.

"Keep a tight rein monsieur. I fear that some members of our company are beginning to get a little lary." Gadifer said, pointing Perrin out with a nod of the head.

"I will monsieur." Berthin replied with a roll of the eyes. "The sun´s gone to his head I wouldn´t wonder. I´ll sort him out now."

"Good man! Well, if all´s in order with you out here, I will go and make history in there." Gadifer turned and marched away to join Bethencourt who along with the Priests and the savages were entering the large hut at the other side of the clearing.

Berthin waited until they had all entered before ordering the men to stand down. They began to disperse, seeking shade between the huts. Old trees grew around the huts, their branches swayed and whispered in the wind. The sun was at its highest point. Waves of heat rose from the baking surface of the plaza. Berthin escaped the heat, following Big Perrin and William around the back of one of the huts. Both men collapsed against the rough bark of a fat trunked old tree.

"Berthin!" William hailed noticing Berthin behind them for the first time. "Join us for a touch of refreshment." He reached inside his tunic and pulled out a small flask. Perrin snatched it away. "Oi!" William complained. Perrin unstopped the flask and took a swig. He coughed and spluttered, spilling half a mouthful down the front of his tunic.

"That's disgusting." he said before taking another deep swig and belching loudly. "That's better." he said thumping his chest and holding the flask out to William who snatched it back. He took a quick swig before offering it to Berthin. Berthin could see the fumes of the brandy escaping the neck of the flask and declined.

"Your loss." said Big Perrin snatching the flask back and taking another drink.

"Go easy." Berthin warned, "We might still have to fight our way out of this place."

"I'll need a drink if I have to come up against that giant. Did you see the size of him?" William said, taking back the flask.

"He's nothing." said Perrin, spitting a big glob into the ground. "I've had bigger than him before."

"When?" asked William.

"Lots of times."

"And the Virgin Mary's my sister."

"I've had bigger than her too." William shook his head and took another drink.

"Seriously though, how much do you think a big fucker like him would fetch?"

Berthin's mind was asking the same question.

"It will be a lot more if he's undamaged." he said, fixing Perrin with a level stare.

"What do you mean?" Perrin asked, snatching the flask back from William.

"You have to rein yourself in and stop antagonising the monkeys."

"Me!" Perrin spluttered. "*I do not antagonise anybody.* Show me anyone who says I do and I'll batter them." He tilted his head back and took another drink, grumbling under his breath.

Berthin waited for a second to see if any irony was intended. He suspected not.

"He has got a point." William said.

"What's that?"

"This isn't what we expected when we signed up. *A quick in and out. Bash some savages, take their gold.* That's how you sold it to me."

"Well, that's how I heard it." Perrin said.

"It hasn't turned out that way old friend. It looks like we are going to be here for a very long time, and we cannot draw attention to ourselves." Perrin puffed up, a look of hurt crossed his features. William continued in a tone laced with sarcasm. "Yes! yes I know you're only fooling around, having some fun."

"That's all it is:" Perrin said, his face as innocent as a little boy who just ate all the pies.

"But not everybody shares your humour." William continued turning to face Perrin "How many times have I told you the same? We must tread carefully from here on in, and that does not mean picking fights with every monkey in the yard. We need them to come to us when the time is right, not run away from us."

"Even the Old Man has noticed you pulling faces." Berthin added.

"Who? Gadifer?"

"The very same. And if he's noticed you, you can bet it won't be long before the Peacock swivels his eye towards you too. I… We do not need that kind of scrutiny if we have any chance of success. If you can't keep a low profile, I'll have no choice but to drop you."

"Drop me! You wouldn't fucking dare."

"Try me."

"We should fucking drop you, you jumped up… Do you know how many years we've been at this?"

"I do, that's why I consider you an asset. But as soon as you become a liability, you become useless to me."

"Listen to him Perrin." William said, seeing a blackness in Berthin's eyes that chilled him to the bone. "I'd prefer to be with you than without you."

"What you saying? You'd ditch me too?" scoffed Perrin.

"I´m here for the money old friend. You can see for yourself what´s happening here. Gadifer and Bethencourt treating with the monkeys. They´ll get everything, we´ll get nothing but endless guard duty. We´ll be stuck here until the Priest has baptised them all. No! That´s it for me. If this man tells me he´s got a plan to get me rich quick, then I´m taking it and getting off this shithouse rock. With or without you."

Perrin cowed. He folded his arms and looked away. "Fucking charming." he harrumphed.

Berthin gave a swift nod to William, grateful for his intervention and help dealing with the big fool. He turned and walked away, stopping at the edge of the central plaza where he paused to look around.

Most of the savages were standing next to the meeting hut. Some had drifted closer to the knights sheltering in the shadows. Martin stood to the left and had a small crowd of curious savages pointing and peering at his trumpet. Martin lifted it to his lips and blew a note that sounded like a wet fart. His audience of savages fell about laughing.

Berthin switched his gaze to the other side of the square where a pair of Gadifer´s old knights were tempting a small group of savages closer by holding out strips of meat. One had the bravery to accept it and then the temerity to give the knight a strip of meat from his own pack in return. Berthin shivered with disgust and looked away.

Something caught his attention in the blur of his eye and he refocused to see a savage staring straight back at him. It was the same one he had warned Perrin about earlier. The one who looked as if he understood their words.

An enormous roar drew his attention back to Gadifer´s men, one of whom had the unfortunate gift of sounding like a charging bull when he laughed. He stood clutching his balls and pointing to the meat his companion was biting into.

Berthin looked back to find the staring savage. He was no longer there.

****

"Alfonso." Guadarfia said for the third time before pointing to Isabel.

"Is-a-bel." she pronounced clearly.

"Isabel" Guadarfia repeated then nodded, asking something else in his language, making Nichel scoff into his sleeve. Isabel turned to Father Verrier.

"Mence Guadarfia asks if everybody will be required to take a God name."

"It is the way, once you are baptised and brought under the protection of God´s Holy Light. You are reborn and therefore require a new name." the Priest answered.

Guadarfia spoke again directing his attention to Jean, Isabel translating as he spoke.

"I heard that in your land, Tyterogaka is named *The Island of Lancalote*. My mother told stories of a man called Lancelote who came here and tried to claim the island as his own. He named himself King. Do you know this man?"

"No your Grace, I do not, but I know of him. A Genoese gentleman, or rather charlatan, who lied and stole his way around the world. The island was named for him on maps drawn by his own countrymen, later changed to Lancarote on subsequent charts. We have not come to force names upon you nor your island. We come in peace, offering the protection of our sponsors to you and your people."

"You come in peace, dressed for war?"

"We are prepared for war, but war with your enemies. We come with our steel to protect you from those who would do you harm. The slavers who take your people and the pirates who take your food. We have come dressed and armed to face them, to make this island a haven, safe from the scourge of their craven ways.

"I have fifty heavily armed men with me on one ship. Each and every one of them bastard dogs of war who go where I point them. Good King Enrique has over one hundred such ships, each with another hundred iron warriors on board, all directed by him to where he wants them to go. King Enrique has the strength and the power to protect you, or to crush you."

"If I accept this protection, what will you ask for in return?"

"Trade."

"We already have trade."

"Not at the moment you don´t. The pirates take what they want and leave you with nothing. I will take everything you produce and pay you well for it. All the dragon´s blood, leather, tallow, lichen, salt you can produce. I will guarantee that it finds its way to market. You will be paid in silver and gold, and when Your Grace, you have silver and gold in your hands, you can have anything you like. That is if, and only if you accept the protection I am offering."

"If we do not?"

"Then others will come and take everything by force. Alfonso and Isabel have seen with their own eyes the size of the armies and navies the Northern Kings control. They are ruthless, without compassion, they will come and lay waste to your island and culture." Jean was pleased to see Alfonso nodding. Guadarfia saw it too and sat back.

"Only under King Enrique´s protection, enforced by my knights, blessed by the Holy Church of Rome, will your future be secure. I am offering you the choice between life with us, or death at the hands of others."

Nichel began furiously whispering into Guadarfia´s ear. Jean turned to Isabel and Alfonso for a translation but the two of them sat stubbornly watching the Holy Man without offering to translate. Guadarfia looked at Jean and held up a hand to quiet the agitated holy man. He took a deep breath and addressed Jean one more time.

"I have much to discuss with my people. You may return to your camp with your men. I will deliver my answer to you there when it is decided."

He stood quickly, followed by Beselch and Nichel. Jean got to his feet and bowed quickly, taking the dismissal with as much humility as he possessed. Father Verrier, Bontier and the two translators stood too. Gadifer clanked to his side, he had been stood up for the entire meeting.

"I look forward to hearing from you." Jean said holding out his hand. Guadarfia looked at it, not knowing what to do until Alfonso explained. Guadarfia half smiled and took Jean´s hand inside his massive fist and squeezed. Jean swallowed and tried his best to return the smile while the bones in his hand cracked painfully.

21

Eagle Claw Bay, Lancarote,
August 23rd, 1402

The King gifted land to Jean around Eagle Claw Bay. Jean decided to name it Rubicon. He told Gadifer it was in honour of the great general Julius Caesar when dedicating it, which seemed to please the old warrior tremendously.

Work had gone on a pace to begin constructing a small fort, come chapel on the site. Many knights had discarded their weapons and armour for aprons and tools. From dawn till dusk there was the constant sound of chipping and banging as the artisan knights shaped rocks into building blocks. The camp bustled with as many Majos as knights, sent by Guadarfia to help with the construction. They dragged huge blocks of stone on wooden sleds to the masons who split them and sent them to the builders to lay.

With the Majo´s help, the stonework progressed at a swift pace and already the outside walls of the fort were nearly complete. It was a square structure built on the axis of the compass with large turrets jutting out of the four corners. Beneath the main hall a rough cellar had been scratched into the ground to house an armoury, a crude dungeon and food store. Several large trees from the north of the island had been felled to make the roofing joists. A team of carpenters were chipping away with chisels and planes, watched by a group of curious natives.

Gadifer saw one of the carpenters demonstrate to a pair of natives how his plane shaved a length of timber. He showed them what to do and then handed his plane to one of the onlookers. Gadifer was impressed to see the young native copy the carpenter's actions carefully before handing the tool back.

"Well done." said Gadifer under his breath. He was about to go cast his eye over another group of workers when Bethencourt's man Philip caught up to him and told him to meet with Bethencourt down on the beach. Jean was pacing up and down the high tide mark when Gadifer found him, digging a furrow in the sand with his bare feet.

"You asked to see me?" said Gadifer coolly.

They had crossed words a few days earlier when Jean had insisted on taking Martin and three other knights with him to attend the native Beñasmen festival at Guadarfía's palace. Gadifer had argued that the men were needed on the building site, but Jean had insisted they accompany him to the feast. Gadifer was annoyed in no small part because he hadn't been invited to attend the feast himself. Jean had explained that Gadifer was originally invited but Jean had declined the invitation on his behalf, explaining that he was needed on site to oversee the building works.

Gadifer's ire had abated somewhat by the time Jean returned the night before, only to be reignited when Jean paraded into camp with gifts from the King. There were several vats of rich goat fat, bushels of fine leather and baskets filled to the brim with orchil and dragon's blood. It was a king's ransom in trade goods and would go a long way towards paying Gadifer's men, but Jean had squirreled the goods away in his own personal store. He appeared to be busy working on fortifying his own personal fortune while everybody else was hard at work constructing the fort, and Gadifer didn't like it.

"Ah Gadifer, yes." said Jean stopping his pacing to face him. "I see the works have progressed well in my absence."

"Yes, we should get the roof joists in place by the end of the week. I imagine we'll be able to use the chapel within a fortnight."

"Excellent." replied Jean. "In that case, I think it high time we pressed on with the next part of the mission."

"But we haven't finished here yet." Gadifer protested.

"I disagree. The island is tamed."

"Hardly tamed Monsieur. We still have defences to build."

"Defences against what? The natives are practically doing all the work for us. There must be over a hundred of them up there labouring. Father Verrier is happier than I've ever seen him, Guadarfia has virtually ordered his people to attend catechism classes. He sits in his palace now trying to decide on his own *God Name*. What more is there to do that we can't leave to Berthin to manage while we go and explore Erbania?"

"I suppose I could free up a dozen or so men."

"That is all we need to scout the land and find where the natives are before leading a full invasion force. It took us how many... three or four days to conquer this island? I can't see it taking much longer than that over there. Hells, we might even have them eating out of our hands before the roof is put on the chapel."

"With respect Monsieur, we got lucky here. The pirates and slavers drove them into our arms. It wasn't so much conquering we did here as provide them with a service they needed."

"And are willing to pay us for."

"Us? Pay us? The only goods I have seen come to us have gone directly to your personal store."

"Ah! I see now. That has upset you." Jean said making Gadifer twitch uncomfortably. He had been goaded into going on the offensive and he didn't like it. Past battles were won by forcing his opponents to do the same thing. His face coloured, embarrassed to lose his composure, albeit briefly. "The goods I have locked away are items of tribute, from one King to another." Jean explained. "From Guadarfia to King Enrique, to show good will. They are not *mine*."

"King Enrique? And what of our own dear King Charles?"

"When our *own dear* King Charles provides us with funds and men, he will receive tribute of his own."

"I have to say, I am not completely comfortable treating directly with the Castilian King. I swore my oaths to France and the protection of her borders."

"And France will benefit too one day, but for now we owe Enrique more. Listen, when we have everything built here, the fort, the chapel and the trading posts, we will have more than enough to go around, enough to keep everyone happy, including our own King Charles. In order to reach that stage we need solid foundations beneath us. We need to advance our plans and reach our goals quickly and efficiently.

"As I look around, I see some knights stood doing nothing, you and I included..." Gadifer let that one go. There was only one of the pair doing nothing and it wasn't him. "...which is why I suggest we load up the ship with a small expeditionary force and move on to our next objective. A dozen or so men will suffice for one week of exploration. We could leave tomorrow and be back before anybody notices we've gone."

"If your mind is made up to go, then why wait until tomorrow? We could be there this evening and begin searching at first light."

"Even better. Do you think you and your men could be ready to leave after lunch?"

"My men and I are always ready."

"Then let us be gone. You organise your men and I will brief Father Verrier and Berthin."

"Very well." said Gadifer.

Jean nodded curtly and marched away up the path to the camp. Gadifer watched him until he was out of sight, his chest puffed out like a strutting cock. Gadifer's blood was up. Jean had a way of irritating him as no other could. He was impatient and reckless and it didn't sit well on Gadifer's shoulders to feel that way.

He walked along the beach to where the ship's dinghy rested on the sand. There should have been a man with the boat but Gadifer couldn't see him. He kicked the side of the dinghy in frustration. An angry seaman jumped up from the bilge where he had been asleep beneath a pile of empty sacks.

"What the... who the?" he screamed before seeing Gadifer looking down at him with his hands on his hips.

"Did you sleep well boy?" Gadifer asked.

"I wasn't sleeping Monsieur, I was looking for leaks."

"Did you find any?"

"Find any what?"

"Never mind. Just row me out to the ship."

Gadifer bent to start pushing the dinghy down the beach. The seaman leapt out and helped push. Gadifer sprang aboard gracefully when the dinghy hit the water and sat down on the stern bench. The seaman splashed a few more feet before springing aboard. He slotted a pair of oars into the oarlocks and began rowing feverishly.

"Careful boy." Gadifer roared, "You´re splashing water everywhere."

The seaman calmed down a little and dug the oars deeper, straining to look over his shoulder to avoid looking Gadifer in the face.

The dinghy bumped against the side of the ship and Gadifer flew up the ladder onto the deck. Not a single member of the crew was visible, not even a watch posted up in the crow´s nest, if there was one there he was sleeping. The air hummed with the stench of grime and neglect. Gadifer curled his nose in disgust. He stormed through the door in the stern castle and made directly for the Master´s cabin.

He burst through the door without knocking.

"Monsieur le Brument, if you please!" Gadifer barked loudly. A cursing jumble of cotton and flesh erupted from the stained bed in the corner of the tiny cabin.

"You damned..!" le Brument sat up, tugging his shirt down to cover his cock with one hand, he lifted the other to push the greasy mop of hair away from his face and stared at Gadifer through red rimmed eyes. Clumps of white pasty sludge gathered at the corners of his open mouth and collected in his thick beard. Spittle flew as he yelled.

"Where in hell do you think you are." he screamed, scrambling from his bed and grabbing his britches from the floor. "A knock on the door of civility wouldn´t go amiss Monsieur." le Brument said as he strained to fasten his britches. "What the hell gives you the right to come crashing into my cabin without being invited, in such an aggressive manner?"

"This is my ship. I have the right to go wherever I choose upon it. You, in case you have forgotten, are employed by me to maintain it. Your primary task is to see to the basic upkeep and cleanliness on board. From what I see monsieur, you have control of neither of those things at the moment, lounging in your cabin like a spent whore while rats run wild through the hold."

"In case you have forgotten monsieur, you have failed to pay me to run *your* ship for many weeks now." le Brument spat back testily.

"The debts accrued in lieu of payment to me and my crew are substantial, indeed we are owed more than this ship is worth."

"Why you!" Gadifer reared up menacingly in le Brument's face. "You will be paid exactly what you deserve. Which, seeing how little you and your men are actually doing, will not be much."

"Oh really. So you intend to renege on our contract?"

"You monsieur, have already *reneged* on your side of our deal. This ship is an absolute disgrace, as are you. I should drag you out of here and hang your worthless arse from the top of the mast." Gadifer screamed at le Brument, his nose an inch away from the Master's. "We sail for Lobos and Erbania today, and as God is my witness, if this ship isn't shining from top to bottom when we embark in three hours' time, I will have you keel hauled and flogged. Do you understand me?" he said, punctuating every syllable with a poke in le Brument's shoulder.

"I asked if you understand me monsieur." Gadifer hissed as le Brument trembled before him.

"I ASKED IF YOU UNDERSTAND ME MONSIEUR!" Gadifer roared, le Brument jumped back and raised his hands.

"YES I UNDERSTAND YOU MONSIEUR!" he screamed back, sweat dripping from his face.

"Good." Gadifer turned round abruptly and marched from the cabin.

****

Norstar saw Gadifer sat upright in the back of the dinghy as it rowed back to shore. The ship burst into life behind him with men swabbing the decks and climbing through the rigging. The big man climbed out of the dinghy as soon as it hit the beach and stumbled across the sand back towards the camp.

"Sand is the great leveller." Rayco chuckled. "Even the mighty warrior walks like a child to cross it."

Norstar laughed.

"He doesn't look all that mighty to me." Fayna said, wrinkling her nose.

"He looked mightier in his metal suit." Norstar said. "They all did. But I will give them this, they are fine builders." He looked over at the fortress growing steadily upon the bluff like a wart on a chin. Piles of cut stone and timber surrounded the site, picked over and moved from one place to another by Majos. He had heard that many had answered Guadarfia´s call to help the French, he hadn´t thought it would be this many though.

The tent village adjoining the fortress site had also grown and was almost entirely surrounded on the landward side by the stone wall. It was much taller and wider since Norstar had last seen it. A couple of stone huts had been built and a guardhouse added next to the gate, even a new kitchen block had been built, from where steam billowed into the air carrying the smell of stewing meat through the camp.

There were certainly more tools on display than weapons, but Norstar did notice a few pairs of guards shouldering pikes and wearing chain mail wandering around.

"We should go and take a closer look."

They walked down to the gateway in the middle of the wall. A rough wooden sign hung above the entrance with the name "Rubicon" carved into it. Two guards stood leaning heavily on spears, sweat rolling down their faces from beneath their helmets.

"Three more bloody savages for the working party." one of them commented. His companion chuckled. Norstar smiled dumbly and nodded. The guard lifted a tired arm and waved them through the gateway.

They picked their way through the mess of guy ropes between the tall cylindrical tents. The place smelled musty, thick with the hum of stale piss and sweat. They passed a tent with the flap open wide and saw a pair of men squaring away bedrolls and packing clothes and weapons into canvas sacks. The wall of the tent next door suddenly dropped to the ground, revealing another pair of knights with their belongings bundled up around them.

One of them called out and pressed Norstar, Rayco and Fayna into helping bring down the rest of the tent.

The men thanked them graciously when, ten minutes later, they had the tent and poles rolled and tied on the ground. They continued on their way and soon stepped past the last row of the tent village and saw the full vista of the building site open up before them.

There were artisans working everywhere, chipping and sawing. The air was heavy with the dust of wood and stone, it covered everything. Majo workers wore it like a second skin as they laboured carrying stone blocks between masons and builders.

Norstar spotted Isabel standing quietly at the Priest's shoulder in the centre of the site. They stood with a pair of Normans, the Priest was pointing to a plan one of them held in his hand. The other was shaking his head and stroking his chin as the Priest talked.

Rayco stepped towards them. Norstar grabbed him by the elbow and pulled him back.

"Not now Brother."

"I have to speak with her."

"There will be a time, but not now." Rayco appeared to relax and Norstar let his arm go. He turned round to find Fayna. She stood behind them looking in the other direction, watching a young man in a makeshift forge pounding on an anvil, beating a glowing iron peg into shape. He held it up to his face and examined his work. He caught sight of Fayna watching and stared back at her. His face slipped into a friendly smile and Norstar saw his eyes wander up and down his daughter's body.

"Fayna." he growled. She whipped around to face him.

"What!" she asked sharply.

A loud hiss dragged their attention back to the Smith. Steam billowed from the bucket at his feet. He pulled the spike from the sizzling water and lifted it to his face, doing a poor job of pretending to examine it while appraising Fayna. He bit his bottom lip seductively. Norstar felt the urge to drive the metal spike through his sooty face.

"Let's go!" Norstar snapped. Fayna stepped up to his side and nodded ahead. Norstar turned to see Rayco had already covered half the distance to Isabel.

"Shit!"

He broke into a run and reached out a second too late to catch Rayco before the Priest turned and saw them.

"Ah! Rayco isn't it, and Norstar?" the Priest said with Isabel translating. "These are Monsieur Avago's sons." he said to the Frenchmen who simply nodded and carried on looking at the plan.

"How is your father?" the Priest enquired. "We haven't had the pleasure of his company for several days."

"We have seen less of him than you. He is with King Guadarfia."

"Yes I know. Charming fellow. And who is this you have brought with you?" he asked, noticing Fayna stood behind Norstar. Norstar nudged her forward.

"Fayna." Rayco said, "The daughter of my brother."

"Your brother is truly blessed to have such an angelic daughter." The Priest said bowing his head. There wasn't a trace of angelic in the look Fayna gave him in return.

"I am very pleased you have all come to help us today." He turned to the Frenchman. "You see messieurs, ask and the Lord shall provide. The two pairs of hands you said you were short have arrived."

He turned back to Rayco and Norstar. "If you two strapping young men could help Messieurs Salerne and Maulcon up on the high wall, it would be very much appreciated. As for you my lovely young lady, I have a special task for you. If you would like to accompany Isabel and myself."

Fayna huffed, ready to complain but Norstar hushed her with a *Tsssk*. She lowered her head and followed the Priest and Isabel back to the tents. Norstar and Rayco went with the two Frenchmen to the seaward side of the fort where a small wheel crane hoisted blocks up to the top of the wall. They climbed up a ladder and were directed with pointing fingers and mimed actions to assist the men unloading stone blocks from the crane's cradle.

It was hot heavy work and they toiled for hours without rest. Just after midday when the sun was reaching its highest point, a commotion in the tent village caught Norstar's attention. Everybody stopped work to watch as Bethencourt and Gadifer strode out of the camp followed by a line of knights. Behind them trailed a crèche of servants and squires, heavily laden with canvass bundles. Brother Bontier and Alfonso the translator brought up the rear.

The procession marched down to the beach where boats were waiting. In two trips everything was ferried out to the ship. As soon as the last man climbed aboard, the sails bloomed and the ship came to life. She swung around and let the wind take her off to the South.

Norstar casually sidled up to two masons sat watching the ship leave and listened to them talk.

"…no, it's most of the Gascons, Gadifer's men."

"I saw. It would have been nice to be offered though, get away from here for a few days."

"You are not wrong my friend."

"We should have all gone. There might be some real fighting to do over there."

"Bethencourt's got the idea that all the other islands will be as easy as this one to break. I hope he's right, it's too damn hot to fight in this weather. Peaceful is good for me."

"Really? I thought you would have jumped at the chance."

"I did when I took his coin but now, I'm not so sure. Maybe I'm getting old, but the more time I spend here the more I like it. I could see myself with a small homestead one day. Maybe even plant a little vineyard, take a new wife and start a new life."

"Bollocks. You'd never grow good grapes in this shit."

"They had some fine local wines in Cadiz. I don't imagine it's any hotter and dryer here, especially up in the hills."

"Wait and see what the winter brings."

"We'll see where we are come winter. We might have to go rescue Gadifer and the Gascons."

"We might need rescuing ourselves with young Berthin left in charge."

"Ach! Don't go too hard on the lad. He's a bit eager that's all. Weren't we all at his age?"

"Maybe, but I've been hearing a few things about the donkeys he's gathering around him."

"Didn't one of them, the swarthy one, William. Didn't he talk to you last night after supper?"

"He did. He took five minutes to ask me anything but the question he wanted to ask. I don't trust him. He's a sly one alright."

"I haven´t spoken to him."

"Best thing you could do."

"Speak of the devil and he shall appear. Here they come."

Berthin walked out of the tent village leading five guards wearing mail shirts and carrying long pikes. They picked their way through the building site and made for the cliff top next to the fortress. They stopped to look out to sea just below where Norstar stood. He ducked out of sight as Berthin looked up at the fortress.

"Oi! What are you doing?" one of the masons yelled at Norstar. He thought quickly, picked up a stone block lying at his feet and hoisted it on his shoulder. He glanced back over the wall and was horrified to see Berthin staring straight back up at him. A chill ran down his spine.

"Give it to me." said the mason impatiently. Norstar hefted the stone into the mason´s arms and then hurried off to the other side of the fortress. He didn´t see Berthin again for the rest of the afternoon.

Tools went down when one of the cook´s mates wandered up to the edge of the site and bashed a huge ladle against a metal pot to announce it was time to eat. The whole site just upped and left en masse.

Norstar climbed down from the roof of the fort and waited at the foot of the ladder for Rayco.

"What is it brother?" Rayco asked, "Are you not hungry?"

"What? Yes, No." Norstar managed to spit out, "I´ve got an uneasy feeling about something, it´s taken my appetite away."

"Tell me." Rayco enquired, suddenly serious.

"Remember the sly one from the meeting with Gadifer?"

"The one who couldn´t stop staring at you?"

"The very same."

"Go on."

"He´s here, and from what I´ve heard he is now in command. He is dangerous. He has a viper´s look in his eye. Have you seen Fayna?"

"She was giving water to the men earlier, I haven´t seen her since."

"We should find her and go. This man has placed his evil eye upon me. I need to wash it off. Find Fayna and bring her down to the beach, we´ll leave that way."

Rayco nodded and made his way into the camp. Norstar watched him go, making sure he wasn't followed. The coast appeared to be clear. There was nobody left at the building site or lingering around the tents, so he made his way down to the beach.

There were a handful of people in the water rinsing away the smell of work and dust. It looked so inviting that Norstar couldn't resist the temptation to kick off his moccasins and dive into the water. The cool clear water was invigorating. He could smell the dust in his nostrils as the salt water flooded every part of his body, purging his skin and soothing his aching muscles. The water rushed over him and found a couple of blisters on his palms. He felt the sting as he scrubbed his fingers through his hair, working right down to the scalp to dislodge tiny stones trapped next to his skin. He dived down again and again, stretching his limbs with a few long strokes under the water before bobbing back up to the surface. He kicked hard and stroked furiously with his arms for a few seconds to loosen his shoulders before making his way back to the beach. The last of the people were walking up the path to the camp as his feet hit the warm dry sand.

He bent over and shook the water from his hair before whipping it back over his shoulder. He opened his eyes and froze.

Berthin stepped out from behind a rock twenty feet in front of him, cradling a loaded crossbow. His right forefinger tapped the side of the trigger.

"Well, what do we have here?" Berthin drawled. His words slow, sly and dripping with malice. Norstar stood rooted to the spot while Berthin edged closer. "I see you my little savage. I remember you well. You are not the same as the others. I see it in your skin and your eyes. You understand every word I say don't you savage?" Norstar stood still, mute, his eyes fixed on the crossbow.

"I've asked about you," Berthin continued, taking another small step closer, "but nobody seems to want to tell me anything about you apart from your name. Norstar." His finger continued a rhythmic tap on the trigger guard. "Even your name is different from the other savages. Norstar... *North Star*... Why is that?" He cocked his head to one side. "Did you fall from a ship and get washed up here? Where are you from *North Star*?"

Norstar felt the pull of the knife on his hip. It was calling out for him to bury its blade in the chest of this sneering weasel. He forced himself to be calm, staying as still as a statue while Berthin took another small step closer.

"I don´t trust you *North Star*." The words oozed out of his mouth like puss from an open wound. "I feel the eyes of a spy upon me every time you are near. Have you been sent by your King to spy on us North Star? I hope not."

The sound of falling stones brought Berthin to a halt. Fayna and Rayco were coming down the path to the beach.

"Savages." Berthin said, turning to watch Fayna and Rayco clamber down the path. "Some of my men would love to take turns fucking your women but I can´t see the appeal myself. Grubby little creatures, I bet their cunts have teeth. Maybe I´ll ask this one for a look,"

Norstar´s hand jerked towards his knife, but Berthin was quicker. He raised his crossbow to aim between Norstar´s eyes.

"I knew you understood me *North Star*." he said triumphantly. A cruel smile twisted his lips. "All it takes is the right key to open the lock. She is not your woman, far too young for that, your daughter perhaps?" Norstar´s breath was quickening, blood rushed to his face. "Ah yes! Daughter. Maybe I´ll introduce her to Big Perrin. I´ve heard he has quite the gift for breaking wild young fillies."

Fayna and Rayco were now only a few short paces from where the two men stood facing each other. Rayco reached for the hilt of his knife but Norstar signalled for him to still his hand.

"Very wise." Berthin said. "I would hate to have to kill you all now. You are worth so much more to me alive." He raised his crossbow and turned to look Fayna up and down. "Take your little bitch and your friend and be gone from here. If I catch you snooping around here again, I will put a bolt through your heart and serve your girl up to my men. You understand?" Norstar didn´t move. "Of course you understand me. You may be brighter than the other monkeys on this rock, but you are still just a savage to me… North Star."

Berthin casually turned and began to walk away slowly, lifting the crossbow to rest on his shoulder.

Rayco and Fayna rushed over to Norstar. He shook his head to stop them speaking and led them away. He was still shaking with rage as they slipped over the cliff at the far end of the beach, well beyond the camp wall.

"What just happened?" Fayna asked.

Norstar turned to her, his eyes bulging, the veins standing out on his neck. "The bear has shown his teeth." he said looking back in the direction of the fortress. "Take one last look if you need to. You will not be returning."

****

Berthin was strutting like a bull entering a field of cows when he arrived at the kitchen block. He paused to look around the trestle tables where the company sat tucking into their evening meals. There were as many savages as French sat mopping up their stringy goat stew with stale flat bread. Much to his dismay, they were sharing tables and trying to communicate with each other. When the works started a few short weeks earlier, the two peoples didn´t mix, but now they shared bread like old friends. The sight dulled the joy Berthin was feeling.

His joy dulled further when he spotted the Priest sat next to the translator girl, deep in discussion with a group of savages. It was a shame they hadn´t gone to Erbania with the Peacock and Gadifer. He didn´t care for the Priest. He found him patronising and superior, like he always knew better than everyone else. Hearing the old fool´s voice now scrubbed the final spark of elation from Berthin´s soul. His authority wouldn´t go uncontested with that pious piece of shit questioning him at every turn.

At the last table in the row sat a small group of men, notable for the lack of savages amongst them. Berthin pulled up a stool and took his place at the end of their table. A young serving girl passed by and thumped a bowl of stew and a chunk of bread down on the table in front of him. He grabbed her arm as she turned away and ordered her to bring more wine.

Jacquet the baker brought a fresh jug of wine a few moments later and forced his bulk onto the bench next to Berthin.

"Did you do it?" he asked leaning on his elbows and shoving his waxy face far too close to his own for Berthin´s liking.

"It´s done."

"How?"

"I told him if I were to see him around here again I´d let Big Perrin fuck his little daughter… over his twitching corpse."

"That would work." nodded Jacquet approvingly sitting back and rubbing his belly. "Where is monsieur le Big?"

"Walking the walls with Gillet." William answered from down the table. "It´s best if he´s not in the same space as the monkeys for too long." The men chuckled quietly into their food, "It´s for his own good."

"I see." Jacquet said vacantly. It was clear he had no idea what William was talking about. "So, when do we make a move?" he asked, leaning forward again.

"When the time is right." answered Berthin filling a cup from the wine jug.

"Why not now?"

"Because now is not the right time." Berthin answered, giving Jacquet a hard stare. "I´ve told you. All is in hand."

"I don´t see why we don´t go now with Gadifer, Bethencourt and most of the Gascons away." Jacquet persisted.

"Will you keep your fucking voice down." Berthin hissed. "Do you want everybody knowing our business?"

"No of course not." Jacquet said leaning further forward. "I just don´t see why we can´t strike now."

"Because now is not the right time." Berthin said through clenched teeth. "We have no ship and still need more men. Speaking of which, how is the recruitment going?" he asked wanting anybody else but the Baker to speak.

"I´d say we´re having some success." said William. "Pernet and I had a good talk with Jean le Brun today. He´s getting tired of lugging rocks around."

"I wondered about him. What did you tell him?"

"Nothing much."

"Keep it that way. I just saw him talking with Courtille, Gadifer's minstrel."

"Yeah! We talked to him too. He's not happy that Martin is getting all the attention. These musicians are more precious than a tower full of princesses."

"Their loyalty evaporates like a shallow puddle on a hot day. See who else is not happy, but be careful. The Priest is still here and could get in our way."

"So let's just *off* the Priest then." Jacquet said matter-of-factly.

"Will you just stop talking now and fuck off back to the kitchen." Berthin said, rubbing his eyes.

"What's wrong with that?" Jacquet asked, his voice rising to a squeal.

"Dealing in slaves is one thing, everybody does it." William answered for Berthin who was struggling not to punch the portly baker. "Even the Pope has slaves rowing his barges. But killing his Priests! You'd be hunted down and crucified by the Pope's enforcers."

"It can always be made to look like an accident."

"I really need you to fuck off now before I accidentally stick my knife in you." said Berthin, the look in his eye leaving Jacquet in no doubt that leaving would be his best option. His knee smacked the table as he struggled to step over the bench knocking several cups over. He was followed from the table by an earful of curses.

"Why do we have to put up with that fool?" Pernet the Blacksmith asked, mopping spilled wine from the table with his sleeve.

"We need every man we can get," Berthin replied, "until we don't need them anymore." he added under his breath.

22

Port of Lobos, Erbania,

September 1st, 1402

Gadifer led the men back to the beach, the hot sun beat down on their backs. They had spent seven days camping in the shadow of an ancient volcano searching for natives. Despite finding many trails and signs of life, they didn´t see any of the elusive tribesmen. They decided to return to the ship and sail further south to a river marked on the charts, believing they would stand a better chance of finding Erbania´s Majos near to a fresh water source, rather than continuing to wander aimlessly through the desolate northern wastelands.

They trudged through the deep sand towards the bay where the ship waited. The cooling hues of the deep blue sea beyond the hot white sand was welcoming on the eye but cruel on the rest of the senses. After a punishing hike across dry, arid land, it was fresh water and wine they craved more than anything. The beautiful turquoise water in the bay might as well have been acid for all the good it did them. Hardly a word was spoken, they didn´t have enough energy to speak.

The sun burned patches of skin on the back of Gadifer´s neck itched. His face was bombarded from all angles by flies. They rattled and buzzed under the rim of his helmet, exacerbating his mood. By the time they reached the rendezvous point he was at the end of his tether. He ripped off his helmet and threw it down in the sand, shed the pack from his back and emptied the last drops of water from a canteen over his fiery red neck.

He was disappointed to find no boats waiting on the beach to meet them. Gadifer looked around to make sure he was in the right place. The remains of their campfire from the first night were still visible under the shifting blanket of sand at the back of the beach, so this was where they landed. He looked out into the bay. The ship swung lazily on its anchor in the turquoise water, no more than six hundred paces away.

Gadifer lifted his hand to shield his eyes from the glare of the sun and squinted to see a couple of figures on the poop deck looking his way. He called out to them and began waving his arms in the air, the men didn't move. Before long, what appeared to be the entire crew joined them above decks. They stood staring back across the water at Gadifer and the bedraggled line of knights behind him.

After what seemed like an inexplicably long time, the ship's dinghy finally rowed out from behind the ship. Gadifer was surprised to see Colin le Brument, the Master's younger brother sat at the tiller. Like his brother, he had been at sea so long that his knees splayed out to the side. On dry land, the pair waddled like ducks carrying baskets of eggs, but on an open deck in a rough sea, they were as sure-footed as cats.

Colin remained seated as the dinghy hit the sand and slid to a stop. The two oarsmen leapt out and steadied the little boat, one either side of the prow.

"Brument! What in Hell is going on?" Gadifer walked forward to meet them. Colin lifted his head and mumbled something.

"Speak up man!" Gadifer roared.

"A w-w-word if you please." Colin managed to splutter. "Here on board... in private if you will."

"What?" Gadifer's head was in danger of exploding with the pressure of the outrage building inside it.

"I am not to come ashore. I have orders from the Master." Colin answered a little more confidently.

"This is ridiculous!" huffed Gadifer as he stomped round the dinghy and climbed aboard. He stood with his legs braced against the sides and looked down at Colin who shrank back into the stern rail. "I am here as you requested, now start talking."

"P-please be seated Monsieur." Colin stammered.

Gadifer gripped the hilt of his sword and took a step forward. "I'll..." was all he managed to say before a shrill whistle sounded down and to his right. He looked around to see one of the oarsmen taking his fingers out of his mouth.

"What in God's name?" Gadifer muttered.

"That was one whistle." Colin answered. "At three whistles, my brother leaves."

"Wha..! This is absurd."

"Not absurd at all Monsieur. It is the final straw. You have left us with no choice. If you please, be seated and we can get this over with."

"I ought to have you all flogged." Gadifer growled.

"Is that worth a whistle?" piped up the other oarsman, his fingers hovering close to his mouth. Gadifer turned to him staring incredulously.

"Nah, we´ll give him that one," replied his mate, "but keep your fingers ready." Gadifer turned back to Colin dumbstruck.

"Please Monsieur." Colin held out his hand inviting Gadifer to sit.

Gadifer took two slow deliberate steps forward and sat on the bench directly in front of Colin, their knees almost touching. Gadifer´s ice blue eyes didn´t waver as he stared into Colin´s face. Le Brument looked away, wringing his hands, his head ticking nervously as he searched for the words he´d practised. He took a shallow breath and began to speak, his head turned slightly away from Gadifer.

"Master le Brument will no longer be taking orders from you until you pay what is owed to us."

"In full!" piped up one of the oarsmen.

"Yes… In full." agreed Colin. "And I have been instructed to tell you that until such a payment is made…"

"To us all." the oarsman chipped in again.

"Of course to us all!" snapped Colin, "Will you be quiet and let me speak."

"Get on with it then."

"I will if you stop interrupting."

"For Heaven´s sake… This is absurd." Gadifer blustered getting to his feet and reaching for his sword. The oarsman whistled. "Will you stop that!" Gadifer turned and stared down at him.

"I will when you sit down." he replied, breaking out into three-toothed grin.

"Is there a problem?" Bethencourt called from up the beach where he stood huddled with the other knights.

"No. No!" answered Gadifer, "Nothing to worry about. We'll be on our way soon." Jean waved back and shrugged. Gadifer turned back to Colin and sat down.

"The Master…" Colin resumed, chewing the inside of his lips furiously, "no longer supports your little adventure…" Gadifer flinched. He almost reached for his sword again but checked himself. Colin made a show of turning to the oarsman and shaking his head quickly.

He leaned forward and looked down before lifting his sallow eyes to meet Gadifer's

"I implore you monsieur. Do not test my brother in this. Look to the ship and you will see that he has men in the tops ready to drop the sails." Gadifer glanced and saw that Colin spoke the truth.

"He'd leave you behind too." Gadifer sneered.

"We'd tip you overboard and be away long before any of your men could reach us." Colin answered cockily.

"This, monsieur, is mutiny. A dishonourable and shameless act. You will all hang for it."

"This *monsieur*, is business. The Master has a proposal."

"Pah!" barked Gadifer.

"We shall fulfil our obligation to convey you and your companions safely back to Rubicon. But no further, until you see fit to pay us."

"I have told your brother time and time again that you will be paid on completion of our mission, just like everybody else."

"But it's not like everybody else is it monsieur." Colin stared defiantly into Gadifer's eyes. "The good knights and their squires were paid handsomely before embarking on this… this… treasure hunt! One hundred francs a man, and more. We all heard him say it."

"Heard who say what?" Gadifer asked confused.

"One of your knights came and supped with us one evening, all friendly like. Drank most of our brandy and bragged about how much you gave him for doing nothing. How do you think that made us all feel eh? You paid us nothing and yet we have done everything. We haven't been paid enough to buy the holes to make nets with."

"Which knight spoke to you? Was it one of those here?" Gadifer asked, furious that a noble knight could act in such a manner.

"No no no. He isn't here, but that's hardly important right now. We will allow you the time it takes us to row back to the ship and bring back the longboat to decide if you want to leave with us on our terms, or stay here forever."

"And what terms are those?"

"That neither you, nor your son shall set foot upon the ship lest you seek retribution against my brother and the rest of us. We are honest sailors, not battle-hardened knights. We can't fight you, we have to use other means. We demand nothing more than what you promised to us."

"I find your timing incredible. What exactly do you need silver for down here? There are no brothels, no fighting pits to take your wagers!"

"That's not the principle, it's the right... I mean it's not the right, it's the money... no... It's not the point. There are always trades to make, debts to pay, some of us have families to feed. We are only asking for what is rightfully ours. Until we get it, neither you nor your son will be boarding the ship."

Gadifer felt like reaching across and throttling the smarmy little bilge rat, to hell with the consequences. He could grab Colin and hold him as a hostage, but reasoned le Brument would happily leave the slimy little turd behind and sail away. They had him over a barrel. He could surrender his ship to them and be humiliated, or be abandoned on this desert island, condemned to die with twenty innocent men. There was only one decision he could consciably make.

The Brument brothers were proving to be very shrewd operators despite their slovenly appearance and lax attitudes. Gadifer was amused to realise that in another life he would have been impressed by the brass balls they had shown him this day. In this life however, he would nail those brass balls to the mast at the first opportunity.

His face broke into a sinister smile causing the hairs to rise on the back of Colin's hand and the cocksure expression on his face to melt away.

"We shall discuss this further when we are all safely back in Rubicon." he said, a hint of menace in his tone. He stood abruptly causing Colin to jerk backwards. "Go. Return with the longboat swiftly. I want to sleep in my own bed tonight." He jumped down from the boat and walked away.

The oarsmen heaved the little boat back into the water and leapt aboard. Gadifer turned to watch them row back out to the ship. The squat form of Master le Brument stood on the poop deck watching. Gadifer snarled, cursing the day he had hired the fool. He turned to find the other knights led by Jean, walking down the beach to meet him.

"Gadifer! What on earth is happening?" Jean asked. "My God man! You're as white as a sheet!"

"Gentleman." Gadifer began, "I'm sorry to inform you that our expedition to further explore the island is indefinitely postponed. The crew has mutinied under le Brument's direction. They refuse to take us anywhere but Rubicon until they are paid a ransom."

The knights erupted with a barrage of questions and protests. Gadifer held his hands out and appealed for calm.

"Gentlemen. Gentlemen. Please! They have us at a disadvantage. I have no other option but to accede to their demands for now. I have given my word that no harm shall befall them."

"You have given *your* word, not mine." Remonet proclaimed, gripping the hilt of his sword. "I'll take these curs apart for slurring your honour monsieur."

"I thank you for your fealty, but unfortunately, Hannibal and I are to be held hostage to prevent that very thing happening. We will be in the dinghy, towed behind the ship back to Rubicon. Any sign of trouble and we are to be cut adrift."

The knights erupted once more. Once more, Gadifer tried to calm them.

"Gentlemen... Gentlemen... If you please. Please! I suggest we gather our things and be ready to depart when the boats return. I believe Master le Brument is quite serious and would have no qualms about leaving us all here to die."

****

Jean closed his eyes and felt the spray hit him in the face. It was so refreshing to feel cool water on his skin after baking in the dusty hills of

Erbania all week. His face tingled delightfully, but not enough to mask the sickness he felt in his stomach. He turned to look at Gadifer riding in the dinghy astern. He sat bolt upright on the stern bench next to Hannibal, an indefatigable smile twisted his lips into a madman's grimace. Both men were drenched to the bone. In a small way, Jean was enjoying Gadifer's discomfort. He deserved it. After all it was *his* failure to manage his affairs properly that had caused them to be hostages in Master le Brument's little game. But, these little games, whatever the cause, were threatening the whole mission with failure.

From his vantage point at the rear starboard quarter of the poop deck, Jean could see the greasy Master poke his head out from time to time. He cowered on the quarterdeck behind four of his largest men. Colin, the Master's slimy little brother stood with an axe poised over the rope tethering Gadifer's dinghy to the ship.

Jean had pushed his way past le Brument's men and climbed up to the poop deck as soon as he boarded, too tired and angry to be intimidated by them. The rest of the knights stood or sat in small groups on the main deck. Their mood was dark. Every time le Brument wandered into their line of sight, they jeered and cursed him. Jean knew he would have to intervene before the mood on board turned from dark to ugly. If things went too far and Gadifer cut adrift, they would all be lost.

He strode to the front of the poop deck and leaned against the rail.

"Master le Brument." Jean called down.

"Monsieur." le Brument answered, his head popping out from the shelter of the tiller house.

"A word if you please, in private." Le Brument thought for a moment before agreeing. He stepped out into the open and crossed to the steps.

"Shame on you!" called out a voice from the main deck.

"Craven dog!" called another. Knights hissed and booed as le Brument scurried up to the poop deck. Jean steered him towards the stern, the uproar from below tailed off as the pair ducked behind the sail and out of sight.

"This has all got terribly out of hand now Monsieur." Jean turned to le Brument. "You have made your point. It is not serving your cause to have Monsieur Gadifer spend any more time being humiliated in such an undignified manner."

"Monsieur please. I am protecting the lives of my crew by leaving him where he is. You heard them just now. If Gadifer were on board I would be dead by now and the rest of you would be floundering off the coast of Canaria, if not already sunk. And please. Undignified? Are you aware how little dignity we have been afforded by the honourable monsieur Gadifer. He has gone back on his word to pay us and can no longer be trusted."

"Nonsense man! He lives by his word. If he has promised to pay you, he will. There is no need for this… this display of childish petulance."

"There is only so far a rope can be stretched before it breaks monsieur. We are way past that point now."

Jean looked back at Gadifer sat in the tiny dinghy like a wet bear. He looked a sorry sight despite the fury boiling behind his strange smile.

"I am aware that relations are strained between the two of you, but why humiliate the man in front of the entire company like this?"

"The man struck me in front of my crew. Was there any need for that humiliation?"

"When was this?"

"The day we left Rubicon. Punched me in the face he did, in front of all my men. They all saw it."

"Ah! I see. This is your revenge."

"Oh he had it coming long before he hit me. He owes us, has done for a long time."

"We are here to make history man, on one of the most important voyages of discovery in modern times. What worth is silver when historians will judge you on the nobility of your deeds?"

"When history books are written, they won't be written about men like me who carry people like you on our backs." Le Brument's eyes were clear, he stood as tall as his bent legs would allow. "Besides, how is it that *we* were the only ones to be overlooked when you and Gadifer scoured the noble houses *paying* knights to accompany you on your *adventure*? One hundred francs a man I heard. Where is our hundred francs each eh? We have all embarked on the same crusade yet we, my

228

men and I, have nothing to show for it. Promises were made, and promises have been broken… Will that be written about in the history books?"

"You are paid handsomely for what you do. A price you agreed to before we set sail. It is you who have broken your promise and failed to honour your side of the agreement. You, and you alone have threatened the future of this crusade by stealing this ship from under the feet of its owner."

"This ship is our home. That man there" Le Brument pointed angrily at Gadifer, "does nothing but sign his name and send us on our way. He wasn´t with us when we were attacked by pirates off the coast of Corsica. He wasn´t the one who had to lash himself to the mast in a fifty-foot swell in the Bay of Biscay. We risk our lives to enrich that man. Every time he disrespects us with broken promises, he humiliates us, treats us no better than slaves. He hit me! I ask you! Is that a way to treat an experienced Ship´s Master? Enough is enough. He can sup on his own medicine." He turned and spat over the rail.

Jean felt like an unwilling passenger riding on the wave of Brument´s ire. He bit his lip and let the bitter little man have his moment. He talked for an age, about what exactly, Jean couldn´t be sure, he had stopped listening. There were many blowhards like le Brument in the world and Jean had had the displeasure to meet many of them. He knew it was a pointless exercise to try reasoning with the man. He had a deep store of long held grievances to air and as God was his witness, he would make sure someone heard them all.

Jean was so tempted to just throw le Brument overboard, but he knew men were hanging in the rigging with crossbows and itchy trigger fingers. Slaughter would ensue if he raised his hand. Even if they survived a barrage of crossbow bolts and managed to take over the ship, they would then have to find Gadifer. Colin would cut him adrift at the first sign of trouble. It was a big ocean in a boat without oars. The knights were not sailors. They wouldn´t be able to turn the ship around quickly enough to save the old man from the sea.

It was difficult to decide which of the two men made him angrier. Le Brument for being a small-minded fool, or Gadifer for letting the situation get this far out of hand. Jean had thus far refrained from interfering in Gadifer´s business, believing, wrongly as it would appear, that the old man had his side of things under control.   His incompetence presented Jean with yet another problem to resolve. The whole sorry incident fortified Jean´s dislike of dealing with other people.   They always waited until the moment you needed them most to let you down the hardest.

Le Brument paused his monologue long enough for Jean to make him a proposal.   The Master agreed before hurrying off to tell his crew. He hobbled back down the steps to the quarterdeck.   Jean joined in with the booing and hissing this time as the Master ran the gauntlet of abuse from the knights below while crossing the open deck to the safety of the tiller house.

Jean took one more look at Gadifer and shook his head.   He walked to the front of the poop deck and sat down on the steps. Lancarote´s mountains rose out of the sea ahead.   The island looked so welcoming with its cap of fluffy clouds over the highlands.   It was going to be hard to leave it behind at such a crucial time.

The fortress of Rubicon came into view.   Jean was relieved to see figures moving about the building site.   The exterior of the fortress appeared to be almost complete.   It made a menacing sight from the sea.   The dark stone and timber walls stood tall and imposing against the soft pastel hues of the wilderness beyond.   Jean imagined rows of archers safe behind the battlements, spitting arrows down on any brigand foolish enough to attempt an assault.

The sound of chipping, sawing and banging faded.   Workers downed their tools and wandered to the top of the bluff to watch the ship ease into its anchorage.   Jean couldn´t help but notice more than one arm point to Gadifer in the dinghy, he even heard a couple of loud guffaws from one group of men.   It was nothing like the victorious homecoming he had hoped for when they left.

The knights and their men climbed down into the longboat and rowed ashore towing Gadifer and Hannibal behind in the dinghy.   They hit the beach with a jolt.   Jean almost fell in his haste to scramble over the side.   He regained his balance and splashed through the shallows and up onto dry sand.

Father Verrier and Berthin stood waiting.

"Welcome back Monsieur. How was it?" Verrier asked, looking over Jean´s shoulder at Gadifer sat in the dinghy.

"As well as could be expected, under the circumstances." Jean answered kicking his feet in the sand.

"Did you come across any natives?" Berthin asked.

"Not a one I´m afraid to say. Not for the want of trying though, we walked a long way across the island." He turned around and looked across the deep blue water to the mountains of Erbania in the distance. He pointed. "We camped there, beyond the tallest peak. Looking at it now, we didn´t walk very far at all." He let his arm drop and turned round to face Father Verrier and Berthin. They weren´t paying any attention to him, they were watching Gadifer. Two knights were pulling his little boat closer to the beach.

"And how are things here?" Jean asked to the side of Father Verrier´s head.

"Wha…?" Father Verrier turned round to look at him. His eyebrows arched high over his wide-open eyes.

"I trust everything ran smoothly while we were away. The fortress looks magnificent from the seaward approach." Jean asked again.

"Yes, yes. King Guadarfia himself brought a whole army of workers to help the day after you left. He set up camp just outside the wall."

"King Guadarfia! Is he still here?"

"Yes. Isabel has gone to fetch him." the Priest said smiling.

"Good. Good." Jean was glad he would be able to tell Guadarfia in person that he was leaving.

The dinghy hit the beach, Gadifer and Hannibal jumped down onto the sand. Jean snatched them away before they had a chance to speak. He led them across the beach and up the pathway to the camp with Father Verrier and Berthin behind, trotting to keep up.

They arrived at the top of the path at the same time King Guadarfia stepped out from between the tents at the far side of the building site. Avago walked on his left side, Isabel on his right. A small band of armed Majos followed closely behind. People fell over themselves to clear a path before the King as he strode through the site. Jean smiled genuinely for the first time in many days.

He walked forward and used the few Majo words he knew to greet the King. Guadarfia delivered one of his rare smiles while responding in kind. The two men shook hands. Isabel stepped up to translate their conversation.

"I am glad you have returned in one piece." Guadarfia said.

"It gladdens me to see you here, in Rubicon." Jean swept his arm around, leading Guadarfia´s eyes to the fortress. "She is looking magnificent. I have to say she looks very intimidating from the sea. Any pirate will think twice before landing here."

"Why is it *she*?"

"A very good question. She is a *she* as a ship is a she. She is our mother when we are away from home. She protects us as a mother protects her children."

Avago and Guadarfia gasped when Isabel finished translating. Avago said something quickly to Guadarfia who nodded and smiled.

"Avago says we are not so different. Majos also worship the Mother." Isabel said smiling up at Jean. Jean found their happiness infectious. He laughed and reached across to clap Avago on the shoulder.

"I never thought of it like that." he said, although he had. He knew perfectly well the names of the native Gods and the significance of each. "It is one of the common links that bind us together." he said, turning around and taking a long look at the fortress.

Guadarfia spoke. "I am impressed by the skill of your people. The palace looks very … straight." Jean nodded.

"It would not have been possible without the help of your people. You should be proud of them. Hard-working, fast learners all. They are a credit to you." Jean replied with a small bow.

"Are all buildings where you come from built this way?" Guadarfia asked.

"This is nothing compared to the buildings back home. One day I will take you to see the magnificent castles and halls of my country. Towers and cathedrals soar into the sky as high as your mountains. Some are so huge they take generations to build."

"I would like to see them."

"You shall my friend, you shall. Come, let us take refreshment. I need wine to rinse the taste of salt and sand from my mouth."

Jean led them through the camp to the kitchen block where they all took seats around a long table. Jean called for drinks. Gadifer sat at Jean's side as meek as a scolded dog. Jean had felt everyone's eyes upon them as they walked through the camp. They were all witnesses to the old warrior's humiliation. The camp would already be alive with gossip and rumour. Let them talk. Jean had too much to do because of it, he didn't want to waste time explaining it.

Kitchen helpers brought jugs of wine and water to the table and filled cups for everyone.

"To Lancarote! The jewel in the Canary Islands' Crown." Jean raised his cup, touching it to Guadarfia's who sat mirroring his actions from the other side of the table. Jean closed his eyes as he drank, savouring the acid bite of the wine rinsing his mouth, reinvigorating his salt-burned tongue.

"That's better." he said, smacking his lips and taking another quick sip. He watched Guadarfia drinking. The Majo King appeared unsure whether he liked the wine or not, but he was willing to keep trying.

"I am glad to find you here Your Grace." Jean said. "There is something I need to tell you. I will be leaving the island for a time." There were more than a few splutters and exclamations of surprise at Jean's sudden announcement.

"Due to events beyond my control, I must return to the mainland to settle a dispute. It is nothing to worry about, merely a inconvenience that I must resolve personally."

"I will be sad to see you go. But look forward to your return." Guadarfia said, appearing to be sincerely aggrieved. Jean noticed the reaction and was moved by the King's affection.

"I trust the peace and good will that is blossoming between French and Majo people will continue in my absence. I am leaving Monsieur Gadifer here to oversee the works on the fortress, aided by Berthin. Until the work on the chapel is complete, I understand Father Verrier would like to visit your villages to begin teaching the Word of Our Lord. Am I correct Father?"

"Yes indeed. Both Brother Bontier and I are eager to meet your people and see more of this wonderful land." Father Verrier clasped his hands at his chest.

"I will agree to it only if you come to my home first. I would like my family to listen to these words." Guadarfia answered to the delight of Father Verrier who nodded enthusiastically.

"It would be my honour to teach you personally."

"Perfect." Jean sat up straight and clapped his hands. "I hate to be rude Your Grace, but you must excuse me. I have many matters to attend to before embarking this evening. I would like to invite you to share a meal with me before I leave. The cooks can prepare something."

"My cooks already have hogs roasting over our fires. Come to my camp and we shall make it a feast of farewell."

"That is an offer I cannot refuse." Jean replied, nodding his thanks. They stood up from the table together. "I will see you there presently." Guadarfia strode away, followed by Avago and his huddle of guards.

Jean watched them go before walking around the table to face Gadifer and the others. He sat down slowly and leaned heavily on his elbows. The pleasant demeanour he had shown to Guadarfia evaporated. His features hardened as he lifted his head to speak. His voice was low, with a hint of fire in its tone.

"As you have all no doubt seen, we suffered a humiliating blow while in Erbania. Master le Brument has taken control of the ship. In order to amend the situation, I find myself in the unenviable position of having to return to Cadiz. I am forced to trade the goods we have accumulated thus far to pay le Brument and his crew." Gadifer bristled and was about to interrupt. Jean shot him a sharp look, freezing the words in his throat. "The works will continue as a priority, I leave Monsieur Gadifer here to make sure the fortress and chapel are finished with all haste."

"Will you be making the journey alone?" Father Verrier asked.

"I will take a handful of knights to assist me, no more. I hope to return as soon as possible with more men, ships and supplies. I will speak to each of you individually before I leave. In the meantime, if you wish to have any letters delivered I suggest you prepare them quickly."

"Berthin," he said before anybody could ask any more questions. "You are to take some guards and supervise the loading of the ship. Make a record of everything that goes in and comes out. Hannibal has the manifest. Work together. Make sure le Brument gives you all the weapons, tools and supplies from the hold. Bring everything ashore and lock it away." He turned to face Gadifer who was grinding his teeth behind bloodless lips.

"Monsieur Gadifer, I will speak with you now. The rest of you may leave."

Father Verrier scuttled away with Isabel close behind. Berthin and Hannibal stalked off in the opposite direction leaving Jean and Gadifer alone. Jean sat back and regarded Gadifer closely. The man was visibly shaking, whether it was with rage or the chill of his sopping wet clothes Jean couldn´t be sure. He didn´t care. He worried a splinter free from the edge of the table with his fingernail. He peeled it away slowly, rolled it into a ball and flicked it away.

"Master le Brument was very forthcoming." he said leaning forward until his face was inches from Gadifer´s. "I had the displeasure of listening to his bile for a large portion of the return journey."

"I saw." Gadifer´s voice was low, it crackled in his throat.

"This whole episode has put me in a very uncomfortable position. It is not for me to judge how you conduct your business monsieur, but this… altercation has placed everything in jeopardy and for that, I am deeply concerned. Nay bloody furious!"

"The man is a fool and a coward." Gadifer snapped.

"He may well be, but that is not my concern. The fact that he refuses to obey you is what concerns me right now. The value of that ship far outweighs the value of the men aboard her, but without sailors to crew her, she is of no use to us. I cannot afford to run the risk of any harm coming to le Brument and his men, so I must leave immediately." Gadifer looked away. Jean continued, "We need silver for a new crew. I have barely a franc left in my chest. I suspect you are in a similar position."

"I have funds, but not here, and certainly not to pay that filthy pig. Look how he cowers on my ship afraid to step ashore."

"Why would he want to? To die? He may advocate altruism when he speaks and claims to act for the welfare of his crew, but we both know he doesn't possess the courage to martyr himself for them."

"The welfare of his men is not in jeopardy, or rather it wasn't. We had an agreement which *he* has reneged on."

"Yes, he has, but under provocation. A noble knight spreading rumours. I believe le Brument's brother told you the tale." Gadifer nodded. "I would have liked to have been forewarned by you about that little detail. It left me at a disadvantage when he brought it up." Gadifer looked down. "I'll wager it's the same traitor who stirred up trouble on the voyage down here. I need him found before he brings ruin down upon all our heads. I thought we left all the bad eggs behind in Cadiz."

"As did I."

"While I am gone, ferret this weasel out. See to it personally this time."

"And le Brument and the ship?"

"Leave le Brument to me. Do you have contacts in Cadiz?"

"I have an associate in Seville who could organise things for me."

"Very well. I suggest you prepare letters to authorise and pay for a new crew to bring the ship back again… and of course to compensate me for your share of the expenses I will incur with this unnecessary diversion." Gadifer looked like he was about to object to the final caveat but backed down quickly.

"Good. Then let that be an end to the matter."

Gadifer nodded and took a sip of wine.

"I don't imagine I'll be gone for more than six weeks. I hope I can rely on you to maintain order while I am gone."

"Of course! Once le Brument and his dogs are gone things will settle down."

"Things will not settle down while we have a traitor in our midst monsieur." Jean leaned over and hissed in Gadifer's ear. "Find him."

****

The afternoon sun was racing towards the western horizon by the time the ship was ready to leave. People lined the bluff watching. Berthin stood alone on the fortress roof. He had a clear view of the Peacock stood on the poop deck with a handful of men, looking forlornly back to shore. Master le Brument strutted into view, stepping out from the shade of the tiller house. He yelled up to the men on the high spars. There was a brief flurry of activity and the topsails dropped and filled. The ship wallowed around in a slow circle before picking up her anchor and swinging around to run with the wind. She ploughed a deep furrow to the south before switching heading to the north-west.

A strange hush descended when she disappeared around the distant headland. A rigged longboat on the beach was all that remained of her. People shuffled away with their heads down. The ship was their lifeline back home and Bethencourt had taken her away. Berthin was overjoyed to see so many lose heart; the disenchanted were always the easiest to influence.

He shouldered a long spear and left the fortress, walked along the edge of the bluff and across to the eastern end of the perimeter wall. He climbed over a flat-stone stile set in the end of the wall and dropped down to the other side. He paused for a moment to enjoy the cool shade out of the sun´s glare before beginning a slow, perfunctory patrol around the camp perimeter.

It felt good to be alone. The afternoon spent with Hannibal supervising the loading and unloading of the ship had sapped his will to live. Gadifer´s bastard was possibly the dullest man Berthin had ever met. He checked, double-checked and then triple-checked everything he did, before checking it again and writing it down. And then he would check what he had written. In the end, to keep from losing his mind, Berthin excused himself, saying he had to relieve one of the guards. He left Hannibal to finish the job alone. Unfortunately, he had to follow through with his lie in case he was seen. He donned his mail shirt, jerkin and helmet and wandered aimlessly around the camp. It made for a hot uncomfortable couple of hours wearing all that weight and carrying his spear, but it had got him away from work, and Hannibal.

It did feel good to be out of sight for a while, anonymous in his guard uniform. It allowed him time to let his mind wander. He imagined all the things he could buy with the mountain of silver coming his way. He scoffed at the ignorance of Bethencourt running away to find extra funds. A fortune in slaves camped just outside the gates, picking lice from each other's hair and grunting like animals. If the Peacock hadn't been such a pious fool, they would all be rich by now. They should have been ferrying ship loads of savages back to the block for the last two months instead of building a chapel for them.

A small sound up ahead stopped him in his tracks. It sounded like a girl weeping. He gripped his spear tightly with both hands and crept forward. Within a few short paces around the curve of the wall, a wretched figure came into view, crouching down holding his head in his hands while his body heaved, gulping down air between back-breaking sobs. Berthin couldn't quite believe his eyes when he realised who it was.

"Philip. Is that you?" he asked, approaching the curled-up bundle of misery.

Philip flung his head back suddenly. His face was a mess of tears and snot. He smiled manically, his eyes wide open, looking anywhere but at Berthin. "Yes it's me." he said in a high, hysterical voice.

"Why are you here and not on the ship with Bethencourt?"

"Because, monsieur Bethencourt has decided to leave me behind. He told me he wishes to *examine the work of some Castilian tailors.*" I ask you. Castilian tailors are good for hacking up bad cloth. I spit on them! Pah! I am an artist. And he discards me like a used brush." He collapsed once more into a snotball of hacking sobs. His head fell back into his hands and he began to wail like an injured banshee. Berthin hurried past, amused and slightly disgusted by the sight of the cocky little tailor brought so low. He would be a good recruit, if he ever stopped crying.

The camp of the savage King came into view a hundred paces inland of the gateway into Rubicon. It was beginning to come to life as the sun drifted off to the west and the air cooled. Children's laughter carried in the wind and soon the sound of singing voices lifted to join the sound. Berthin smelled roasting pork. His mouth watered at the thought of anything else but goat stew. He hadn´t realised how hungry he was until his stomach rumbled.

The unmistakable figure of the savage King, accompanied by his lap dog Avago strolled through the camp. They made a striking pair. Lean and fit, backs ramrod straight atop strong, powerful legs. The King alone was worth his weight in silver. Fifty more like him and Berthin would never have to work again. He watched as the King said something to old Avago who smiled, turned away and ran from the camp.

"You look like a man in a market choosing which hog to bring home for supper." Big Perrin snorted from the gateway where he was standing guard with William, or rather leaning against the wall and banging the butt of his spear into the ground.

"That´s exactly what he´s doing." William answered. "The Big King gets bigger every time I look at him. We could sell him as meat and get enough to keep you in whores for a year."

Big Perrin roared with laughter.

"Keep your voices down." Berthin growled, hurrying over. "Someone will hear."

"There´s nobody around, they´re all eating." Perrin whined.

"There´s always someone ready to overhear careless talk. Just be careful, especially now we´re so close." He glanced past William and saw one of the cook´s helpers hurrying over from the kitchen block. He was struggling to undo the chord keeping his britches up, obviously in some distress. "You see." Berthin said, as the youngster burst through the gate taking William and Perrin completely by surprise.

"The little shit!" Perrin said. "Where did he come from?"

"It´s one of the little bastards from the kitchen." said William, leaning out to watch the lad go. "Be careful what you say around that one, he´ll be pissing in your stew when you´re not looking."

"Both of you be careful." Berthin said, cutting their mirth short. "All it would take is a word in the wrong person´s ear from someone like that kid and we´re all sunk." Berthin growled, William looked up and nodded.

"The little shit!" Big Perrin muttered and kicked the wall.

Berthin shook his head and walked through the gateway and into the camp. Weariness descended on him like a shower of warm water. The sound of Big Perrin´s voice and the words he said with it, tired him out. He couldn´t wait until this caper was over and he would never have to see Perrin´s pink jowly face ever again. He wandered over to the kitchen block to get some food but turned away before he got there. The unmistakeable aroma of goat stew and the sound of scraping knives and loud conversation wafted over him and drove him away. The din tore rents in his head, the smell brought bile to the back of his throat. He began to feel dizzy. His eyes throbbed and his mouth went dry. He needed to lie down.

Thankfully, his tent wasn´t far away. By the time he arrived there he felt as weak as a kitten. He ducked inside and pulled the flap closed behind him. He dropped his spear on the ground, undid his sword belt and let that fall to the floor. He slipped his jerkin over his head and threw it onto a stool. The room started to spin, light began to drain away, he gasped for breath as he felt his chest tighten. He thought for a moment about stripping off his mail shirt and britches but needed to lie down quickly before he collapsed.

He threw himself onto his cot and closed his eyes. He reached up with his hand to touch his forehead. It felt cold and clammy under his fingertips. He hadn´t felt like this since he was a small boy. It had happened frequently then. His nanny would cradle him in her arms, singing gently as she rocked him, telling him to think of happy thoughts until the dizziness passed.

He scrunched his eyes tightly shut and searched desperately for images of happiness. *A fat leather purse overflowing with silver and gold. A huge cart, straining to bear the weight of the jewels heaped upon it. He imagined fantastic castles he would build, filled with servants and beautiful concubines ready to obey his every command. There would be stables and horses. His horse would be a jet-black stallion, he would teach it to stamp and piss on his father´s grave…*

He passed out.

He came to a little later, how much later he couldn´t be sure. He opened his eyes and was relieved to find the wave of malady had passed. His breathing was back to normal and the tent was no longer swirling. He rolled over onto his side and closed his eyes. He was about to drift off to sleep when a scraping noise against the tent flap brought him back to wakefulness.

"Is someone there?" he asked sitting up and swinging his legs onto the ground.

"Monsieur!" A willowy young girl pulled the tent flap aside with one hand. She held a wooden platter bearing a steaming pie and a mug of ale in the other. "My father sent me with some food for you." she said, her eyes wide and voice tiny.

"Your father?"

"Monsieur Jacquet. The baker." she answered.

"Of course. Come in and set it down on the table." Jacquet was a royal pain in the arse, but occasionally he was able to justify his existence. Berthin was hungry, but not necessarily for food anymore. He watched the young girl cross the tent and bend over to set the platter down on the table. She was young, but not too young for Berthin's tastes, if anything she was a little older than he usually liked. He had seen the young girls and boys around the kitchen block but had no idea any of the little bastards belonged to Jacquet.

She was a skinny thing. Reed thin arms poked out from the sleeves of her blouse and looked ready to snap. Her mousy blond hair was pulled back from her face and bundled under a thick white headscarf. Berthin eyed her skinny rump through the thick material of her long skirt and felt a stirring in his loins. The girl stood, turned and offered a small curtsy to Berthin before making to leave.

"Wait!" Berthin ordered. "Turn around and let me look at you." The girl stopped and turned slowly to face Berthin who uncoiled from his cot and rose to face her.

"What's your name?" he asked.

"Nicol." she answered meekly, her eyes rooted to the floor.

"And how old are you Nicol?" Berthin's voice was as dripping with bitter sweetness.

"Fifteen next Birthday." Berthin felt the blood rush from his head down to his cock. She was young and unmarked by pox, unlike the other hags who hovered around the camp hoping to catch the knight's eyes. He heard them most nights screaming fake bliss, encouraging the men between their legs to drain their sacks before taking coins from their purses.

Berthin stood back and appraised Nicol. She was very pale. The sun had barely coloured her soft skin. Her breath quickened as he continued to stare at her, her budding breasts pushed against the grubby material of her blouse.

"And why haven´t I seen you before?" he asked, lifting her chin between his fingers. Her eyes still wandered a little as she struggled to find words.

"I have been working inside the kitchen Monsieur. My father doesn't like me to wander around the camp. He says the men would take advantage of me."

Berthin smiled. His cock was straining the stitches of his britches. "But your father is a very dear friend of mine, you shouldn´t be afraid of me."

"No. He speaks very highly of you monsieur. He has told me that I am to please you in any way you ask." He felt her tremble. He loosened the grip on her chin and brushed her cheek with the backs of his fingers. She looked up. Her eyes were huge and round, a beautiful light brown colour flecked with gold. Her mouth was small, sat above a delicate pointed chin. A little pink tongue poked out between her dry lips and moistened them. Berthin nearly burst. He reached up and removed her headscarf. A few strands of hair fell across her forehead.

"You are very pretty Nicol." he said. The girl blushed and looked down again, her hands clasped tightly in front of her.

"Thank you monsieur."

"There is one thing you can do for me."

"Yes monsieur." she said eagerly. "Anything."

"Sit on the bed."

"Monsieur?" Nicol fidgeted nervously, looking down at the cot and back to Berthin.

"Sit there on the edge." The girl sat down pertly on the wooden edge of the cot, her hands still clasped in her lap and her legs pressed firmly together.

"Look at me Nicol." She looked up, her big eyes were looking fearful now, only serving to inflame Berthin´s desire. "I need you to do something for me, but it is to be our secret. Do you understand?" The girl nodded. "You cannot tell your father he will be very angry with you. Would you like that?" The girl shook her head like a little bird.

"Good. But I need you to swear on *his* life that you can keep *our* secret. Can you do that?" She nodded. "I need to hear you say it Nicol. I´m afraid your father would have to die if you told anybody. Do you understand?" The girl nodded, tears beginning to form in the corners of her eyes. "Say it!" Berthin hissed.

"I – I – promise not to tell."

"On your father´s life."

"On my father´s life."

"Good." Berthin stood up. He squeezed the girl´s knees between his own and tugged the mail shirt above his waist. Nicol´s eyes opened wide and she tried to pull away.

"No." Berthin scolded reaching over to grab a handful of her hair. "Am I to tell your father you disobeyed him?"

"No monsieur. Please. I will do anything you ask."

"Good girl." Berthin said undoing the laces of his britches with his free hand.

****

Norstar checked and double-checked that no part of the boat was visible from the top of the wall overlooking the secret harbour. French patrols were crossing the island a little more frequently these days and finding new caves and settlements daily. He did not want them to stumble across his boat. It hadn´t been in the water since the invaders arrived, although he had been sorely tempted on many occasions to push it out through the waves and tear up the coast. He missed the sensation of skimming across the waves with a fresh wind in the sails. It was the nearest thing to flying, a sensation of freedom he never experienced doing anything else. His children all inherited his love of sailing. Fayna had begged him to take the boat out that morning, but common sense, or rather Gara´s will had prevailed. She explained how the sight of the sail would bring every French soldier running from miles around. That was enough to keep them on dry land for the day.

Apart from a few coracles on the southern coast, Norstar´s was the only boat on the island. The Majo people hated water. Norstar had heard the songs about the Great Upheaval, when the land sunk between the waves killing all but a few of their ancestors. The peaks of the mountains they clung to, to escape the rising water formed the islands they lived on. They believed the upheaval was a punishment from the Gods and it would happen again should they ever attempt to cross the seas between the islands.

He had been disappointed not to get in the water, but the day in the harbour had been enjoyable nonetheless. It felt like a return to normality for a brief moment. Norstar had scraped the boat´s hull and given it a fresh coat of tree sap resin while Gara and Fayna oiled the ropes and pulleys. Boyo and Nayra helped as much as infants could help when working next to a swimming pool on a hot day. They spent hours exploring and playing. Norstar was happy to let them enjoy their freedom after all the time they had been entombed with Iballa in the deep caves. His wife´s mother spent the long nights telling the children stories about monsters and demons, waiting outside the cave to gobble them up. She had scared them so well it took a surprisingly long time to persuade them to leave the safety of the cave that morning.

Norstar jogged along the path and caught up with Gara and Fayna. The little ones had scurried on ahead, eager to get back home as the deep shadows gave way to twilight. Gara heard Norstar coming and stopped to wait. She held out her hand, Norstar took it and gently kissed the back of it before letting go. He patted her on the backside as she turned back and carried on walking along the narrow track.

"When do you think it will be safe to sail?" Fayna asked from up ahead.

"I don´t know." Norstar replied truthfully. "I am still not convinced the invaders are as full of good intentions as Guadarfia would have us believe."

"He has been charmed." Gara said. "He always was gullible, even when we were small."

"Mence was small?" asked Fayna.

"He was smaller than me for many years until his balls dropped, and then he turned into the giant he is now." Gara answered, Fayna sniggered.

"Don´t tell me, he was another boy who was madly in love with you?" she said rolling her eyes.

"Every man who ever laid eyes on your mother fell madly in love with her." Norstar answered. "I was the most unpopular man on the island when I won her heart."

"What was he like when he was younger?" Fayna asked.

"Who, your father?"

"No, Guadarfia."

"He was very serious, a little bit too serious at times. Even more so when he became Mence."

"Why is he so much bigger than everybody else?" Fayna asked.

"Ha Ha!" Norstar laughed. "He gets his size from the pirate who slept with his mother Ico and planted Guadarfia in her belly. Some say Guadarfia should not be king because he is not of noble blood."

"Pah!" Gara spat. "It was proved that story was made up by Princess Ico´s enemies to discredit her."

"Proved how?" Fayna asked.

"It was proved by Ico´s trial by ordeal that she spoke the truth."

"She was smoked in a hut and didn´t die." Norstar added. "She was clever enough to hold a wet cloth to her face and didn´t succumb to the smoke in the spirit house. She was obviously telling the truth."

Gara stopped and turned to face Norstar. The look on her face told him to be careful. He held his hands up and smiled. "That´s what I was told." he said. Gara turned around and carried on walking.

"It was suspected for a while that Guadarfia was Ico´s secret twin brother." she continued. "Mency Zonzamas kept his wife and children hidden in the deep caves. I suspect this is why her skin was pale. Even in later years she chose to live underground rather than be subjected to the stares and the gossip of the people."

"I heard she was a witch and stayed below ground brewing potions." Fayna said.

"Gossip." Gara spat. "Stories like those become the truth if told by enough people. Never tell and listen to stories if you wish truth to guide you. Nobody really knows why Ico stayed hidden, which is why everybody made up the stories. She only showed herself when called upon to defend Guadarfia's claim to the throne, dying shortly afterwards, her heart shattered by poisonous words.

"Guadarfia shared her pain for many years. He found it difficult to trust the men who pursued her so mercilessly. Guañarmeñe Nichel was one of those. He caused her to scream in pain on more than one occasion. It doesn't surprise me that Guadarfia is finding the new men and their God so appealing. He blames the old Gods for causing Ico to suffer."

"Did you know her?" Fayna asked.

"I saw her when we were young. Avago had close ties to their family. We went to the palace regularly before you were born, Ico was there sometimes."

"The visits stopped when I showed up. My strange face reminded them of the cuckold pirate." Norstar chirped in and instantly regretted it as Gara stopped and turned to face him again with her hands on her hips.

"Not as many are guided by mistrust and hatred of strangers as you would have us believe." she scolded.

"You don't feel their stares upon your back all the time. I don't think many will mourn my passing when I go."

"You get worse as your hair gets thinner old man. Nobody on this island thinks poorly of you. They only treat you differently when you speak out of your arse."

"My arse speaks all the sense I need." He cocked his leg up and let rip with a loud fart. Fayna burst out laughing behind Gara who stood looking at her husband with her mouth open. "That one said "I love you" in Danish." Gara turned around and began walking away, trying her best not to smile.

A peel of screeches up ahead caused them all to look up. Avago was trotting down the path towards them. Boyo and Nayra raced into his outstretched arms. He gathered them up and carried them back down the path, laughing as they battled to tell him as many things as they could within the shortest time possible.

Fayna ran to meet him.   He bent to let her kiss his cheek and tried to put the little ones down.   It only made them cling tighter around his neck.

"Boyo! Nayra!   Let him go, you're killing him." Gara said as she reached the old man and gave him a kiss.   The children reluctantly let go and dropped to the floor.

"It is good to see you." Norstar said, shaking Avago's hand. "Has Guadarfia left the French camp?"

"No.   He leaves tomorrow for Zonzamas.   I am home for two days before I join him there.   He asked me to pass on some news."

"What news?"

"Bethencourt is gone."

"Dead?"

"No.   He returned from Erbania this morning and left to the North in the afternoon."

"Has everybody gone with him?"   Norstar asked hopefully.

"No.   He only took a few men and those who live on the ship. He told Guadarfia he will return soon."   Norstar was crestfallen.   "He has left Gadifer and the holy men in charge.   The man who threatened you on the beach is still here."

"Shit."

"Guadarfia trusts Bethencourt.   They spoke today like old friends. He told me to tell you if Bethencourt vouches for the man then he must have some good within him.   Nevertheless, he asks if you will return to watch the camp while Bethencourt is away.   Observe Berthin.   Do not confront him."

"The man cannot be trusted.   He reminds me of a shit house rat." Norstar spat.

"He may have over-reacted with you on the beach.   Bethencourt vouches for him.   Can he be as bad as you say?"

"I can't be sure if I can trust Bethencourt either."   Norstar's words hung in the air for a long moment.

"Pay him no mind Pa.   He trusts nobody today."   Gara slipped her arm through Avago's.   "If we only have you for two days let's make it a happy two days."   Norstar stood in silence as Gara led Avago away. He began to wonder if he was searching too hard to find reasons to justify his mistrust of the invaders, misreading signs, looking for enemies and dangers that didn´t exist… Perhaps his judgement couldn´t be trusted because of his prejudice.

Fayna skipped back down the path and linked her arm with his. She began pulling him up the path behind Gara and Avago.

"I believe you Papi. I saw this man´s eyes too. If he wants to harm you, he will have to go through me and every other Majo who loves you first. We are many."

"That´s what worries me." Norstar replied quietly.

23

Rubicon, Lancarote,
September 21st, 1402

Berthin´s father was calling his name when he jerked awake from the dream. The voice still echoed around his head even with his eyes open. It was not yet fully light but past dawn judging by the level of gloom inside the tent. He stirred slowly and then sat bolt upright as he realised the voice was not coming from his dream at all.

"Monsieur Berthin!" the voice called again from outside the tent.

"Who is it?" Berthin snapped.

"Hannibal."

"What do you want?"

"My Father requests your presence at the fortress."

"I´ll get dressed and be there soon." Berthin replied grumpily. He lay back down and squeezed his eyes shut to try capture the end of the dream, but it was no good, it had disappeared leaving no trace in his memory. He shook his head and climbed slowly out of his cot. The air was cooler than it had been for months. The long hot summer was finally relinquishing its hold on the island. Berthin knew it should make him happier not to be constantly sweating but this morning it annoyed him. Everything annoyed him and he had only just opened his eyes. It looked like it was going to be another miserable day.

He stood up and stretched his arms above his head, took a deep breath before bending to splash some water on his face from a wooden bowl set up next to his cot. His britches had slipped from their hanger in the night. They were crumpled and damp on the floor. He had nothing else to wear so he stepped into the damp britches and pulled them up to his waist, shivering when the clammy cloth stuck to his legs. Climbing back into his cot was all he wanted to do but he couldn´t. He picked his boots up and sat down on the edge of the cot just staring into space.

Lack of sleep did not improve his mood. The fort was all but finished and the majority of native workers had drifted away. A small core stayed behind and helped the artisans, adding details and flourishes to the chapel's interior. The savages learned quickly, many of them were able to hold short conversations in French. Berthin saw their block value rise with every recognisable grunt they made. Unfortunately, only a dozen or so of them were still hanging around. He needed at least forty to hand should the slavers suddenly turn up.

He eventually pulled on his boots, donned his tunic and strapped on his sword. He left the tent and picked his way through the camp to the fortress. Passing beneath one of the high arrow slits in a corner tower he heard the sound of snoring coming from inside. It was one of his men on guard duty, sleeping in the snug comfort of the tower.

How he missed sleeping behind good, strong, stone walls. The cacophony of bodily expulsions and exertions seeping through the canvass walls of his tent every night made it difficult to sleep. By mid-afternoon he was usually exhausted and had to fight to keep his eyes open. Unfortunately, his tent was hotter than an oven in the middle of the day when the sun was at its fiercest. There was little rest to be found under the canvass ceiling. His eyes would close but the heat would be too intense to sleep for more than a few snatched moments. If he could find the energy to do so, he would hate this island even more than he already did.

Rounding the edge of the fortress, he saw Gadifer standing with Hannibal up on the battlements looking out to sea. Cursing under his breath, he doubled back to the fortress entrance on the other side of the building. Passing the snoring arrow slit, he drew his sword and banged it several times against the edge of the hole. Whoever was inside woke with a start, he heard them curse and swear. It was the first time a smile had threatened his face all morning.

Hannibal was turning to say something to Gadifer when he spotted Berthin strolling around the edge of the roof to meet them. He tapped Gadifer on the shoulder. The old man turned to watch Berthin walk the final few feet and climb up to join them on the allure behind the battlements. Berthin felt Gadifer's eyes on him and it made him uncomfortable. For a fleeting second he imagined pushing Gadifer and his moronic simpering son over the edge.

"Ah Good! Berthin. Take a look over there." Gadifer pointed out to sea. "It appears we have company. They are just slipping behind Lobos, there on the right. Do you see?"

Berthin squinted through the light haze and saw a tiny white speck disappearing behind the island of Lobos four leagues away.

"Have you any idea who it is?" he asked eagerly.

"It looked Spanish to me judging by the rigging. What do you say Hannibal?"

"Yes Spanish, definitely Spanish. Or Portuguese."

"They could be bringing word of Bethencourt." Gadifer said. "We must send a delegation over to deliver…"

"I´ll go." Berthin blurted out. It had to be Ordoñez and the Tajamar.

"Well in sir!" Gadifer smiled. "Inaction getting to you is it my boy?"

"I am finding things a little tedious at the moment monsieur."

"I know exactly what you mean. I remember when I was your age. Nothing would have kept me cooped up for this long without searching out distraction. It was during a time like this, between skirmishes with the English that I met this one´s mother," he flicked an eye towards Hannibal. Berthin and Hannibal both shifted uncomfortably. "You see, even while doing nothing I had to be doing something." Gadifer laughed at his own poor joke. Berthin felt obliged to smile politely in response.

"I will have a letter prepared immediately for you to deliver." Gadifer said. He waved with his fingers and Hannibal scampered away. "Will you be ready in an hour?"

"Certainly monsieur."

"Excellent. One other thing, the matter we talked about. Are you getting any closer to finding the craven dog who stirred up le Brument and his men?"

Berthin nearly laughed out loud. Le Brument and his men didn´t matter anymore, not with the Tajamar close by.

"I´m still searching monsieur, but he is a wily character this one. I suspect he knows we are on to him."

"Ah well! Keep at it, keep at it. I want him found before Bethencourt returns."

"I have a feeling it won´t be much longer before we discover his identity." Berthin replied.

****

Berthin stood in the prow of the longboat as it pulled around the headland and slipped into the lee of the tiny Island of Lobos. Fat seals lay on the rocks, their barks mingled with the screeches of the gulls whirling through the air above. The ship came slowly into view and Berthin was horrified to see it wasn´t the Tajamar. It swung around on its anchor and presented its stern. Berthin saw the name Morella painted in big, bright letters. Warning shouts rolled across the surface of the water as the Morella´s crew spotted the longboat heave into view. In seconds, the gunwales and masts were crowded with sailors.

"Is this them?" Big Perrin asked, he stopped rowing and turned around on his bench to look forward.

"Not quite." Berthin answered quietly.

"What do you mean *not quite*?" Big Perrin asked and spat over the side.

"Just row." Berthin said impatiently.

"Are we on a fool´s errand here?" Perrin asked, his eyes narrowing to slits as he leaned over his oar. "This lot are hunters and fishermen, not slavers. You can see they´ve already got their tackle out. They´re here for seals and whales, not monkeys."

"Keep your back to your work and your voice down." Berthin shot back turning around to stare at the back of the big man´s head. "The only fools here are the ones who don´t see fresh opportunity when it arises. Concentrate on your job and leave me to mine." Big Perrin harrumphed and shook his head.

"You in the boat, identify yourselves!" Berthin looked back to the ship where a man stood on the poop deck with a speaking cone held up to his mouth.

"I am Berthin de Berneval of Normandy, come to offer greetings from Gadifer de la Salle, Steward Protector of the island of Lancarote."

The man turned to speak to someone just out of sight. After a few moments, he turned back and raised the speaking cone back up to his mouth.

"You have permission to board Señor. Your boat will stand off." he called. The scourge of piracy in these waters made every sailor over-cautious.

The longboat pulled round to the Port side of the ship and nudged against the stout timbers of the hull with a dull thud. Berthin jumped onto the ship´s ladder and climbed on deck while the boat pushed off beneath him. The man who had hailed them was there to meet him. He was short and barrel chested, his head and chin shaved clean with a wide unsmiling mouth in the centre of his face. He stood with his hands clasped behind his back looking like a martial bullfrog.

"Señor de Berneval." the frog offered a clipped bow. "I am Master Ximenes. First Officer of La Morella." Berthin was surprised to hear the man speaking in flawless, if slightly accented French.

"Captain Calvo awaits you in his stateroom if you will follow me." Ximenes led Berthin across the gleaming deck. Sailors stood and watched him pass. Berthin walked as steadily as he could under their gaze. He couldn´t help but notice the vicious hooks many of the sailors held in their hands. These boys were strong, used to hauling heavy carcasses around. Berthin thought quickly, there was still a chance he could make this visit work to his own advantage.

Ximenez knocked twice on the stout wooden door at the end of the passage below the quarterdeck before pushing it open. Ximenez invited Berthin to enter the small cabin before him. Calling it a stateroom was a bit of an exaggeration. It was barely ten feet square and completely bare save for an oak desk battened to the rear wall under a row of tiny portholes. The shutters were all open. Air and light flooded into the cabin, devoid of decoration save for a small crucifix hanging on one wall.

A man sat at the desk blotting notes in a ledger with his back to the door. He closed the heavy book and pushed it to one side before standing and turning around. He was a head taller than the frog. His thick peppered hair brushed the planks of the ceiling above. His style matched the cabin he was in, austere without adornment. He wore simple yet well-made clothes on his square torso.

"Captain Francisco Calvo, may I introduce Monsieur de Berneval. He comes bearing greetings from the expeditionary force currently occupying the island of Lancarote." Calvo looked down his nose as Berthin bowed politely, returning the bow with the shallowest nod Berthin had ever seen.

Ximenes produced a chair from behind the door and invited Berthin to sit. He sat and reached inside his jacket for the sealed letter Gadifer had written. He offered it to the captain who gestured for Ximenez to take it. Ximenez did so and cracked the seal. He read the first few lines quietly to himself before translating it smoothly into Catalan for the Captain.

Berthin spoke a little Catalan but not enough to understand every word Ximenez said. He watched Calvo closely while he listened to his First Officer speak. His dark rugged features and deep, almost black eyes betrayed not one hint of emotion. He seemed too alert to be disinterested, but Berthin sensed this meeting was a distraction the captain could do well without.

On closer inspection, the captain's clothes were not as pristine as Berthin had first thought. There were frays around the cuffs of his jacket and small scars covered his strong hands. Berthin guessed he was eager to get to work on his bloody harvest. Seal skin, blubber and meat fetched a high price on the mainland, but not high enough to spend time idle.

Ximenez finished reading and placed the letter in the captain's hand. He scanned the neat handwriting quickly before placing the letter on the table behind him. He began to speak with a surprisingly quiet voice. The words tumbled from his mouth far too quickly for Berthin to understand even a syllable. He finished speaking and flicked his eyes at Ximenez.

"The captain thanks you for bringing the letter of welcome from Señor Gadifer. However, Captain Calvo would like you to know that he and his crew have plied these waters for many years and have no need of monsieur Gadifer la Salle's blessing to continue to do so in the future. He has no plans to visit Lancarote at this time and carries no word from Señor Bethencourt." Berthin watched the captain closely as Ximenez spoke. Something in his eyes alerted Berthin. They brought to mind the look the spy Norstar affected when pretending not to understand French. The *honourable* captain wasn´t quite as honest as he would have everyone believe. Berthin smiled.

Ximenez finished. Before Berthin had a chance to speak, Calvo let fly with another barrage of words.

"The captain enquires how your Priests are faring educating the natives, and also asks if you have had any contact with the tribes of the western isles?"

"Teaching the savages the Word of Christ is as pointless as trying to teach a dog to walk on its hind legs and speak." Captain Calvo raised an eyebrow. "And no. We have not yet been to the western isles."

"Captain," Berthin said leaning forward in his seat. "I can see you are a busy man and eager to get to work. I understand, seal hunting is a hard and thankless task. Up to the elbows in blood and stinking flesh for days on end and for what…? A handful of silver pennies a tonne?" The captain leaned forward slightly in his own chair. "What if I were to tell you that a far more profitable cargo awaits you on Lancarote? One that requires little effort and delivers far greater reward." Berthin waited while Ximenez translated. Calvo regarded Berthin coolly.

"I am offering the opportunity to partner with me and earn enough to buy a brand-new ship, hell, two ships. In return, all I ask is a little help to round up the cargo and give conveyance to my men and I to Portugal, or even Aragon." He finished talking and nodded for the Frog to translate.

Berthin sat back and watched Calvo´s face. The captain turned around and picked up Gadifer´s letter again while Ximenez spoke. He unfolded it, his eyes scanned across the small, neat handwriting. Berthin felt electricity crackling through his veins, even his hair fizzed in anticipation. Within a week they could be away from this interminable place and sailing home with a hold full of dusky gold.

"Berthin de Berneval. Do I pronounce that correctly?" Calvo looked directly at Berthin. His French was as Berthin suspected, flawless. He rewarded his perception with a tiny smile and nodded to the captain.

"Oui monsieur!"

"I shall remember that name and what you have proposed here today. The crusade your Lords lead is well spoken of… and may I say, very welcome in the ports of Castile. Were you aware of that?"

Berthin shook his head. "No Señor I was not."

"I am even more in awe of their accomplishments now, knowing that men conspire against them from within their own ranks. You are neither worthy of my time nor my words. Señor Gadifer on the other hand," he said lifting the letter, "I could tell him many things and possibly should, but I fear anything I write would only be tossed in the sea. I will keep this letter and remember what you proposed here today, asking for my help to wreck the noble works of señors Gadifer and Bethencourt for a purse full of blood-stained silver."

Berthin's stomach lurched as Calvo stood up. He got clumsily to his own feet to face him.

"We are finished. Leave now."

Berthin opened his mouth to speak. Calvo fired a thunderstorm of words at Ximenez.

"Señor!" Ximenez grabbed Berthin by the shoulders and manhandled him through the door. He dragged him down the short corridor and pushed him back out onto the open deck.

"I suggest you call your boat señor." he said, rubbing his hands together.

"We could be very rich men." Berthin turned to face Ximinez. "Talk with your captain."

"Call your boat or swim to it Señor." Ximenez said, walking slowly forward, forcing Berthin to back away to the top of the ladder. The boat lay only a few feet from the side and started sculling over as soon as Berthin appeared.

"I suggest you row away without looking back señor. You have offended my Captain. Do not cause him to run you down and send you to the bottom of the sea. He has done it before and I would willingly help him to do it again… for you." Berthin looked beyond

Ximenez and saw the deck and the rigging crawling with sailors brandishing hooks, knives and even one or two cutlasses.

"I was merely offering an opportunity, to you all, to enrich yourselves." Berthin said as he took a step down the ladder. "Think about it!" he said climbing down low enough to leap aboard the boat.

"Row." he hissed when he landed on the prow bench.

"How did it go?" Big Perrin asked from the stern where he gripped the tiller, obviously too tired to row anymore.

"Just fucking row!" Berthin nearly snapped his own teeth with the force of air he pushed through them.

They sculled away in silence. Every man aboard the Morella looked down on them as they slid away. Berthin glanced up and saw the grim face of Captain Calvo looking back at him through his stateroom window. Berthin despised the man and wished he had a crossbow to hand to shoot him with. *Leave integrity to the bastards with titles you fool!* he shouted defiantly in his own head before looking away.

The mood was dark on the little boat during the choppy crossing back to Lancarote. Berthin brooded the entire time. Miraculously, Big Perrin kept his mouth shut. He was too busy fighting the tiller, which bucked like an over excited dog all the way back.

Berthin was dismayed to see Gadifer waiting for them on the beach below the fortress.

"Say nothing to anybody about what has passed today." Berthin said quietly, climbing up onto the prow bench. "We will meet after dinner in the usual place. Bring everybody. We may be forced into action sooner rather than later."

The boat lurched forward as it rode high on a small wave and scraped up onto the beach, far enough for Berthin to stay dry as he leapt out onto the sand. He walked to meet Gadifer who waited well above the high tide mark. The men hauled the boat up behind him before scurrying up the hill to the camp.

"How did it go my boy?" Gadifer asked. "Are they friend or foe?"

"Seal hunters from the mainland Monsieur. Not the most amiable bunch I've ever met. They have no plans to come here anytime soon."

"I see." Gadifer sounded deflated.

"Can I be candid Monsieur?"

"Of course."

"I didn´t trust the captain. I found him duplicitous. He pretended not to understand me yet spoke perfect French. Also, he sent no reply to your letter which I find highly irregular and rather rude if I´m honest."

"Very strange." Gadifer mused. "And did they have any news of Bethencourt? Is there any word at all?"

"They claimed to have heard of him. They suggest he is being, shall we say, flamboyant, in the cities of southern Castile. Notorious even. He is well-known. They bring no word from him for us."

"Disappointing." Gadifer said, deflating further. "Did you find out why they went directly to Erbane?"

"From what I saw they were there to hunt sea wolves."

"Seal skins and hunting" Gadifer brightened instantly. "What I wouldn´t give for a spot of hunting. There is nothing on this island wild enough to make sport of. Perhaps an excursion to the island of Lobos is in order, to procure leather for our shoes."

"A very good idea Monsieur. If I might make a suggestion though?"

"Of course."

"It would be prudent to wait for the other ship to leave before visiting the island again. I got the impression the Captain of La Morella and her crew would attack first and ask questions later if anyone got too close."

"You speak well my boy. We cannot spoil his hunt, however much of a miscreant he may be, it would be most unsporting. We will wait until they leave. Did you find out how long that might be?"

"As soon as their hold is full. They´re hauling flesh, I expect they will want to make haste to the mainland before it rots."

"Good. Then I will gather a hunting party. Perfect!" He rubbed his hands together and smiled. "Now Berthin my boy, I know that you would like to come with us, but I need you here to keep an eye on things while I´m gone."

"Truly a shame that I can´t come monsieur. I miss the thrill of a good chase with a spear in my hand."

"As we all do. Good man, good man. Now hurry away and see that your men are fed and watered. I think I will bathe before dining this evening."

"Monsieur." Berthin hurried away as Gadifer began to undress.

******

Norstar's curiosity was piqued. He sat in the dunes watching as knights left the camp in twos and threes and made their way directly to the wells on the other side of the headland. Knights didn't collect water, servants did. They gathered there, waiting for something or someone. Norstar was about to suggest creeping closer when Fayna grabbed his arm. She pointed back to the camp where Berthin and the foul-mouthed fat man had just come through the gateway. They walked the same path as the others down to the wells. Berthin didn't look happy and for once the big man was silent. He looked to be in some discomfort, stopping and clutching his ribs every few steps.

"We need to get closer." Norstar whispered to Fayna. She nodded and followed closely as he slithered through the coarse dune grass and crabbed his way across to the left. Suddenly Fayna grabbed his ankle. He looked back at her. She held up two fingers and pointed away to the right. Norstar crept to the top of the dune and was horrified to see two armoured guards walking directly towards them.

He cursed and slid back down the dune.

"We have to move!" he said urgently. He had no idea whether the men were looking for him or just out on patrol. He couldn't risk capture, especially with Fayna by his side and Berthin within shouting distance.

He told Fayna to stay close and ran crouching in a direct line away from the approaching men. They kept low and moved swiftly, soon rounding a small hillock. Norstar climbed to the top and looked back the way they had come. The men stood where he and Fayna had been hidden moments before. They pointed at the ground, tracing tracks in the sand. Norstar managed to duck down just before they lifted their heads to see him.

He raced back down the hill and collected Fayna. They sprinted a few paces before slipping into a shallow gully, a sunken path leading away from the coast. It´s length choked by clumps of razor-sharp dragon plants, one nicked Norstar on the thigh as he passed by. He cursed as he felt a drop of blood fall to the ground. He spat on his fingers and pressed down on the cut, urging Fayna to move quicker. After a hundred paces or so, the gully intercepted a large dry valley. They crossed this quickly and climbed up to the lip on the other side, where a tortured old tree grew out of the cracks in a stand of rocks. They leapt behind the tree and looked back down the length of the gulley.

The two guards come into view. One of them skidded down the side of the gulley and bent over to look closely at the plants and the ground. He said something to his companion who turned towards the well where Berthin and his men were meeting. He waved his arms in the air and called out to get their attention. Norstar´s stomach lurched. He looked back to the man´s companion who was walking slowly up the gulley, scanning the ground. He stopped and pointed at the ground again and said more words to his companion. The two of them almost in unison swung crossbows from their backs and took a few seconds to prime and load them.

Norstar turned to Fayna and saw the look of horror in her eyes. He pressed two fingers of his right hand into his left palm, telling her to stay in his footprints. She nodded quickly and he took off, running doubled over to keep low, using rocks and trees as cover until they slipped into another deep gully further up the hill.

They scrabbled down into it and began moving upwards, hopping from rock to rock to avoid leaving prints in the earth. They made quick progress up the cut before vaulting onto an overhanging tree branch, using it to climb out of the gully. They paused again next to the tree´s trunk and risked another look back down the hill.

Two heads popped up at the point they had entered the little valley a hundred paces away. The two men climbed over the edge and dropped down onto the rocks. The leader crouched down to study the ground again before looking up the valley directly at the tree Norstar and Fayna hid behind. He said something to his companion who lifted his crossbow. Norstar was mortified to see the man aim directly at them. Fayna let out a small squeak.

"Quiet. Don't move." Norstar whispered. "Stay perfectly still, they can't see us. It's just a trick to try and flush us out."

The man who was reading the tracks in the earth started moving slowly up the hill, stepping carefully on the tops of the rocks, checking with his lead foot before shifting his weight forward on to the next one. Norstar watched every move waiting for an opportunity to escape. The man with the crossbow didn't waver, he looked ahead while the other scanned the ground. Suddenly a shout from further down the hill rang out. Crossbow man turned his head away to acknowledge whoever had called. Norstar didn't waste the chance to move. He ducked down dragging Fayna with him.

He looked around desperately, searching for an escape route. There was a pathway leading up to the mountain tops a short sprint away, but it was open all the way to the summit. There was no way they could climb it without being seen. He thought about doubling back the way they had come, sliding down the hill on their bellies on the opposite side of the gulley to the hunters, but it was too risky.

Fayna suddenly tugged at his arm. He turned to see her pointing over to the right to a small dark hole in the rocks twenty feet away. The mountains were full of such holes. Some were no more than shallow depressions, too small to provide shelter for a sleeping dog. Others led deep underground, linking to the cave systems that crisscrossed the entire island. Norstar nodded to Fayna to lead the way hoping it was one of the latter and not just a scratch in the earth.

Fayna set off quickly on all fours with Norstar following close behind. They reached the hole and saw that thankfully it sank down a fair way before chinking off to the side. Fayna dropped straight down without hesitation. Norstar followed, lowering his weight into the blackness as silently as he could. The tree they had been hiding behind a moment before shook. An arm appeared around the trunk.

Norstar ducked down quickly and wriggled blindly into the hole beneath him. His shins scraped past a rock that protruded into the shaft. He gripped the rock tightly and twisted his body at an awkward angle to fit around it. He cursed as his bow scraped against stone. It sounded so loud in the close confines of the cave.

His feet touched dirt and he dropped into a low crouch. A shallow layer of earth and stones covered the floor of the cave. His eyes adjusted quickly to the gloom and he saw dim outline of Fayna just a few feet away. She was facing him beckoning him to follow. He shuffled forwards, crouching to avoid scraping his bow on the rock above. In a few short paces, the tunnel opened out into a small chamber. There were two black openings side by side on the opposite wall. One of them sloped downwards to a round black hole in the ground. The other was tiny and appeared to snake upwards before twisting around a horn shaped rock and disappearing.

He pointed at the smaller one and Fayna leapt into it. She wriggled up and squeezed around the horn shaped rock. She disappeared from view and then her head popped back out into the passage urging Norstar to follow. Norstar tried but couldn't pass the horn with his bow on his back. He backed out of the hole and shrugged the bow and quiver off. He passed them to Fayna and started to climb.

A shower of stones fell down the entrance shaft behind him. He was squeezing around the horn when he heard the sound of heavy feet land on the cave floor. With an almighty heave, he dragged himself over the horn shaped rock and popped into a small lava bubble. Fayna pressed herself into a corner away from the opening giving Norstar just enough room to lay flat next to her. He pulled his feet in and held his breath.

The sound of walking feet got closer. Norstar unsheathed his obsidian knife and held it tightly to his chest. He was coiled like a viper, ready to strike.

"They had to come this way." a muffled voice said.

"Can you see anything?" asked a man much further away.

"Nothing. There's a passage leading down, but I can't see where it goes. We need torches."

"Shit. These fuckers are like rabbits. Come back up, we'll get some wood and smoke them out."

"Drop me one of those big rocks."

"Why?"

"The cave goes down a big hole, I'll drop it on their fucking heads." A muffled laugh came from outside followed shortly by a loud thud.

"Careful you idiot, you nearly hit me." Norstar heard a grunt and then some scraping, shuffling and cursing.

"You dirty fucking monkeys. Come on, I have a treat for you. HNNNGH!" The rock struck the walls as it fell, bouncing from side to side, dislodging others as it plummeted into the blackness. Norstar felt as much as heard when it hit the bottom of the shaft.

"It must be fifty feet straight down."

"Did you hit anything?"

"I don't think so, but who knows. It might have smashed their skulls in before it hit the bottom. There's no way to see. Go back and get some rope and torches."

"Is it worth it?"

"Berthin wants them caught. You can explain how we let them get away if you like. His face already looks like thunder today."

There was the sound of feet crunching away followed by more grunts as the guard climbed up and out of the cave, and then silence. Fayna breathed out loudly. Norstar put his hand up to shush her. He twisted his body around as quietly as he could and peered down the hole past the horn. The shadows were still. He could hear the sound of conversation from outside but not the words.

"We need to keep moving!" he whispered.

"Where?"

"Down. We have to go before they come back."

Fayna nodded.

Norstar eased his bulk around and backed down through the tight tunnel. He landed on the cave floor and took his bow and quiver from Fayna who crawled out after him.

"Follow me closely." he said at the edge of the black hole looking down. "Make sure your hands and feet are well braced before going down further. We go slowly and steadily." Fayna nodded. "Don't fear little one, we'll find a way out of here."

"I was about to tell you the same thing." she replied.

Norstar climbed down into the dark hole. About fifty feet said the Frenchman, a little less guessed Norstar. He could only hope that at the bottom of this shaft was another tunnel to lead them away. If not, they would have no other option but to fight.

The rock was cold and rough to touch. Looking up he saw Fayna lower her legs over the edge above him. She lay on her stomach on the cave floor, her toes feeling for a foothold. Norstar reached up and guided her foot into a hole. She found another by herself and followed him down into the chimney.

They made painfully slow progress, testing every hand and foothold with fingers and toes. Looking up, Norstar could see some grey light bleeding underground, but below was a pitch-black void. It seemed like an eternity before his outstretched toe scraped the bottom. He dropped down, got to his knees and felt around with his hands. He found the large rock hefted by the Frenchman surrounded by some smaller stones that had been smashed out of the chimney wall as it fell.

He stood and helped Fayna down the final few feet before taking out his knife. He unscrewed the round pommel from the end of the handle and shook it. A soft leather bundle fell out. Within that was a small thumb-sized lump of flint.

"Hand me your steel knife." Fayna removed her bow pouch from her back and opened a small pocket on its side. She reached her fingers in and slid out a small-bladed hunting knife. She gave it to Norstar.

"Watch your eyes." he warned before striking the flint against the blade.

A small arc of lightening leapt from the steel. Norstar repeated the action three more times, a different direction each time. He saw they were standing at the head of a narrow tunnel leading deeper into the mountain. He struck the flint again and saw the tunnel carry on for about twenty paces then bear off to the right.

"Let's see where it leads." he said striding across the rocky floor. He struck the flint every few paces but saw no other openings along the tunnel wall.

Just before they reached the bend, they heard voices. A burning torch suddenly clattered down the chimney behind them. It landed in a shower of sparks before settling to burn at a steady lick. The voices mumbled again. Seconds later, a thick coil of rope thudded down next to the flaming torch.

"Move!" Norstar hissed. They followed the tunnel round to the right and on a few paces before Norstar dare strike the flint again. He bent low to avoid hitting his head on the ceiling which was getting lower with every step. He kicked his toe painfully against a rock and had to bite the back of his hand to avoid yelling out.

The tunnel twisted to the right again and got even tighter, it then quickly turned to the left and ended at a small hole. Norstar squeezed through the hole and popped out into a huge cavern, leading even deeper below the mountain. Its end was too far to see by the light of the flint. There was a clear smooth path leading down through the boulders piled up to the left and the right. Fayna started to run along the path before Norstar hissed, stopping her in her tracks.

"Climb!" he whispered, striking the flint several times and nodding to a steep pile of boulders on the right of the path. She slung her quiver over her shoulder and climbed up and over the rock fall behind Norstar. He risked striking the flint one more time to reveal a small tight gap between the top of the rock pile and the roof of the cavern. They squeezed into it moments before the cavern ceiling exploded with colour. The shadows fled before the spluttering orange torch light from below.

"Holy Mother of God!" a voice called out. "Look at the size of this place."

Norstar held his breath. He lay as still as he could, pressing himself into the rock, transfixed by the orange light dancing across the ceiling. He heard running steps and saw the glow on the roof split into two.

"Don´t stop you fool," called out a second, much deeper voice. "We´ve got some rabbits to catch." The glow on the ceiling ran away with the footfalls. Norstar had no idea if the cavern ended in fifty paces or five hundred, the men could come racing back and discover them at any moment.

He tapped Fayna on the leg and quickly and quietly led the way back down the boulder pile. They popped back into the small tunnel and felt their way around the first two bends. Norstar froze when he saw a dim glow around the final corner. He hoped it was the torch on the floor and not another guard waiting for them.

He gave Fayna her knife and plucked his bow from his shoulders, taking an arrow and nocking it snugly onto the string. Fayna stood behind him, her knife held high. They crept forward together on silent feet. Norstar pulled back the bowstring and pivoted around the final corner. He let out his breath when he saw a spitting torch laying at the foot of the shaft and not a guard.

"Let's go!" he whispered flipping his bow onto his back. They sprinted to the chimney and found the rope still hanging down. Norstar virtually threw Fayna up it and followed her. She pulled herself up effortlessly, with her knife clenched in her teeth.

They emerged into the top cave and found the end of the rope looped around a large boulder. Fayna gripped it and was about to slice through it when Norstar grabbed her arm.

"They'll know we were here if you cut it. Let them believe they were chasing shadows."

He led the way back along the entrance tunnel, listening carefully for the sound of more guards outside. He heard nothing so climbed slowly up and out of the cave and into bright sunlight.

The heat of the sun felt like a warm blanket wrapping around his body. He scanned the mountainside quickly to see where the other Frenchmen were. Incredibly, he saw no others searching the slopes. The camp showed no sign that any alarm had been raised. He stood on his toes and could see Berthin and his men gathered by the wells. Whatever they were discussing must have been more important than helping their companions to search for intruders.

Fayna crept up behind him.

"What is it?" she asked.

"It's quiet."

"Leave it to sleep. We must go. Now!"

"Lead the way." Norstar said, following her onto the path leading up the mountainside. Their skin was the colour of the land, in moments they disappeared from view.

They were high in the peaks before they stopped running. The strong wind on the mountaintop dried their sweat and cooled their bodies. They looked back along the length of the path. Fayna pointed out the tree next to the hole. They watched with grim satisfaction as their pursuers emerged from the hole a short while later. One had the rope coiled around his body and was waving his arms in the air and stamping his feet. He heaved the rope from his shoulders and threw it at the other man before stomping away in a huff. The other stood watching him go with his hands on his hips, barking at his back like a dog on a chain. Eventually he stopped shouting and shook his head. He bent down to pick up the torches and rope from the ground. Standing up he turned to look at the mountain peaks towering above him. His head scanned slowly from left to right and back again. He shrugged his shoulders, dropped his head and sloped off after his companion.

"Your mother is going to kill me!"

"I won´t tell her if you don´t."

"She´ll know as soon as we walk in."

Fayna chewed on a fold of skin on her hand. She was worried more by her mother´s wrath than by the four hundred pounds of steel and violence that had chased her underground in the dark.

"I really cannot bring you again. They will be more alert now."

"But you need someone to watch your back."

"I´ll bring Rayco, Jonay, or one of the other men from the mountain."

"Which one? Breathless Besay or Heavy Foot the Vincible?"

"You may be quick, but speed isn´t everything. If we´d taken a wrong turn down there and been caught, there´s no telling what those bastards would have done to you."

"I wouldn´t have given them the chance. I would have sliced their cocks off faster than they could blink."

"Words are far easier to wield than a weapon, especially in the rush of a fight. Those men wore chain, if you missed with the first strike, they would have smothered you before you got the chance to strike again. Remember that these are fighting men, not boys with sticks."

"Well, we just made them look like boys."

"We were lucky."

"They were clumsy."

"They won't be next time. Nothing makes a man more determined than humiliation. We were lucky today that they didn't look into the first hole. If they had seen us, we would be dead or captured now."

Fayna huffed her shoulders.

"If we killed one, or both of them do you think that would have been the end of it?" Norstar continued. "No. It would have been the start of a war. The French would have slaughtered us all. I have seen with my own eyes the devastation men like these leave in their wake,"

"Why can't we just load up the boat and leave?"

"Because this is our home. If we leave now we might have nothing to come back to when we return."

24

Cadiz, Kingdom of Castile,

September 24th, 1402

The walls were pressing in, but it was preferable to be alone in his little wooden box than out on deck with le Brument. Jean heard the distinct sound of the Master´s shoes shuffling across the planks above his head. *Scrape, bang, scrape, bang*, a pause while he looked over the rail, turn around and then *scrap, bang, scrape, bang* back again. He was doing it more and more as the days wore on.

Jean was beginning to worry about Martin and the other knights. It was taking too long. Almost two weeks had passed since he sent them on their way with instructions to find Sir Robert. He could have gone ashore himself, but feared as soon as he was off the ship that Master le Brument would sail away. He wasn´t as much a prisoner of le Brument, as much as le Brument was a prisoner of his.

There was a knock at the door.

"Enter." he called.

The Master´s brother Colin slid back the door and pushed his way inside.

"What is it Colin?" Jean felt a judder of revulsion, this oily character made his skin crawl.

"My brother… Master le Brument has requested your presence on deck."

"Concerning what?"

"Just come with me and see for yourself."

"I´ll be there presently."

"You don´t understand, you are to come with me now."

"I am under no obligation to you Monsieur. Be gone, and I will follow when I am ready."

Colin paused for a moment, his face contorting while he made up his mind up what to do. Eventually, he left, trying but failing to slam the door behind him.

Jean let out a sigh. These brothers and their crew were proving to be more tiresome every day. No doubt the *Master* wanted more reassurance that his silver was on the way.

Jean sat back and looked at the ceiling for a moment. *SCRAPE, BANG, SCRAPE, BANG*. Le Brument was pacing again. Jean chuckled when he heard the muffled roar when Colin told him he had to wait. They really were insufferable fools. Jean looked forward to the day when they received their *payment*, in full.

He took his time dressing, making sure the sash holding his sword hung at just the right angle across his chest. It took far longer than was necessary, but it meant less time in le Brument's company.

He climbed the steep steps to the poop deck and saw Colin whispering in his brother's ear over by the stern rail. The Master waved him away irritably when he saw Jean approaching.

"Monsieur le Bethencourt. Pleased you could join us." he said, holding out his hand.

"I imagine you are." replied Jean testily, ignoring le Brument's outstretched hand. "What can I do for you this time?"

"You can explain that to me." He pointed over the rail. Jean walked over and saw three boats rowing towards them. "Isn't that your man sitting in the lead boat?"

Jean looked and was pleasantly surprised to see Martin stood in the prow of the first boat. He was even more overjoyed to see Sir Robert in the second boat. His face was ruddy and vibrant. Piquet sat huddled next to him, his arms as usual filled with a bundle of papers and scrolls. Not for the first time Jean wondered why he didn't put them all in a bag.

"Those are the colours of the Castilian royal guard if I am not mistaken." Le Brument said pointing to the third boat with a squad of guards sat on its benches. "Why would he be bringing Castilian soldiers to a business transaction?"

"I imagine because the amount of silver he is carrying warrants extra security." Jean replied. "I suggest you call your men up on deck. This is what you have all been waiting for."

The Master harried Colin to rouse everyone from below. Jean could hardly stifle a smile as he walked down the steps to the main deck. Le Brument followed so closely that Jean felt his sour breath on the back of his neck. He stopped at the port gunwale and waved to the approaching boats.

"Bethencourt!" Sir Robert called. "A pleasure to see you monsieur!"

"To you too Sir Robert." Jean answered. "Please, you are most welcome on board."

"Do you mind monsieur." Le Brument bristled. "It is for me to decide who is welcome on board my ship."

"Master le Brument." Jean smiled and dropped his head. "Please. Extend your invitation."

"You've already done it now." le Brument huffed. The ship's crew began spilling out on deck and gathered in an untidy gaggle behind the Master. Jean turned away shaking his head. He reached out his hand to help Sir Robert climb the last two steps up to the deck.

"I hear good things my boy." Sir Robert said, gripping Jean's hand. They moved away from the top of the ladder to make room for the others to follow.

"I will tell you everything once we have dealt with Master le Brument and his men." Jean answered.

"Ah yes! Le Brument. That I imagine is you monsieur." Sir Robert turned to study le Brument who stopped attempting to arrange his men into an orderly line and shuffled forward, his hand held out. Sir Robert regarded the hand as if the man was offering him a turd. Le Brument pulled it back quickly.

"And these are all your men?" Sir Robert asked turning round, collecting a piece of paper from Piquet, which he passed on to le Brument. "Could you confirm that they are all listed here and are present." Le Brument took the paper and read quickly.

"You're missing one. Blind Fabrice the lookout." Piquet took the paper from him.

"Add that name to the bottom." Instructed Sir Robert redundantly, Piquet was already fishing in his coat pocket for his stylus and ink. A dozen guards formed a line and passed three hefty strongboxes from the boats, up and onto the deck. They laid them at le Brument's feet. They hit the deck with a satisfying clunk.

"There you go boys. I told you I'd get us what was owed us." Le Brument crowed triumphantly. He approached the first chest licking the tips of his fingers. He looked up at Sir Robert. "May I?"

"One moment. Piquet?" Piquet came rushing forward with the amended paper and laid it out on top of one of the chests.

"If you could sign your name at the bottom please." Piquet said holding out the stylus to le Brument. Le Brument snatched it and scribbled his signature quickly. Piquet took the stylus and quickly blotted the ink before whisking the paper away and showing it to Sir Robert. Sir Robert nodded and Piquet disappeared behind the guards.

"Be my guest." Sir Robert waved his hand over the chests.

Le Brument got to his knees in front of the centre chest and fumbled the clasp in his haste to undo it. He cursed somebody's mother at length before eventually sliding out the bolt and flinging back the lid. There was no silver waiting to light up his face inside the chest, only cold grey iron.

"What is the meaning of this?" he demanded shrilly.

"Your reward." Sir Robert answered dryly. "One set each. Guards!"

The guards lowered their spears as one. The points tickled the chins of le Brument's men. They looked down the sharp blades, their faces contorted with terror and confusion.

"Acting on behalf of Charles, King of France with the blessing and cooperation of his Grace Enrique of Castile, I hereby order your arrest Master Robin le Brument. Along with all the co-conspirators listed here." Piquet stepped forward and put the paper back in Sir Robert's outstretched hand. He squinted as he read "Including *Blind Fabrice the Lookout*. For the crimes of mutiny, kidnap, theft, blackmail and attempted murder."

"B b b but…" le Brument began.

"Monsieur, I believe you have nothing to say. The charges are clear and verified by many witnesses. You will be tried, judged and convicted in very short order. I will recommend your immediate execution if I hear one more word out of your mouth."

Le Brument could only stare dumfounded as iron cuffs were clamped and locked around his wrists. Tears were falling from his eyes freely by the time he was prodded down the ladder into the boat.

Two boats filled quickly with guards and prisoners and shoved off. Jean remained on the ship with Sir Robert, Martin and Piquet. They watched the sorry looking mess of human flotsam being rowed across the harbour, off to spend the rest of their sorry lives in one of King Enrique's deep, dark dungeons.

"What a thoroughly disagreeable chap!" said Sir Robert.

"A scoundrel to be sure." added Jean "I'm not sure how much longer I would have been able to stand his company before throwing myself overboard and swimming to shore."

"Well, I for one am glad to find you still here." said Sir Robert thumping him on the back. "You handled that whole unfortunate situation with a cool head Monsieur. I am proud of you. Now tell me there is something to drink on this tub. We have much to discuss and I would find it easier if my mouth were lubricated."

"Certainly." Jean answered. "Go below Martin and see what you can find in le Brument's cabin."

"Best go with him Piquet, secure the logs." Sir Robert added.

Martin and Piquet hurried off. Jean led Sir Robert up the steps to the poop deck where they had a clear view of the longboats rowing back to shore. Jean saw le Brument huddled over like a cowardly rat. Far different from the cocksure slob who had skulked in his cabin for the last few weeks, barking at a crew too dim-witted to realise they followed the orders of a misguided fool.

Sir Robert brushed the glossy wood of the rail with his fingertips. Satisfied it was clean enough he turned around and leaned against it. He appraised Jean for a moment.

"I've got to say you're looking slightly dishevelled my boy. We are going to have to get you smartened up if you are to be presented to the King." he said smiling.

"Is he here?" Jean asked, standing up straighter and pulling at his slightly worn coat.

"He is making for Seville as we speak, if he hasn´t already arrived. I imagine he will be most interested to learn how your crusade is progressing, as am I. How did you leave it down there?"

"Stable. I left Gadifer in charge."

"The same Gadifer who nearly lost his ship?"

"The very same."

"Instances of mutiny tend to have one thing in common, a weak leader."

"Yes. I thought the same, which is why I left Father Verrier to keep an eye on him."

"I worry about his ability. It takes a very special talent to have one´s crew risk their lives to mutiny. If Gadifer were to lose control on the island, chaos would reign. I hear from your man that there is already one seditious voice within your company who makes mischief."

"I left Gadifer to rout him out with young Berthin´s help."

"Ah! The infamous Berthin. How is he shaping up?"

"Adequate for the most part. Some of the men appear to have taken to him quite well. Although at times I find... I find him, no... He makes me feel... I can´t quite put my finger on what it is about him. It is most strange."

"Strange how?"

"He is there when he´s there, the rest of the time he is nowhere, it´s like he lives in the shadows between my thoughts. Blink and he is gone." Sir Robert looked at Jean curiously before the sound of footsteps coming from below diverted his attention.

"Ah! Perfect timing. Messieurs." Sir Robert stood and tugged down the back of his tunic. Martin and Piquet were climbing the steps. Martin carried a decanter of ruby red wine and two cups, Piquet struggled with even more papers and a thick ledger wedged under one arm."

"Share a drink with me Monsieur and tell me everything. Tell me of the dusky warriors who wander around the island as naked as the day they were born."

Jean laughed. Martin passed cups and splashed wine into them.

"To which King shall we drink today?" Jean asked.

"How about to the Ruler of the Canary Islands my boy." Sir Robert replied tilting his cup to Jean.

"Guadarfia. A truly noble gentleman." Jean answered raising his wine.

"He is only a King on one island. I drink to the ruler of all seven islands." Sir Robert said watching Jean closely over the rim of his cup.

25

Rubicon, Lancarote,
October 13th, 1402

Gadifer stretched, but it didn´t dull the pain in his knee. The changing seasons brought heavy showers and a chill to the air causing his joints to complain bitterly. He walked around the parapet of the fortress looking down into the camp. The heavy building work had shifted from the fortress into the camp itself. Tents were moved to make room for some more permanent structures. Shells of new buildings lined a central avenue linking the fortress with the gateway in the wall. Work was progressing achingly slowly as there were only a handful of natives left in camp to do the heavy lifting and carrying.

Gadifer was on his third circuit of the parapet when he spied movement across the water. He stopped and turned to see a puff of sail against the hazy outline of Erbania heading west. The hunters were leaving Lobos.

The pain in his knee disappeared. He crossed the roof and skipped down the steps to the gate room. He hesitated at the door, deciding to offer a quick thanks to God before going off to hunt, it couldn´t hurt.

The chapel was empty, as he liked it. Light bled into its dark interior through a cross-shaped arrow slit in the wall above the rough sandstone altar. Gadifer walked forward and knelt on one knee. He bowed his head, lifted it again, crossed himself and stood up. It was a short prayer. The hunt was calling.

Turning to leave he was surprised by Father Verrier who stepped out of a dark corner holding several small books clasped to his chest.

"Ah! Monsieur Gadifer." he said smiling broadly. "I thought it was you."

"Father." Gadifer replied with a stiff nod.

"I was hoping to run into you today."

"Really?"

"Yes. I was wondering if you might have a word with young Berthin. He has seconded Pierre and Guillaume for extra guard duty. I was hoping to leave in the morning for the western settlements, but my knights appear to be unavailable."

"I was heading over to see Berthin anyway. I will speak with him about your men."

"Thank you."

"Now if you will excuse me Father, I have some good news to spread. The Spaniards have left Lobos."

"Ah! I see. When will be leaving?"

"As soon as the boat is packed."

"And you say it´s leather for shoes you are going for?"

"Indeed. We should be gone for no more than five days, a week at most."

"Perhaps I should stay here while you are gone, to keep an eye on things."

"I don´t think that will be necessary Father. The builders know their task and Berthin is proving to be more than adequate at organising the guards."

"Perhaps you are right. Yes, go and do what you must and leave me to find and minister to my flock."

"Good hunting." Gadifer said, bowing quickly and hurrying for the door.

"Yes, thank you. The same to you I suppose." said Father Verrier to his back.

Once outside, Gadifer made a beeline for the tent of Remonet. He found his old friend sat with a small group of Gascons around a collection of feathers, hooks and string spread out on a white sheet. They were concentrating so hard on the intricate lures they were tying that they didn´t notice Gadifer creep up behind them.

"Good to see you all keeping busy." Gadifer said quietly in Remonet´s ear.

"What the...!" Remonet started, turning round and seeing Gadifer´s smiling face over his shoulder. "Don´t creep up on me like that, scared me half to death you old fool." Gadifer laughed.

"Why are you tying freshwater lures?" Gadifer asked.

"We´re getting desperate. The cook´s boy caught a big one yesterday and challenged us to beat it." Remonet held up the lure he was wrestling with for Gadifer to inspect. "I reckon with a bit of Gascon knowhow and engineering, we´ll be reeling in some of the monsters we´ve seen beyond the western headland. Would you care to join us?"

"Normally I would. But I´m hoping to get a spot of hunting in."

"Have they left?" Remonet asked eagerly.

Gadifer nodded. "Sailing west as we speak."

"Marvellous." Remonet said throwing down his half-finished lure.

"Don´t break it, bring it along. You might catch a monster over there."

"Do you really think there´ll be any fish worth catching with a pack of wolves on the prowl."

"Probably not." laughed Gadifer. "Gather the men and fill the boat. We leave within the hour." The little group cheered. Gadifer left them throwing their lures onto the sheet and hurried away. It felt good to deliver some good news for a change. It buoyed Gadifer´s mood as he picked his way through the camp to find Berthin.

He stopped at the kitchen block to inform the cooks that there would be at least a dozen fewer dining for a few days. While there, he checked the stores. They were getting low on oats and barley, but there was a healthy supply of dried meat and fish, sweet dates and milk, with enough wine for another three months at least. His small barrel of vintage wine was untapped. He considered taking it along but decided against it. They would save it for the celebration when Rubicon was complete.

Satisfied, he left the kitchen and walked past the long line of dining tables. He noticed Brother Bontier with Isabel, teaching a small group of natives at the end of one table. Gadifer paused to listen to the lesson for a moment. He heard a pair of natives stumble through several passages of the bible study book Bontier was using to teach them. He was impressed with the progress they had made within a few short weeks. He lingered for a few moments before making his way to the gateway where he found Berthin stood with four guards dressed for patrol. After a couple of uncomfortable attempts to draw more than a grunt from the men, Gadifer led Berthin away to speak in private.

"The Spaniards are leaving Lobos," he began once they were out of earshot. "I´ll be taking a dozen men with me hunting, which means I´ll be leaving you in charge for a few days."

"I will do my best to maintain order in your absence." Berthin said quickly.

"Yes, I´m sure you will. There are a couple of issues I need you to address while I´m away. Firstly, your guards need to find the idle slobs who have been defecating inside the walls. I need you to find the culprits and stop them. We´ll be overrun by vermin if it continues."

"Yes Monsieur, I´ll get right on it."

"See that you do. Another thing, I have just been talking with Father Verrier. He tells me you have pressed his knights into extra guard duty."

"Yes Monsieur. I need them to cover the gate while my men are out on patrol."

"I understand that, but Father Verrier is eager to leave and round up his flock. I would prefer if he was accompanied by guards outside the walls. The natives appear to be peaceful but it´s best not to take too many chances."

"Very well, I will see what I can do."

"Skim men from your patrols. How many are you sending out?"

"Three rotations of four men per tour."

"Why so many? Is there a threat from the locals?"

"No Monsieur. I´m merely doing as you suggested."

"I suggested?"

"Yes Monsieur. I recalled the time you gave me the duck speech. *The legs are busy out of sight, while the body glides peacefully across the surface.* This could be one of those instances monsieur. It all appears quiet, but the natives could be working furiously below the surface to upset things. The presence of our knights could well serve to dissuade them if they are indeed plotting against us."

"Hmmm yes." replied Gadifer, buffed a little by Berthin´s reverence. "Well remembered my boy. But in this instance, I believe the chance of insurrection is slight. This Guadarfia fellow seems to be a rather decent chap. I am worried however, about the threat from within. Tell me. How has the search for the bad apple been going? You haven´t reported anything for some time."

"There is nothing to report Monsieur, everything appears to be quiet. I can only conclude that the man stirring up the trouble left to the mainland with monsieur de Bethencourt."

"I suspected as much." Gadifer agreed. "Let us hope Bethencourt discovers the man´s identity and leaves him in a Castilian cell to rot."

A shrill whistle coming from the gate interrupted them. Berthin turned to look to the guard who had sounded the alert, he was pointing inland. Berthin looked and saw a flash of sunlight glinting off a metal helmet.

"It seems that one of our patrols is coming back early. Do you mind if I…"

"Lead the way." Gadifer said. The pair hustled back to the gate where the guards stood watching the four-man patrol trotting towards them through the waves of heat rising from the ground.

"Something must be afoot." commented one of the guards. "They weren´t due back until later this evening."

"Let´s wait and see." Berthin said with a glare at the guard.

The small patrol soon arrived. Gadifer walked forward to meet them with Berthin at his shoulder.

"Gentleman. Why the haste. Is there a problem?" Gadifer asked before Berthin had chance to open his mouth.

"Erm! No monsieur." answered William de Blessi, the leader of the patrol appearing to be ill at ease addressing Gadifer and not Berthin. "Everything is as it should be."

"Then why have you returned early?"

"We finished our circuit quickly and were eager to get back monsieur. We saw nothing out of the ordinary."

"Very well." Gadifer said. He was pleased there was no emergency to keep him tied to the island. "I will leave Berthin to debrief you. Berthin, come and see me on the beach when you have finished." He turned abruptly and marched back through the gate, eager to be packed and on his way.

280

****

Berthin watched Gadifer until he was completely out of sight before turning to William.

"Tell me." he said.

"The ship has arrived. We saw it this morning, must have slipped in last night and anchored in the bay at Graciosa."

"Can you be sure it´s them?" Berthin asked.

"We were too far away to see the name, but it flew Castilian colours and had a black hull as you described." William reported.

"Excellent. It appears that the stars are finally beginning to align in our favour. You are not to say anything to anyone about this ship." The guards all looked back at him nodding. "…and I mean not a single word, until Gadifer is off the island."

"He´s leaving?" William asked

"The Morella left a short while ago. Gadifer is taking his men and going to Lobos in the boat. If he learns that another ship arrived in the night he won´t go. We need him gone, so keep your mouths shut. We leave for the North as soon as his boat leaves. Meet back here then, ready to march."

With that he turned on his heal and hurried off to his tent. He was dismayed to find the girl Nicol loitering outside, obviously craving some attention. She had slipped into his tent several times since their first encounter, seeming to possess a taste for the depravities Berthin had delighted in inflicting upon her young body. He had no time to enjoy her muffled screams now though, his mind was on other things.

"Monsieur." She attempted a demure courtesy as he approached.

"This is not the time girl. Be off with you." Berthin said gruffly, pushing past her and storming into the tent.

"But monsieur…" Nicol said, following him inside and closing the tent flap behind her.

He rounded on her, grabbing her roughly by the throat.

"I said that this is not the time. Leave now." He pushed her away. She tripped over her skirts and fell on her back. She let out a small whimper. Berthin pounced on top of her and clapped his hand over her mouth.

"I have neither the time nor the patience to deal with you right now girl." he hissed into her face. His anger seemed only to excite her. She looked up at him through hooded eyes, bit the rough salty palm of his hand and raked her nails across his back.

Berthin closed his eyes and opened his mouth to scream. Nicol clapped a hand over it and squeezed. Berthin felt a strong stirring in his loins and realised suddenly that he did have some time to spare after all.

****

Norstar leaned forward as far as he could over the edge of the lookout nest to see the black hulled ship fouling up the waters of Graciosa. It's stench was visible, infecting everything surrounding it like a plague mark on young skin.

"Are you certain?" he asked. "No boats have left the ship?"

"No brother." Rayco answered. "Not one since I have been here."

"We should get a message to Guadarfia, get him up here." Norstar said, not taking his eyes from the unwelcome visitor.

"I sent a runner as soon as I arrived."

"What about Beselch?" asked Norstar.

"Him too, they should both be here soon."

"We should get a message back home too. Tell them to make for the deep caves."

"Jonay's already on the way."

"Good. Who was here when you arrived?" Norstar asked.

"Two of Beselch's. Snoring under furs. I sent them to Guadarfia and Beselch."

"Everybody has gotten too lax." Norstar ruminated.

"They don't feel the need to bother anymore. The French promised to protect them." Rayco leaned out to get a clear look at the black ship.

"So they did. Let us see if they are good to their word."

The sun dipped below the clouds to the West, bathing them in a warm orange glow for the briefest time before it disappeared. King

Guadarfia, Avago and a handful of heavily armed men slid down beside them just after dark. Fat heavy clouds slammed into the cliffs in the middle of the night. Thunder rolled and lightning strobed. Hail and raindrops followed, washing the heat out of the earth.

26

Sky Bird Lookout, Lancarote,

October 14th

A dozen French knights arrived just after dawn. Norstar and Rayco watched them light a small fire on the headland across the strait from the black ship. A boat detached from the ship and collected a small delegation, led by Berthin. They were below decks for a long time before they were ferried back to the Lancarote shore.

They left immediately and struck out along the path leading back to Rubicon, followed at a distance by a large group of Majos. They were a long way inland before Guadarfia ordered everyone to hide. He walked forward with Avago by his side and hailed the Frenchmen. Norstar crouched behind a boulder, an arrow nocked and ready in his bow. Rayco lay at his side fingering his tenique.

Norstar almost hoped the French would turn hostile, he had a clear shot of Berthin. The conversation was brief however and Berthin appeared to be pleased to meet with Guadarfia. After only a few moments, their conversation ended and the French continued on their way. Norstar watched until last knight ambled out of sight around a bend in the path before leaving his hiding place. He joined the others thronging around Guadarfia demanding to know what was said. The Mence waited until there was silence before speaking.

"The one named Berthin tells me he met with the leader of the slavers. They say they are only here to make repairs to their ship, and then they will move on."

"Why doesn´t he stay to watch them?" Beselch spat. "He is running away from the slavers to the safety of his fortress." Beselch´s outburst got a roar of approval.

"He will return with more men tomorrow."

"Why did he not leave any of his men watching the black ship today?" Beselch asked. "They told us when they came that they were here to protect us from this, yet at the first sign of any threat they turn tail and run. Where is your colourful friend, Bethencourt, the leader, the one who made all the promises, took plenty from us, and left? Where is the warrior with the shiny suit, Gadifer? Why hasn't he come? Why have they sent this boy, Berthin?"

"I would like to know the same." Guadarfia answered, turning to look over everyone's heads and fixing Norstar in his gaze. "Have you seen anything?" he asked, catching Norstar a little by surprise.

"I saw Gadifer the day before yesterday, standing on his fortress roof. Yesterday I was on the cliff top with you all." Norstar answered.

"Pah!" scoffed Beselch turning back to face Guadarfia. "I have told you to ask *my man* to spy for you." He turned around and grabbed Alfonso by the shoulder. He dragged him forward to face Guadarfia.

"Your man hasn't left his village for nearly two moons. It is difficult to see Rubicon from your daughter's hearth." Guadarfia's answer raised a ripple of laughter. It was common knowledge that Beselch was encouraging his youngest daughter to woo Alfonso.

"He will go now." Beselch snapped irritably. "He will discover the answers to our questions. He will be better than your spy was." Beselch said, pushing Alfonso further forward.

Norstar didn't appreciate the slight but saw the wisdom in the suggestion. Alfonso could move around the camp freely and had the ear of the Priests. They would tell him all they needed to know.

"Would you do this?" Guadarfia asked Alfonso who looked anything but ready to return to Rubicon.

"Of course he will!" roared Beselch. Alfonso nodded weakly.

"Then so be it. Until we hear from him we will continue to watch the black ship." Guadarfia proclaimed before Beselch interrupted, addressing Alfonso directly.

"Leave now, but tread carefully. Do not be discovered as Norstar was." Norstar's mouth dropped open. Over Beselch's shoulder he saw Beselch's idiot son Belicar sneering over at him. Rayco touched his arm and shook his head. Norstar closed his mouth and laughed to himself.

"Go." Guadarfia said to Alfonso. Everybody looked on in silence as Beselch made a big show of packing an unenthusiastic

Alfonso off on his way before marching the rest of his men back along the path to the cliff tops.

When they had gone, Avago excused himself from Guadarfia´s side and walked over to Norstar and Rayco.

"I am glad you refused to let Beselch goad you just now." he congratulated Norstar.

"It is a game he feels he must play. He will tire of it if I refuse to play it with him." answered Norstar. "It sounded like he was beginning to play the same game with the Mence there for a moment."

"Beselch has been testing the Mence´s patience for many moons now. He is gaining strength and support in the North. Nichel counsels him. I fear they plot to challenge Guadarfia´s leadership."

"They would do that?" asked Norstar, surprised but not shocked.

"Beselch and his tribe control the orchil and dragon´s blood. He has begun to trade directly with the French using Alfonso as his personal translator. With Bethencourt gone, Guadarfia has lost some of his influence over the French. Nichel is also working against him, persuading the older ones that Guadarfia is giving up our religion and the old ways too readily. It is a view that has a lot of support in the North."

"If this is known to Guadarfia, why doesn´t he challenge Beselch?" Rayco asked.

"The Mence is reluctant to use brute force to get his own way. He holds out hope that Beselch will realise that dividing the island will only weaken us."

"I would have Beselch beaten and that would be the end of it." Rayco spat.

"And that, my son, is why you are not the Mence. A beating would not be the end of it. I thought the same for a time until I realised how deep the bad feeling runs with the northerners. There would be war between us. The French would watch us kill each other and then have total control over the island. We need to work together as one for our very survival, not allow the greed and ambition of one man to put our future at risk."

Guadarfia appeared at Avago´s side.

"Mence!" Rayco said.

"Rayco, Norstar." Guadarfia boomed quietly. "Are you ready to stand watch with me for one more night?"

"We are Mence." Norstar replied, feeling a sudden wave of affection for his King.

****

Berthin was pleasantly surprised when he arrived at the wells. Courtille, Gadifer´s trumpeter had done an excellent job of rounding up extra men. All but four of Gadifer´s knights had turned up for the meeting, there must have only been a half dozen men left in Rubicon. Philip, the Peacock´s diminutive tailor puffed his chest out. He had persuaded a couple of Norman heavyweights to attend and was grinning up at Berthin seeking his approval like a cat with a mouse.

Berthin ignored the little man and counted the heads of the knights present. Gadifer was on Lobos with twelve men. The Peacock had taken five to the mainland. The Priest´s knights couldn´t be counted on so nobody had tried tempting them. Out of the thirty-three knights left in Rubicon, he had over twenty of them. With the thirty scrappers he had been promised from the Tajamar he had more than enough men to get the job done.

He walked confidently into the midst of the throng and an expectant hush descended.

"Gentlemen!" he called when all chatter had ceased. "First of all I would like to thank you for coming this evening. Before I begin, I need you to swear that not one word of what is to be discussed here this evening will be spread around the camp." A low murmur of assent answered him.

He waited for silence once more, his fingers stroking the pommel of his sword.

"We stand here, abandoned." he began quietly, "We few, who have risked our lives and reputations to follow our leaders on *their* quest for glory. One of our *glorious* leaders has taken some... not all, just a select few, to take sport and vacation with him on another island. The other openly flaunts our bounty around the cities of Castile, courting King

287

Enrique, and telling tales of how he, the mighty warlord, single-handedly tamed this island of savages.

"When I, like most of you, swore my oath to become a knight, I swore it to God, His Saints and to my King, King Charles of France. I feel sullied by having my loyalty sworn to another without my consent, and I resent being left here to build walls in the sand while Monsieur de Bethencourt curries favour with his foreign king. The Castilians hold our leashes as if we were their dogs, here to do their bidding without hint of reward. I feel ashamed to be in this position."

There were rumblings of assent coming from his men.

"This is horse shit!" spat one of the older knights, Jean the Mason the master builder. "How can you say that monsieur Gadifer works against his own country?"

"And that monsieur Bethencourt has duped us?" said the knight stood next to him, Jean le Chavalier, another old knight in the autumn of his years. "We have won an honourable victory here without bloodshed, all thanks to the wise leadership of Gadifer and Bethencourt."

"Gentlemen," Berthin answered raising his hands. "I have said what I have said and believe it to be correct. The evidence is there for all of you to see. I am not here for a discussion but to make a proposition. You are at liberty to leave whenever you choose."

"Then I will take my leave now. I will hear no more of your seditious tripe." Jean the Mason spat before walking away from the gathering followed by le Chevalier and two other knights.

Berthin watched them go before turning to address the ones who remained. "If any others wish to leave, now is the time." None did. He took a deep breath before continuing.

"There is a ship anchored off Graciosa. I have secured passage to France where I will petition King Charles for men and arms. I intend to return, with his blessing, and take this rock from the current tenants for the Glory of France."

The crowd voiced their approval. One man stood still in a small huddle of Gascons with his arms folded, looking askance at Berthin.

"Monsieur Siort, is there a problem?" Berthin asked him.

"I was wondering why, if your plan is so simple, do you need our help?"

"I need your swords for one night. I need to secure certain goods from the savages to pay for passage back to the mainland. I ask for nothing more."

"One night of sword play?" Siort asked.

Berthin nodded. "One night, for the glory of France and our King. That is all I ask."

The men surrounding Siort looked to him. Siort took a moment, staring into the distance before looking back into Berthin's face. He nodded once.

Berthin walked forward and shook his hand warmly.

The air was split by the sound of an arrow zipping over their heads. Berthin ducked and swung around to see William with his bow arm raised, reaching over his shoulder to take another arrow. He stepped forward, his eyes locked on a target in the distance.

"What are you doing man!?" hissed Berthin.

"That monkey who escaped us last time. I just saw him back there in the dunes." Berthin swung around to look where he was aiming.

"Go! Bring him to me." he ordered.

William sprinted away through the dunes followed closely by young Gillet and Big Perrin.

"Is there something we should know?" Siort asked suddenly, concern creasing his brow.

"Nothing at all." answered Berthin, smiling to cover his anger. He should have tracked down that Norstar character and gutted him like a pig a long time ago. "Just a young savage who has been following our patrols and goading us. Savage by name and savage by nature."

"I thought they were meant to be harmless." Siort said.

"You haven't been patrolling the interior. We face them every day and have witnessed many deprivations. Acts of aggression we could never do anything about while Bethencourt kept our hands tied. Well I for one have had enough of kowtowing to these animals. The time has come to prove our dominion over them."

****

Alfonso ran as quickly as his legs would carry him. He dropped down to the beach where he hid in a small cleft in the rock wall. He pushed himself as far back into the darkness as he could and lay there, trying to listen over the beating of his heart for any sound of pursuit.

The arrow had missed his head by a hair's breadth and scared him half to death. There was no way he was going to continue spying for Guadarfia if his life was the price. He decided to abandon the camp and sneak away under cover of night. There were plenty of places he could lay low for a while until it was safe to return to his home in the North. Beselch would forgive him in time.

He waited until it was fully dark outside before creeping back out onto the beach. The journey back to the camp took an age as he stopped every few paces to make sure he wasn't being followed. Eventually he snuck back into Rubicon over the perimeter wall and was relieved to find the tent he shared with Isabel where he left it.

A lot of changes had been made to the camp since his last visit. The most notable being how much quieter it was. There were hardly any bodies moving around, French or Majo. Isabel would tell him why when she returned from wherever she was. He decided to wait to speak to her, get the information he needed for Guadarfia and then leave. That would be better than running away with nothing.

He settled down on his cot to wait for her to arrive. His eyes closed for a moment. They stayed closed for the rest of the night.

27

Sky Bird Lookout, Lancarote,
October 15th, 1402

They came at first light, two boats crowded with dark-skinned men with black hair and hearts to match. The sun glinted off the cutlasses they wore tucked in their belts. They were quiet and menacing, with the lean hungry looks of those well acquainted with violence.

Norstar stood with Guadarfia watching them cross the strait and land on the beach below. Two messengers were immediately despatched to Rubicon to inform the French. Other runners left to spread word to every corner of the island to tell the people to get to the deep caves.

"There are only thirty of them." Norstar said to Guadarfia when the runners had all left. "We could knock them off the side of the cliff without losing any of our men."

"We wait. We will see if the French are good to their word." Guadarfia replied sombrely, not taking his eyes from the beach below.

There were two paths up and over the cliffs from the beach. One led directly up the twisting Giant's Staircase to the eastern side of the island. The other traversed the face of the cliff, leading west to Acatife and Zonzamas. Norstar and his men had prepared rock falls on both paths months earlier, before the French arrived. Huge hoppers were filled with stone, ready to be dropped on the heads of any unwelcome visitors walking up exposed sections of the pathways.

Beselch and his son Belicar slithered down the scree wall into the lookout nest. Beselch elbowed his way between Norstar and Guadarfia. He visibly paled as he saw the slavers below. His people lived in settlements in the valleys behind the cliffs. His own home, nestled in the most fertile of these valleys would be the first the slavers would encounter if they took the staircase path.

"We should spring the traps now, stop them from climbing." Beselch said.

"We don´t yet know which path they will take." Guadarfia replied.

"But if we block this one, they will be forced to take the other." Beselch reasoned.

"And if we block this path now, they will know we are watching them." Guadarfia parried. Norstar saw by the way he chewed the inside of his mouth that Beselch´s belligerence was beginning to annoy the Mence.

"If we trigger the trap now, they will suspect the other is also rigged and simply put ashore further down the coast." Norstar added. "If we wait until they begin climbing, we can crush them all."

Beselch was without words for a moment.

The atmosphere inside the nest was charged. Every emotion stretched to breaking point with so much tension in the air. Norstar couldn´t just stand around doing nothing, he had to move, do anything.

"I should go and prepare the traps." he said, his fists clenching and unclenching, the adrenaline rush was even making his scalp itch. Guadarfia simply nodded without turning.

Norstar shared a look with Avago. The old man nodded and put his hand over his heart. Norstar grabbed Rayco by the arm and the pair climbed up and out of the nest.

****

Berthin arrived at the gateway where two natives stood waiting to speak to him. He sent one of the guards to fetch a translator, annoyed that they hadn´t thought to do it already. By the time the guard returned with a dishevelled and twitching Alfonso a small crowd had gathered around the gateway, including the Priest and Friar.

Berthin listened as the savages spat out their guttural words, trying his best to appear shocked and angry as the savages explained that the slavers had landed. By the time the story had been told, the rest of the camp crowded round the gateway listening.

"You visited with the slavers yesterday?" Father Verrier turned on Berthin. "Why is this the first I am hearing of it?"

"I did indeed visit with them, to warn them that the island was under our protection and to leave. I didn´t tell you Father because monsieur Gadifer left strict instructions that I should use my judgement on all martial matters. I saw no reason to consult with you before acting." Berthin replied haughtily.

"But this matter concerns us all." Verrier protested.

"Father, please forgive me for being blunt, but I would not expect you to ask my advice when teaching the heathens the ways of the Church. By the same logic, I would not expect you to instruct me on the best way to deploy my men. Now if you will excuse me." Verrier opened his mouth to reply but Berthin pointedly turned away from him and addressed Alfonso.

"Tell these men to hurry back to their King and inform him that I will follow immediately with a force to repel these invaders. We will meet with him in Acatife." He waited until Alfonso had finished speaking. The savages simply nodded, turned and sprinted away. Berthin noticed a look of longing in Alfonso´s eyes as the messengers ran away. He smiled to himself. He had completely forgotten about the translators. They would fetch a fine price on the auction block.

He took a deep breath and turned to face the crowd gathered at the gate.

"I am going to speak with these Spaniards and as God is my witness, if they refuse to listen to me, I am willing to kill or be killed to see that they leave the island. Those of you with me collect your things and meet back here." He finished speaking and barged through the crowd, not giving any a chance to question him.

It took no time to collect his things from the tent, what little he cared for was already packed and ready to go. He grabbed his spear and helmet and hurried back to the gateway. All twenty-five of his men were there waiting. The Priest and the Friar were stood talking in a huddle with their knights, Pierre and Guillaume. Berthin strode up to them and broke into their conversation.

"I need the translators if I am to speak with Guadarfia." he said, nodding to Isabel and Alfonso who stood behind Brother Bontier.

"Very well." Verrier replied. He turned to Isabel and Alfonso and sent them away to collect their things. He turned back to Berthin.

"I ask you to reconsider this action." he pleaded gently. "You cannot and should not draw blood on this island in the name of the Lord. I insist you allow myself and Brother Bontier to accompany you to talk with these slavers."

"The time for peaceful negotiation has passed Father. These slavers have no respect for the words of men or God, they only respond to the whisperings of cold steel. My blade, and those of my men shall sing to them the sweetest of lullabies to send them into a deep sleep."

"At least send word to Gadifer and seek his counsel."

"And how are we supposed to get word to him when he possesses our only boat? No. I am committed. This is the way it must be." Berthin finished, looking down into the soft, pitiful eyes of the Priest.

The little man turned to lead his pious party away, shaking his head and wringing his hands. He stopped at the gateway to bid farewell to the translators who had returned from their tent carrying travelling packs.

Berthin waved for the two savages to hurry. They ran forward and Berthin placed them in the centre of the line of Knights stood waiting to get underway.

Berthin ordered the column to move. He watched them file away then turned back to look at the Priest's party framed in the gateway with the fortress at their backs. A smile threatened his face when he realised that this was probably the last time he would ever have to set eyes upon the tawdry little place and it's people ever again. They could all rot in the heat and stink. He was going home.

****

The sweat poured off Gadifer's brow. He inspected the freshly scraped skin stretched upon the tanning rack and decided it was time to take a nap to wait out the midday heat. The others were already sitting under the makeshift parasol they had made from the boat's sail.

He washed his knife in a bucket of bloody water at his feet and wiped it dry, inspecting the blade carefully before putting it back in the sheath on his hip. He picked up the bucket and walked over to a rock pool where he washed his hands and rinsed the bucket out. Slithers of seal flesh slid from the bucket and slopped into the pool, before Gadifer had walked half a dozen paces away the rock pool was engulfed by squawking gulls fighting over the scraps of meat.

Gadifer dropped the bucket next to the rack and climbed up a low hill to his right and squinted into the distance across the sea to see the amber peaks of Lancarote. The centre of the island had a belly of dark cloud hovering above the mountaintops. One cloud released a curtain of rain so thick it obscured the land below and beyond it. Gadifer wished for a downpour to replenish the water barrels. They had a surplus of rich seal meat to eat but drinking water was in short supply.

The hunting was providing ample diversion for them all. The sea wolves were quicker than the fat seals of the north, agile and ferocious. Their corpses were heavy and cumbersome to manoeuvre but the leather from their hides was supple and tough. The only downside to their little expedition was the heat. It was so much hotter and much more exposed on the little island than on Lancarote. There was neither sweet water nor vegetation to freshen the air. The wind, swirled around Lancarote and slammed into the little island, it was relentless and loaded with salty sea spray. It gave some relief from the scorching sun during the day, but it made the nights bitterly cold and uncomfortable.

Despite the harsh conditions, the trip had put mettle in his men´s hearts and a spring in Gadifer´s step. The feeling of camaraderie was immensely rejuvenating. He didn´t relish the idea of returning to Lancarote and the endless drudgery of camp life, but the lack of drinking water was becoming problematic.

He debated packing up and taking the men back to Rubicon to restock. If he did, there was no telling how long it would be before he could get away again. The alternative would be to send a small party back in the boat to collect more supplies.

Tomorrow I will decide he thought as he climbed back down the hill and strolled over to the welcoming shade and conversation of his companions. *What difference will one day make?*

****

Norstar looked down from his vantage point high on the cliff. He and Rayco were alone in a spot directly above the slavers. He couldn´t understand why they just sat on the beach, prepared for action but seemingly unwilling to take any. The day was wearing on, if they didn´t start moving soon it would be too dark for them to see the trails.

Suddenly, the tiny sound of a peeling bell carried on the wind. Rayco grabbed his arm and pointed. The slavers were starting to move. They formed up into a long column and began a slow march across the scrubby little headland toward the base of the cliff, making for the point where the path split into two.

Norstar and Rayco couldn´t see the path´s junction from where they watched so sprinted back to the lookout nest. They slid down into the nest and joined Guadarfia and the others craning over the lip to see which path the slavers would take.

The air was thick, nobody was able to breathe, let alone speak. Norstar looked across at Beselch hunkered down next to Guadarfia, it was the first time Norstar could ever recall the little Northerner being this quiet for so long.

The slavers arrived at the junction. The leader hesitated for a moment before leading his men to the right. Beselch released his breath loudly. His home was safe. Norstar, Rayco and Avago looked at him with disgust.

"We should go to Acatife and warn everybody." Beselch said quickly.

"You go! I will follow later. Send a messenger if you receive any word from the French." Guadarfia ordered.

Beselch wasted no time, he and Belicar scrambled up and out of the nest.

"Please Mence, now is the time for action." Norstar pleaded. "We could knock them off the path. Just give the word."

Guadarfia was silent for a long moment.

"Come, we will follow them." He led them out onto the top of the cliff.

They ran to the rock fall in silence. Norstar allowed himself to let his hopes rise as the King greeted the Majos stood guarding the traps. Guadarfia walked around the rock piles and inspected the sturdy logs holding them up. He picked a sharp stone from the top of one of the hoppers and looked to the horizon deep in thought. Norstar waited by his side, forcing patience into his raging mind.

"Do you really think this will work." Guadarfia asked quietly.

"It does work. We tested it many times. It will destroy the path and send all those upon it crashing down into the sea."

Guadarfia looked deep into Norstar's eyes, scraping his very soul with the intensity of his stare.

"I will be the one to release the rocks." he said finally. "I cannot expect another to carry the burden of ending so many lives. The responsibility is mine."

Norstar was too stunned to reply. He nodded dumbly.

"You tell me when the time is right, and I will bring the mountain down on their heads."

Norstar flashed a look at Rayco who was bouncing on his heels, eager to go. They ran in opposite directions, Norstar off to the right where he could spot the slavers entering the killing zone, Rayco to the left to a place where he could relay Norstar's signals up to Guadarfia.

Norstar climbed down carefully to a ledge a hundred feet above the pathway and crouched down. He looked across the cliff face and saw Rayco settling down into his position, high and to the left. Norstar peeled the quiver of arrows from his back and set it down at his side. He inspected his bowstring and then settled down to wait.

It wasn't long before the sounds of the slavers scuffing along the path reached Norstar's ears. He tensed, not daring to move a muscle. They appeared around a bend down and to the right, walking steadily but slowly in single file. The path was wide enough for two, but its outer edge hung over a thousand-foot sheer drop. Some of the slavers were wary and stuck to the inside of the path, others brazenly stepped as close to the edge as they could, looking down at the sharp rocks and crashing waves below with indifference.

Norstar heard a strange clanking noise, a hard, miserable sound that carried clearly up to his vantage point. He looked closely and saw cruel chains hanging from the shoulders of every fourth man. Others carried collars of cold, black iron. Norstar shuddered.

He looked across at Rayco and waved quickly to let him know the lead invaders were entering the killing zone. Rayco acknowledged and repeated the signal to Guadarfia.

Norstar turned back to the path and began counting the slavers filing past. By the time the thirtieth had passed by, his hands were beginning to shake. He held them out to steady them and counted to ten. He picked up his bow and turned to give Rayco the signal to let the rocks drop.

He wasn't there.

Norstar scanned the cliff face frantically searching for him. He found him higher up the cliff than he should have been, gesturing for Norstar to climb. The traps hadn't been sprung, no rocks were falling, something must have broken. He threw his bow across his shoulders and climbed as fast as he could to the top of the cliff. He sprinted to where Guadarfia waited with Rayco and Avago. The other Majos were busy re-chocking the rock piles to make them safe again.

Norstar skidded to a halt next to Guadarfia.

"What's wrong?" he asked.

"The French are coming." Guadarfia answered, a smile threatening his lips. "We are to meet them in Acatife."

****

Berthin was feeling as miserable as sin. The sweat rolled down his back and between his legs, the thin leather of his vest rasped against his skin. To top it all off he was soaked on the outside too. A series of torrential downpours had drenched them as they crossed the Great Divide. But the cold and damp were not the things that fouled his mood the most.

There was nothing to hear other than his own breathing and the scape of the knight's boots in the dirt. There were no barking dogs or bleating goats, the only savages he had seen all day were the two translators. *The damned rabbits have all run back to their holes.* Berthin needed savages. His deal with Ordoñez was for the delivery of at least forty slaves. There was a chance that things would turn nasty if Berthin failed to deliver any.

The further they marched the worse Berthin´s mood got. Even on the final stretch up to the village of Acatife the land was devoid of life, save a solitary cock standing on a wall at the entrance to the village. It crowed loudly as the knights passed by.

Berthin cursed Ordoñez for putting his men ashore too early and frightening the savages underground. All hope rested on his messages to the King getting through. If nobody waited for them in the meeting hut the whole escapade would be doomed to failure. There was no way his men would be able to pry any of the savages from their deep holes. He wondered for a moment if Ordoñez and the Tajamar crew had already raided the island and carried off the best of the merchandise without waiting for him.

He led his men through the outskirts of the village and onto the square of tamped earth in front of the meeting hut. He was relieved to see the door of the hut stood ajar and a young man sat in front of it apparently snoozing. The sound of the approaching knights woke him. He sprang to his feet and disappeared inside the hut.

He reappeared a moment later leading no more than eight mature Majo males outside. Five of them were a lot older than Berthin would have liked. One of the younger males was a big ugly brute with a broken nose. He yelled a loud greeting to Alfonso the translator but was hushed unceremoniously with a slap to the face by an elderly man standing at his side. Berthin was disappointed that neither the King nor his man Avago were anywhere to be seen. If this sorry selection proved to be all he had to trade with all his scheming would be for nought. His knights might end up fighting the slavers after all.

He called on his men to halt and summoned the two translators to his side. The broken-nosed giant and the old man who had slapped him shuffled forward.

"We are glad to see you." Berthin said smoothly, the smile on his lips not carrying to his eyes. Isabel translated but didn´t convey his breezy tone. She sounded flat and lifeless. "Where is your King…Guadarfia. Where is your King?" Berthin asked loudly.

The old man pointed to the North. "He is watching the slavers." Isabel translated for him.

"I need him here, do you understand?" Berthin said to which the old man nodded enthusiastically and explained that he had already been sent for.

"Good! Good!" Berthin said clapping his hands together.

"Please, drink something. You must be thirsty." The old man babbled on gesturing to the well at the side of the meeting hut.

"Yes. Thank you. That would be most welcome." Berthin acted gracefully before turning his back on the old man and addressing his men.

"Gentlemen! It appears we have some time before the King arrives. The kind – er gentleman, has suggested we take refreshment and fill our flasks from the well. See to it now and then rest, we have a very long night ahead of us." The knights grunted wearily and trudged over to the well.

Berthin watched them go and turned back to the old man who was deep in conversation with the translator Alfonso.

"What are you saying?" he interrupted loudly, "What are they saying?" he pressed Isabel.

"Beselch was telling me that all the people are safely underground." Alfonso replied testily.

"Yes, we had noticed a lack of people in the fields. Still! We are here now. Surely they have nothing more to fear and can come back to their homes. Are they far? The people from the town… Are they far from here?" Berthin pressed.

"They are safe and will come back when the black ship has gone." Alfonso answered looking defiantly into Berthin's eyes. Berthin noticed he spoke without asking the old man, a demonstration of familiarity and contempt that might need beating out of him later. He let it slide for now, excused himself and walked over to the well leaving the translators speaking to the old man.

William poured a full canteen over his head and swept his hair back. He shivered as the water found its way down his back. Berthin sidled up to him and spoke quietly.

"I need a quick word."

"What is it?" asked William smoothing drops of water from his tidy beard.

"When the King gets here I need you to go and intercept Ordoñez´s men before they get too close. They´ve already fouled the plan by coming ashore too early. We need them to stand off and give us more time to draw as many flies into the web as we can."

"I understand."

"Take Big Perrin with you, they should recognise the pair of you from yesterday´s meeting." William nodded and began refilling his canteen. "One other matter," Berthin raised. "Who carried the wine today?"

"Who do you think?"

"Shit, not Jacquet."

"Who else."

"Shit." He stopped talking and pushed his way through the throng of men straight to Jacquet the baker who stood talking with Michelet the cook.

"Good." he said, pulling them both gently by the sleeves away from the others. "Just the men I want to talk to." He stopped and released them.

"I need you two to prepare some food."

"What!" spluttered Jacquet.

"You heard me, food for all, and wine, at least a cup for every one of the savages."

"But there won´t be enough to go around." protested Jacquet.

"Then make it go around, twice if you can, and if there is any left make sure to give it to the King. We need that big bastard as docile as possible." Jacquet answered with a petulant shrug, his bottom lip threatening to stick out.

"What shall I cook, and where?" asked Michelet.

"You´ll have to make what you can with what you can find. Take the woman Isabel to ask the old men where the larder is. There must be something around here somewhere. Kill that damned chicken if you can´t find anything else."

"I could make a pot stew with dumplings if we can rustle up some flour." Michelet said stroking his chin.

"Make whatever you can. I don't need the details." Berthin cut him short. "And don't *you* drink any more wine." he hissed at Jacquet. "We need every drop."

******

Norstar dropped his head into his shoulders, trying to disappear in the middle of the pack following Guadarfia and Avago down the track into Acatife. They entered the village from the north and saw the French knights milling around by the well. A small group of Majos stood in front of the meetinghouse. The translators were there talking with Beselch and Belicar.

The French knights sprang to alert when the Majos appeared, watching the natives stroll past them with their heads held high. The one named Berthin pressed his way forward and hurried to meet Guadarfia. He scuttled to the head of the group of Majos and intercepted Guadarfia. Even pulling himself up to his full height he was still way shorter than the Majo King.

Norstar listened carefully as the Frenchman began to speak, peering through Rayco's hair which hung loosely to his shoulder.

"Your Grace. I am glad you remain whole." he began. Guadarfia stood impassively, looking down at him, not wasting words with an answer when Isabel finished translating. "Let me assure you we have your safety well in hand. As I explained yesterday, I have brought enough men to chase the slavers all the way back to where they came from. I would like to invite you and your people to dine with us before we go and deal with these brigands."

While Isabel translated, Berthin peered around the bulk of Guadarfia and appeared to be counting heads. Norstar shuffled uncomfortably as the Frenchman's gaze swung in his direction. He ducked out of sight behind Rayco.

The Frenchman began talking again.

"We have brought the finest wine to sup with our food. Please come, you are all invited."

The booming bass of Guadarfia's voice filled the air.

"You are here to protect us, not feed us. We have been watching the slavers all day. Are you not interested in their position and number?"

Norstar noticed movement out of the corner of his eye. Two of the French knights had broken away from the group by the well and were heading north. Norstar blew on Rayco´s neck to get his attention. He pointed out the men with a nod of his head. Rayco nodded once and turned back to face forward.

"Your Grace, if you please. I have sent scouts to shadow these slavers. We do not fear them. They are a rabble, no match for our steel and discipline, each of my men is worth ten of theirs. We will rout them at our leisure." He drew his sword dramatically and held it aloft. It rang as it was pulled clear of its scabbard. "This sword and all those of my men are pledged to smite down any who dare to challenge us in the pursuit of our duty." He brought the sword whistling down with a strong, swift, backhand slice. Berthin twirled it deftly around his wrist and presented it, handle first to Guadarfia.

Guadarfia was transfixed by the flashing, shiny blade. He reached out and took it from Berthin. It looked like a pocketknife in Guadarfia´s massive hand. He lifted it to examine its sheen closely and tested the sharpness with his thumb before taking a slow swing down and across his body. He handed it back to Berthin who accepted it with a bow of the head.

"We will accept your invitation to dine. I would like you to tell me how you plan on defeating the slavers." Guadarfia said. Berthin swept his arm in a shallow bow and invited Guadarfia and Avago to enter the meetinghouse ahead of him.

The older tribal leaders followed with the rest of the Majos close behind. All save two. Norstar and Rayco had slipped away unseen. They skirted around the huts of the village and used a long low wall to hide them as they ran back around to the North. A copse of trees shielded them once out of the village. They kept low to the ground before slipping into a long dry gully, which cut a winding path to the top of the cliffs.

They spotted the pair of Frenchmen easily. The second of the two was the big fat man with the foul mouth. He was slow and clumsy and made more noise than a herd of goats shuffling up the hill, complaining all the way.

It took no effort to keep pace with the knights, indeed it took a bigger effort not to get too far ahead of them. Before long, Norstar and Rayco decided to forge ahead and look for the slavers. They flew across the land using gullies, rocks and clumps of sparse vegetation to shield them from view and were soon a long way ahead of the knights. They gained the top of the cliff at the head of a dry valley. They looked down along the length of the valley and saw the slavers standing at another junction. If they took the left fork, they would climb up through the valley along a steep track ending a few feet from where Norstar and Rayco stood. The right fork led to Zonzamas along the Great Divide.

Norstar and Rayco ducked out of sight and crabbed along the left lip of the valley, soon finding a suitable hiding place from where they could watch the slavers below and see the pathway along the cliff top. The pair of French knights came into view a short while later. They headed directly for the head of the dry valley and stood at the top of the switchback path. The smaller man was pointing down, urging the fat man to follow him. The fat man refused, simply perching his bulk on a large boulder and folding his arms across his chest.

"Look!" said Rayco pointing downwards. "The slavers are moving again."

Norstar's heart sunk. "And coming this way."

****

Berthin pushed his way out of the meeting hut door. As soon as he stepped into the open air, the smile on his face disappeared like smoke in a gale. He scowled as he stomped around the side of the hut to where the knights waited.

All talking stopped. Berthin scanned the men quickly, singling out young Gillet and Pernet the Blacksmith to follow him. He led them away from the other men talking quietly.

"Have you noticed any savages wandering around out here?"

"No. I can't say that I have." Gillet replied, shaking his head.

He looked to Pernet who was also shaking his head. "Nope. Nothing."

"There are two missing." Berthin hissed. "They must have slipped away before we went inside."

"They probably just wandered off. You know what these savages are like." Pernet offered.

"These ones do not just wander away. These are the Monkey King's guards." Berthin snapped back. "Has there been any word from William and Perrin?"

"Not since they left." Gillet answered.

"Damn!" cursed Berthin. "If these men stumble on Perrin and Blessi talking with the Spaniards we'll be sunk. I need you two to get after them and warn them to keep an eye out. If you see these two savages anywhere I need you deal with them quickly and quietly."

"Kill them?" Gillet asked.

"Of course not. We don't get paid for dead meat. If you must, wound them a little, but only enough to slow them down. Leave them with Ordoñez's men. We're a few shy of the number I promised, we need every single one of them." Berthin was starting to feel lightheaded. "Hurry, get your things and find the others, we haven't got much time."

Gillet and the Blacksmith hurried back to the well, collected their packs and disappeared up the cliff path.

Berthin caught sight of Courtille, Gadifer's trumpeter, sat a little distance away from the others. He was staring into space and mouthing something while he swayed, tapping his hands lightly on his knees.

Berthin walked over and tapped him on the shoulder. Courtille nearly jumped out of his skin.

"Is something wrong?" Berthin asked.

"Nothing at all." Courtille answered amiably. "I was just practicing in my head and praying for an appreciative audience." He smiled nervously.

"Hmm!" Berthin sniffed. He'd never had any truck with mummers and musicians. He understood neither their language nor their motivation. He couldn't fathom the appeal of music, to him it was just noise. But he did understand how the sound of music affected the savages. It transfixed them, hypnotised them. He needed the King as tranquil as it was possible to be without being dead.

"It's time." Berthin said simply.

Courtille stood and rummaged through his pack, picking out a small flute and a horn wrapped carefully in soft chamois. He puffed out his chest and panted three hard breaths before following Berthin back round to the entrance of the meeting hut.

"Remember." Berthin whispered. "Keep their eyes and ears on you." Courtille nodded.

He pushed open the door and led the young musician inside where the overpowering hot, damp smell of male musk was staggering. It mingled with smoke from the fire and the steam rising from the bowls of chicken stew and dumplings Michelet the Cook was handing around.

A buzz of anticipation filled the dark hut as Courtille stepped into the light of the fire. He placed the horn down on the floor at his feet and lifted the small flute to his lips.

The first notes he blew were shaky at best, but he soon settled down and started to play a haunting melody. Berthin observed with satisfaction as the savages settled down to listen, completely absorbed in the music.

Berthin caught the eye of Guadarfia who was sat next to Isabel. She still looked miserable Berthin noted. The King bowed his head to Berthin and smiled, before turning away and giving his full attention to Courtille who swayed gently in the light of the fire as he played.

Jacquet the baker brushed past bearing two large jugs of wine and water. Berthin caught him by the elbow and whispered in his ear.

"Make sure they drink it. Extra for the King remember."

"I remember. Don't worry. I've watered it to hell to spin it out. We should have enough." Jacquet replied.

Berthin nodded and let go of Jacquet's arm. His senses were beginning to overload with the sights, smells and sounds swirling around inside the dark hut. His head was starting to burn up, he needed fresh air to cool it down. He stole a quick glance at the King as he walked to the door. He was captured by the music. Very shortly, he would be captured in another manner, one which would be much more rewarding for Berthin. A genuine smile creased his face at the thought as he pushed his way out of the hut.

****

Norstar shifted slightly to improve his view of the slavers who were climbing the final few steps up the steep path. Suddenly Rayco grabbed his arm and dragged him down into the dirt. A heartbeat later, an arrow shattered the trunk of one of the tabaiba plants they were hiding behind.

Rayco pointed frantically away to their right. Norstar chanced a quick glance and was horrified to see two more French knights approaching. One had another arrow already nocked and aiming directly at Norstar, the other was running at an angle to cut off their escape, gripping a sword in one hand and a heavy hammer in the other.

The archer let his arrow loose and it thudded into a plant next to Norstar´s head. Norstar ducked back down and heard the Frenchman yelling to the other two knights at the top of the path.

"We have to get out of here now." hissed Rayco.

"Lead the way brother." Norstar answered. He raised his head to risk a quick look back to the men at the top of the path. The smaller man had already nocked an arrow in his bow and let it fly as soon as Norstar´s head appeared. It whistled overhead and clattered harmlessly on the rocks behind them. Norstar was horrified to see the fat man running towards them drawing a heavy sword as he ran. For a fat man he moved fast and had already covered half the distance between them.

"Go now!" yelled Norstar.

Rayco burst from the ditch with Norstar at his heals. Another arrow whizzed past them, sticking in the ground just ahead of their feet. The one with the sword and hammer was yelling, changing the angle of his run to coral them on the edge of the cliff. Another arrow whizzed past Norstar´s nose, so close it caused him to stumble slightly to his right. Another arrow split the air to his left and sliced Rayco´s left shoulder. Blood splashed onto Norstar´s face from the cut. The sting urged Rayco to run even faster. He veered off to the right and jumped over the edge of the cliff. Norstar followed and tensed for a hard impact. They landed on a narrow goat path a few feet below the edge. They followed it as it meandered around the contour of the cliff, it swept around to the left and descended steeply. Another arrow clattered harmlessly on the ground behind them as they careered down the steep slope, hopping from rock to rock. The path twisted around a rocky outcrop and took them out of sight of the men on top of the cliff.

A shout rang out behind and below him. He looked under his arm and realised they were now in full view of the slavers climbing up the dry valley. A couple of the slavers lifted loaded crossbows and fired. The bolts clattered harmlessly against stones a few feet away.

The pathway jinked back to the left and across a steep gulley, out of sight of the slavers. Rayco abandoned the path and leapt into the gulley. Norstar followed without question, their feet barely brushing the tops of the rocks on their mad, barely controlled descent. A huge boulder blocked their path. They vaulted over it and slid down its other side and stopped. Norstar listened but couldn't hear any pursuit, for the moment they were safe.

Rayco tore a strip of leather from his waistband and wrapped it around his left arm. Norstar reached across to help pull it tight over the cut in his shoulder before taking a quick look around the boulder to make sure there was no one on the path behind them.

"We have to get back to warn the others." he said.

"We will have to double back and climb the cliff." Rayco said, he spat a glob of saliva into his hand and rubbed it around his cut. "We can't go back the way we came, they'll be waiting for us. We can't go along the Divide, that is the way they'll expect us to go. We must climb up behind them." Rayco said getting to his feet and shaking his arm.

"Can you climb with your arm like that?"

"I could climb better than you if I lost both arms and had cramp in my legs." Rayco smiled over at Norstar who laughed despite everything.

"Then let's get moving quickly before they come looking for us." he said, standing and shifting his bow on his back.

They set off crabbing to the left, keeping as low as they could to stay out of sight from above. They soon came to the foot of dry valley. Peering up through a patch of flat-headed cacti, they saw the last of the slavers cresting the top of the valley, others were spreading out along the cliff top, looking down. Norstar led Rayco a little further down the hill where a low ridge shielded them from view as they crossed the valley on their bellies. It was a relief to make it to the other side unseen. They got to their feet and climbed back up to the path which wrapped around the cliff.

They sprinted along the narrow path following the contours of the hill for a few hundred paces before turning right and scrambling up a steep rocky slope to the vertical cliff face soaring high above them. The weather worn cliff bore deep, vertical gashes in its surface. Unfortunately for anyone climbing it, the constant attack from the sea air left many soft spots where rocks crumbled out of the cliff at the slightest touch.

Norstar rushed to begin climbing as soon as they arrived at the face. He placed his foot on a crumbling rock after climbing only two feet. It gave way beneath him sending him crashing back into Rayco´s arms.

"I will lead, you follow." Rayco said calmy. Norstar nodded slightly embarrassed. Rayco and his brother Jonay were prolific climbers. Their love for scaling impossible rock faces matched Norstar´s love for sailing. This was Rayco´s kingdom. Even with a weakened arm he moved with confidence and fluidity. Norstar followed as closely as he could but soon fell behind. Rayco waited for him every few steps to direct his hands and feet onto secure footholds.

About halfway up the face, Rayco pulled his body into a deep cleft in the rock wall and leaned out to help Norstar. Norstar was relieved that there was enough space to stop and rest a while on a narrow ledge inside the cleft. His whole body was shaking. His fingertips were numb and his toes hurt from gripping rocks. He leaned out to take a quick look back down the cliff face and suddenly wished that he hadn´t. The height made him feel slightly dizzy, he thought for a moment that if he were to slip it would mean certain death, a thought he hadn´t allowed to enter his head while climbing. He steadied his nerves by looking out to sea and fixing his gaze on the distant horizon.

A gull floated past and turned its head to look at Norstar. It was close enough to touch, riding on the swirling air currents. It let out a raucous *cawl* and shifted its weight, turned in a tight circle and shot off back the way it had come with a single flap of its wings.

"Come on." Rayco called. Norstar turned and looked up. Rayco was already climbing again, up the inside of the cleft wall.

Norstar rushed to catch him but slipped after only a couple of steps. He berated himself and forced his limbs to move more slowly and deliberately. It was far easier to climb up the interior of the rock chimney, it gave them a bit of respite from the wind, it also provided several places where they could brace their backs against the wall and relieve the pressure from their hands.

By the time they reached the top of the chimney, Norstar's fingers were throbbing and his legs were starting to turn to jelly. It didn't please him immensely therefore when Rayco explained that they had to swing out of the cleft and back on to the exposed cliff face. It was the most perilous move of the climb so far, it didn't help that Norstar was literally shaking with fear. His muscles were reaching the end of their limits of endurance, but he had no choice but to follow Rayco. He pressed himself into the rock, his cheek scraped across the rough stone surface as his left hand searched for grip. It found a crack big enough for three fingers to slip inside. The wind battered him as he pulled his body out onto the sheer rock wall. Rayco spoke softly, directing Norstar's movements, wary that the older man was tiring. They climbed slowly and steadily until suddenly the vertical wall started to level out.

Relief flushed through Norstar. He was able to relax a little as he scrambled up the last few feet to the summit. Rayco waited for him at the top grinning. He offered his hand. Norstar accepted it gratefully and allowed himself to be pulled up the final few steps.

They crested the climb amongst a stand of pale rocks, furry to the touch, covered with bright green moss and lichen. There was no time to breathe. They worked their way around the rocks and peered out across the plain at the top of the cliffs. A couple of hundred paces to their right was the head of the dry valley path where a few of slavers stood milling around. The rest of them were scouring the cliff top in the other direction, past the point where Norstar and Rayco had leapt down onto the goat path.

"Can you see any of the Frenchmen?" Rayco asked.

"I can see two of them over there, where we were hiding. The fat one and his friend." The two knights were easy to spot, dressed in much brighter colours than the slavers. The late afternoon sunshine glinted off their helmets. The other pair were nowhere to be seen.

Suddenly, Norstar heard the crunch of footsteps and the clang of metal on rock only a few feet to his right. He dragged Rayco with him to the ground. They squeezed into a gap between two rocks and held their breath. The shuffling feet got closer and then stopped. It then sounded like a weight dropped to the ground on the other side of the rock.

Norstar almost jumped out of his skin as a sword belt fell to the ground inches from his head. He and Rayco pushed themselves back even further into the hole. A hand reached down and picked up the sword accompanied by some mumbled French curse words. Norstar eased his knife from its sheath as silently as he could.

A huge fart rented the air followed by the unmistakeable sound of shit splatting onto the ground. Whoever was there taking care of business let out a huge groan of relief, and then the smell hit. Norstar nearly threw up.

Someone called out from too far away to hear the words.

"Would you prefer it if I shit in my britches?" roared a voice only a few feet away.

The other replied, sounding irate, the wind carried the words away.

"I´ve finished, calm down!"

The man shuffled. Norstar could clearly hear the sound of a mail shirt chinking as it dropped down over the man´s waist. A moment later, he heard footsteps crunching away. Norstar and Rayco waited for a moment before creeping out of their hiding place. They cautiously lifted their heads above the rocks and saw the other two Frenchmen walking away from them to the left, back along the path to Acatife. The larger of the two was adjusting his belt while he walked, the other stormed ahead, not waiting for him. Words were being exchanged but the distance too great to hear them. Before long, they slipped out of sight.

Looking back the other way they saw the other pair of French knights shaking hands with one of the slavers before striking out for Acatife. They didn´t walk along the path but chose to take a direct path through the wild scrubland back to the village. Norstar kept one eye on them, the other on the slavers who were all beginning to drift back to the top of the dry-valley path. The Frenchmen soon disappeared behind a clump of bushes.

Norstar and Rayco didn´t waste any time. As soon as the knights were gone, they hurried along the cliff top, staying low to keep out of sight. Acatife soon came into view. They crept closer until they crested a small hill with a clear view of the village below them. They watched the two pairs of knights walk back into the village where they were met by the man Berthin. He appeared to have heated words with all four of them before dismissing them and storming back into the meeting hut.

The sun had already sunk below the horizon and the sky was getting darker. Norstar and Rayco inched closer to the village until they brushed up against the huts on the outskirts of the village. They danced around the buildings until they found themselves at the very last line of huts stood facing the meeting hut across the square. They climbed quietly onto the roof of one and lay flat on its domed surface.

They had a clear view of the meeting hut doorway. It stood slightly ajar allowing the orange glow of the fire within to seep around its edges. A lone flute was playing a melancholy tune within. The sound drifted to Norstar who thought he recognised it from his youth although he couldn´t remember the words that went with the melody.

It was almost completely dark. Suddenly the door of the meeting hut flew wide open and the unmistakeable silhouette of Berthin stepped into the frame. He stood there for a few seconds just looking back into the hut before turning and closing the door behind him. Norstar felt every type of hatred for the man and was tempted to send an arrow into his throat. It would have been an easy shot. He stayed his hand and watched as the hateful man slipped round the outside of the hut to where his men waited next to the well. He said something and the men all got to their feet. Norstar looked on in horror as he saw one of them pass lengths of rope amongst the others.

Norstar was getting more and more anxious. He thought of sprinting across the square and warning all those inside the meeting hut to flee, but he wouldn´t make it in time. The French knights were too close and were all armed. Norstar nearly screamed out a warning as Berthin began to usher the knights through the door. The flute was still playing its haunting melody as Berthin slipped inside the hut following the last of his men. He closed the door behind him.

Norstar checked carefully to make sure there were no knights loitering outside before he tapped Rayco on the arm. The pair climbed back down to the ground and sprinted across the square to the meeting hut. They flattened themselves against the wall next to the door.

"What are we going to do Brother?" Rayco whispered.

"I don´t know." admitted Norstar, the exasperation in his voice conveying all the feeling he was getting from his churning guts. Avago was inside with the King and twenty more of his people, surrounded by armed and armoured knights. What could they do?

The sound of the flute drifted through the door. It was slowing to the tune´s sleepy conclusion. Norstar suddenly remembered the song. It was a lullaby his mother used to sing to him on cold nights when the wind howled at the door. *"And the birds will come home, home to roost."* He closed his eyes and heard his mother´s voice in his head as the final note drifted away into the night sky.

Suddenly a yell went up from within the building followed by screaming and the sound of an almighty uproar. Before Norstar could react, Rayco sprang to the door, flung it wide open and sprinted inside.

"NO!" Norstar cried, running through the door after him. The world slowed down as he crossed the threshold.

All about the walls of the hut, steel flashed, reflecting the glow of the fire burning fiercely in the centre of the room. Isabel was stood against the wall screaming as blades were pressed to the throats of the Majos sat around the fire. Norstar noticed Beselch sat down to his left with his eyes open wide, his skinny arms shaking in the air beseeching mercy from the knight who stood in front of him waving his sword in the old Majo´s face. His son Belicar lie face down on the floor, a knight knelt on his back, one hand gripped his hair shaking his head, the other holding a dagger to Belicar´s eye. Belicar was screaming out for his father, the knight began to pound his head on the floor.

Norstar spun around when he heard Rayco cry out from the far side of the hut. He saw him launch himself at a knight who held a knife to Avago´s throat. Avago was resisting, gripping the man´s knife arm and forcing it away from his throat. Rayco put all his weight and momentum into punching the knight in the face. The Frenchman flew backwards, already unconscious as his head hit the wall behind him with a dull crack. His body slumped lifeless to the floor. Rayco dragged Avago to his feet and pushed him towards Norstar. Norstar caught him, flung him around and propelled him out through the open door.

Norstar turned back to see Rayco punching a gloved hand which had reached out and grabbed him around the wrist. Norstar leapt over the fire, drew his knife and plunged it into the back of the hand. The stone blade didn´t break through the leather of the gauntlet but struck it hard enough to make it release its grip on Rayco´s wrist. A huge roar of pain rang out. Norstar turned to see Berthin drawing his injured hand back. His left arm clung around the neck of Guadarfia who was pinned by three armoured knights. Their combined weight forced the mighty King´s chest down to his knees while they struggled to drag his arms behind his back. Berthin´s arm was trapped between Guadarfia´s neck and bulging thighs, he was pulling with all his might to free himself. He looked into Norstar´s face and snarled like a rabid dog.

"YOU!" he called, bloody spittle flying from his mouth. Norstar pivoted around on his leg and kicked the raging Frenchman in the face, catching him across the jaw with a stunning blow.

"Run!" roared Guadarfia "RUN!"

Rayco grabbed Norstar and pulled him away as one of the knights on Guadarfia was lunging towards him. Guadarfia grabbed the knight´s arm as Norstar and Rayco leapt over the fire. They ducked to avoid a sword swinging at their heads from out of the gloom and sprinted through the door. They cut to the left as soon as they were outside and ran to where Avago waited at the edge of the clearing.

"Guadarfia?" he asked as they approached.

Norstar shook his head. Avago bowed his head, turned and ran with them.

The trio ran as quickly as Avago could go, heading downhill to the south before dropping off the path to their left and jumping into the bottom of a deep gulley. The deep cut jinked all the way to the top of the volcano overlooking Acatife.

After a short while, Norstar stopped and paused to listen. Nothing. No pursuit… Yet! They had to keep moving.

Soon they arrived at the yawning crater of the volcano. They crouched down in a high perch just below the crown, facing north, high enough to see down into the centre of the village. A slice of moon illuminated the valley below in a soft silver glow, but not for much longer. Heavy clouds were rolling in from the sea.

****

Berthin slapped Isabel across the face.

"I said be quiet!" he screamed into her ear. She was the last of the heathens to be bound and had the temerity to question him.

"When you finish tying her hands, gag her." he ordered Gillet who was holding Isabel´s arms behind her back.

Berthin looked around the hut. All the Majo´s were lying on the floor in various states of distress, from the fully aware and frightened old men babbling incoherently, to the King, lying unconscious with extra ropes binding his arms and legs.

For the most part, Berthin´s men had escaped unscathed. The Gascon Siort, had been the unfortunate one to be on the receiving end of the savage´s fist when Avago was freed. He was still groggy, laid out flat where he fell, unable to sit up without seeing stars.

Berthin rubbed the back of his hand where the knife had struck him. It was badly bruised if not broken. If not for his gauntlet, it would probably be lost. He clicked his jaw and shook his head. Thankfully, the bastard who kicked him was wearing soft shoes, otherwise he would have taken his head off. He dearly wanted to meet Monsieur *North Star* again before he left the island. He had cost Berthin a valuable slave and quite possibly a tooth.

Gillet forced the translator roughly to the floor before turning to Berthin. "All done Monsieur." he said.

"Were those the same two you lost in the hills?" Berthin asked.

"I couldn´t be certain Monsieur. I only saw their backs and you know, they all look the same to me."

"You fool!" barked Berthin. "Of course it was them. It´s always them. Take some men and see if you can find them, but don´t dawdle. We have to start moving the rest of them down to the ship."

"Monsieur." Gillet dismissed himself, grabbed three men stood by the door and pulled them outside.

Berthin´s mood was foul as he counted the bodies trussed up and face down on the floor. Twenty-three. A worthy haul and worth a small fortune on the block, but woefully short of the forty he´d promised Ordoñez. He stormed out of the door into the night, kicking a prone body in the chest as he passed by.

William the Bastard followed him outside. They walked around the side of the building to the well where Berthin lifted a large jug and poured water over his chin and into his mouth to wash away the blood. He handed the jug to William.

"We can´t wait for Ordoñez´s men." he said while William took a drink. "We have to start moving them now before that damned spy rouses the whole island to come after their King."

"How do you want to do it?" William asked, handing the jug back.

"Wake the King and take him first. Get him to the Spaniards then bring some of their man back here to help with the rest."

****

From their perch, high up the volcano Norstar watched as the unmistakeable figure of Guadarfia was pushed out of the hut. Three knights carrying blazing torches surrounded him. They tripped and prodded him, one slipped a rope around his neck and began to drag him along the pathway leading to the North.

"Where are they taking him?" Avago asked.

"Delivering him to the slavers." Norstar answered.

"We have to help him." Avago said.

"I´ve tried to help him for months." Norstar replied bitterly. "He didn´t listen to me, which is why he´s where he is now."

"Do you stop picking up a child after it´s fallen a dozen times, or do you continue to help it until it can walk unaided?" Avago asked.

"A child will eventually learn to walk and not fall anymore." Norstar replied.

"A child keeps on falling throughout its life, and you never stop picking it up." Avago said leaping from the nest. He set off hopping down the mountainside.

"Wait!" Norstar shouted after him.

"Let´s go brother." Rayco said, climbing to his feet. "We may have to save the old fool again before morning." He leapt out of the nest and chased Avago down the mountainside. Norstar shook his head and followed.

Thick cloud rolled over the moon before they were halfway down the side of the volcano. By the time they reached the foot of the steep slope, fat raindrops began to fall. Soon the heavens opened and sheets of water lashed across the earth.

Avago led the trio around the eastern side of the village, well out of sight of any knights who lingered there. They began running up the other side of the valley and soon saw the spluttering torches of the men leading Guadarfia away to their left. Avago angled his run to intercept the men as the path entered a small copse of wind-bent trees. Norstar plucked his bow from his back as they ran and gripped an arrow in his other hand, rolling it in his fingers, feeling for the slit with his thumbnail. Avago unwrapped the sling from his waist and bent to pick up a fist sized stone from the ground. Rayco pulled the tenique from around his shoulders and started whirling it´s heavy end in a tight circle.

Both groups of men arrived at the end of the little copse at the same time. The knight´s torches spluttered and fizzed as fat raindrops hit the flames. Avago burst onto the path ahead of the knights, swinging his sling about his head. Rayco followed and let his tenique out to its full length. With an almighty swing he smashed it into the hand of the knight who held the rope around Guadarfia´s neck. Bones snapped under the force of the blow and the knight let go of the rope. Norstar leapt onto the path and raised his bow, aiming an arrow into the face of the young knight behind Guadarfia who was reaching for his own bow.

"Don´t move!" Norstar shouted in French, stunning the knights into silence. The sling and tenique whirled through the air, whistling as they whipped around. The knight who cradled his broken fingers in his good hand backed away from Rayco´s tenique as it flashed before his eyes.

The fat knight behind Guadarfia suddenly lunged forward, pulled his sword and held it over Guadarfia´s shoulder.

"Release him." Norstar said, "and live."

The knight began to laugh. Guadarfia suddenly bent his legs and threw his head backwards, into the knight´s face. The knight stumbled backwards and tripped over a rock. With an almighty roar, Guadarfia flexed his huge arms and shoulders and burst the ropes tying his arms behind his back. He surged forward towards Norstar and the others. The knight with the broken hand whirled around and lifted his good hand to stop him. Rayco´s tenique smashed into the side of his helmet, dropping him like a puppet with its strings cut.

Norstar pulled back on his bowstring as the fat knight regained his balance and took off after Guadarfia. He bellowed like a bull and charged. Guadarfia stopped running, turned and sent his clenched fist smashing into the knight´s face with such force it lifted the fat man off his feet. He rose and fell heavily to the ground, his face stoved in by the force of Guadarfia´s mighty fist. Guadarfia turned and started running again, Rayco reached out, took his arm and guided him off the path to the right. The pair ran off into the scrubland and soon disappeared in the black night and the rain.

Norstar stood braced. He looked down the shaft of his arrow at the knight left standing. His hand hovered over the pummel of his sword, a bow rested on his back. Avago stood next to Norstar, swinging his loaded sling above his head.

"Go!" Norstar snapped at Avago. "I´ll keep you covered."

"No! You go and I will cover you." Avago replied.

"Just GO!" Norstar shouted.

Without another word, Avago backed up a few paces and leapt from the pathway. He plunged through the darkness after Rayco and Guadarfia. Norstar began to back away slowly from the Frenchmen. The two on the ground wouldn´t be walking anytime soon but the one left standing could shoot with the bow. He´d nearly hit Norstar earlier in the day. He wouldn´t miss from this short distance. As angry as Norstar was he couldn´t kill the man in cold blood. He thought about shooting him in the leg but paused a second too long.

He heard a foot scuff along the path behind him.

"I told you to run!" he shouted without looking back. The young knight with the bow smiled.

"I said I told you to run!" Norstar shouted once more.

"Que?" said a voice at his back.

Norstar spun round quickly, but not quickly enough to see the club coming out of the darkness to slam into his temple.

28

Graciosa,

October 16th, 1402

The wind picked up as dawn broke, hurling cold salty water at the men in the longboat as they battled the current to reach the black hull of the Tajamar. From where he sat on the prow bench, Berthin could clearly see Master d´Ordoñez scowling down at the boat from the ship´s quarterdeck. He shifted uncomfortably under his gaze. The boat nudged the side of the ship and Berthin climbed the ladder up to the main deck. A man with a face that looked as if it had been on the receiving end of many an angry fist led Berthin up to the quarterdeck. Ordoñez stood waiting for him with his hands in the pockets of his big black great coat.

"Señor!" Berthin greeted with a hurried bow. The Master made no effort to acknowledge or return the greeting. "I trust you are content with the merchandise?"

"The quality is adequate, the quantity is not. You promised me forty bodies and delivered only twenty-two. One of those is next to worthless with his head all bashed in." Berthin winced a little. Even near death, the spy Norstar could still cause problems.

Berthin and William had arrived at the scene of the King´s rescue moments after Guadarfia had fled and found Norstar unconscious on the ground. Young Gillet was the only one of his men left standing. Big Perrin was a gibbering wreck. The King´s almighty punch crushed his nose and broke the bones of his cheek and jaw. Bloody tears rolled down his face as he keened like a blubbering child through his shattered mouth. Pernet the Blacksmith fared only a little better. His head had swelled inside his battered helmet, blood ran down his neck into his tunic. He himself was the only man with the skill to remove the helmet but was unable to use his shattered right hand to hold any tools. Berthin exploded with rage and kicked Norstar again and again. He would have smashed the bastard to a pulp if William and a couple of the slavers had not pulled him away.

"To make things worse," continued Ordoñez, "You have turned up with double the number of men we agreed passage for."

"Twelve of them will not be coming with us." Berthin said quickly.

"Do they know that?" Ordoñez answered, "Because they wait over there on the beach, trying to climb aboard every boat that goes over there."

"They should know of course." Berthin blustered, "I agreed with their leader that they were only needed for one night's work. I never said that they would be leaving with us."

"You have proven to me that what you deliver is not always what you promise." Ordoñez admonished, Berthin bristled. "As I see it," the Master continued. "You have not fulfilled your end of the bargain. Only half the merchandise has been delivered at double the cost to me. Give me one reason why I shouldn't throw you and your men off the ship and leave without you." Ordoñez pulled his hands from his pockets. In one, he held a stout wooden club. He smacked it into his palm. Bloodshot eyes leered at Berthin through greasy, straggly hair. His nostrils flared, even the pits on the tip of his bulbous red nose appeared to swell and threaten Berthin.

"I-I-I can make up the shortfall." he stuttered, desperation seeping into his words.

"Go on." said the Ordoñez, slapping the club once more into his meaty palm.

"There are stores, substantial stores of arms and supplies back at Rubicon. There may even be a few more savages to add to the tally. If you were to send your men to Rubicon…"

"Send my men, to fight because you failed to deliver?" Ordoñez spat. He took a step closer.

Berthin held his hands out. "No of course not." he blustered. "I will return and secure the stores. But I will need the help of your men to carry everything."

"What sort of goods?" Ordoñez asked.

"There are dozens of ash bows and new crossbows, with enough parts to make dozens more. Crates of bow strings, arrows and bolts lying in the storerooms. I dare say there will be swords too, and wine."

"I trade in livestock, not arms."

"There are women." Berthin said hurriedly. Ordoñez calmed down slightly and smiled. Or rather his face contorted into what his mother would have called a smile, but to Berthin it was only slightly less intimidating than staring into the face of an angry bull.

Suddenly a lookout cried out from the top of the main mast.

"Sail!" he shouted. "Off the port quarter."

Berthin felt a moment of panic as Ordoñez pushed past him and crossed the deck to look.

"Where is it?" he bellowed.

"Due West, making straight for us." the lookout answered, pointing.

Berthin joined the Master, hoping in his heart that it wasn´t Bethencourt returning. He saw the sail after a few moments, tiny in the distance, appearing and disappearing as it bobbed up and down in the heavy swell.

"Shit!" cursed Ordoñez.

"What is it?" Berthin asked.

"La Morella." Ordoñez answered banging his fist on the wooden rail.

Shit, Berthin echoed in his mind. He had hoped never to meet Captain Calvo again. He almost wished it were Bethencourt. "Do you know them?" he asked casually.

"We´ve met. The Captain´s a self-righteous bastard who looks down his nose at the likes of us. I imagine he´s heading here to shelter and wait for the wind to change before making a run for the North."

"Shouldn´t we leave before he gets here?" Berthin asked hopefully.

Ordoñez turned to face him, "We have business to conclude before we leave."

****

Berthin saw the boat approaching Rubicon while he was still a half league from the camp.

"Is that Gadifer?" William asked.

"I hope not." Berthin answered. "Let's pick up the pace." he called out. He had all his Normans with him except Courtille the trumpeter, who volunteered to stay and watch over Big Perrin and Pernet the Blacksmith on the Tajamar. For a Gascon, Courtille was proving to be very able in Berthin's mind, unlike Siort and his ragged band, who refused to budge from the headland opposite the ship, demanding Berthin allow them to escape on the Tajamar. Berthin had almost laughed in Siort's face when he admitted they were afraid of returning to Rubicon and facing Gadifer's wrath.

The camp was virtually deserted. Berthin and his men jogged through the gateway unmolested and made their way directly to the bluff overlooking the beach where the boat nudged ashore. Berthin was relieved to see only three men on board. Gadifer's friend Remonnet was at the tiller with two other knights manning the oars.

"We need that boat." he said to William who nodded and took off with the rest of the men following him down the path to the beach. Berthin was watching the two groups come together when the sound of slapping sandals alerted Berthin to the approach of Father Verrier who was hurrying from the direction of the kitchen block.

"Berthin!" hailed the Priest. "I didn't know you had returned." He glanced down and saw the longboat. "Ah, good. Monsieur Gadifer has also returned."

"Look again Father." Berthin said, a thin smile threatening his lips.

"Oh! I see. That's Remonnet isn't it? What on earth is going on?" The sound of steel sliding across steel sliced through the air as Remonnet and William drew their swords. Remonnet brandished his high in the air. William matched his movements, mockingly holding his own sword high and wobbling his wrist. The Normans all laughed, provoking Remonnet to lung at William who casually swatted the blade away. Remonnet attacked again with an almighty swing, William ducked under it easily, looking as calm as a man dealing with a boy with a stick.

"This can't be right, I demand to know what is going on!" shouted Verrier.

"Nothing to concern you Father." Berthin replied, not taking his eyes from the fight. "Unless of course one of them dies, and then I suppose you will be asked to say some prayers over his grave." He winced as Remonnet took another wild swing missing William by a hair's breadth. The Bastard leapt forward, attacking Remonnet with a flurry of swings, taking the older man by surprise with the ferocity and speed of his flashing blade. Remonnet backed away, flailing desperately to parry the blows raining down on him. He stumbled in the sand and swung his blade recklessly in a wide arc as he tumbled to the ground.

William stood back and waited for Remonnet to climb back to his feet. The older man surged forward, chopping at the air frantically. William dodged the attack effortlessly without raising his sword until the very last swing when he stepped inside a wild backhand swing and struck Remonnet in the face with his cross guard. The old man stumbled backwards once more. He touched the blood flowing from his nose and looked at it incredulously. He charged at William, all pretence of poise and grace abandoned. Their blades came together with a dull clang. The two men pushed against each other, swords locked together. Berthin could hear William laugh as Remonnet grunted and heaved with all his might, pushing Blessi back a step before he twisted his hip and tripped the old man, sending him crashing to the ground. Remonnet let loose another wild swing from the sand which Blessi swatted away before rapping Remonnet's sword hand with the flat of his blade. Remonnet cried out, his sword fell into the sand. William casually placed the tip of his blade under the older man's chin.

"Throw down your arms." William called out to Remonnet's companions. "Or your friend dies." They dropped their swords and stood helplessly by as Gillet and Philip heaved the boat back into the sea. They climbed aboard and rowed out beyond the waves before resting on their oars.

"I demand to know what is going on." The Priest said, clearly agitated and confused.

"You demand?" Berthin spoke quietly. "Unfortunately Father, you are not currently in a position to demand anything."

"But why? I don't understand. What have you done?"

"I am leaving this company. I am no longer willing to leave the reigns of my destiny in Monsieur Gadifer's hands. He who would have us starve while we wait for Monsieur Bethencourt's return."

"But Gadifer is abroad fetching meat and leather for shoes, we will all benefit by his actions."

"*Gadifer*," Berthin spoke the name with as much distaste as he could cram into three syllables. "Gadifer is away enjoying a hunting trip with friends while we are laid up with neither purpose nor direction."

"This is ridiculous." said Verrier shaking his head. "What has come over you? And where pray tell, are the rest of the men you left with, the Gascons, and Isabel and Alfonso? Where are they?"

"I have treated with the Spanish ship. They are looking after your translators while I conduct business here."

"Looking after? These people are slavers… No!" The Priest crossed himself and stared at Berthin as if he was the Devil himself.

At that moment, Remonnet reached the top of the path, William walked behind him, driving him forward with the tip of his sword. Remonnet's companions followed looking dishevelled and defeated. Jacquet the Baker seemed to be dancing with excitement as he pushed and harried the knights up the path, clutching their swords to his chest.

"What shall we do with them?" William asked.

"Throw them in the castle store. But make sure to remove all the weapons from inside before locking the door." Berthin replied.

"Traitor!" Remonnet spat at Berthin's feet. William cuffed him around the head with the back of his hand.

"Take him away. Old fool." Berthin ordered, kicking dirt in Remonnet's direction.

"This is an outrage!" said Father Verrier. "If Monsieur de Bethencourt were here he would have your head for this… this… "

"I will go to Monsieur Bethencourt in Castile and I guarantee you this Father, he will thank me for what I have done. As will you all. I have staked as much if not more in this enterprise than any other. I am taking what is rightfully mine and leaving before the savages succumb to the call of their nature and slit our throats while we sleep. We cannot and should not ally ourselves with animals. We should be ruling over them with an iron fist, as I shall show when I return from France with the King's army."

"Your ridiculous notion of acting with noble intentions may have won you allies amongst the weak minded, but I see you Berthin de Berneval…"

"You see nothing Father. You are blinded by devotion, whereas I am free to see the whole truth. Now, if you will excuse me, I have work to do." Berthin left Verrier stood in apoplectic shock as he stalked over to the fortress.

He followed the sound of voices to the storeroom under the main hall. The last of his men was squeezing through the door as he arrived. Berthin followed them inside. The tiny room was no more than a stone box, ten feet square, scratched out of the ground beneath the fortress. The floor was uneven and cold. The only light came from a spluttering candle on a rough-hewn table in the centre of the room. Barrels, crates and sacks were stacked around the walls. Remonnet and his companions huddled in an empty corner with Jacquet standing over them, clutching a sword in each hand, grinning like a weasel on its hind legs.

"Get all of this down to the boat quickly, then lock the door and bring the key to me." Berthin instructed before turning to leave. Father Verrier arrived with Brother Bontier and blocked the door.

Berthin sighed.

"This is an outrage!" Verrier spluttered, "These stores are not yours to take." The Priest's face turned redder with every word.

"I have invested heavily in this expedition; I am only taking what is mine by right." replied Berthin.

"You didn't invest anything in this mission. You were paid to come, the same as everybody else." Verrier was shaking his head, a look of disappointment on his face.

"You know nothing of the sacrifices I made to be here. Monsieur Bethencourt would agree with me if he were here."

"But he isn't. You cannot commit heinous acts in another man's name if they are not here to repudiate your claims."

"Have you ever spoken to God Father, or do you just claim to?"

The room went silent, the accusation hung in the air like a bad smell. Berthin threw his head back and laughed.

"Pray for me Father." he sneered.

"I fear your soul is already lost." Father Verrier answered shaking his head.

"Take everything," Berthin snapped, "even the table and the candle. If anybody tries to interfere, kill them." he turned around to scan the faces of his men. "Michelet, come and open the kitchen store. Show me what Gadifer has been hiding from us."

Berthin pushed his way past Father Verrier and Brother Bontier and climbed back up to the gate room with Michelet in tow.

Leaving the fortress they encountered the Priests´ knights, Pierre and Guillaume running the other way.

"Berthin." Pierre said. "When did you return?"

"A short while ago. I´ll be leaving again before nightfall. Excuse me gentlemen."

"Wait." Pierre grabbed Berthin by the arm. Berthin snatched his arm back angrily and rounded on the knight.

"Disrespect me again Monsieur and it will be the last thing you do." He turned on his heal and stormed away leaving the pious knights perplexed.

"Ha!" Michelet sneered as he walked past Pierre and Guillaume and trotted after Berthin.

The two of them marched unhindered to the kitchen block. They didn´t see another soul anywhere inside the camp until they were crossing the dining area. The kitchen helpers sat around one of the long tables, sipping tea and listening rapt as Jacquet´s wife regaled them with a tale of royalty and rose cakes. She abruptly stopped talking and stood up. The others around the table craned their necks to see and got to their feet when they saw Berthin and Michelet hurrying past.

"As you were." Berthin said without looking back. He strode purposefully up to the kitchen storeroom and waited while Michelet fumbled under his tunic for the key. He pulled it out and unlocked the door. Berthin pushed his way inside. Jacquet´s wife had followed them to the door. She asked Michelet if she could collect some things from inside.

"Not now." Michelet said curtly before following Berthin inside, half closing the door behind him.

The storeroom was dark and cool. The only light came from the doorway. Joints of cured pork hung from hooks in the ceiling, filling the air with their heady aroma. Barrels of biscuits and sacks of grain were stacked against one wall. Barrels of wine and jars of herbs and spices lined the opposite wall. Two huge, sweating cheeses wrapped in muslin sat on a table at the far end of the room. A small barrel was partially hidden beneath a pile of sackcloth under the table.

"What's this?" Berthin asked, touching the side of the barrel with his toe.

"That's Gadifer's good stuff. He was saving it for a special occasion." Michelet answered.

"I would think this constitutes a special occasion, wouldn't you?"

"Yes, I think you may be right." Michelet answered smiling, his eyes open wide, nodding like a daisy in the wind.

"Bring an empty cask."

Michelet grabbed a small one from a pile of empties near the door.

"Fill it for me. Take the rest down to the men on the beach. They can enjoy it while we wait for the others to arrive."

"Help me then." Michelet said, lifting the little barrel onto the table. He squeezed and pulled the cork, releasing a rich fruity aroma into the air. Berthin's mouth watered as the smell teased his senses. Together they tipped the barrel and filled the small cask. Michelet reached a high shelf and pulled down a stack of cups. He offered one to Berthin. Berthin took it and filled it to the brim from the barrel. He took a sip and smiled. The rich, deep red liquid tasted divine compared to the horse piss they drank every day. He let it roll around his mouth before swallowing it. It felt as warm and comforting in his belly as it had on his tongue.

Michelet helped himself to a cupful and sipped at it.

"It truly is something special." he said smacking his lips together.

"Truly." Berthin agreed. He enjoyed one more mouthful, stamped his feet and picked up the small cask. "Off with you to the beach." he ordered Michelet. "Leave the door unlocked when you leave." Michelet nodded from the depths of his cup, Berthin pulled open the door with his foot and stepped outside.

Jacquet´s wife stood waiting next to the door. "Take whatever you need." Berthin told her as he walked away.

He went directly to Gadifer´s tent. He checked to make sure nobody was looking and slipped inside. He closed the tent flaps behind him and placed the cask and cup on the ground. The tent was roomy and well appointed, compared to Berthin´s own. Pennants and flags hung from the walls with a small cluster of framed tapestries, which looked to be sewn by children´s hands. Gadifer´s suit of armour stood on a stand next to a rack of well-used tournament weapons. Berthin walked over, lifted the faceplate and spat inside the helmet. He sniggered triumphantly as he slammed the faceplate back down with a loud clang.

Next to the suit of armour were two large chests. Berthin flung the lid of the first one open and rummaged inside. Clothes, shoes, belts, smalls and nothing more. The other contained books, charts, maps, and navigation equipment. There was a smaller locked chest hidden underneath the papers. Berthin lifted it out and smashed the lock with several hefty whacks of his knife. Inside was a tied stack of personal letters and a leather pouch. Berthin undid the drawstring of the pouch and tipped the contents into his hand. There were some small pieces of decorative jewellery, more personal than valuable. He dropped them back into the chest. He spied two rings amongst the other lumps of brass and tin and held them up to examine them more closely.

One, a delicate silver band with a golden nest mounting, contained a diamond the size of a pea. He pocketed that ring and studied the other. It was solid gold, as thick as his little finger with a turtle shell pattern engraved around it´s circumference. An emerald as big as the tip of his thumb sat in a four-leaf mount. He lifted it up to his eye to study it. Light danced through its many facets, the quality of workmanship was equal to the value of the stone. Berthin smiled and tucked the ring deep inside his boot.

Next to a comfortable looking cot made up with clean blankets was a small desk and chair. Berthin yanked open the desk drawer and found nothing but blank parchment, quills and ink inside. He pulled the drawer out completely and threw it on the cot. He thrust his arm into the drawer space and knocked on the wood. There was a hollow sound on two sides, the third rattled slightly when he rapped his knuckles against it. His fingernails found the edges of a hidden drawer. He spent a moment trying to open it before giving up and flipping the desk over. He went to the weapon rack and plucked a heavy mace from its hook. With three mighty swings, the base of the desk splintered and cracked. Berthin pulled the wood apart and found the secret drawer. He lifted it out and put it on the cot. It was a small oak box with a keyhole in its lid. Berthin swung the mace again and the box shattered.

There were two soft leather pouches inside. He lifted them and smiled as he weighed them in his hands. He opened the smaller of the two and peered inside. His smile was nearly as bright as the contents as he tipped them out onto the cot. Seven large, fat gold ingots, stamped with the mark of a crescent moon. He kissed each one as he put them back in the pouch. The second pouch was half-full of silver coins. Berthin was amazed. He didn't count the haul, there was no need, he could tell by the weight that he was now a wealthy man. He tucked the pouches deep into the folds of his tunic and picked up his wine.

"To your health Monsieur." he said raising the cup. "May you rot in Hell!" He guzzled the wine and poured himself another.

He was halfway through drinking that one when he felt the overwhelming urge to piss. He pulled out his cock and sent a hot stream of dark, stinking urine cascading over Gadifer's cot. He tucked himself away and laughed. He drained the rest of his wine and tossed the empty cup onto the cot. He took one last look around the interior of the tent and left.

The wine hit his stomach and head hard when he stepped out into the sunlight. He felt dizzy and needed to lie down before he fell down. He swayed through the camp, gripping guy ropes to keep him on his feet. He arrived at his own tent and was annoyed to find the door flapping open. He always tied it shut. His head cleared as he unsheathed his dagger and crept inside. He cursed when he saw young Nicol laying in his cot.

"What the hell are you doing here?" he asked re-sheathing his knife.

"I saw you by the kitchens," she purred. "It made me hungry for you." She threw back the blanket to reveal her young naked body, stretched out in what she must have imagined to be an alluring pose. Berthin felt repulsed looking down at her skinny limbs, peppered with burns from the kitchen fires. Sallow skin stretched too tightly over her bruised ribs and hipbones. On a normal day, he would have thrown her out, but this was anything but a normal day.

Without a word he dropped his sword belt and britches, got to his knees and dragged Nicol´s legs around him. Within seconds, he was spent inside her. She wriggled beneath him, complaining that her back hurt against the side of the cot.

He got to his feet and pulled up his britches. As he was doing so, the diamond ring tumbled out of his pocket and onto the floor. Nicol´s wide eyes followed it down as it fell in the dirt. She reached out and picked it up.

"Where did this come from?" she asked, casually slipping it onto the end of her finger.

"None of your fucking business." Berthin snapped. He grabbed her hand and snatched at the ring. It slipped out of his fingers and flew across the tent, struck the canvas wall and slid down to the floor. Berthin lost track of it in the air, his head started to spin again.

In a fit of rage, Berthin reached down and dragged Nicol from the cot.

"Get dressed and get out of my sight." he roared.

"But My Lord…" she managed to say before Berthin swiped her across the face with the back of his hand. She fell to the floor clutching her cheek looking up at him defiantly. He bent over her and raised his hand once more. The threat was enough. She scurried across the floor, gathered her clothes and dressed quickly as Berthin flopped down on to the cot. He raised his arm to cover his eyes. His head was throbbing. He needed to close his eyes for a few moments.

He awoke with a start sometime later, how much later he couldn´t tell. His mouth was dry and his eyes gritty. He sat up and rubbed them but it made them worse. He thought about sinking back down into the sweet oblivion of peaceful sleep. It was then the shouting started. Suddenly remembering where he was he leapt from the cot, strapped on his sword belt and ran from the tent.

He followed the noise to the front of the fortress where he found Jean the Mason with Chevalier, yelling "*ALARM!*" at the tops of their voices. They stood half-dressed, each clutching fishing lines and strings of fish. Chevalier was pointing to the West, dancing on his tiptoes as if he was one of his precious horses. Father Verrier and Brother Bontier came racing around the other side of the fortress followed by their knights, Pierre and Guillaume.

"What is it?" yelled the Priest.

"Nothing good." Chevalier answered pointing to a dark longboat, sculling towards them, brimming with wild men with too much hair and not enough teeth between them.

"You may want to get dressed messieurs." Berthin said quietly. "We have visitors to entertain."

"Who is it?" Jean the Mason asked.

"It looks like a boatload of Iberian slavers to me." Berthin smiled grimly.

"You fool!" Father Verrier shouted at Berthin. "What have you done?"

"Nothing anybody else wouldn't have done in my position Father."

"Pah!" The Priest turned and grabbed Brother Bontier by the arm. "Run! Run and tell the Majo boys and girls to flee for the hills. Go now!" The friar took off at a sprint.

Berthin walked away. He jogged down the path to the beach where he found his men around the loaded boat. They were enjoying Gadifer's wine and were in good spirits, laughing and joking while watching the Tajamar's boat get closer.

"Messieurs." Berthin hailed them. "I suggest you collect anything of value from your tents before these gentlemen set about their business, for believe me, these slaver boys are going to be like locusts through a wheat field when they get into the camp."

And so it proved to be.

The slavers landed and immediately launched into a thieving frenzy. They looted every unguarded tent. They didn't pause to fight, they had no need to as almost all the tents stood empty. Jean the Mason and Chavalier stood in the doorways of their adjacent tents with swords drawn, watching in disbelief as the Spaniards stripped the camp clean all around them. Processions of possessions wandered down to the beach for hours on top of legs that got more shaky as more wine was drunk. Both boats were soon full of plunder. The armour, tunics, boots and weapons that wouldn't fit inside the boats were piled up on the beach. Men picked them over, searching for hidden treasures.

Berthin left the beach with William and Young Gillet to watch the slavers at their business. The trio stood by the fortress doorway commenting on the antics of the men, rolling around drunk, trashing the camp before their eyes.

The pious knights Pierre and Guillaume barred the fortress door from the inside and stood watching from the parapet. The Priests cowered behind them praying. The slavers didn't even pause to test the strength of the fortress, they had far easier pickings elsewhere.

By the time night fell, there were drunken slavers waddling between the tents draped in heralded flags and pennants. One man even marched through the camp wearing Gadifer's shiny suit of armour. His crewmates roared with laughter, striking the armour plates with their clubs as he passed by. He discarded it piece by piece until it lay scattered throughout the camp like fallen petals in the dirt.

Suddenly, Jacquet the Baker stumbled into sight making a beeline for the fortress dragging Nicol by the arm. She was kicking, screaming and trying with all her might to break free, but his big pink hand gripped tightly round her skinny arm. A small, sloshing cask was tucked under his other arm.

He stopped in front of Berthin and yanked her around, sending her crashing to the ground at his feet. Jacquet twisted her wrist, causing her to scream out. He put the cask down gently and used his free hand to prise open Nicol's clenched fist. After much huffing and puffing he stretched out her fingers and squeezed them tightly. He thrust the hand up to Berthin's face.

"See this!" the baker hissed. Nicol fought like a wild animal trapped in a snare. "Shut your mouth whore!" Jacquet screamed and kicked her in the ribs, cracking more than one by the sound of it. Nicol could no longer breathe enough to scream.

"See what?" asked Berthin.

"This ring here."

"What about it?"

"She said you gave it to her."

"Why would I give *her* a ring like that?" he squinted and looked at it carefully. He was furious when he recognised it as the silver diamond ring that had fallen from his pocket. She must have snatched it from the ground before leaving his tent.

"Exactly what I thought." Jacquet gripped the ring and yanked it off the girl's finger. She shrieked in agony as he pulled the finger bones from their sockets with the ring. "Filthy fucking whore!" He cast her arm away and kicked her once more. She fell to the ground gasping, nursing her broken finger. Her hair stuck to the snot and tears on her face.

"Filthy, fucking, Whore! Just like her filthy, fucking, whoring mother." Jacquet screamed down at his wretched daughter. He lifted the ring to his face, trying to focus his drunken eyes enough to study it. He gave in and shoved it deep into his pocket. Berthin watched carefully which pocket he put it in, he would get it back when Jacquet passed out later.

"The pair of them have been tomming for trinkets since we got here." Jacquet spat. "They've got a stash somewhere that they think I don't know about." Berthin suddenly felt a little uncomfortable. The Baker went on, "I'll wager that there isn't a noble cock that hasn't been inside my sweet little girl. Between her and her mother, I'm willing to bet they've given every man here a dose of cock rot."

Berthin noticed out of the corner of his eye as William shifted awkwardly and reached down to touch his groin. Young Gillet stroked his chin, looking anxious. Jacquet dragged Nicol to her feet. He led her sobbing to a pair of slavers who had been watching and laughing a few paces away.

"Here. You want her?" he asked them. They smiled through broken teeth and asked him "Repit plis"

"You take girl. Take her. Go on!" he said like a hawker, offering his daughter up to them like an old coat. The slavers´ faces lit up. They took one arm each and dragged Nicol down to the beach.

"Go on! Take her! Fuck them all you sons of whores, may the sores on your cocks be as big as cherries in the morning." And with that he staggered away without looking back.

As darkness fell, the camp lay in tatters. A glow radiated from the beach where huge bonfires spat flames into the air. The slavers sat around them digesting their feast of pillage and rapine. They continued to gorge themselves on wine and women through the darkest hours of the night. Every woman from the camp was dragged down to the beach, stripped and raped, by lines of eager men. Their screams softened to silent whimpers as the night wore on.

Berthin slumped down on the fortress steps next to William. They were both hopelessly drunk. Young Gillet stretched out at their feet snoring fitfully. William attempted to fill their cups from a small cask and ended up spilling most of it in the dirt. Berthin leaned down and picked up his cup, took one drink, fell back against the door and dropped his cup. He was asleep before the cup hit the floor.

****

Gadifer sat with his men on the peak of the small volcano at the western end of the little island of Lobos. They stared wordlessly across the strait to Lancarote. They sat in silence watching the glow of the fires burning on the beach below Rubicon. There was nothing left to say that hadn´t already been said.

Down below them, a pack of sea wolves lay on the rocks where the volcano met the sea. They barked loudly into the night sky. Gadifer couldn´t help but think they were laughing at him.

****

At first it was a sound. A creaking and a murmuring of indistinct voices. Then the sound of lapping water… and pain… everywhere. Sensations began creeping through his skin. He was lying on wooden boards. Something soft and damp was under his head, damp from his own sweat, or blood. He shivered once. It sent pain shooting through his broken body. His head felt like it was going to burst open. He squeezed his eyes tightly shut against the pain.

A soft hand touched his brow gently. A woman's voice whispered his name.

"Gara." he tried to say, but his mouth couldn't form the word. He tried to swallow but it hurt too much. Somebody touched a damp rag to his lips and he relished the moisture. Even though the touch caused pain, it also brought relief.

"Gara." he tried to say once more.

He sensed a light coming nearer. He tried to open his eyes but the pressure was too great. He attempted to lift his head but the small hand touching his brow pressed it back down.

"Gara?"

"Gara isn't here Norstar. It is I, Isabel." *Isabel…* The name sounded familiar somehow. But why?

He gripped her wrist as another spasm of intense pain wrapped around his head before shooting through his entire body…

And then all went black again.

28

Lancarote,

October 17ᵗʰ, 1402

Fayna sat looking down on the two ships sheltering in the bay of Graciosa. Her father lay injured in the belly of the black ship. She longed to see him. Just a glimpse would be enough. She knew deep inside that he still lived. He was too strong to die.

Rayco stirred next to her, wrapped in his cloak against the wall of the lookout nest snoring gently. The bruise on his face looked painful from where Gara had punched him the day before. It had taken the combined strength of Jonay, Daida and Iballa to pull her away from Rayco when he returned home and told them of Norstar´s capture. If Guadarfia had been with him Fayna had no doubt her mother would have killed him on the spot. Gara blamed the whole sorry mess on the Mence and his failure to heed Norstar´s warnings from the beginning.

Fayna had left the cave and ran as fast as she could to the lookout nest high in the cliffs. She watched the black ship, not daring to close her eyes in case she missed a glimpse of her father. Rayco had followed her and cautiously joined her just before sunset. She didn´t have any words for him. She had been tempted more than once to shove him out of the nest when he got close to the edge. She, like her mother, was a raging ball of fury. It focussed her mind and fuelled her determination.

Around midday, a flurry of activity on the black ship caught her attention. She kicked Rayco´s foot. He woke with a start and rushed over to join her. Two boats were rowing around the headland from the East. Even from this far away, Fayna could spot the foul creature

Berthin stood at the prow of one of the boats. They watched as the boats pulled alongside the black ship and were unloaded. Barrels, crates and sacks of all shapes and sizes were transferred onto the deck of the ship.

When they were empty, the boats pushed away again and crossed the strait to the beach below the lookout nest. Fayna watched as a group of knights on the beach surged forward to meet the boats. They didn´t appear to receive a warm welcome and soon were embroiled in a massive shouting match with the oarsmen. Their arguing stopped suddenly as another large group of men appeared walking from the cliff path to the beach. Their backs bent beneath the weight of chattel they carried. They shuffled down the path on tired feet. Upon arrival at the beach, they pushed the knights aside and climbed aboard the boats. They pushed off and rowed back to the black ship while the knights looked on.

Sometime later, the two holy men from Rubicon appeared from the cliff path accompanied by five more knights. They walked to the knights on the beach and spent a while in what appeared to be unfriendly conversation. The knights eventually broke away from the Priests and retreated to a small camp they had set up inland, still arguing.

The Priests began waving furiously to the other ship. After a few moments a boat left that ship and collected the holy men from the beach.

"We need to get closer." Fayna said, standing and putting her bow over her shoulder.

"Why?" asked Rayco.

"Because we can´t do anything to help my father from up here."

"We can´t do anything to help him from down there either."

"Stay here then." Fayna shrugged and climbed up and out of the nest.

****

Berthin paced up and down the deck, getting more irate as every minute passed. The Tajamar´s crew were bustling around him, driven by Captain Ordoñez´s orders to clear the decks and prepare to sail. The longboat was hoisted on board and lashed to the deck behind the main mast. The boat from Rubicon was tied up alongside the ladder. Two men hopped down into it and began tying lines to its lifting hooks. Suddenly the lookout at the top of the mast shouted a warning. A small boat had left the Morella with the Priests on board and was heading straight for them.

Berthin raced up to the quarterdeck where Ordoñez stood like an island amongst men surging all around him.

"We need to leave now." Berthin said, dancing from foot to foot.

"We leave when we are ready." Ordoñez replied in a low growl.

Berthin seethed and stormed to the port rail. The priests were nearly at the ship, shouting at the men attaching lines to the Rubicon boat. Ordoñez walked over to stand next to Berthin.

"What is it?" he said gripping the rail, his knuckles turning white.

The Morella's boat surged across the water and swept alongside the ship. Brother Bontier leapt from the prow of the moving boat and landed heavily inside Rubicon's boat. He struggled to his feet and began haranguing the men tying the lines to the lifting hooks. They cursed him in return but were reluctant to raise their hands to the holy man.

"What do you want friar?" Ordoñez bellowed over the side.

"This boat is our property. You have no right to take it."

"And who says it's yours?"

"The man standing next to you for one." Bontier answered, flicking his head with disgust towards Berthin.

"I have no idea what you are talking about." Berthin answered haughtily.

"No. I imagine propriety and the notion of right and wrong are lost on you. I will pray for you. But in the meantime..." he reached across the sailor stood in the stern and grabbed the line attached to the lifting hook. "... I will be taking back what is ours." The sailor looked up at Ordoñez, unsure how to react.

Bontier tugged the rope and the slipknot untied. Ordoñez shook his head and gestured for his men to abandon the boat and get back on board the ship. They scrambled up the side as Bontier reached the bowline and released it.

"What are you doing?" Berthin hissed at Ordoñez. "Throw him in the water and be done with it."

Ordoñez turned and stared down at Berthin. "I have asked myself many times why I haven't gutted you and thrown you overboard little man. If I did, who do you think would miss you? Eh! Who would ever know? Eh! Eh!" Berthin blanched, Ordoñez continued. "If I so much as sneeze on a Priest there isn't a port in all of Christendom I could dock at. I would be crucified on my own mast, if I was lucky. If you wish to tip the friar in the water then be my guest. I'll leave you here with them."

Bontier threw both lines up to the ship's deck as the Morella's boat finished a tight circle and came back alongside. Father Verrier stood in the bow, looking directly at Ordoñez.

"You Señor!" he hailed.

"What is it Priest?" Ordoñez replied, standing back from the rail and folding his arms across his chest.

"You have friends of ours chained up in your hold and I demand their release."

"Friends of yours? All I have are two dozen monkeys in cages which I will be taking to market as soon as you get out of the way."

"You are committing a heinous crime against humanity, and you know it."

"I am committing no crime! This is my business, has been for as long as preaching has been yours. I find and sell slaves. I have even been known to sell the odd skin to your father, the Pope, to row his barges. If what I am doing is a crime, then why does he pay me to do it?"

Father Verrier looked crestfallen, frustrated and angry, all at the same time. Berthin rejoiced. It felt good to watch the sanctimonious old priest getting slapped down. Verrier looked at Berthin's triumphant smile and breathed deeply before turning back to Ordoñez.

"You have taken our translators with the others. They are baptized, they are Christians. You cannot sell them as slaves."

"Says who?" Ordoñez scoffed. "The Christians buy the Pagans, the Pagans buy the Arabs, the Arabs buy the Christians. They are all the same to me Holy Man."

"I implore you. Please leave us our translators. While we are here unprotected, we have no way of speaking to the natives. If there is any humanity left in you, I beg you to grant us this favour."

"And what's it worth Father?" Berthin couldn't resist chirping up.

"It is worth your soul Berthin de Berneval." Verrier answered smartly. "Master Ordoñez, there is still hope for your salvation. I beg you, grant us this tiny boon."

"You can have one." Ordoñez grunted.

Berthin looked up, about to protest. The look Ordoñez's returned brooked no argument. Berthin withdrew.

"Release Isabel." Father Verrier cried.

"The woman?!" Ordoñez answered. He looked at Berthin. "That will cost more!"

"I'll pay the difference." Berthin offered quietly. He knew Ordoñez had planned to gorge himself on the woman once upon the high seas. It was a small victory to deny him that one thing. With Gadifer's gold and silver, he could afford it. Ordoñez scowled down at Berthin.

"Release the woman. Toss her overboard!" he shouted. Two men stood at his shoulder rushed off to do his bidding. Ordoñez looked away from the Priest, just as he was about to speak again. "Ximenez!" he called to the man manning the tiller of the Priest's boat. "How is my friend Captain Calvo?"

"He's well." the sailor answered curtly.

"Send him my regards." Ordoñez said, curling his lip and snarling.

At that moment, Isabel was dragged from the door beneath the quarterdeck. She cursed and hissed like an alley cat at the two men holding her arms.

"Give her to them." Ordoñez ordered. The two men walked Isabel to the side and hurled her overboard. She plunged into the water and sank like a stone before kicking briefly back to the surface. Her arms splashed wildly as she fought to stay afloat, but the weight of her dress pulled her back down. Her head disappeared again. Bontier leapt in the water after her and managed to catch her hand before she sank out of sight. He kicked and pulled back to the surface where Verrier and Ximenez caught his arm. With an almighty heave, he pulled Isabel to the surface. She was crying as she was pulled into the boat.

"Now would be a good time for you to back away." Ordoñez called down from the ship. "We are leaving. I wouldn´t want your boats to be damaged when we come about." He disappeared from the rail. Berthin smiled his serpentine smile down at Father Verrier one final time before walking to the stern gunwale. He lifted his eyes to watch the men on the high spars, unfurling the topsails.

The sails felt the wind and the ship swung around. Berthin heard the calls of the men from the capstan winding the anchor in and suddenly they were off, cruising across the turquoise water for the final time. They slid past the Morella. Berthin saw Captain Calvo stood on his quarterdeck, four square with his hands clasped behind his back. *Foolish man, this could have been his.* Berthin thought as he saluted across the water. Calvo scowled back at him.

Before long, they had cleared the islands to the North and were being battered by the Atlantic swell. The wind increased and the skies darkened. Berthin stood at the stern rail and looked back at Lancarote shrinking over the horizon. The island was nought but a dark smudge beneath the clouds. The ship lurched beneath his feet. He tightened his grip on the rail to avoid being thrown overboard. Heavy rain came out of the air from nowhere and started to hammer the deck. It was so intense and so sudden it drenched Berthin to the bone. The ship lurched again then shuddered as the bow dug into a massive wave.

Berthin lost his hold on the rail and fell forward. He ran into the solid back of Master Ordoñez who was fighting to control the tiller.

"What the hell are you doing man!" Ordoñez screamed. He shrugged Berthin away as the forecastle lifted to climb another wave. Berthin went reeling back to the stern rail. It hit him hard just beneath the shoulder blades. He screamed in agony and crouched down, bracing his body between the deck and the rail, hanging on for dear life.

The stern rose again and then crashed back down. Berthin felt an instant of weightlessness before the hardwood deck rose to slam into his backside.

The sea calmed for a moment, Berthin pulled himself back up onto his feet and began to rub away the soreness in his back. He winced in agony as he twisted around to look to stern.

The island had disappeared.

****

Fayna saw the black ship depart and chased it for as long as she could until it turned to the northwest and disappeared over the horizon. Rayco found her curled in a ball, weeping uncontrollably. She fell into his arms and sobbed until her body ached, and then she cried some more.

And then the tears stopped. Her face changed. She held her jaw high, her eyes narrowed. Determination hardened her features.

Rayco followed her without question back along the path down to the beach.

As they got closer, they watched the holy men and Isabel row to shore. The knights gathered on the beach waited until they were all ashore before twelve of them broke away and heaved the boat back into the water. The holy men and their knights watched on helplessly as they rowed off to the east into the open sea.

The old man Verrier shook his head sadly and began to lead his companions back inland. They crossed the headland and began to climb the cliff path.

Fayna and Rayco were marching down the pathway towards them.

The knights reached for their swords, but Verrier stopped them from drawing steel. Fayna´s eyes didn´t waver from Verrier´s face.

"Where is my father?" she called.

They didn´t even realise until later that she had asked them in their own language. Isabel stepped forward.

"Who is your father?" she asked.

"Norstar."

"Norstar is alive."

"Where is he?"

"On the black ship."

"Were you with him?"

"I nursed your father.　He is strong, he will live."

"But where?"

"That I couldn´t say."

"You were taken, and you came back.　Where did they take you?"

"I was sold in a land to the north called Portugal, and then from there I travelled a lot."

"Do you remember all the places you have been?"

"Why, yes."

"Then I will speak with you as we walk Isabel."

"Why?"

"Because I need to know all that you know if I am to find my father."

29

Seville,

October 19th, 1402

Jean sat back in the overstuffed chair while servers bustled around the table clearing away the remains of dinner. It had been a fine meal. The chicken fell from the bone with just the lightest encouragement and filled his mouth with the most marvellous collage of sensations. It was a meal that made his palette demand more, despite his stomach telling him clearly that more was impossible to cram inside.

The steward placed a large glass in front of him and filled it from a crystal decanter. He did the same for Sir Robert who sat across the table, before backing away and leaving them alone in the private dining room.

Jean reached out and cradled the ornate glass in his palm. He inhaled the fumes rising from the fiery liquid. His nose came to life as his eyes relaxed. He took a small sip and rolled the brandy around his mouth. It burned and made his gums tingle.

"What did I tell you old boy," said Sir Robert from across the table. "The best food in the whole kingdom." He raised his own glass and began rolling the brandy around, watching the trails of sweet alcohol stick to the inside of the glass.

"Yes indeed, a rare treat." Jean took another sip.

"Of all the wonderful eateries in Seville, I believe this to be the most sublime. A true beacon of civilisation in a world of barely tamed savagery." Sir Robert continued.

"I have to agree, and I have only seen a small portion of the city. The last time I was here I saw little else other than the inside of the Palace of Justice."

"Yes, yes, a most disagreeable turn of events, but well behind you now old chap. The next Palace you visit will be the King's own, Alcazar."

Sir Robert put his glass back on the table and sat back.

"Is there any news of King Enrique?" Jean asked.

"Indeed, there is." Sir Robert smiled and leaned forward. "His Grace is extremely busy with court affairs at the moment but hopes to meet with you before the end of the month. He has asked me personally to see to it that you have the best reception here in the city during your stay. When your good lady wife arrives, you are both to be his guests in the palace. Her Grace, Queen Catherine is looking forward to entertaining Lady Bethencourt personally."

Jean couldn't help himself, he barked a quick laugh and then stifled it quickly.

"What amuses you so?" Sir Robert asked.

"The wife."

"Go on."

"Well, to be brutally honest, or honestly brutal in her case, my dear lady wife has always been my loudest and most devoted critic over the years. I look forward to seeing her face when the coach pulls up outside the palace."

"Indeed." Sir Robert chuckled. "I always find the best pie served humbly."

"A dish I must dip into myself to remind me our task is far from complete. Lancarote was a good beginning, but it was only that... a beginning."

"A strong beginning!" said Sir Robert leaning across the table. "A foothold on the islands no other nation has managed to secure. And you managed it without significant loss. Hells, you lost more of your company in Cadiz than you did in Lancarote. Now that Enrique's peace treaty with Portugal is ratified, he is willing and able to throw some real weight behind you to support your endeavours. Men, ships and silver. Speaking of which, what is happening with Gadifer's ship. Did you find a new crew?"

"They are aboard her and preparing to sail here. They should arrive within days. Although, word of our adventure has spread amongst the tradesmen of Cadiz, the old tub has acquired a somewhat legendary status. I've had to turn down several very generous offers to buy her. I might have been tempted had she been mine to sell, but I imagine Gadifer wouldn't be best pleased if I did."

"Maybe now is the time to think about commissioning a ship of your own and then you wouldn't be so beholden to Gadifer."

"He should grant me ownership papers for this one considering I wrested it from the hands of *his* mutinous crew."

"Long may they rot in jail." Sir Robert added lifting his glass.

"I'll drink to that." Jean raised his glass and took another long pull of brandy.

The two of them talked until the decanter was nearly empty. Jean's speech had started to slur a little by the time Sir Robert made his excuses and left. The steward returned and cleared the table before turning down Jean's bed in the adjoining room.

Jean looked through the window onto the dark street below and smiled when as saw Sir Robert leading Piquet away into the night. The diminutive secretary was swaying from one side of the street to the other. Jean suspected he'd enjoyed the inn keeper's hospitality a little too enthusiastically in the public lounge downstairs.

He watched until the darkness swallowed them both up. He undressed and sank down into the deep, soft bed and pulled the crisp linen sheets up to his chin. In the moments before sleep took him, he allowed himself to imagine his triumphant return to the island at the head of a colourful procession of ships.

The mighty Guadarfia kneeling before him as he steps ashore. Gadifer with his knights, resplendent in their gleaming armour in a long line behind him. Father Verrier and Brother Bontier stood with a choir of angelic Majo's on the bluff above the beach, singing thanks and praises up into the blue, blue,

Blue…

Blue…

cloudless sky…

30

Northwest Barbary Coast,
October 20th, 1402

They had rowed through the night, taking it in turns with the four oars in the boat. The light of dawn revealed a slither of dull yellow land creeping over the horizon.

"What did I tell you messieurs. Africa, dead ahead." Siort crowed triumphantly from the stern where he gripped the tiller tightly. The men stopped rowing and turned around to see. The other bodies began to stir between the benches and lift their heads. A couple of knights at the bow stood to get a better view.

"Steady there!" Siort called. "You'll have us over." The men sat back down quickly. The waves had rocked them mercilessly, coming steadily from the larboard side throughout the night. The wind was fresh. Rain and sea spray had drenched the men to the bone. They all wore their armour-plated tunics to keep what little warmth they could inside their bodies.

"Put your backs into it men." Siort encouraged from the stern. "Just a little further and we'll be back on dry land. A short walk up the coast and we'll catch a ship back home."

The men rowed with renewed vigour and within a short time were just beyond the outer break of a long golden beach. Beyond the beach, low sand dunes stretched away into the distance. Siort steered to starboard to run with the waves, looking for slack water between the breakers.

"Riders!" called a man laid in the prow, pointing away to his left.

"Shit!" Siort cursed as he spotted a half dozen men on horseback galloping along the beach towards them. He pulled the tiller arm close and the boat started to head for shore. "We'll have to take our chances with them. We won't outrun them in this. Get your swords ready."

"What are you doing?" shouted Labat on the bench next to him. "We can´t fight men on horseback. Are you mad?"

"We can´t outrun them and we can´t go back out to sea. This is our only option." Siort gritted his teeth and looked back over his shoulder, a large wave was building behind them.

"It is not our only option." spat Labat, leaning over and pulling the tiller from Siort´s grasp sending the boat turning sharply to starboard.

"NOOOO!" Siort screamed, leaping from his seat just as an enormous wave curled around the boat. It hit them side on, lifted them smartly and then dumped them over beneath an avalanche of white water. Siort tumbled head over heels under the weight of the almighty wave rolling over him. He fought to turn upright but had no idea which way upright was. His back hit the sand and he dragged his fingers through it to slow down. He span around and levered his legs under his body and pushed off as hard as he could.

His head broke the surface long enough to take a lung full of air before another wall of water broke over his head, driving him under once again. He struggled to rip his plated tunic away, tearing at the buckles with shaking fingers before he was slammed into the sand once more. He found his feet and managed with an almighty heave to rip his tunic from his back before kicking to the surface.

He saw the next wave coming and dived beneath it, kicking his boots off in the process. He continued swimming through the waves, shedding his clothing until after what seemed like an eternity, it was shallow enough for his feet to stand on the sandy bottom with his head above water. He began wading to the beach, exhausted and beyond bedraggled. He fell to his knees when the water was only as high as his shins and cried with relief.

He turned around and sat down to face the waves. He saw the boat bobbing behind the waves. It had righted itself and drifted away on the rip tide, it´s oars flapping lifelessly from the oarlocks. There was nobody left on board. They were all in the water.

Siort got anxiously to his feet and scanned the sea on both sides. Nothing. Not a sign of any one of his companions. Suddenly, away to his left he heard a cough and a splutter. He looked and saw Labat floating through the waves on his back. He splashed over to him and dragged him roughly to his feet. He flopped around like a rag doll in his hands.

"Labat!" he screamed into his face as he held him up by his undershirt. "For God's sake man. Labat, wake up!" Labat slowly came to and was able to stand unassisted. He bent over and coughed a belly full of seawater down his legs.

"Where are the others?" he managed to ask between coughs.

"There are no others. Just us. In our fucking underwear."

A horse snickered from somewhere up the beach. Siort followed the sound. Six Moors sat on horses, their flowing robes blowing in the wind, revealing gleaming scimitars on their hips.

Siort fell to his knees and bowed his head. He clasped his hands to his chest and began to cry once more.

"I think it's a little late for praying." Labat said, standing to look at the horsemen.

"This isn't praying my friend. This is begging for forgiveness."

31

The Royal Alcazar, Seville, October 30th, 1402

Jean was walking on air. His first meeting with King Enrique had gone even better than Sir Robert said it would. Jean offered the prize of the Lancarote to Enrique at a lavish banquet thrown in his honour. The King played his part flawlessly in front of his court of nobles, graciously accepting Jean´s gift and rewarding his loyalty with titles and riches. Jean was granted permission to tax all merchandise from each island he tamed, one fifth of the value of all goods exported from the islands would be Jean´s. The King offered stewardship of the entire Canarian archipelago to Jean with permission to mint his own coins. The look on Madame Bethencourt´s face had been a sight to behold when she realised just how wealthy and powerful her husband was about to become. She had even crept into his chamber in the middle of the night to show just how impressed she was with his achievement. Jean smiled at the memory as his prick jumped a little inside his cod.

"In here señor." said the guard leading Jean along the mosaic-lined corridors of the palace to a small meeting room off the main entrance. The guard had to duck to fit the plumes of his helmet beneath the lintel. Jean followed him into the room, sparse save for a tall writing desk in the corner. Light entered through a narrow, barred window set high in the wall. Two men waited in the centre of the room flanked by two more liveried guards. They stood up smartly as Jean entered the room.

"Gentlemen!" Jean said, stopping two paces from the men and clasping his hands behind his back. "You asked to see me?"

"Monsieur Jean de Bethencourt, of Lancarote?" asked the taller of the two, a serious man with a thick main of peppered hair making him seem even taller.

"The very same." Jean answered with a slight bow. "And you are?"

"Captain Francisco Calvo of La Morella, and this is Ximenes, my second." He indicated the squat man stood at his side who delivered a crisp smart bow as Jean turned to him.

"At your service señor." said Ximenes.

"We are recently returned from the Canary Islands where we encountered members of your expedition." Captain Calvo continued.

"Ah! Wonderful news." Jean beamed with delight. "Did you lay over in Rubicon? Did you meet Gadifer? Father Verrier?"

"I did not meet Señor Gadifer face to face, Ximenes did. I met with your priest, Father Verrier. I also had the misfortune to deal with your subordinate, Berthin de Berneval. He is the reason we have come directly from the docks to speak with you señor, even before securing our load."

"I see." Jean was stunned. As Calvo went on to recount the tale of Berthin's dastardly betrayal, Jean felt his legs getting weaker and weaker. Every word Calvo spoke was another nail in the coffin of Jean's euphoria. He nearly exploded with rage when he learned of the capture and subsequent enslavement of the Majos by Berthin and his men. The only relief came with the news Guadarfia had escaped their clutches.

"And you say you know this slaver, Ordoñez of the Tajamar?" Jean asked.

"I've had the displeasure to cross his path from time to time."

"Where is he taking them?"

"My guess is Aragon. That's where he'll get the best price at his time of year. Although he will have to stop somewhere to take on more supplies with that many people on board. I imagine he'll go to Cadiz. If there are buyers there he could look to make a quick sale without going further North."

"But he left before you. He could have already been and gone."

"Not in that ship señor. The Tajamar's got a heavy midriff. In the weather we encountered, against the wind, with a full hold, I can't see him making Cadiz for at least another two days."

"Then I must make haste if I am to intercept them there and rescue our friends. Captain, I cannot thank you enough for your assistance. If there is anything I can do to repay you?"

"Right this wrong señor. That will be payment enough. Our trade depends on the good will of the natives in the Canary Islands. There are many of us who appreciate the task you have undertaken there to make it a safer place for us all. If you need supplies delivering to Rubicon, we will be ready to return there within the week."

"I thank you Captain and will consider your offer. But first, I have urgent need of swift horses and a few dozen swords."

32

Cadiz, Kingdom of Castile, November 2nd, 1402

Berthin´s bruised and battered body seemed to slump with relief as the Tajamar sailed into the still water of the channel to the dock. The journey had been a relentless assault on his senses, a nightmare of creaks and bangs on a restless, canting deck. He was wet and miserable and had prayed for the mercy of a quick release on many an occasion as the ship was tossed around like a toy on the Atlantic´s mighty waves. His knees were black and swollen from the numerous times he was hurled to the floor during black, stormy nights.

It seemed to take an age for the ship to finally stop. Ordoñez steered her into a secluded anchorage near the animal pens and tied her alongside a pair of similar ships, with black timbers and grimy sheets. He set the crew to work swilling out the water tubs and flushing the slave decks before seeking out Berthin.

"We´ll be here for two days before heading North." he said gruffly.

"Can we not sell them here?" Berthin asked in a thin whiney voice. "You told me there were auctions here."

"There are, just not now. Look around. No sellers, no buyers. It´s the wrong time of year for trade here. We´ll have to go to Aragon."

"And how long will that take?"

"Maybe a week, two. Depends on the wind."

"Ah! The wind. The fucking wind. I think I´m beginning to miss its constant howl in my ears." Ordoñez could have smiled beneath his moustache, Berthin couldn´t tell.

"You need a night ashore." Ordoñez grunted. "Take your men and go. You foul the air with your misery. Give my crew a rest from your constant bellyaching."

"You really believe me to be a fool." Berthin replied haughtily. "We go and you go. What´s to stop you from slipping off and taking all the merchandise?"

"The tide for one." Ordoñez batted away Berthin´s question off-handedly. "This whole bay is going to be a huge mud flat in less than two hours. And we need supplies, we won´t get everything we need until the morning. Besides, I have business in the city to take care of myself." He looked at Berthin with the most menacing twinkle in the depths of his dark eyes. "I don´t want *you* on board alone, with all those valuable trinkets to sell."

"Ha! Finally the truth." Berthin puffed a little to think Ordoñez might have some respect for him after all. "Very well. I shall take my men into the city for one night, we shall return before the morning tide."

******

Jean wrinkled his nose at the cloying, musky air rising from the street. As soon as they rode through the gates and into the city the aroma of too many people crammed in too small a space assaulted Jean´s senses. He rode with Martin at his side leading a column of thirty guards. Their hot sweaty horses steamed and snorted, eager to drink and rest after a hard ride from Jerez, the last leg of their dash from Seville forty leagues away. People thronged the narrow streets and reacted angrily to being barged out of the way by the horsemen. Jean paid them no mind and urged his horse onwards to the office of the Harbourmaster, a squat, two storey stone building on the edge of the quayside. From the crenelated rooftop, it was possible to see every mast in the port. There was usually at least one guard patrolling there, but not now. The office looked deserted.

Jean leapt from his horse, passing the reins to Martin. He walked over to the office door. A tall character dressed in a heavy black coat, with a weather-beaten tricorn on his head, leaned against the wall watching Jean approach. His dark eyes were in deep shadow, a thick beard started high on his cheeks, stretching down to two well-oiled ponytails tied below his chin with black cords, tipped with silver.

"Good evening to you señor." Jean said, tipping his cap to the stranger, who barely lifted his head and grunted in response. Jean reached out for the door handle and tried it. The door was locked.

"Damn!" Jean cursed. "Do you know where he´s gone?" he asked the man in black.

"It was locked when I got here." Jean kicked the door and turned around to face the man.

"Do you work here?" he asked.

"No. Just passing through."

"Have there been many ships coming in today?"

"I couldn´t tell you, like I said, I just arrived."

"Where from?"

"I don´t think that´s any of your business." said the man pushing himself away from the wall and squaring up to Jean. Martin and the Captain of the guard hurried over to Jean´s side.

"Is there a problem here Señor Bethencourt?" asked the captain.

"I shouldn´t think so." answered Jean raising his hand to still the over exuberant Captain who stared threateningly at the man in black.

"Bethencourt?" the man growled from somewhere behind his thick beard.

"That is correct." answered Jean amiably.

"I´ve heard of you. Canary Islands."

"Indeed señor. The very same." Jean couldn´t help but stand a little taller and puff his chest out. He really was enjoying his newfound fame. It was rubbing his ego in all sorts of pleasant ways he never knew possible. That this strange character should have heard of him amused him no end. "And you are?" he asked.

"Late." the man said, casting his eyes over the throng of guards stood behind Jean. He shrugged his shoulders, turned and began to walk away without another word.

"Well I say. How rude." Jean said watching the big man haul his bulk over the quayside and descend an iron ladder to a small dinghy waiting for him at the bottom.

"Señor Bethencourt?" Jean´s attention was drawn away from the man in the dinghy to the stocky figure of the Harbourmaster, who was hurrying along the quayside towards him, his thick white mutton chop sideburns flapping in the wind. Two well-armed, uniformed men followed in his wake carrying lanterns on poles, trotting to keep up.

"Señor Rodriquez." Jean beamed at the Harbourmaster, welcoming him with a hearty handshake.

"Have you been causing trouble again?" Rodriguez said pointing at the guards filling up the quayside.

"Ha! No, not me this time. This time they are with me."

"Come inside, come inside." Rodriguez said smiling and pulling out a large iron key to unlock the door. "I was all the way on the other side of the dock when I heard you all arrive. It has been a very busy day." He shouldered the door open and pushed his way inside the building with Jean close behind.

"We've been riding hard since yesterday." Jean said. The Harbourmaster moved around an enormous, leather-topped desk in the centre of the room and began turning up the wicks of the lanterns spread around the room. Martin and the Guard Captain entered the office behind Jean, pushing ahead of the Harbourmaster's guards. The stern looks on their faces didn't welcome argument, none was offered.

"Please, take a seat." Rodriguez invited Jean to one of the two wooden chairs in front of his desk.

"Thank you." Jean said, lowering his stiff backside onto the seat with a small grimace.

Rodriguez looked amused by Jean's discomfort. "That's why you'll never get me on a horse." he commented with a little chuckle.

"We had little choice, our business is most pressing."

"It would have to be." He sat down across from Jean and leaned forward. "What can I do for you?"

"I need to know if a certain ship has called here recently."

"We've had plenty in and out this last week. Does the ship have a name?" Rodriguez said, pulling a thick ledger from a drawer and dropping it with a thud on the desktop. He flipped it open to the last written page.

"The Tajamar, skippered by a Fernando d'Ordoñez." Jean said.

"I don't need this." Rodriguez scoffed, closing the ledger and pushing it away. "She came in a couple of hours ago. You were talking to Master Ordoñez as I was approaching."

"You mean that big man in black was him?"

"The very same."

"Damn!" Jean leapt to his feet. "Where will the ship be anchored?"

"He usually ties up by the animal pens. He'll be back at the ship by now if he rowed straight there. The way by road is a lot longer."

"Show me. It's imperative we catch him before he leaves." Jean was virtually hopping on the spot, harrying the stout Harbourmaster to his feet. "Captain, find this man a ride." he said pushing Rodriguez out the door ahead of him.

"Har... yes." The Harbourmaster blustered, unable to complain as the guard Captain took him by the elbow and propelled him towards his waiting men. He virtually threw him onto the back of a horse behind one of his men. The Harbourmaster wrapped his arms tightly around the guard as Jean called to him, already swinging his leg over his own saddle.

"Which way?"

"We must go all the way around. The quickest way is round the back of the loading sheds." No sooner had the official raised his arm to point the direction, Jean spurred his horse into a reckless gallop. Thirty armed guards on broad chested warhorses rode behind him. The light was failing fast. Lanterns burning in warehouses threw a carpet of light along the route the horses took. The sound of thundering hooves echoed through the streets and up into the night sky. Curious faces peered out from doorways and windows as the equine wave swept through the docks, they flashed by in an instant, making the ground shake beneath them.

They emerged from the backstreets and out onto the waterfront, only halfway around the harbour. They slowed slightly as the ground changed. The horses felt smooth stone flags beneath their hooves, shiny and slippery with use. Suddenly, Rodriguez began pointing and shouting.

"There, at the end of the wharf. They're pulling away. He hasn't paid his docking fee yet!" the Harbourmaster spat with disgust. Jean followed his gaze and was horrified to see what must have been the Tajamar dropping topsails at the end of a very long wharf. He dug in his heels, urging his horse into another gallop. It was sweating heavily and breathing huge frothy breaths as it tore along the waterfront. Fishing baskets and people flew in all directions before them. More than a few were tipped in the water as Jean and his men bulldozed a path across the stone flags.

Jean raged inside, fuelled by the memory of the promises made to the Majo people to protect them. He drove on with righteous abandon. His horse nearly went from under him as they rounded the final sharp bend and struck out along a wide wharf leading to a dark corner where the masts of the Tajamar could clearly be seen sliding away. She was picking up momentum as she felt the current of the ebbing tide pulling at her hull.

Jean spurred his horse into one final lung-bursting gallop, the horses head was dipping up and down wildly as it was nearing the end of its stamina. It slid to a halt at the end of the wharf. Jean leapt to the ground before it fully stopped and vaulted over the rail of the ship tied up there. He sprinted across the ship's deck and hurdled the rail on the starboard side, landed lightly on his toes on the deck of a ship tied alongside. He let out an agonising wail as he slammed into the starboard gunwale of that ship, looking out and seeing the Tajamar's stern, only twenty feet away. It might as well have been twenty leagues away.

Martin arrived at Jean's side followed by the Guard Captain and several of his men. They pulled crossbows from their backs and levelled them at the departing ship.

"You on board. I say you of the Tajamar!" the captain yelled, cupping his hands around his mouth. There were a few figures running through the rigging high above the slaver's deck, but there was no sign of anyone on the quarterdeck. Ordoñez was probably crouching out of sight behind the tiller. "You there, Master Ordoñez." The captain persisted. "I order you to return to the dock in the name of the King!" his challenge went unanswered. "I order you to cease Señor or I will be forced to order my men to shoot."

"Shoot what?" Jean said at his side. The deflation in his voice was heart-breaking. He shook his head and put his hand on the captain's shoulder to still him. "There is nothing we can do until they land again.

There's no way we'll be able to track them through the night. They've won this time." The men watched on in silence as the clumsy black hulk waddled into the stronger current in the middle of the channel, within minutes it was riding out of the bay and into the open sea.

Jean hung his head, unable to lift it with the weight of shame, anger and sorrow pounding through it.

"We might not have lost everything just yet." Martin said beside him.

"What?" Jean asked looking up at him, his eyebrows rising slightly.

"Look. Back there." Jean turned to look where Martin pointed at the quayside. The guards there had stopped a man and were arguing with him. Jean recognised him immediately, even in the gloom of the early evening his mop of unruly blond hair was unmistakeable.

"Courtille?"

"None other!" Martin replied, smiling from ear to ear. The two men began to cross the ships' decks back to the quayside.

"What is he doing here?"

"He was keeping an eye on Berthin."

"Keeping an eye on Berthin? What do you mean?" Jean said, climbing over the rails between the ships.

"We suspected he was up to no good a few weeks ago but didn't like to say anything until we knew for sure. You can't go around accusing noble knights without strong evidence to back it up. Courtille stayed behind in Rubicon to find that evidence when you brought me here."

"You two are friends? But I thought you were rivals."

"There is a musical rivalry between us, there has been since we studied together. We have been friends for many years. Not in a way many people can understand. We don't openly flaunt our friendship."

"I see." Jean said, genuinely touched that Martin should choose to share such a confidence with him. "By the looks of it, your *friend* has some news of import to share with us." Courtille grinned broadly as the two men approached. Jean could have sworn he saw a twinkle in the blond knight's eye as he looked at Martin.

******

Berthin couldn´t last much longer. The inside of his mouth remained dry and furry, no matter how much wine he poured into it. He knew he would be shaky at best when it came time to get to his feet. There were only four others left standing, or rather hunched around the table; William Blessi, Jacquet the Baker, Young Gillet and a semi-conscious Big Perrin, whose battered head was swaying like a sunflower in the wind. An incredibly ugly sunflower, his face looked grotesquely out of shape. The bruises had changed from purple and black to a fist-shaped shit-brown splodge in the middle of his face. He still couldn´t use his jaw and had it strapped up with a filthy bandage. It dripped wine drops onto the table from under his chin. William reached across non-too steadily and held his cup under Perrin´s chin to catch a drop. One plopped in and the two men fell onto each other, giggling like children.

Berthin had no idea where the rest of his men were. They had drifted off one by one through the privy door, soon after devouring an enormous meal of chicken, potatoes and fresh bread. They were drunk on the food alone, and then the wine started flowing. Berthin wouldn´t have been surprised if they were all passed out on the privy floor. He really didn´t care if he never saw any of them again. He despised every single one of them and resented the fact he would have to share the slave bounty with them. He considered walking away and leaving them behind but knew they would be after his blood when he got back home to France.

He reached inside his tunic, as he often did when thinking, and found his purses of gold and silver. He liked to feel the edges of the coins, he could see the glimmer of the gold ingots in his mind´s eye every time his fingers brushed against them through the soft leather purse.

The tavern door opened. Berthin looked up and saw Courtille push his way inside followed by two men with hoods drawn up to cover their faces. They went off to a table at the other side of the room while Courtille crossed the room directly to Berthin. Berthin pulled his hand out of his tunic quickly and leaned forward to take his cup.

"Where´ve you been?" snarled Jacquet the Baker as Courtille got to the table.

"Out walking, enjoying the feel of the earth beneath my feet." Courtille replied, shrugging off his pack. Jacquet pushed himself to his feet and swayed for a moment before belching loudly and launching himself towards the privy door. Courtille watched him crash though the door and laughed before turning back to the table. He reached inside his pack and pulled out a small wooden flute.

"Do you mind?" he asked, holding it up.

"If you must." slurred Berthin, reaching forward and grabbing the jug from the centre of the table and sloshing some wine into his cup. He sat back hard and watched as Courtille sat on a small stool and started to play. Before he had played a half dozen phrases, William and Big Perrin were snoring, leaning against each other cheek to cheek.

Young Gillet smiled gormlessly, enraptured by the notes Courtille played. Berthin tried hard to concentrate but was starting to see double. The noise coming out of the flute was nauseating. He hiccupped and felt a little sick come into his mouth. He grabbed his cup and swilled his mouth with wine. He shook his head to try and clear the fuzz a little. The door opened, a few more men walked in and walked over to the table next to theirs, settling in behind Big Perrin and William.

"I love this song." Young Gillet said, closing his eyes and sitting back. The door opened and another couple of men walked into the tavern. It was getting crowded inside the small room. The low beams of the ceiling seemed to get lower as the heat increased. Nobody talked. They all listened to the damned flute.

Berthin took another swig of his wine. Try as he might, he couldn't escape the pull of the music. With no other noise in the room, it filled every corner. The tune reminded him of something. Then Young Gillet started singing softly.

"...and the winds will cease,
and the birds will come home,
home to roost."

Courtille was looking Berthin directly in the eye as he played the final note. He lowered the flute and the room erupted around him.

The men behind William and Big Perrin stood and flung a noose about the sleeping men's necks. They pulled the loop tight, pressing the men´s faces together. They woke with a scream. One of the three men behind them produced a stout club and silenced them with a smart crack on their heads. The hollow sound sickened Berthin who turned away to see Young Gillet on the other side of the table, held fast between two huge men. They looked like they could tear the Young Knight in two if they wanted.

Berthin made to stand but a sword pricked his throat. He turned to his left where another guard stood, the point of his sword held an inch from Berthin´s eye. He looked around and saw Courtille stood over the table holding a cocked crossbow in his arms.

"What´s going on man?" Berthin hissed with all the strength he could muster. Courtille didn´t even attempt to respond, he just stood there looking down on Berthin with an indefatigable look on his face. Berthin felt piss flowing down his leg, he was paralysed with fear… and then loathing. Had Courtille found out about the silver and gold and paid these thugs to steal it from him?

He was about to speak when the two hooded men at the other side of the tavern got to their feet and walked slowly across the floor.

"Who are you?" Berthin asked hoarsely. The first pushed his hood back. "Martin. What…?" The two men stopped in front of the table. The second man pushed his hood back.

"Bethencourt! Jean! I am so glad. I have been looking for you." Berthin stammered. Bethencourt didn´t even look him in the eyes. He simply nodded to an unseen man at Berthin´s back who reached down and hurled Berthin forward and slammed him onto the tabletop. His arms were pulled back and bound with a coarse rope from wrist to elbow.

"Monsieur!" Berthin grunted, he could taste the wood of the tabletop in his mouth. "Why is this happening Monsieur? I did everything for you!" He screamed in agony as he was lifted from the table by the rope binding his arms. A sweaty ball of dog-chewed material was forced into his mouth, it was so wide it felt like it would break his jaw. He tried desperately to bite it smaller but couldn´t. He tasted the blood flooding his mouth from his torn tongue and suddenly felt lightheaded as an unseen hand dragged a sack over his head and tied it around his throat.

He was prodded and pushed to the door. He felt the cool night air through the sack as he stumbled outside. He tripped on something and fell heavily into his chest, cracking his head on the cobbles painfully. Someone grabbed his arms from behind and yanked him to his feet. They untied the sack from his head and dragged it roughly up and over his face. A hand grabbed his hair from behind and forced him to look down at the ground. There, trussed up like hogs to the slaughter, all his men lay in a long line. The unconscious forms of Big Perrin and William were hurled down to join the others.

Berthin could feel the tears burn his eyes as the sackcloth mask was dragged back over his face and tied tightly around his neck. Suddenly he felt hands on his body, moving around his side and under his tunic.

"NOOOO!" he tried to scream, twisting away from the probing hands. Suddenly the rope around his neck jerked tightly, lifting his feet from the floor, punches flew into his body from all directions. He was powerless to resist, unable to protest. He felt as the gold and silver pouches were taken from him, and then everything went black.

****

Norstar woke when the ship began to pitch and yaw. He had enjoyed a few hours of glorious sleep while the decks had been still. He sat up painfully and began to twist and stretch his body to give what little relief he could to his aching limbs. Thankfully, no bones had broken under the boots of the slavers, but his body was taking a long time to heal. It hadn´t helped being tossed around like a ragdoll for endless days, as the ship battled it´s way North through the Atlantic swell. Norstar had felt every wave as he was lifted and slammed back down onto the planks beneath him. During the worst of the storms, the Majos had been forced to cling to the bars of the cage to keep from flying across the deck when the ship pitched violently over the waves.

The Majo´s cage was on the lowest forward deck of the ship. It was barely high enough to sit up in and was lit by a solitary candle during feeding times. The rest of the time it was dark and cold. The Majos huddled together to keep warm during the cold, damp nights. The temperature barely rose enough during the day to stop their shivering.

"Are you awake?" a voice came out of the darkness.

"I hope not. I want this to be the dream and I wake up a free man."

"As do we all." It was Beselch. The old man´s resilience had impressed Norstar. Their confinement drew them all closer, old resentments long since forgotten as they helped each other to survive each new day of horror.

"Did I sleep for long?" Norstar asked. Since the beating, his sense of time was sketchy at best, not helped by being shut up in a dark cage. He was prone to fall fast asleep for long periods of time, blacking out completely while his body fixed its deepest injuries.

"No longer than usual. We sailed at sunset… without the French."

"Without the French?"

"Berthin and his men didn´t come back before we left. What does that tell you?"

"They may have had an argument, or the Master is double crossing Berthin. Anything could be possible. Ruthlessness is treated like a blessing in this world, a virtue to value one´s worth with. This is what you allowed to enter our island by not driving away the invaders when we had the chance." Norstar immediately regretted his words. Beselch was suffering his own personal recriminations for his early inaction. It wasn´t fair for Norstar to pile resentment onto Beselch´s shoulders too. The old man sat still, Norstar heard a gentle sigh of sadness.

"I am sorry Beselch." Norstar said, placing his hand on Beselch´s shoulder. "That was uncalled for. You have no more guilt to bear than I for all that has become of us. My anger is coming to the surface more with every league we travel North."

"You are sure we go North?"

"We sail into the Mediterranean. A sea of pirates. Every ship on this sea is looking to steal from everyone else. There are men who sail these seas who would slice out your heart because he wants your teeth."

"I have heard you say this before. It doesn´t worry me."

"Why?"

"I only have two teeth."

Norstar laughed out loud for what seemed like the first time in months. The sound of his own laughter filled him with a joy he had feared he would never feel again. His sides began to hurt and he struggled to breathe but he just couldn´t stop. The laughing spread like wildfire and soon, every soul in the cage was rolling around, clutching their bellies, happy tears washing clean tracks down their filthy cheeks. A few in the dark cried softly when the laughter eventually died.

"Where do you think we are going?" Beselch asked softly.

"Aragon or France. I am hoping for France." Norstar answered. It is the land of my mother. There is every chance I can talk us out of this when we get there."

"Do you really believe that?"

"I have to believe it. And if it fails, I have to believe in the next thing, and then the next thing, and all the other chances that follow that one. If I give up believing, I am accepting I will never go back home and hold my wife and children again, and that I can never do."

Beselch grunted his approval and the two settled into a companionable silence while the sea rocked the boat relentlessly, up and down, up and down.

The moon rose and illuminated a shimmering path of light across the surface of the water between the Pillars of Hercules. The Tajamar turned to the east and followed the path into the Mediterranean Sea.

By the time dawn spread her light over the horizon, the Tajamar was gone.

Printed in Great Britain
by Amazon

12092394R00210